THE
CONSPIRACY
GAME

A TULLY HARPER NOVEL

THIS TIME I WON'T
BE LEFT BEHIND

ADAM HOLT

D1307940

The Conspiracy Game: A Tully Harper Novel

ISBN 10: 1940873010
ISBN 13: 9781940873015

ACKNOWLEDGMENTS

It took several million keystrokes to write *The Conspiracy Game;* however, those keystrokes wouldn't amount to much if not for these fine folks: Peggy Turlington, whose wisdom and encouragement shaped the story; Kristen Ball, my capable editor and steadfast friend, who finished the work Peggy began in exacting, Kristonian fashion; Denny Holt, my technical adviser, NASA historian, and father, who filled those roles beautifully and introduced me to Lagrangian Points; and the Koehlers, who went out of their way to support me in launching a new career.

Then there is the cast of folks who funded the novel via Kickstarter. Benevolent Benefactors include: Carson Dunn & Family, Simon Mayhew, Jim & Lennie Diaz-Granados, the Stones, the Duffys, the Pellegrinos, and Mom & Dad. Helpful Conspirators include: Julie Gallington, Jan Dunn, Sara Fitzgerald, Charlie Pellerin, Mark Stewart, Linda White, Ernie & Gina Harvell, Mary Dunn, Peggy & Buddy Beaird, Marilyn Bullard, Chad, Krystal, & Case Collins, and Max Harberg. And Taylor Cole, the Aussie I met in the Louvre, who ran a one-man campaign for my book half way round the world for no other reason than he likes sci-fi and is generally a great guy.

I must also acknowledge the inspiration for this novel—the 3 year old that sat through the "R" rated movie *Prometheus* on opening weekend. As her mother explained to me when I asked her why she brought a toddler to a gory sci-fi blockbuster, "Oh, she loves scary movies." At the time I felt powerless to do anything about the situation, but now I don't. I wrote you a book, little girl. I'll never know your name, but I'm sorry that all those awe-inspiring yet captivating images invaded your sweet mind before you could appreciate their meaning and artistry. I hope that one day, when you're old enough to read this book, your view of space will be redeemed. It's a place that some of my readers, maybe even you, will one day explore. Have fun out there, share your journey, and bring back stuff from the stars that will make us all more human, more like the good God that created the Heavens and Earth.

Finally, you'll notice that I didn't thank any of my students. If I tried to recount all those names or any of what they've given me over the past decade, it would stretch into another novel. And then what if I forgot to mention someone by name? Frankly, Kevin, that would be unfair.

-A
October 20, 2013
Friendswood, Texas

July 21, 2069.

It's been one hundred years
since Neil Armstrong
first stepped on the Moon.

Also, it's one month
before I try
to sneak into space.

THE DARKNESS AND THE DEVICE

After the explosion, darkness consumed the aircraft hangar. Silence hung over the place like a cold fog. But the lights wouldn't stay off for long. I had to get out of there fast.

Calm down, Tully. Get yourself together. You've got a second. No one knows you're here.

I checked myself for injuries. My ears rang. My eyeballs felt like they'd been stabbed by the sun. Other than that, all the body parts moved okay. My favorite jeans were not in great shape though. Not cool.

You can explain a pair of ripped jeans. Now what happened? Why did all the screens disappear?

Only moments before, hundreds of floating computer screens filled the middle of this enormous hangar. They had a purpose. They hid me from everyone else in the room. Scientists, astronauts, politicians, shady looking guys in black suits. None of them were worried about intruders though. Their real problem was projected on those screens. Their real problem may have caused this explosion, and it could do a lot worse.

The scientists had been pointing from screen to screen. They discussed what they saw. Every screen, in all sorts of colors and lights spectrums, focused on one thing – a swirling red ball of gas hovering at eye level with me. It defied understanding – just a bit bigger than a basketball but loaded with enough energy to power entire cities. Through the maze of screens I could just make out the real thing, trailing red mist onto the floor.

My dad and others from the Space Alliance wanted to understand this thing. They had scratched the surface of its power. They wanted to dig deeper and run more tests. The whole world waited for the news. Not me. I needed to see it now, and for myself. After all, it was my dad's discovery.

He encountered this thing during his last mission to Mars. It almost killed him. Instead, it made him a legend on Earth. They named it after him. The Harper Device.

Usually his spaceship occupied this hangar, but now his discovery did. This Device almost took my dad's life. I felt like I should face it for myself.

Now I had experienced its power up close. I checked my phone. It was dead.

Stars, now I know why the screens vanished. That wasn't an explosion. It was a power surge. The Device knocked out every piece of electrical equipment in the building. Just get a good look and get going, Tully.

Actually, that was easy. I had a perfect view. Without the screens, only the darkness stood between me and the Harper Device.

My eyes adjusted. The Device cast a freaky red glow over the entire hangar. Beautiful, dangerous, strange. I could hardly see the others all sprawled out on the floor, wondering what went wrong with their tests.

Nobody likes to be tested, not even stuff from outer space.

I staggered to my feet with my backpack slung over my shoulder. I wanted to run but my feet felt stuck. A red mist swirled around my feet and seemed to hold them in place. Weird.

Then reality set in. Murmurs and shouts arose from the other side of the hangar.

"Get the President out of here!"

"Get the lights back on!"

"Shut this thing down! Destroy it!"

"That settles it. We launch it back into space on the next possible flight."

Take it back into space? Who's crazy enough to get in a spaceship with that thing? Who's crazy enough to sneak in here? I guess you are, Tully Harper. Now find an exit before someone finds you.

I pulled myself away from the mist and headed for the exit, but before I reached it a hand clamped down on my shoulder. Inhumanly strong, it whirled me around. Two cold blue eyes examined me.

"Tully Harper," said a voice. "Been here long?"

"Uh, just walked in," I said.

"I doubt it. Elevated heart rate and blood pressure. Constricted pupils from an electrical flash. Nervous sweat from stress and lying."

"What are you talking about? What's going on?"

"Save your lies for someone who believes them. You are fortunate that I noticed you here, and not someone else. You meant no harm. I can keep secrets, and this secret is safe with me."

The hand shoved me toward the exit. I left the hangar without another word – confused, scared. But also satisfied. An idea was forming in my mind. This was one small step toward a bigger plan. That plan changed my fate – and the fate of the solar system.

This story begins a few months before that hand clamped down on my shoulder and pushed me through the door. It's a story that begins several thousand miles away in a forest and then goes rocketing several million miles in another direction. Somewhere in the middle I made some discoveries of my own. And learned to play the Conspiracy Game.

Part One: "Go, and do not delay."

March 27, 2069.

It's been exactly one hundred years
since The Soviet Union launched
a secret probe toward Mars.
It launched
and then exploded
in our atmosphere.

Also, it's five months
before I try
to sneak into space.

IN TWO PLACES AT ONCE

"Tully, what time is it in Alaska?" Dr. Vindler asked when I materialized in his Science classroom one Monday morning.

"About 5am, sir," I said, rubbing my gloved hands together and checking the time. *Whoops, 5:02am. Oh, no.*

"It's 8:02 here in Houston. You're late, but I must say, those two extra minutes of beauty sleep are working wonders for you! Class, don't you agree?" Dr. Vindler sat on his desk and hiked up his khaki pants to reveal his favorite socks, which read "Science Rocks My Socks." He was winding up for one of his classic "late to class" speeches. They were like birthday cards—he personalized each one. My classmates were getting out their pens and journals to take notes during his lecture, a few of them sneaking into their seats while I had his attention. He continued. "All of you have two more weeks to prepare for my final exam, which 18.6% of last year's class failed. Now *that* is something to lose sleep over! So, Mr. Harper, let me give you this amazingly insightful suggestion. You may sleep until noon this summer, but materialize into this classroom no later than 4:59am your time."

"Yes, sir," I said. Only Dr. Vindler could get excited about failed tests and sleep loss.

"And finish your review packet. Did you know that many students do homework even when they're away from home? You can, too. Janice

Chan did Review Worksheet 8.9 on a hyper flight back from Paris last night. Didn't you, Janice? Trés bien! Can you imagine anything more exciting than memorizing the periodic table of elements while traveling at twice the speed of sound? Can you?"

"Um, maybe finding a new element?" I said.

"Yes, you could name it after me. Vindlerium! But if you don't finish these last few assignments while you're in Alaska, you can name it Summerschoolium!"

This was life when my dad was on a mission. He always shipped me off to my Aunt Selma's cabin in the Alaskan wilderness, but I still "attended" my 8th grade classes at Space City Junior High in Houston. It was a new school program called Holoclassing that allowed students to attend classes from virtually anywhere. "Traveling astronaut dad" is a pretty good reason for Holoclassing, so they issued me the very first pair of hologlasses in the program. When I put on the glasses and a pair of earbuds, my aunt's cabin seemed to disappear. After a few seconds of dark silence, Dr. Vindler's classroom appeared in front of my eyes, and my classmates saw a hologram of me in my assigned seat. They called me "HoloTully" and said the hologram looked amazingly real. My body was definitely in my aunt's rustic cabin though. The rest of the class wore t-shirts and shorts, but I was shivering, wearing an "I Love Alaska" sweater, my hands around a cup of coffee to stay warm.

Dr. Vindler began to describe his grueling, two-hour final exam. He was a tough tester, but Science was my favorite class because of him. He was about fifty-five, had spiky "mad scientist" hair, and more energy than any teacher or student at Space City. His class was high energy, too. He made Science feel like a game, and his experiments often involved lasers and minor explosions. Discipline wasn't his specialty, but he was just the right combination of scary and funny to make me listen.

After finishing his speech, he pulled a stack of papers from his ancient briefcase. "Most of you probably realize that we only have two weeks of school left. Who would like to improve their final grade?" Every hand went up. "On the desk behind me is a periodic table with 120 blank spaces. Your task—if you choose to accept it—is to fill in the names of the elements. You'll have five minutes. Break into teams of three and fill in the periodic table from memory. Winners receive two bonus points on the final exam. Well, what are you waiting for? Go!"

That could take me up an entire letter grade! I thought. A lot of people felt the same. Chaos ensued as students broke into teams of three. Chairs and desks went flying.

My hologram image sat still. There was no reason to command him to move yet. He could never have grabbed the paper or written down a single answer, but that was okay. I already had a team. I sat between Sunjay and Tabitha, my two best friends, and we knew how to work together.

Sunjay Chakravorty was my next-door neighbor. He was my best friend since our first day of kindergarten, where he introduced himself to me and decided we should be friends. When we went to recess and played soccer, he would only pass the ball to me, even if I weren't on the field. We were inseparable from then on. He was constantly asking questions and tossing his shaggy, black hair out of his eyes.

Tabitha Tirelli moved down the street from us a few years ago. For some reason she hung out with us all last summer, even though she loved dance and drama while Sunjay and I liked sports, martial arts, and video games. She had zero interest in the first two activities, but we got her hooked on video games, especially *Cave—In!*. She hit a growth spurt last year—one that I completely missed—so she was about a head taller than me. She's quirky, gutsy, and insightful—I could go on with adjectives, but you'll see.

Back to the Vindler's pop quiz. Our team flew into action. Sunjay threw back his hair, and then his chair, hurdled a desk, grabbed the blank periodic table, and returned before most people had formed their teams. Tabitha was waiting with her pen, and when Sunjay threw down the paper on her desk, she started neatly filling in the elements with no help from us. That didn't stop Sunjay from shouting every element he knew. "Hydrogen, oxygen, helium, boron..." I shouted a few fake elements to throw off our competition. "Hexablom, Frankfurtium, oooh, don't forget Baconium. Did you write down Baconium, Janice Chan?" Janice frowned. She never approved of anything that I did.

Tabitha slowed down when she reached the noble gases, so Sunjay took over and madly scribbled in the last few symbols. Finally, he threw her pen across the room, hopped a fallen desk, and slammed down the paper on Dr. Vindler's desk.

"Done!" he yelled. Work continued around us. Dr. Vindler pushed his oversized glasses up his nose and glanced at our work. Something was wrong.

"Names?" he said. *Are you kidding? We forgot to put our names on the paper?* Tabitha saw it coming though. She had already retrieved her pen and tossed it to Sunjay from across the room. He scribbled our names on paper and guaranteed our victory.

"Yes!" I yelled, thinking about those two extra points. "Trés bien!" Janice rolled her eyes. I floated toward the ceiling and started dancing on the light fixture. Being a hologram has its advantages sometimes.

But before Dr. Vindler could announce our victory, something happened that changed my life forever.

A three-toned chime sounded in the classroom. We had only heard the sound once before during the year, when the Presidential election results were announced. As the lights dimmed I floated back to my seat, wondering what the announcement might be this time. A 3-D image sprung to life in the middle of the room—a news studio with the words "BREAKING NEWS FROM MARS" flashing behind the female newscaster.

"There has been an incident on the Red Planet this morning," she explained. "An asteroid impacted Mars a few hours ago. The crater is near where Commander Mike Harper and his crew are continuing their search for water."

An asteroid? That was big news, but at the mention of my dad's name, every head in the room swiveled toward me. My face flushed, even though it was freezing in my aunt's cabin.

"Whoa, an asteroid hit Tully's dad!" someone shouted.

"That's incorrect," Dr. Vindler said. "Now keep quiet."

The newscaster continued. "We expect more information and live coverage from the Space Alliance soon, but we do have video. A high-Earth orbit telescope captured the moment of impact."

The newsroom disappeared and the planet Mars arose in its place, casting an eerie, red light upon the entire room. Then a small speck of white appeared on its horizon, burned through the atmosphere, and landed silently on the surface. A dust cloud rose. Everything looked so harmless from a million miles away.

"Broadcast freeze!" yelled Dr. Vindler. His voice made me jump. He hopped off his desk and approached the now-frozen image. With his finger he drew two circles. "This is the impact crater, students. This second circle is clearly *The Adversity*. What a name for a spacecraft, don't you think? But have no fear. It's roughly thirty miles away. Quite safe." He pushed his oversized glasses farther up his nose and squinted. Then he drew a third circle right next to the crater. "No, wait. This—a white spot with four black dots—what are those? They look like wheels. Something right next to the impact. That is a most likely a Space Alliance rover. That could be trouble. Broadcast unfreeze."

The video ran again, and we saw a dust cloud cover the third circle. My heart thumped against my shirt, and I felt a tingling sensation in my hands. Vindler scratched his chin and glanced at me.

"Students, let's take a moment for the explorers on this mission. Focus your good thoughts and prayers on those people and their commander, Mike Harper, and on our friend Tully, too."

Most of my classmates bowed their heads but kept peeking at me through half-closed eyes and whispering to one another under their breath. The impact video ran again and again.

Tabitha never closed her eyes. "It will be fine," she mouthed to me. She leaned in to grab my hand, but her hand went right through my holographic arm and rested on the desk. I was just a ghost to her. About that time Counselor Jenkins entered the room and motioned for me. I was about to get up to talk to her, but I heard my Aunt Selma's voice cutting into my Holoclass. Then I felt a yank on my hologlasses and Dr. Vindler, my friends, and the video disappeared.

THE CRATER

"Stars, Tully! I told your dad space is risky business." Standing in front of me now was my aunt in her overalls and work boots. She dragged me into her living room where we plopped down on her couch. She was watching the breaking news on her television. I felt like I was in a time machine. She's the only person I know who owns a working TV anymore. I mean, it's the year 2069. I still didn't know what was going on, so I tried to stay positive.

"Come on, Auntie. Scaring a moose out of your garden—now that's a dangerous job. You could have left me in class for a while."

"I was about to pull you out of class to chop firewood anyway. I guess we can watch some TV first." Ah, the beauty of having a dad that travels for business, even if it is space! My aunt considers herself a survivalist. She lives in the Middle of Nowhere, Alaska. That's the name of the town. Middle of Nowhere. Population: 5 (or 6 when I'm there).

"Ooh, this doesn't look pretty, Tullyboy," she said. "Not pretty at all."

"Dad's not looking for pretty rocks on Mars, Auntie. He's looking for water."

"Well, they found trouble, not water. Here on the TV they're saying something about an asteroid impact on Mars," my aunt yelled.

"Yeah, we already heard."

"Well, the reporter just said they couldn't find your dad."

"What?" I looked at her television. "MARS DISASTER 2069" scrolled behind the newscaster as she started to read the updates.

"Breaking news from Mars: there has been an apparent asteroid impact on the red planet. A Space Alliance ship was in the vicinity. All seven crew members are accounted for except Commander Mike Harper, who was searching for water on the South Pole of Mars by himself."

"By himself? Dad, what were you thinking?"

I pictured the third circle that Dr. Vindler had drawn. It must have been my dad's rover. Over the next hour the news went from bad to worse. The media didn't have any more information, but that didn't stop them from reporting. They showed all sorts of asteroid craters from around the solar system. They interviewed experts and asked them stupid questions: *Could anyone survive an asteroid impact? What would you see right before an asteroid hit you? Isn't that what killed the dinosaurs?* They ran animation of an astronaut getting blown through the air by an asteroid impact. Like I needed help picturing the explosion. Thanks, guys. Then they mentioned me: "It appears Commander Harper is a single parent. He has one teenage son. Our thoughts and prayers go out to that brave young man tonight." That brave young man felt numb, sitting on his aunt's couch and praying.

My aunt made me some food, but I wasn't hungry, especially not for the only three things she ate: canned asparagus, potatoes, and caribou meat. She mumbled on and on.

"I told your father a million times there's nothing in space worth risking life and limb. He wouldn't listen though, Tully. Wouldn't hear a thing about it from me." She made some coffee and rubbed my shoulders, but I shrugged her off.

I walked into the bathroom to escape the world and looked at myself in the mirror. The same guy as always stared back at me—messy brown hair, brown eyes, and a scar on my chin where I fell when I was a toddler. Just some kid who used to feel like life wasn't all that fair. *Now I know life isn't fair. My dad is gone. The universe took him from me. I will be stuck in Alaska forever.* Those thoughts didn't stay with me very long. *Don't give into that,* I told myself. *Thinking like that won't help. Be strong like your dad. Be strong for him.*

My aunt yelled for me again, and I returned to my spot on the couch. The newscasters finally had something to report. A shaky video appeared on the screen. A banner above it read "LIVE FEED FROM MARS!"

"Stars, they can't get anything right," I said.

"What do you mean?" Aunt Selma asked.

"This won't be live. It takes thirty minutes for the signal to travel from Mars to Earth, Auntie. Whatever we're about to see happened thirty minutes ago." But the newscaster continued.

"…Yes! We have a live feed from Mars. The other astronauts have almost reached the asteroid crater. You can see the red dust still hanging in the air from the recent impact. We do not see any signs of Commander Harper or his vehicle, but we must warn you, folks. This could be graphic. Harper is feared dead." The camera was obviously attached to a Martian rover, kind of like a dune buggy, because the image bounced up and down. I thought I was going to be sick from all the movement and mayhem. *Be strong, be strong.*

The Martian rover finally neared the edge of the crater, which was was about the size and shape of a baseball diamond. We couldn't judge the depth.

"Mars One, this doesn't look good." It was Buckshot Lewis, my dad's pilot on the mission. The camera panned toward the remains of my dad's Martian rover. It was flipped over and covered in dust. A boulder had crushed one side.

"This isn't happening, this isn't happening," I said to my aunt, over and over again.

Buckshot leapt from his vehicle and bounded over to my dad's wrecked rover, covering ten feet with each step in the Martian gravity. He scanned the accident scene and reported back. "Mars One, I don't know where the Commander is. His rover is a total loss. We will check the crater."

"Uh, that's a negative, Buckshot. That could be dangerous. Search the area but do not approach the crater."

Not approach the crater? My dad might be down there. I imagined my dad, struggling to breathe or to push a monstrous rock off his leg. How could they waste any time? Fortunately, Buckshot didn't listen to instructions.

"Mars One, sorry. Couldn't hear you there. You said to check the crater, right? Will do."

"That's a negative, Buckshot. Buckshot, repeat, negative."

"No, that's a positive, Mars One. I am checking that crater whether you like it or not."

Buckshot leapt over the edge of the crater. The other astronauts followed behind him in the rover, the camera bouncing like mad. Suddenly Buckshot spoke again.

"Mars One, we have a problem," said Buckshot. "Do you have visual?"

"No, not yet. What do you see?"

"I have no earthly idea. Get visual! Guys, bring that rover down here!"

More terrible images flashed through my mind. I couldn't close my eyes. I couldn't pray. It was hopeless. My aunt rubbed my shoulders, and this time I didn't have the energy to shrug her off. The screen kept bouncing. Finally, the camera settled at the edge of the crater. Half of it was in darkness and half in light, but the picture was fuzzy.

"Buckshot, we have visual. It's fuzzy on our end. Please describe what you see."

"Bless me, if that ain't Mike Harper standing down there."

My heart almost exploded. My dad was alive.

"Buckshot, what's going on?"

"Good golly, I don't know, Mars One."

"Where is the asteroid?"

"Forget about asteroids! Get that camera adjusted right, Lewis. Houston, give us a second and you can see for yourself." The images went from fuzzy to crystal clear. I crawled off the couch toward the TV for a better view.

My dad wasn't the only thing in the crater. What was with him would shape the history of the solar system forever.

THE UNEXPECTED

A shadow shrouded half of the red crater in black. In the middle of the crater, right on the edge of that shadow stood an astronaut. Red dust covered his white spacesuit. He was looking at something glowing in the shadow. His helmet—the only thing protecting him from death—was tucked into the crook of his arm. He turned toward the camera, looking calm, composed, unfazed, with his blonde crew cut and sharp blue eyes. There was a pause in which the universe held its breath and considered that impossible scene.

The pause felt too long for me though. My dad's life was on the line—or it had been thirty minutes ago. "Don't just stand there, you idiots!" I finally yelled at the TV. "Make him put on his helmet. He's going to die!" But he didn't, even though there's practically no oxygen in the Martian atmosphere. How was he alive? What was he looking at in the shadows?

The camera adjusted and scanned the crater to find what held my dad's attention. In the shadow a few feet from my dad a shape emerged—a red sphere came into focus. It rotated slowly in place. A red mist trailed from its surface. The object looked like a miniature planet, suspended in mid-air. An occasional spark lit the sphere like a lightning strike viewed from many miles away. Under the glowing sphere was something equally surprising—a small fountain of water—exactly what my dad had been looking for on his mission.

The whole thing looked like some mysterious surreal painting. *He should be dead*, I thought. *What is keeping him alive? Is that really water?* I couldn't understand it at all. Nobody could.

"Houston, it appears Mike found water on Mars," said Buckshot. "And then there's that glowing ball down there. That ain't no meteor. Mike appears to be breathing, but I have no idea how. We're going to get a helmet on Commander Harper and get him to safety. We'll report back when we can."

In that moment my dad went from "meteor victim" to "world famous explorer." I went from "orphan" to "son of a hero." I was exhausted.

My aunt hugged me. "I told him space was dangerous! I just say it all the time. That darn fool and his missions of doom and disaster. And now he's gone and found something useful for once—a fountain of water on dusty old Mars. But shouldn't he put on that helmet?"

For the first time ever I agreed with my aunt.

"Auntie, what is that other thing in the crater? That's not an asteroid. Nobody's ever seen a thing like that."

That "thing" didn't even have a name at first. I had no idea that what was floating in the middle of that crater would change my life forever.

After that my aunt was on the phone constantly. She has one of those phones that attaches to the wall with a cord, and the thing rang like a crazy church bell for hours every day. Like her TV, it's ancient. Anyway, she answered every single call. Out of the first one hundred calls, only one of them was a friend of the family. The rest were reporters, strangers, or weirdoes all wanting to know the same thing—Is Commander Harper okay? Why wasn't he wearing a helmet? What was that thing in the crater? Do you believe in aliens? Will you give us a movie rights to his story? It drove me crazy.

I couldn't talk directly to my dad either. He was on his way back from Mars. That was 140,000,000 miles away. It would take nearly a month to get home. And it wasn't like I could just call him on my holophone. Instant messaging and calls were impossible. Messages took time to go between Earth and the *Adversity*, so we used email. It felt way too formal, but it was good to hear from him. He even sent me a video at one point.

It was short and grainy – the Space Alliance didn't waste money on high definition family videos – but Dad looked like himself.

My aunt, in the meantime, enjoyed all the publicity. Suddenly she loved my dad's job and called him a hero after all these years of calling him a fool. Jeez. I did chores, went to school, and tried not to check the date every five minutes. Those next few weeks stretched out forever.

But finally we received a call from the Space Alliance. The *Adversity* was close enough for live communication. They asked me if I wanted to contact my dad on board *The Adversity*. Are you serious? Of course. And great news. The Space Alliance used hologram technology for official reasons, like beaming an engineer on board to look at a problem. However, they made an exception for me. Sometimes being an only child with one parent pays off.

The next morning I took a deep breath, put on my hologlasses and earbuds, and waited while the Alliance established a connection on board my dad's ship. It was the same routine as school. The glasses locked on to my gaze. A soft voice spoke from the earbuds: "Audiovisual uplink beginning." Suddenly my surroundings went black. There was a dead silence. Then I heard a phone ringing and a distinct click. "Uplink confirmed," said the voice. Moments later, "Uplink complete." Fuzzy shapes began to emerge before my eyes: a bed, a desk, and a man. Soon after I found myself in my dad's spacious living quarters on board *The Adversity*.

He sat at his desk wearing his Astros baseball cap. I noticed a picture of us fishing together on the wall, along with one of his favorite Latin quotes: "AD ASTRA PER ASPERA." *Through hardships to the stars*. He looked like he had been through some hardships, too. Wrinkles appeared under his eyes when he smiled. I jumped up to hug him but my arms went right through. We were just ghosts to each other until he got home. It made me angry so I threw a punch instead.

"Oh, a holographic hug and punch combo. Thanks, Tully."

"That's not funny. What were you thinking? Never go out alone again, dad. You know better than that."

"No risk, no reward, son."

"No risk, no asteroid victim. On TV they were showing astronauts getting smushed by asteroids."

"That's never happened, and this wasn't an asteroid."

"Well, what is that thing? It almost killed you."

"It sure did. It knocked me unconscious and made quite a crater. I have my theories on what it is, but I don't know. The only thing I know for sure is that there's water on the South Pole of Mars. We achieved our mission. Humans can colonize this planet more fully than ever. There's enough water here for millions of people."

I sat back down on the bed and calmed myself down. "That is pretty cool for you, dad. Uh, good job."

"It's cool for all of us. Just think: the solar system is getting *smaller*, not bigger. The planets are just like continents used to be. Who knows? Your children might one day live on Mars."

"My kids may be Martians, huh? They might like Martian football. The MFL?"

"Sure. Why not?"

"But what about that thing in the crater?"

"You sound like your buddy Sunjay with all these questions—or maybe Dr. Chakravorty. We will hand it over to researchers when we return."

"Wait, you're bringing it back to Earth? After it almost killed you?"

"Not my first choice, but we've already brought it on board at the Alliance's request. Researchers are stumbling over themselves to prepare for our arrival. Sunjay's father will lead the research. 'Mike,' he said, 'you found an object that produces oxygen, finds subterranean water, and creates and stores energy in novel ways. Bring that back to me and I will end world hunger.' He's probably overstating things, but I hope he's right. If the Alliance can tap into that energy, it could solve problems on Earth as well as help us explore space. Oh, and we can stop calling it 'it.' They decided on a name—the Harper Device. I didn't vote for that either, but they want to use our family name so people will remember how it was found."

"You mean how it almost flattened you? Someone said you were almost the world's first 'flatstronaut.'" I said, shaking my head.

My dad grinned. "Flatstronaut. Buckshot loves bad puns. I'll have to tell him that one."

"Yeah, real funny. I was about to start planning your funeral! So you're going to get interviewed by a zillion reporters and the paparazzi are going to chase you around and everything."

"I guess, but I'd rather just be an astronaut and a dad. The Space Alliance understands this was a tough mission. Because of that, they did promise me something—the rest of the year off."

"No way! So we'll be in Houston for the rest of the year?"

"Yes."

"No more caribou and asparagus?"

"Roger that. We could both use a good Tex-Mex meal. Please tell your aunt hello for me. Just give us a few more weeks to get home and I'll see you back in Houston."

That was the best news ever. No more "public relations" and chopping wood and scaring moose out of the garden, just hanging out with my dad. Back to Houston, back to summer, and back to my friends, Sunjay and Tabitha. Maybe the Harper Device was a blessing in disguise. Life seemed like it was about to be simple again.

WEIRD THINGS ABOUT FAME, HOLOCLASSING, AND DOODLES

Life did not get simple again. I had to stay in Alaska two more weeks before returning to Houston, and for the next two weeks my aunt kept up her "public relations campaign" for my dad. The phone rang. The doorbell rang. Aunt Selma answered every single ring or knock. She was either at the door or on her old-timey phone doing interviews. It didn't matter if it was one of her friends, a reporter, a politician, the mailman, a friend of our family, or just some curious stranger. She sat on her recliner in her big work boots, jeans, and a heavy flannel shirt and talked all day about her brother the hero, discoverer of the Harper Device and water on Mars. She went on and on: "Oh, honey, that old Harper Device is something else. I bet it will cure cancers and make for world peace." "Oh, yes, I'm sure he's fine. My brother is a hero and all. He's tough as pack mule." "You can bet your boots we're excited about the big discovery. Water on that dusty old planet? Just amazing." Tuning her out was impossible. I didn't want to think about my dad's near-death experience. I just wanted to have him back home.

Finally I asked her, "Auntie, would it be okay if you didn't take every single call? Or at least don't invite everyone in for tea. This is driving me crazy."

"Well, honey, we don't want to be rude, do we?" she asked.

"Yes, let's be rude! Then maybe they'll stop calling or coming by."

"Tullyboy, that's no way to talk to your Auntie! Everybody's excited right now about your daddy and you'd better be, too. He's alive, for goodness sake! Maybe you'll be more excited to go split firewood until sunset," she growled. "You better take the heavy gloves. It's below freezing right now."

"When is it *not* below freezing in the Middle of Nowhere!" I yelled.

She was about to ground me or make me cut down the entire forest, but her phone rang—the first call I was thankful for all day. I walked out of the room hoping she would forget about the firewood. Fortunately she did. I still had some nasty blisters from my last trip to the woodpile.

Finally I convinced her to limit her public relations. After all, I needed a quiet environment to study for my exams. You can convince adults to do a lot of things if it's school-related.

I hadn't been to class in a few days, and I was looking forward to returning. I hoped everyone would treat me like they had for the first few weeks of holoclassing. Back then Tabitha had pretended to be my manager. "Ladies and gentlemen, HoloTully has entered the building!" she would announce. Then Sunjay would hide behind someone's desk. I would search for him. Suddenly he would pop up and do a roundhouse kick at my head—he is really good at martial arts. Everyone liked trying to high-five a hologram or throw a pen right through "HoloTully." I threw on my glasses and hoped for the best.

It was 5:02 again, but Dr. Vindler skipped his tardy to class speech. Sunjay and Tabitha awkwardly waved hello. Maybe they were trying to make me feel normal, but I felt out of place. The class went by at a snail's pace, and I focused on note taking like never before. Finally, Dr. Vindler made an announcement: "Class, our plans have changed. We'll still do our exam review sessions, but our movie schedule has been cancelled." Everyone moaned. *Really? Why?* I thought, but Vindler explained. "We've got something more important to discuss here at the end of the year. The Harper Device!"

Whenever he said "Harper Device," he gestured toward me, like I was some sort of celebrity. My classmates all eyed me, like it was my fault that we wouldn't be watching movies. They tried to treat me like all was normal, but we all realized the discovery meant more work. They resented the extra work. I couldn't blame them for that, but why did they blame me? From then on my classmates always got quiet when I appeared in the back of the room. I was some kind of annoying celebrity—or an alien. When I appeared, people would quiet down and say "Hey, Tully" or nothing at all. They pretended that they hadn't been grumbling about the extra work or the Device. My dad's picture was everybody's screen-saver though. It's weird when your dad is a screensaver.

Only Sunjay and Tabitha really got back to normal. Tabitha twirled her scarf and smiled at me. No matter what time of year, Tabitha wore a scarf. She passed me random doodles. One doodle was a thousand dollar bill. Under it she wrote, "Dear HoloTully, this is your manager, the one who made you dire famous. You owe me loads of money now and a ride in your dad's spaceship. XOXO, Tabitha."

Sunjay did what he does best. He asked a thousand questions: "How are you doing? How's your Dad? When are you getting home again? Does Alaska smell like Texas?" He could ask a thousand questions about anything. Sunjay was the master of getting people off track. His ridiculous questions usually drive teachers crazy ("Does this count for a grade?" "Can I do that for extra credit?" "Did you hear my new ring tone?"), but sometimes he gets on a roll in Science. Sunjay's parents are both researchers at the Space Alliance. He's like a clone of his dad. When he and Dr. Vindler talked about the Device, most everyone listened except Tabitha, who ignored everything. She made straight A's, but she was off in space most days, reciting lines from a play in her head. That was Tabitha.

Fortunately Sunjay helped me dodge most of the tough questions about the Harper Device in Science until the last day before exams.

"Tully," said Dr. Vindler, "we've been discussing your father and the Harper Device for days instead of watching movies, yet you haven't said a thing. I'd like you to summarize some of our discussions at least, if you would."

"Right now?" I asked.

"Yes, right now," he said, giving me a sharp look. "Right now. Stand up, please."

Uh-oh. My hologram image stood up. Everyone turned to look at me. All I could think was how close I was to getting home, but I knew I had to say something intelligent now.

"I'll give you a topic. Tell us why water on the South Pole of Mars is so important."

"Water on the South Pole?" I said. That wasn't so bad. "Because we can colonize *both* poles of Mars, not just one. We already have that colony on the North Pole. Now that we have the South Pole, we can double the population. From there, we can colonize other places, like the moons of Jupiter or Saturn."

"Well said, Tully," Dr. Vindler nodded his approval, but he wasn't done. "Now, tell me what *your* thoughts are on the Harper Device. What do you think is its purpose?"

"Purpose? Uh, we don't know," I said. "It looks like a miniature version of Saturn or something."

"Well, yes, everyone saw that," he said. "But doesn't it seem to have a purpose? Did it help your dad discover water on Mars?"

"Huh?" I hadn't thought about the purpose of the Harper Device, other than it almost crushed my dad.

Vindler continued. "Do you think the Device is intelligent? Was it sent to help your father? How will it benefit humanity? Please give us your thoughts."

Even though it was cold in Alaska, I could feel my face getting hot. How could I possibly know anything about that? It wasn't even back on Earth, and neither was my dad. I felt like I was on a game show where the audience knows the answer but the contestant stumbles.

"I—uh, I'm just glad my dad is safe," I said.

"We all are, too," said Dr. Vindler, "but that's not my question. You've sat in the back of the class and said nothing about this discovery for two weeks. Your thoughts, please."

Vindler hopped off his desk and crossed his arms. I was about to take off my hologlasses and make the whole scene disappear. That's when Tabitha cleared her throat and spoke up.

"Dr. Vindler," she said, "can I be honest with you? I'd really like to hear what *you* think. You know science better than anybody else here," she said, turning toward him. I felt the eyes move back to the front of the room.

He sat on his desk and hiked up his sagging pants. He clearly enjoyed the attention, and I was glad to be out of the spotlight. "Well, what do I think it is? Good question, young lady. I think it's a symbol. We should never, never stop exploring. Like a mountaintop encourages people to climb. Like a rainbow stands for peace. Just imagine—out of nowhere this celestial ball of gas plopped down in the middle of a crater, almost like it wanted us to find water on Mars."

For once Dr. Vindler sounded more like an English teacher than a mad scientist. "Ha! The universe still has plenty of mysteries. That's what I think. I don't really know its purpose either, but it could lead to amazing discoveries. The Space Alliance researchers will know soon enough. Speaking of soon enough, look at the clock on the wall. Just like Mr. Wells has been doing for the last twenty minutes, trying to use his mental powers to make time pass more quickly. Impressive work, Mr. Wells. What time is it?"

"Time to go, sir?"

"Bravo, Mr. Wells! Class dismissed."

Tabitha saved the day. Sunjay packed up and ran to his next class because he had a test. I took a deep breath. I was about to take off my hologlasses and disappear, but she was still packing up beside me.

"How's *Romeo and Juliet?*" I asked.

"Ugh, not so good. I have to kiss Romeo at the end to get the poison off his lips so I can die. It's not that hard to fake my death but the kiss thing is terrible."

"Is he a bad kisser?"

"I guess not, but he eats a peanut butter and jelly sandwich before every show and I feel like I'm really going to die. I'm allergic to peanuts. Bad breath of death for Juliet."

"Well, keep up the good death, I guess." I felt relieved. I mean, what if Tabitha fell in love with Romeo? She wouldn't have time for me and Sunjay.

"Oh, but how are you! You'll be home soon. Super excited?"

"Definitely. It's freezing up here right now."

"I can tell. Your breath." She puffed up her cheeks. "It's frosty when you talk. Hey, don't get embarrassed about all this space stuff. Your dad is a hero," she said. "That's dire cool."

"I guess so," I said. "Thanks for distracting Dr. Vindler. He drives me crazy sometimes. It's just—"

"I know. Teacher teacher, not a mean creature, and poor HoloTully goes all red in the head. Cheer up! Space shrinks every day."

That is what Sunjay and I called a *Tabism*. It was sort of like this accidental riddle that Tabitha spouted off at least once a day. She expected you to "get it," but you never really did. You just had to wait for her to translate it into English. I cocked my head and looked at her.

"You don't get that one? Vindler is just being Vindler. He isn't trying to embarrass you. He just wants to hear your thoughts. Don't worry. Your dad'll be back soon, and so will you," she said, packing the rest of her bag. "Just in time for summer! It'll be nice to see the real Tully again, not this weird hologram thing." She left the room, with the scarf flowing behind her.

Weird hologram thing. That's what I felt like most of the time my Dad was gone. I wanted to be real Tully again, too. I looked at my flickering hands through the hologlasses. I watched her leave the room. She usually walked out with some of the other girls in class, but I realized something. She had stayed behind that day to talk to me. *That* was dire cool. And for a moment I thought about how much fun we could have in a musical or play together. I wondered how it would feel to stand on stage with her in some major dramatic moment like that, swords in our hands and poison on our lips, pretending like our lives were on the line.

On her way out a piece of paper fell out of her bag. It was folded in half. "Tabitha, your doodles!" I yelled, but she didn't hear. I had no way to pick up her note either. It was a hologram to me. Crouching on the floor, I could see some of the drawing. It was a really good drawing of my Dad in the crater. "DANGER?" was written above it. *Maybe she was paying attention in class,* I thought. Next there was a big rainbow that connected to another doodle. I could read "TULL" but couldn't see the rest of the doodle. My heart jumped. The note was folded. I wanted to see the rest of the doodle but I couldn't make it out. I put my nose on the floor but couldn't read anymore of the note. Dang.

At that moment I heard running in the hall and Tabitha re-entered. She saw me there, with my nose to the floor, trying to read her note. Kinda awkward.

"Oh, my doodly doodles!" she said, crouching for her note, her hair in her eyes. The room was empty and quiet except for the two of us. She pushed back her hair. Our eyes met for a moment as we both looked up from the note. I wanted to ask her what her doodling meant, but I kind of lost my train of thought, seeing her soft green eyes and the freckles on her cheeks.

"Thanks, HoloTully!" she said, smiling. "Did you, could you see that?"

"Oh, your doodles? No, not really," I lied. "I'm just a weird hologram thing."

I took off the hologlasses and was suddenly back in Middle of Nowhere, Alaska, holding a cold cup of coffee. Aunt Selma was in the other room on the phone. "That Tully, he splits wood really good for a little fella. I'll miss having him around."

When I tucked myself into bed that night, I tried to think of three good things from the day. It's a good habit. I kept saying to myself, *A few more days, just a few more days!* I would be back in Houston hanging out with friends, Dad would be home, and I could eat mountains of Mexican food again. Eventually those thoughts subsided, and Science class came back to me: how Dr. Vindler embarrassed me and Tabitha got me off the hook. Tabitha Tirelli, star of Shakespeare's *Romeo and Juliet.* Scarf twirler. Peanut allergy sufferer. Good friend. I thought about our moment in the classroom. *Did she think the Device was dangerous? What did she write about me? Was she thinking about me? Or maybe she just likes rainbows and was thinking about them because we talked about symbols. I missed my chance to ask her, all because of her cute freckles and lovely green eyes. Did I just use "cute" and "lovely" to describe Tabitha?*

Relax, I told myself, *you'll be home soon and it will be summer. Everything will be back to normal* in *a few more days.* My thoughts trailed off as I pictured my dad on his way back to Earth, along with his newfound fame and that mysterious swirling object. *A few more days. A few more...*

ALL HAIL THE PROPHET OF THE UNIVERSE

Finally it was time to head home. I kissed Aunt Selma goodbye and took the hyper flight back to Houston, which was a first. The Space Alliance usually put me on a regular plane, but the hyper flight on Universal Airlines took only thirty minutes from Gnome, Alaska to Houston, Texas. Dad picked me up at the airport in his 1967 Mustang. He may be an astronaut, but he loves antiques. "The car is your older, adopted brother," he once told me. He and the Mustang awaited me outside baggage claim. Dad wore his Astros hat and a purple Space Alliance polo. The second he saw me he revved the car's engine. Then he jumped out of the car, slid over the hood, and nearly crushed me with an enormous bear hug. We stood there hugging for a good two minutes without saying a word. It's what you do when you see somebody you almost lost forever. You don't want to let them go.

"You hungry?" he asked. "Good!"

We drove straight to our favorite restaurant: Pappasito's Mexican Diner. We both ordered beef fajitas and ate until we were full. Then we ordered tres leches cake and ate until we practically popped. After months of caribou and asparagus (Aunt Selma's survivalist diet), it was like heaven. Apparently my dad had the same feeling. "The food printer on *The Adversity* malfunctioned," he explained between bites, "and we could only print tuna casserole and iced tea for an entire month." We were both teary eyed, happy to see each other and happy to eat steaming tortillas filled with beef and cheese and guacamole. Everything felt so normal and happy that it didn't even feel real.

Then reality started to sink in. I noticed the other families around us, pointing and whispering. On the way out a few people wanted photos and autographs, and my dad signed and smiled but tried to make a quick getaway. However, a lot of people followed us to the parking lot. Everyone wanted a picture with the famous astronaut beside his century-old Mustang. Then the crowd got rowdy. They hoisted my dad in the air and started tossing him like it was his bar mitzvah. "Harper! Harper!" they chanted. I was afraid they were going to drop him, but he just tossed me the keys.

"Tully, rev the engine!" he yelled. I hopped in the Mustang, turned the key, and hit the gas pedal. The sound of the roaring engine drew everyone's attention. "No way! A gasoline-powered engine!" someone yelled. I slid into the passenger seat as everyone snapped photos with their holophones and hologlasses. My dad broke through the crowd and jumped into the driver's seat beside me. He laughed and tousled my hair.

"Let's order a pizza next time," I said.

"Good call. We may be eating in until people calm down. I should have realized it. During post-flight debriefing one of the younger guys told me, 'You know, Commander, the Harper Device is kind of a thing right now, and so are you.'"

I guess when your dad is a celebrity, you have to learn to share him with other people, I thought as we made our way home.

The house looked just as we left it—a 2-story red brick house in the suburbs. It wasn't until we got home that I really looked at my dad in the bright light of our kitchen. More reality. Astronauts stay in great shape, and my dad spent hours lifting weights and doing Crossfit to keep himself ready for his job. Maybe it was just the effects of a month of tea and tuna, but he looked thinner than before with a few more wrinkles. When he took off his Astros hat, I was more surprised. As always he had a blonde crew cut, but now there was a diagonal streak of fiery red running through the blonde. I tried hard not to stare.

Other people noticed the red streak, too, but after a few days I noticed another subtle change—this red flicker in his blue eyes when he was laughing or thinking. It wasn't a reflection. It looked like a light coming from inside him. His eyes flickered when I asked him about his mission, the only time he became quiet and serious. "Tully, you've already heard what I told the media, right? I knew you would be curious, but there's not much else I can tell you. Let's just enjoy the summer. We don't need to think about Mars for a while." I guess that's all there was to say. I wanted to know more, but he wanted to get back to normal life. I couldn't object to that.

We blended into a good summer routine. My dad cooked breakfast, read the paper, stayed in shape, and did interviews from his home office. Sunjay bounded through the door by noon and we played video games for a few hours. He taught me his newest martial arts maneuvers, usually a kick that knocked over a chair or a vase, in which case my dad told us to take it outside. He didn't like us sitting inside and "wasting" our summer indoors.

We had a trampoline and pool in the backyard, but we forgot those toys the second my dad brought home a new toy—an Upthruster, a new type of hoverboard. It wasn't available for sale yet, but the creator, a retired astronaut named Dr. Chet Chan, gave us one as a "welcome home" gift. His boards were better than regular hoverboards. Any hoverboard could skim a few feet off the ground, but the Upthruster could fly! Dr. Chan made a few dozen, calling them "surfboards with wings," and that was accurate. The Upthruster was seven feet long, with three fins on the back and tiny thrusters on the bottom and sides. Top speed? 30 miles per hour. Highest altitude? 50 feet. Higher and faster were possible, but he gave us a low-powered version. That was probably for the best. The board also came with a "brain bucket," which had a double purpose. It acted like a safety helmet but could also read brain waves. The brain bucket understood your thoughts, so operation was simple. 1. Put on "brain bucket." 2. Strap leash onto leg. 3. Think about what you want to do and hang on!

Sunjay and I wasted no more time inside. Upthrusting was fun, felt dangerous, and Sunjay and I couldn't get enough. The first days we cruised along the sidewalk, above the creek, or over the treetops in our neighborhood. I mastered the controls pretty quickly, but Sunjay often freaked out and lost his concentration at higher altitudes. I held my breath when he fell off the board, but the leash kept him from plummeting to his death. He hung by one leg as the board slowly descended to the ground, always depositing him in our front yard. The higher he was, the more embarrassing the fall. Every time he fell off—pretty often—I almost died laughing, watching the board slowly bringing him down the street to our yard, often through our neighbor's bushes or past a group of high school kids. Of course I occasionally fell off, too, and Sunjay got his chance to laugh until he cried.

Our skills improved quickly though. We did railslides along the neighborhood fences and shot jumpshots at the basketball hoop from fifty feet in the air. Sunjay even rescued an old lady's cat from a tree. That was his shining moment on the Upthruster.

Those days outside cleared my mind, but when we went in for lunch we listened to the news—anything about sports or the Harper Device. There were editorials about my dad's discovery and what it meant. Sunjay and I read them all. "Research suggests the Device creates enormous amounts of energy. It may even hold the key to unlimited energy," one scientist wrote. "We should fund all the research possible to unlock the keys to its power. Humanity solved so many problems in the last twenty years—global warming, deforestation, overpopulation—and the Device could teach us how to make even more progress."

Some weren't so optimistic. "To bring back something so powerful and mysterious from space could doom us all," said one politician. "The Space Alliance has gone too far, blinded by their thirst for knowledge and hunger for power. This Device is their new 'pet project.' As much as I like pets and 'pet projects,' we still don't know this pet very well. Is it a cuddly kitten or a hungry tiger? Will it help us or destroy us? This isn't a domesticated animal. It's a "stray"—we don't know where it came from or where it was going. We know it almost killed an astronaut. The Alliance should have made sure it was housebroken before they brought it home."

Of course, some people developed crazy ideas about the Device. They thought it was a sign—like the end of the world was near, or aliens were coming to invade. Others thought it was a message from God. Or aliens. Or Napoleon. Or their great-grandmother's spirit speaking to them from "the other side." You get the idea.

A few people even thought my dad was a prophet because he found the Device. For example, I was mowing the lawn one day, and this guy showed up at our house. He wore a homemade t-shirt that read "All Hail Commander Harper, Prophet of the Universe!" Before he stepped onto our front lawn, he took off his shoes. He stepped into the yard in front of the lawnmower, and I stopped the lawnmower. He asked me, "Are you the Son of Harper, Prophet of the Universe?"

I slowly nodded. "Uh, I guess. My name is Tully."

"Well, my name is Xanthar, and I come to serve the Prophet." He pointed at his shirt.

I said, "Sir, I don't think the Prophet of the Universe would make his son mow the yard."

"How right you are!" he yelled. At that point, he came toward me, which scared me out of my mind, this crazy barefoot guy in a homemade t-shirt. But what did he do? He pushed me aside and started mowing the lawn! He did a good job, too, so I made some lemonade and watched him from the hammock.

Pretty soon my dad came home and saw this weird barefoot guy mowing our lawn and me lying in the hammock observing his work. Dad wasn't amused. My dad convinced Xanthar to leave, but only after my dad "blessed" him. I mowed the rest of the yard, and dad sat me down afterward. "Some people look for hope in strange places, son. Promise me you won't take advantage of someone in a situation like that again," he said, his eyes flicking red. I promised. From then on, I mowed the lawn myself, which was better than chopping wood.

My other problem was Tabitha. She was never home because of an acting camp during the day and *Romeo and Juliet* at night. One of her brothers also broke her holophone, and I hadn't talked to her since I returned. I couldn't stop thinking about her or her mystery note, and I was kind of embarrassed to go see her.

Late at night I peeked out my window and saw her light was on, but it was past my curfew. I considered flying over to her window on the

Upthruster and offering her a ride, but I was afraid I might get distracted and dragged home through her rose bushes instead.

I finally got up the nerve to call her on her family phone with my hologlasses. Her parents had a holophone, so I decided to call her one night. It turned out that the Upthruster was a safer idea. Her dad picked up the call. I appeared in her living room. Mr. Tirelli was watching baseball on the couch while her four younger brothers chased each other around. Her dad and brothers were all shirtless, wearing only their boxers. How bad is that? Well, it got worse.

Tabitha's dad saw me and said, "Hey, Tully. The AC is broken right now. Oh, homerun! Yeah, go Astros!" Then he yelled upstairs. "Tabitha! That Harper boy is in the living room!" She ran downstairs and there I was, hanging out in the room with her dad and brothers in their underwear. We both turned lava red.

"Dad, what are you doing!" she said. "Seriously? Sorry, Tully. Our air conditioning is out, so this is 'No Pants Night' at the Tirelli house."

"You wanna join us?" her dad asked me, but Tabitha glared at him.

"Just ignore him, Tully. So *Romeo and Juliet* is almost over. Let's hang out sometime soon."

"Yeah, good to see ya, Tully! You should come over for a game sometime," said Mr. Tirelli, chuckling to himself.

I told them both that sounded fantastic and disappeared as quickly as I could. Mr. Tirelli in his underwear. You'd think he could show some respect to the Son of the Prophet of the Universe—or at least not embarrass his daughter to death. She already had to die every night on stage. I decided to be patient and wait until Tabitha finished her performances, but every time I let my mind wander when I was on the Upthruster, I found myself hovering over her house and wanting to knock on her window.

A Sudden Chill in the Summertime

Getting distracted on the Upthruster was a bad idea. Sunjay dared me to do a rail slide on the roof of my house. I did okay until I looked down the street and saw Tabitha getting in her car to head to rehearsal. When I looked back, the chimney was only inches away. Crack. The chimney gashed a hole in the Upthruster. A few bricks rolled down the roof into the pool. The Upthruster and I slid down the roof after them, but fortunately the Upthruster had enough power left to drop me slowly into the pool below. I chucked him my holophone before I went underwater. Sunjay pulled me out and started to give me CPR for some reason—I was breathing fine. When I limped in the front door with the broken board and a soaking wet shirt, my dad was in the kitchen. He looked up from his coffee and just shook his head.

"It looks like we've got a man down. I guess it's time to air up the bike tires, huh?"

I didn't like that idea, and Sunjay didn't either. We sat down with my dad, and Sunjay seized an opportunity to ask him about the mission to Mars. My dad was one of Sunjay's heroes, and his enthusiasm caught my dad off guard and made him open up about his near-death experience.

"So what happened on Mars, Commander? I've read everything and heard all the interviews, but I just want to hear it from you one time. Just one time, I promise."

"Well, I was out searching for water. That was our mission—to find water on the South Pole of Mars, just like we found it years ago on the North Pole. You know why we were searching for water?"

"Of course," said Sunjay. "My father tells me all the time. Mars is like a big rusty desert. There's still some water, but it's below the surface. The more we find, the more we can expand our colonies."

"That's right."

"So you took off by yourself to explore?"

"Yes. We needed results and weren't getting any. So I finally arrived at one of our better locations. After a bit of scanning and drilling, I found nothing and was about to leave. At that point, I felt something strange. The hairs on my arms stood up and I could feel a tingle in my fingers. I knew that feeling well from my time in the mountains. Lightning was about to strike, which didn't make any sense. So I dismissed the feeling and began the long ride back to *The Adversity*. That's when I saw a bright flash in front of me. Then the ground rumbled, like an earthquake, so I assumed an asteroid hit the planet right in front of me."

"That was the Device hitting the surface?"

"Yes. Then a gigantic dust cloud formed in front of me. The impact caused the dust cloud, and that cloud threw me out of the rover. When I awoke—it had knocked me out cold—I gathered my senses and walked down into the crater that was now in front of me. Of course, you saw what I saw—the Harper Device. I also saw an enormous crack in my visor."

"Your oxygen escaped through it!"

"Yes, I checked my oxygen gauges. My tanks were empty. I should have been dead—you know that the Martian atmosphere is mainly carbon dioxide, no oxygen. At that point I figured I was either dead, hallucinating, or was in the presence of some sort of oxygen source."

"So the Device made oxygen and revealed the spring of water?"

"Yes."

"Okay, but what I don't understand is this: did you discover the water or did the Harper Device discover the water?"

"My best answer is this: the Device, the water, and I all met in the bottom of that crater. I don't know who found whom, but I do know that somehow the Device supplied the oxygen that kept me alive."

"And almost turned you into astronaut applesauce! Did it also give you that funky red streak through your hair?" Sunjay pointed toward my dad's hair.

"Yes, it seems that way. Anyway, I hope your dad has more answers soon. He is one of our top researchers. I just happened to find the Device. Your dad will unlock its mysteries."

"Oh, he wants to! He said it stores and keeps enormous amounts of energy. It could help us build better batteries, cleaner fuels, more efficient machines. But the Harper Device isn't cooperating. It doesn't like to be researched, he said. That's weird."

"I'm sure your dad will figure it out."

"Commander, do you think it's dangerous? Do you wish you left it on Mars?"

My dad took a sip of his coffee and looked out the window. "Yes, I do. It's caused a bit more trouble than we expected."

"Trouble, sir?"

A glimmer of red appeared in my dad's blue eyes. It was a rare slip-up by my dad. As usual, he knew more than he could say, but just this once he said more than he intended. He corrected himself.

"It *could* cause trouble. Your father is a good researcher, son, and he will be more cautious than I was, going off by myself on Mars. That's all I meant."

But it wasn't what he meant. Clearly the Device was causing problems, but not many people knew. We both wanted to know more about the problems, but my dad wouldn't say a thing. Sunjay looked satisfied and moved to his next line of questioning.

"Will you go back to space soon?" Sunjay asked.

"Will you ever stop asking questions?"

Sunjay pursed his lips and thought for a second. "I guess when I get all the answers, Commander."

"Well, you let me know when you have all the answers, Sunjay. Then I can stop flying and we can have some longer conversations." He grinned at me but looked over my head with that strange red glimmer in his eyes. "Now do we still have a trampoline you guys can jump on—or did Tully crash that into our chimney, too?"

"Commander, too funny!" Sunjay died laughing and punched me.

"Dad, you want to jump, too? You could double-bounce Sunjay into oncoming traffic for me."

"That's tempting," he said. "But I've got some things to do in the office."

"I thought you had the summer off," I said.

"Uh, you guys get on out there and trampoline yourselves to death for a while. I'll—we'll chat later."

My dad tousled my hair and jogged down the hall to the home office.

The whole conversation frustrated the heck out of me. My dad answered all of Sunjay's questions. When I asked, he hadn't told me a thing.

But that's not what really got me. I knew that look in his eye and tone in his voice: he wouldn't be hanging out with us today. He would be in his office the rest of the day and maybe the night. He might as well not be there at all. What happened to a summer off? Why was he working? It gave me a sudden chill.

LITTLE SPIES, BIG PROBLEMS, AND A STRANGE COMMAND

My dad wanted the whole truth, but he won't like this part of the account. It's hard to write because *technically* I did something wrong, but what was I supposed to do? I needed to know what he was doing in his office, and I felt betrayed because he told me he was free for the whole summer. So what did I do? I used one of my gifts against him.

The gift was a hand-sized Android, or a Handroid, a miniature robot programmed to walk, talk, and think like a human. Handroids are not as impressive as full-sized Androids because of their limited size and abilities—my Handroid stood one foot tall and wasn't the most profound thinker in the world. He also wasn't a "top of the line" Handroid. I really wanted an Einstein or Schwarzenegger model—one could run science experiments and the other one had all these hilarious one-liners from those ancient Terminator movies—but they were way too pricey. Instead, I settled for the Sir Francis Bacon model, a famous 17th century philosopher and scientist. He looked like the perfect miniaturized English nobleman. He wore a colorful, poofy-sleeved shirt with a frilly white neck collar and a floppy black hat—I named him Little Bacon. Sunjay loved to ask Little Bacon questions, but I didn't find him all that interesting after a few weeks. "LB" had about as much personality as

Wikipedia. I put him in a shoebox in my room until my dad started spending all those hours in his office.

The idea came to me as I sat there eating cornflakes for dinner. Mmmm cornflakes. I was alone in the kitchen with Little Bacon, who sat on the counter and kept me company with science facts.

What's he planning? I thought. *Maybe it's nothing.* It felt like something though. I heard voices coming from his study. A conference call. My mind spun in circles for ten minutes before I looked at Little Bacon sitting there on the counter.

"Little Bacon, you're pretty small. Could you do me favor?"

"A favor is an act of kindness beyond what is usually due," he said.

"I'll take that as a yes. Could you sneak under a door to spy on someone for me?"

"Spies are often used to acquire information that cannot be gathered by traditional means, such as asking or researching."

"I'll also take that as a yes," I said. Little Bacon nodded at me, proud of his definition.

He hopped from the counter to a chair to the floor. I handed him the hologlasses. He scrunched them between his hat and frilly collar, which l hoped was enough to keep the oversized glasses on his face.

"Hologlasses can be used to project a person's image into another place," said Little Bacon.

"You are so right. I need you to be my eyes and ears in dad's study. I'm going to give you some instructions. You're going on an adventure." He was about to define *adventure* before I cut him off. "Can you keep those hologlasses on your face?"

"Yes. Hologlasses can be used to project an image—"

"Yes, I know, Little Bacon, but you can't say a single thing while you're in the room. Just stand there like a statue. No definitions." He nodded and didn't say a word.

Little Bacon and I crawled down the hall like soldiers ducking under barbed wire. I pointed at my dad's office door, and Little Bacon gave me two thumbs-up. He crawled under the door, but his floppy hat and the oversized glasses fell off. *This was a stupid idea,* I thought, but moments later, a small hand reached back and grabbed the missing spy gear. He was in! I ran upstairs to my room.

I turned on my holophone and sat it beside my bed. The screen lit up and projected a 3D image in the middle of the room. I could now see what Little Bacon saw.

I expected to see my dad sitting in his leather chair on a conference call, surrounded by his books and awards. Instead, a room I had never seen appeared before my eyes. My jaw dropped to the floor. Not a single book, chair, or desk was in sight. My dad's study was a virtual room the size of a stadium! Magnificent Roman columns stretched to the ceiling, supporting a beautiful dome that was painted with dozens of spiral galaxies. At the center of the dome I recognized the Eagle Nebula with its famous "Pillars of Creation," three brown, yellow, and red dust clouds blown into shape by the radiation from surrounding stars. Little Bacon scanned the room, unable to find anyone there.

Massive marble statues lined the walls. Some of them I recognized from reading mythology—Zeus with a thunderbolt, Poseidon with a trident, Perseus with a gorgon's head. In between the figures were statues and paintings of great moments in space exploration—Neil Armstrong landing on the Moon, the Apollo rocket launching from Cape Canaveral, the Friendship circling Mars. In the middle of the room was a model of my dad's ship, *The* Adversity. Near the ship I saw a group of people in blue Space Alliance jumpsuits, including my dad.

"Little Bacon, you see them now?" He nodded and focused on the group.

Three of them were crewmembers from his last mission, but the last time I saw them they weren't standing in a virtual wonderland. They were in my backyard at a barbecue before the mission. "Buckshot" Lewis and Sylvia Moreline played water volleyball with me and the other astronaut kids in the backyard. "Redshirt" Anderson helped my dad cook fajitas.

Then there was Gallant Trackman. I recognized him from the barbecue, too. His small features—eyes, ears, and nose—were all shoved close together, leaving him with an oversized, egg-shaped head. He was a high-ranking Space Alliance official. He wasn't on the last mission and wasn't an astronaut, but he wore a blue jumpsuit along with the rest of the crew.

The last member of the meeting I didn't recognize at all. He was thin, athletic, and slightly shorter than my dad. His hands were clasped behind his back like an officer at "parade rest." At first I thought he was just another young astronaut, but something seemed strange about the way he moved. Or didn't move. During most of the meeting he stood as still as a rocket on a launch pad. I never really thought about it until I saw him, but humans are constantly in motion—tapping, swaying, twitching, bending, stretching, coughing, and yawning. We're a little "spastic," like Dr. Vindler liked to say. But not this figure, who exercised perfect control over his every movement. When my dad began to speak, the astronaut turned so that I could see his face. Then my suspicions were confirmed. His glowing, blue eyes gave him away, blinking in perfect rhythm in an effort to make him look more human. He was an Android, a robot in human form, and later I learned his name—Lincoln Sawyer.

Trackman was telling my dad something about the Device, but the presence of a full-sized Android had distracted me. I tried to catch up to their conversation.

"That's correct, Commander," said Trackman in a high pitched voice, "that Device of yours is causing some serious calamity at our center in Florida. Researchers haven't learned much about the Device, but lightning has struck their research facility a few times...a few times every day. We're convinced the Device has something to do with that, so we're moving it to a new location."

"Where's that?" my dad said.

"Houston," he explained in a sharp tone, "to the research facility near your home. Maybe things will go better there. Dr. Chakravorty is optimistic."

Sunjay's dad! I thought.

"Niles Chakravorty is always optimistic. But if you keep having these problems?" my dad asked.

"Well, I don't know, Commander. Possibly we send it to Moon Base Tranquility. There's no atmosphere there for the Harper Device to disturb," said Trackman, turning to admire the columns behind him. "But I didn't gather all of you here to discuss this. I called you here to discuss a major problem. This is classified information, as you might expect."

"Shoot, of course it is," said Buckshot, "it's always classified when you show up, Trackman. You'd tell a waiter at a restaurant to keep your order a secret. So go on then. Tell us somethin' we don't know."

"Oh, I intend to do just that," Trackman smiled. "We've lost all contact with a certain space station. How's that?" Everyone in the group was silent as Trackman continued. "So you and your crew will investigate. This is probably just a search and repair mission."

"Well, that is news to everybody here," said Buckshot. "Which space station?

"I can't tell you."

"Why not? The media will hop on this story like fleas on a monkey's butt."

"No, they won't. We've managed to keep a secret, for once."

"You mentioned it was *probably* a repair mission," said my dad. "What else could it be?"

Trackman sucked air between his teeth and let out a sigh.

"That is also classified," said Trackman. "There's not much more I can say, other than we want you to fly this mission. So, please consider the Space Alliance's offer—you'll all receive *quadruple* pay and a year off upon return. In the history of the Alliance, there has never been a more generous offer. May I have your decisions, please?"

"Say no!" I shouted in my room, wishing my dad could hear me. " Say no!"

Just as I said this, Lincoln Sawyer blinked three times and, for a microsecond, looked right at me. Well, he didn't see me. He saw Little Bacon standing in the corner of the room. Or did he? *Why would he start moving for no reason?* I wondered. Then it hit me. He had a reason. Little Bacon must have taken my shout as a command! He yelled "No!" when I said, "Say no!"

I told Bacon not to say another word in that room. He gave me a thumbs-up. Still, Sawyer glanced toward Little Bacon every few minutes like clockwork. I didn't know what Sawyer could see in that virtual room, but his Android "ears" had certainly heard something. By the time I recovered from that shock, I realized half of the group had accepted Trackman's offer. Buckshot and Sylvia Moreline both seemed ready for another mission, but not my dad or Quentin "Redshirt" Anderson.

"Four times our regular salary?" said Redshirt. "That's a lot for a repair mission, Gallant. Maybe too much."

"Well, we are only giving you four weeks to prepare. It seems only fair. Commander Harper, any questions?"

My dad ran his hand along the red streak in his hair. "Four weeks? This is a tough decision for a number of reasons that have nothing to do with space," he told Trackman. "We just returned to our families, and I wasn't planning on leaving for a while; however, I'm in."

But you just said—wait, why? I thought, sitting alone in my room. *What about taking time off? You lied to me!*

"Then I am, too," added Redshirt. The rest of the crew nodded agreed.

"Splendid," said Trackman, taking a deep, loud breath, but my dad wasn't finished speaking.

"I do have one condition, Mr. Trackman."

"Ah, what's your condition, Commander? Anything for you."

"We take the Device," he said calmly. "If it goes, I go. If it stays, I stay. You said yourself that the Moon would be a good place to research it. So we will take it there."

The entire group fell silent again. *There's no way Trackman will agree to that! Yes!* I thought. But Trackman just nodded and narrowed his beady eyes, like he was trying to hear a faint sound.

"Any reason the Device will be needed on this mission, Commander?"

"To use your words, I am not authorized to say at this time."

Trackman's eyes flashed anger for a moment, but he smiled nevertheless. "Well, it's an unexpected request. It won't be popular with the researchers, but I will see what I can do. While I do not make guarantees, I am quite sure the Device will travel with you on this mission—as will I."

"Hang on now," said Buckshot, "you're suitin' up for this mission? There's no room for space tourists on *The Adversity*."

"If you leave your ego behind we will have plenty of room, Buckshot. I will be Special Adviser to the Commander on this mission. Lincoln Sawyer will serve as ship's doctor and my assistant. Is that a problem for you, space cowboy?"

The scene grew tense. Buckshot looked angry, but my dad held up a hand before he could speak.

"Gentlemen, there is plenty of room on board my ship for respect. Bring that or don't bother coming. Are we clear? I hope so. Mr. Trackman, I will wait to hear back from you about our arrangement. Good day, everyone," said my dad. The virtual room disappeared. My dad stood in his dim, wood-paneled office again. It looked small and dull compared to the virtual world that had disappeared in a flash. He walked over and picked up a picture of the two of us fishing.

I turned off the holophone in disgust. What just happened? My dad just agreed to go back into space! I wanted to run downstairs and punch him, but I took some deep breaths. It was late. I needed to go to bed, and punching him wouldn't keep him on planet Earth. Before bed I tried to calm myself some more. It's a good habit. I kept telling myself, "Don't think about things you can't control. Think about the things you're grateful for. Maybe he will change his mind." I ran down the list: fajitas, sour gummy worms, a trampoline, Sunjay and Tabitha, my house, my dad. I somehow drifted off to a peaceful sleep.

Then the dreams began. At first I pictured myself standing alone in that enormous virtual room, with its marble floor and giant columns. In my hand was a helmet just like my dad's. I felt like an astronaut preparing for a launch! That was cool, but I wasn't really prepared. Instead of a sharp, blue jumpsuit, I wore my regular plaid pajamas. *Stars! Why do you always end up in pajamas in dreams?* I wandered around the room, admiring the bright galaxies that swirled above my head.

Soon I felt a rumbling. It grew. Before long the virtual room shook with earthquaking power. The columns began to crumble, and I ran from side to side, dodging chunks of falling statues. After that the ceiling caved in. I looked up and dodged that debris as well. In place of the golden dome, a beautiful pink sunset appeared in the sky. I gazed in wonder, but the rumbling increased and knocked me to my knees.

Finally, out of the center of the room there rose a spaceship—my dad's ship, *The Adversity*, leaving Earth in a smoking blaze. I stood there, gazing up at the rocket launch with that helmet tucked into the crook of my arm. The ship faded into the sky and the sound diminished. In its place I heard a faint whisper in my ear: *Go, and do not delay*. I spun around to see the speaker, but I was alone in the room.

That dream morphed into another dream. I viewed the Earth from the blackness of space. Our planet was cradled in a bed of stars. Then a small red sphere flew past me toward the Earth. I followed as it rocketed down, down, down through layers of clouds. Finally, it crashed through a familiar roof and plunged into my room. I saw myself catapulted out of bed and across the room. I shielded my eyes. There in the middle of my bedroom was the Harper Device, glowing red and filling my room with a cool, red mist, a brilliant ball of gases defying all the laws of physics, and spinning, spinning, swirling, swirling, sucking me deeper into its mysteries. Once again I heard that faint whisper, a strange command: *Go, and do not delay*.

I woke up on the floor with my back against the bed. I opened my eyes and looked toward the middle of the room, hoping not to see a red glow. Then I checked under my bed, carefully. Nothing. I tried to sleep, but how do you sleep after that? I kept thinking about those words: *Go, and do not delay*. Where was I supposed to go right then? Back to dreaming? Back to sleep?

I knew where I was actually going. Back to Alaska. Dangit. I just wanted to have a normal summer. Yeah, that wasn't going to happen now. Dad had betrayed me. He had four weeks to prepare for another space flight. I had four weeks to prepare for a trip to Middle of Nowhere.

You'll be left behind again, Tully, said a voice in my mind. *Enjoy the launch and have fun chopping wood in the Middle of Nowhere.*

If you're an only child, or maybe even if you're not, you can relate to that voice, right? The one that mocks you and says, "The glass isn't half full, it isn't half empty, it's broken." This is why I hate to be alone sometime. That mocking voice just won't shut up. How great it would be to have a brother or even a sister to talk about stuff like this. I could say,

"Hey, (insert my imaginary brother's name), looks like dad's going back to space. That stinks, huh? At least we've got each other!"

But I didn't have "each other." I had Little Bacon, and if I told him about space, he would say, "Space is the final frontier" or something stupid like that. I also had my dad. Now he was leaving, taking the Harper Device with him. *Yes, it's just you alone. SoloTully, HoloTully. That's who you are. A thousand miles from your friends. A million miles away from your dad.*

"Shut up, Brain Voice! What do you know about me, huh? Solo Tully? Is that all you've got? I can take it," I said aloud, jumping to my feet and clinching my fists. "Go ahead. Say it again. Call me Solo Tully one more time. I dare you."

The voice was silent, but I recalled that simple, strong whisper from my dream. *Go, and do not delay.* I didn't have to be Solo Tully. I didn't need to go back to anything. I could go anywhere, and I didn't need to delay. Where did I really want to go? I knew the answer.

"If dad is headed back to space, then I am, too," I said aloud. "This time I won't be left behind."

I knew it was impossible to do such a thing, but I meant what I said, meant it deep down inside. I kept repeating those words to myself over and over like a prayer: "This time I won't be left behind. This time I won't be left behind."

COMPANY

A few days passed before I saw Sunjay again. I didn't see much of my dad, but it didn't seem to matter. That idea—that my dad wouldn't leave me behind—comforted me and helped me sleep like a rock. Actually, I must have fallen into a coma because I never heard Sunjay jumping on my trampoline one morning. I didn't even smell the pancakes cooking downstairs. No, I was too busy drooling on my pillow. I finally heard something that sounded like a herd of wildebeests running up the stairs. Before I knew it, my door was open and Sunjay was trying to rip off my covers.

"Gimme ten minutes. All I need is ten more minutes," I said, pulling the blankets around me like a worm that refuses to leave his cocoon.

"Oh, buddy, are you crazy? You don't have ten more minutes. You've got company."

"Sunjay, you're not company. You're a disease!" I said, burying myself deeper and feeling him tug the blankets harder.

"Well, am I a disease too, Tully Harper?" I froze. It was a girl's voice, full of swagger and danger and too many summer theater classes. It was Tabitha Tirelli's voice. It was the first time I had heard that lovely voice in person in a long time, and she was in my room.

While I was buried under my covers for a moment, I had a flashback that completely cleared my mind. I pictured Tabitha's younger brothers whipping through the house like miniature hurricanes while her dad sat there in his underwear. I also remembered Tabitha's note and realized she might have a crush on me and I might have a crush on my friend, even if I did have to look up six inches to see into her lovely green eyes. Now she was trying to rip the covers off my bed with Sunjay. Man, summer was getting weird.

I didn't want to look into her eyes right then though. Imagine if you were buried under your covers in your favorite pajamas, clutching your drool-stained pillow: you wouldn't peep your messy hair out to say hello to anyone either.

"Both of you, out of my man cave now!" I shouted.

Tabitha laughed. I could hear the theater in her voice. "Wow, I've never been in a *man cave* before. Fascinating. Sunjay, look at the primitive cave drawings!" she said, poking at a sketch of *The Adversity* on my desk. I like to sketch. She spoke in an English accent, sounding like a Discovery Channel narrator. "A lovely specimen! And see how the caveman leaves his underwear laying around as decoration, Dr. Chakravorty?"

"Oh, yes, Tully, er, the caveman must have recently decorated," said Sunjay. He wasn't going to win an Oscar.

Tabitha continued and tugged on my covers. "Dr. Chakravorty, would the caveman mind if I, uh, take some photographic evidence of this man cave?"

"No pictures!" That was too much embarrassment for one day. Still under the covers, I jumped up and made a mad rush for the sound of their voices, catching both of them by surprise. I wrapped them both in the bedspread before they had time to react. They squirmed around but were trapped in the covers like fajita meat in a tortilla. Tabitha kept up her ridiculous accent.

"Oh, blimey, a giant cave slug!" Tabitha said as she tried to untangle herself. I held them tight. "No! Dr. Chakravorty, a radioactive cave slug bear hug! We are suffocating, Dr. Cha——"

With that I shoved them both out of the room unceremoniously. They slammed into the wall and fell into a heap. I locked my door and looked around. Tabitha was right. My room was pretty well "decorated," and their laughter continued as I threw on my jeans and t-shirt and shoved my dirty clothes under my bed. Where they belonged.

"Truce?" I said through the door.

"Yes, truce," they repeated.

I opened the door and Tabitha stood there in a flowery skirt she had thrown on over a pair of jeans. She twirled her scarf and went into one of her confusing Tabisms. "It's not that hot outside today. So Antony took all the keys off my keyboard. He's the littlest brother. I tried to superglue it back together and now my fingers are stuck." She held up her hand and gave me the okay sign; only her thumb and index finger were clearly stuck together. "Anywho, your trampo is calling my name. I holophoned Sunjay last night when I got home from camp because my dad was wearing pants. So what do you think?"

"So you're here to get some super glue remover?" I asked. She was completely mystifying sometime. Sunjay seemed to understand though.

"No, well, yes. That would be splendid, caveman, but I'm here for video games and trampoline," she said, punching my arm.

"Is your dad's console hooked up?" Sunjay asked.

Of course it was. Dad kept a lot of his old, cool stuff in one room, and we called it Mission Control. Dusty framed pictures took up one wall—anything from celebrities posing with dad to spaceships blasting off to my dad holding football trophies, shiny reminders of his college days. He also collected vintage electronics, like compact discs and video game consoles, and kept them neatly stacked beside a pool table.

Mission Control also had a LiveWall. You may have seen a LiveWall but they're pretty old—I think from the 2020's. The LiveWall took up one entire wall in Mission Control and operated like a giant iPad or a television, depending on how you used it. It was "old school," my dad would say, but still pretty fun. The LiveWall was great for pranks, too. I've scared the pants off Sunjay a dozen times by pulling up a cute cat picture that says, "You're purrrrfect." Then I swipe the screen to the left. A howling zombie fills the entire LiveWall. "GRAAWWL!" screams the zombie, flailing his arms. Sunjay falls over the couch. My dad gave me the idea. He scared *my* pants off with this thing called "The Scary Maze Game," which he made me play on the LiveWall. You could probably still find it, but I've warned you—it'll scare your pants off, too, or you'll need to change them after you play.

Finally, the best part of Mission Control—the brown, threadbare couch. Every time you sit there, the cushions sink in and your butt nearly hits the floor, with your knees at almost eye level. It almost feels like a hammock. It must sound terrible, but believe me; I've fallen asleep on that couch a hundred times and never felt better.

All morning we sat on the big brown couch and played our favorite old video game, *Cave-In!*, on the LiveWall. In the game, you are a spelunker trapped underground in a system of caves. Your flashlight is almost out of batteries. You have to escape before the light dies. Most of the caves aren't connected, but the spelunker can travel between caves using her only tool—a teleporter wand. When she uses the wand, a portal between the caves opens. She can teleport to another cave. It's easy on the early levels. You just find the right wall, jump across a few gaps, use the wand, and you're in the next cave. There's no penalty for entering a room twice. For the advanced levels, the caves are full of elaborate traps and monsters. If you return to a cave more than once, the monsters are waiting for you. You're usually dead meat.

Anyway, the way we played it was a three-person operation. We tucked ourselves close together on the couch with me in the middle. Sunjay was the architect. He created a "mental map" of where we had been and always seemed to know which caves we had not entered. Tabitha was the problem-solver. When we were stuck between choices, she could always find an escape route. And I was the controller because Tabitha and Sunjay couldn't control the teleporter wand and do anything else at the same time, like run or jump or not freak out. We had lost countless lives because Tabitha would walk into walls or off cliffs because she was concentrating on using the portal wand. If a monster were about to eat us, Sunjay would throw the controller and run out of the Mission Control. We would all take turns just for fun, but when the caves got tough, we all knew our jobs.

That morning I controlled for a while but soon let Sunjay take his turn. At first I tried to help, but he kept falling off the same cliff again and again and again. "Sunjay, don't forget. Shoot and jump. Shoot AND jump. NOW! Shoot and jump now!" Then it started getting comical. "Okay, Sunjay, whatever you do, DON'T jump now. Fall off the cliff, Sunjay. Fall off! FALL NOW! Yay, you did it!"

"Stars, stop bugging me, Tully. I know what to do!" he said, but his fingers couldn't prove it.

Finally, I just got bored and started doodling on the sketchpad where Sunjay had been mapping the caves. After a few minutes of doodling, Tabitha peeked over at the page. I had not realized, but I doodled parts of my dream. There was the Harper Device floating in my room, and me on the floor. All those nighttime feelings of loneliness came back to me. Suddenly tears welled up in my eyes. I swallowed hard and tried to get back into the game, but Brain Voice returned. *This won't last much longer. Your dad will leave you and where's your mom? You'll be alone again, Tully.*

"Tully?" Talk about double embarrassment. Tabitha had already invaded my man cave this morning. Now she was watching me doodle and cry. "Tully? What is it?" she asked, frowning and biting her lip.

That's all it took. "I—my dad, he's going on another mission." My voice felt uncontrollable for a moment, but I gathered myself. I explained how I sent Little Bacon into my dad's office, which turned into a virtual conference room. Tabitha listened carefully but Sunjay was excited about all the wrong things.

"Really? A virtual room! Oh, whoops!" yelled Sunjay, dropping the controller and watching our character jump into a pit. "What's the purpose of the mission and when—"

"Sunjay," Tabitha cut him off. "Wrong questions. How long until your dad leaves, Tully?"

"Four weeks."

"Oh, awesome!" shouted Sunjay. "I wish he was my dad. My dad just researches at headquarters and doesn't do anything interesting except he broke his nose at work the other day, which is interesting I guess if—"

"Sunjay!" Tabitha clamped a hand over Sunjay's mouth. "Shut it. This isn't about you."

"Three billion miles away," I continued, "and me stuck in Middle of Nowhere, Alaska, with Aunt Selma, chopping wood and being the weird hologram thing in the back of the classroom. You guys, my dad almost died on his last trip."

"I can't imagine how that feels."

"It feels like I'm a helpless little kid!" I pounded my leg with my fist. "My mind gets stuck on the same bad feelings. I can't think straight. My heart feels like it's full of pins. Not anymore. I'm not going to feel it again. I'm making a plan."

"A plan for what?" she said, grabbing my hand.

I felt this electric charge when she touched my hand, like a big confidence boost for some reason. My tears stopped; I took a breath. "I don't want to stay here," I explained. I pointed toward the ceiling. "I want to go up there." The words came back to me. "This time I won't stay behind."

Sunjay looked confused at first. "No, not the roof! Tully, you already fell off once. Don't do it. I don't want to lose you. I'll miss you so much—"

Tabitha grabbed his hand. "No, Sunjay, he's not jumping off the roof. He's pointing into space!" We all sunk deeper into the couch, thinking, letting the idea swirl inside our heads. A light popped on inside Sunjay's head. He understood at last. Tabitha looked concerned at first, but her face softened. She started to grin, and then she squeezed my hand tighter. The harder she pressed, the more I seemed to relax, and the more I let myself look into her lovely green eyes. Then Sunjay grabbed my hand. His palm was sweaty, but I didn't care. We sat there holding hands. It must have looked ridiculous, sitting on the couch like we were having prayer time or something, but it felt right, sort of peaceful and scary at the same time.

"This time I won't be left behind. I won't be left behind." It felt dire good, like it could actually happen, like I could actually sneak past all the Space Alliance security cameras and guards and right onto my father's ship. Just saying it to my friends made me feel—I don't know—brave. For once, none of the voices in my head challenged me.

Sunjay broke the spell though. "And how will you get on board the ship? Won't you be disobeying your father? What will they do when they discover your plot? You'll be sent to jail." Sunjay spurted questions after question until he could think of no more, and Tabitha kept holding my hand. "What will, how will, where?" Sunjay finally ran out of questions and shrugged. "Okay, well, fine. I'm just glad you're not jumping off the roof to your death."

"He wouldn't do that. Who would get us past this level of *Cave-In!*," Tabitha said. We looked at the LiveWall and watched our character being eaten by a ferocious monster. I did one of those sniffle-laughs that feel good after a cry.

"Okay, Tully Harper," she said, "you won't stay behind. I only have one question," she said, glancing at Sunjay, then back to me.

"What's that?"

"Would you like some company?" she said.

"Company? Oh, you mean it?" I said. Sunjay nodded his approval. Yep, they meant it. I was so glad they wanted to come. My dad had his crew. Now I had my team.

However, if I told my team what had happened to me the day before, I don't think they would have said yes.

NERVE

The day before my dad scheduled a few meetings at the Alliance Space Center. It was a beautiful sunny day. I convinced him to take me along. I wanted to snoop around some more to find out about his mission, but that's not what I told my dad.

"Do you think I can tour *The Adversity* today?"

"Sure, it's in Hangar One, that big building over there. Join a tour group. I'll meet you for lunch in the cafeteria, so don't fill up on candy. You should wear sunglasses and a hat, too. If anyone recognizes who you are, it might make a scene. Hey, bring your football. We can throw later." I said that was fine, threw on some shades and a Houston Rockets hat, and packed my bag. An hour later we pulled into the Space Alliance main campus, which stretched along Clear Lake. Dozens of buildings, warehouses, and aircraft hangars filled the campus. We drove through a security checkpoint. The guard gave us a polite nod and my dad hardly slowed down—apparently no one but Commander Harper drove a one hundred year old sports car to work.

We planned to meet at the Alliance cafeteria at noon. Dad pointed me toward Hangar One, which was the size of a basketball stadium, and headed toward his destination, Hangar Two, which was across a large parking lot. At that point I had a choice to make: stay with the tour group or follow my dad. I needed to find a hiding spot on board *The Adversity*.

I also needed to know more about the mission. Either way I would miss out on something. If only I had someone else to help me, we could have split up and done both. Little Bacon was undersized for this kind of adventure. I yanked some sour gummy worms from my backpack, ate a few, and pondered my predicament. After a moment, I made up my mind. I ran after my dad toward Hangar Two.

He walked across an open area, said hello to a security guard, and entered the side door of Hangar Two. Tiny door, enormous hangar. A pudgy security guard in a black uniform stood watch beside the door. "Howdy, Commander," he said with a strong Texas accent. I ducked behind a car and watched the guard for a moment. Lots of people came through the door. The guard said "Howdy, Professor" or "Howdy, Admiral." Everyone flashed a badge when they entered. I couldn't get in without a badge, and I could tell these were not the kind of badges you could buy at the Alliance Gift Shop. These were VIP's.

To get in, I needed a distraction. My football was in the backpack. *Perfect*, I thought. I can hit the guard in the head with the football and knock him out. Then I could walk right in. Stuff like that worked in the movies, but I couldn't throw a football that accurately. Also, it was kind of a stupid idea. Even if I hit him, would he really slump over and pass out? Uh, no.

I could hit the side of the hangar though. That might work. I stepped from behind the car, reared back, and threw the ball as hard as possible. It hit the metal hangar about fifty feet away from the guard. It made enough noise to get his attention. As he started to walk toward the noise, I dashed from behind the car and through the door.

Like I said, tiny door, enormous hangar—it was the size and shape of a football stadium, bright but totally hollow. The roof towered 200 feet overhead, the walls stretched at least that far in all direction. Everything, including the floor, was shiny and white. It was like a giant cereal bowl turned upside down. If anyone was looking for me, they would have seen me immediately, but everyone in the enormous room—about fifty people in all—was looking at hundreds of holographic screens of different sizes and shapes in the middle of the room. Behind all those screens I saw a faint red glow. Then I looked at the images—all of them same spherical shape rotating slowly and shedding mist. It didn't take long to figure out what was behind all those screens: the Device was there. *That was quick,* I thought. *Trackman must have shipped it here right after that conference with my dad.* I wondered about my dad's request, if they would take the Device on the mission. About that time I heard a rumble of thunder and rain on the roof.

In the middle of Hangar Two I saw a few familiar faces from the virtual room conference—Buckshot, Redshirt, and Sylvia Moreline were all there. I looked around for Gallant Trackman and Lincoln Sawyer, but they were nowhere to be seen. A group of people walked in behind me. *Oh, no,* I thought, but they didn't pay me any attention. They walked toward the Harper Device and I followed them. Someone stepped onto a platform in front of the screens, but I was too short to see his face.

"Houston, we have problems," he said, in a high-pitched voice. "Most of you know we are flying a last-minute mission. The nature of the mission is classified. Fortunately, Commander Harper and crew are up for another mission on short notice. Unfortunately for many of you, they will be taking the Harper Device with them. It's just too dangerous in our atmosphere, and since no one knows why, we have chosen to research the object in a safer environment."

"Where's that?" someone asked.

"The Moon."

The researchers in the crowd murmured in protest. The speaker continued.

"I know, I know. We've only had a few weeks to study this Device, and we have more questions than answers. The only thing we've learned so far is that the Device doesn't like research equipment or researchers very much. Niles Chakravorty was able to measure some the Device's infrared heat signature earlier today, but at a cost. The Device pulsated and threw him across the room. He broke his nose and a collarbone. No pain, no gain, right?" The crowd chuckled, but I gasped. That was Sunjay's dad, one of the Alliance's best researchers. *So that's how he broke his nose. He couldn't even tell Sunjay what really happened.*

"Well, if we don't laugh we'll probably cry. Research will continue on the Moon. Hopefully the Device will be safer there. I can't promise you that, but…"

The group kept talking about other space-related things, but nothing more about my dad's mission. I grew bored. Thunder rumbled and rain started to pound the hangar. Since it was difficult to hear anyway, I decided to get a better look at the Device. *There are so many screens that I can hardly see it, but nobody will see me if I slip behind the screens.* I skirted the side of the crowd and began my descent through layer after layer of colorful images of the Harper Device. The red glow of the Device got stronger. With each step I took, rain pounded outside on the metal roof and thunder shook the building. I could no longer see or hear anyone else in the hangar. Instead, one hundred screens lit my way toward the Device. The hair on my arms felt prickly.

Just as I reached the last layer of screens, I saw a red mist trailing onto the floor. Then I saw the Harper Device—exactly as it had looked in my dream—like a miniature red planet, swirling and beautiful, with dozens of different shades of reds all blending together on its surface. The cold mist soaked through my shoes. I could smell ozone, like before a thunderstorm. For a moment images of the color red filled my mind: apples, stop signs, fire trucks, fires, planets, flowers, blood, and stars. I caught myself walking closer to the Device with my hand outstretched. A few more steps and I would have touched it, but I came to my senses. *Careful, this thing is from another world,* I thought. *It's real, not a dream.* It was spinning more quickly than in my dream and seemed to be accelerating. The hairs on my arms stood on end. I took a step back.

"Lord have mercy! Anybody else feelin' that?" I heard Buckshot shout.

At that moment I heard a tremendous boom. Then another. And another. It took me a moment to realize what was happening—lightning was striking the hangar. Over the sound of the rain and booming I heard shouts from the other side of the room. I ran through a layer of screens looking for an exit, but I didn't get far. With one final tremendous crash, I saw a bolt of lightning break through the ceiling of the hangar. The lightning struck the Harper Device with a sizzle and bang. I didn't know whether to cover my ears or eyes—the sound and sight were too much. A wave of heat washed over me, and all the lights and screens in the hangar went out. A faint red glow lit the room.

The whole world felt sideways. Because it was. I was on my back instead of my feet. One of my shoes felt really hot. The sole felt gooey, like I stepped on a piece of gum. I tried to lift my foot and realized my shoe was melted to the floor. I yanked it up and pushed myself further back from the Device. In the dark, I started to check my hands and arms to see if I broke any bones. I seemed to be okay, but the fall knocked the wind out of me. The Harper Device shimmered in the dark hangar, the only thing unbothered by the freak weather event.

Then suddenly the thunder and the rain stopped. A moment later the lights and screens all came back on. The room looked exactly as it had before except for a tiny scorched part of the ceiling where the lightning entered the room. Through it I could see blue sky outside, like the storm had never happened.

"Everyone okay?" someone shouted from the group.

"Well, that proves Trackman's point," said another voice. "I hate to say it, but we're in over our heads."

The Alliance officials were gathering themselves, and I needed to make a quick exit before someone noticed me. I caught my breath and went for the side door, but before I escaped, an iron hand gripped my shoulder from behind. Spinning around I found myself staring into the luminous blue eyes of an Android. Lincoln Sawyer. He stood so motionless for a moment that I thought he was rebooting or something. Finally he blinked three times and dropped his hand from my shoulder.

"Authorized access only, Tully Harper," he said with a smile.

"Uh, I just wandered in here and realized I was in the wrong place. Sorry about that."

"You don't look like you just arrived." His hands reached for my throat. I flinched, thinking he was going to strangle me. He checked my vital signs instead. "Relax. I'm trained as a medical doctor. Your pulse is 140 beats per minute, but that's not surprising, considering what we just witnessed."

"Huh? I didn't see anything," I said.

"Oh, you weren't knocked to the floor along with everyone else? Blinded by the lightning?"

"No."

"Then why are your eyes dilated as if you've been staring at the sun? Or the Harper Device?"

"I was outside."

"Then why aren't you wet from the rain?"

"Because it's sunny—now."

"Ah, and the sun melted your shoe," he said. "Why did I not think of that? Silly me."

It was no use. I could lie, but he was a step ahead of me and not buying a single word I was saying. He smiled.

"Ha, you have a lot of nerve to sneak into a secure Space Alliance facility and lie to one of its most trusted employees. Tully, you are trouble, are you not?"

"No, I are not. I mean, I'm not. I'm just curious."

"Here is the truth: first, you are indeed curious. A true curiosity, if you follow me. Second, you definitely know more about the Harper Device and your father's next mission than you should."

"My dad is going on a next mission?" I said, looking to cover my tracks and make a quick escape.

"You surely know about this mission, Tully. I can put two and two together to make four, as they say. I can also tell you the square root of 2 is 1.41421356237."

"You don't make any sense," I said. I decided to leave, but before I had moved half an inch Sawyer put his hand on my shoulder again and held me in place. I wasn't sure if he anticipated my turn or had amazing reflexes. Either way, he stopped me cold.

"Stay for a moment and let me explain. A few days ago a virtual conference was held in your father's study. In the corner of that study there stood a very curious figure—a Handroid with oversized holo-glasses who shouted 'No!' when your dad accepted his next assignment. I am very adept at reading people and situations, Tully. Do you know what I read?"

I shook my head and tried to pull away from his grip, but he held me firm.

"In the past, people would have called you a 'misguided youth,' sneaking behind your father's back and lying to cover your tracks. You are the kind of boy who would have hopped on a riverboat just to see where it would take you. Yes, people would have said that you had 'a lot of nerve.' But do you know what?"

"What?"

"I like a lot of nerve. For now, your secrets are safe with me."

He took his hand off my shoulder and gave me a light push toward the side door. I didn't look back.

It was once again perfectly sunny outside though the ground was wet from the rain. I waited for my dad at the cafeteria as planned. *What a day!* I thought. If I had gone to Hangar One, I could have toured *The Adversity*. I might have found a place to hide. That was the easy path, but the journey to Hangar Two was more like my dad's motto: "Through hardship to the stars." Now my hands were shaking. My eyes felt sunburned. I felt lucky to be alive.

I also felt confused. "Lightning never strikes the same place twice," they say. What about four times? It made more sense now why my dad wanted to get it off the Earth.

Finally, Lincoln Sawyer was way too smart, and he knew I was sneaking around. Why did he let me go? I thought that Androids were programmed to follow the rules, but he released me. Maybe he thought my dad had enough on his mind and didn't need to worry about his troublesome son. He also thought I had a lot of nerve. Usually when Dr. Vindler says that to me, it's an insult. *You've got a lot of nerve handing in these incomplete notes, Tully Harper.* Sawyer meant it as a compliment. I guess I did have a lot of nerve, sneaking around and plotting to get on board a spaceship. Maybe Sawyer thought I was brave—or crazy. Or both. *I just hope he never figures out that I want to sneak into space. He won't hide that from my dad.*

I was pondering these questions when I felt a hand on my shoulder again. I jumped like a scared armadillo, but it was just my dad.

"Whoa, easy there, son," he said. "How was the tour? Did you learn anything new today?"

"No, nothing." I said. "Just a pretty basic tour of the ship. And stuff. What about you?"

"Oh, just a bit more than I wanted to know about the Harper Device." He ran his hand along the red streak in his hair.

"Are they going to keep it here?" I asked.

"Tully?" He frowned at me. "Who told you it was here?"

"Oh, you know. That was the rumor," I lied. "But I guess you just confirmed it. Don't worry. I can keep a secret."

He eyed me suspiciously. "Well, we've found a safer home for the Device than where it is now. I'll tell you about it soon enough."

I didn't feel right about lying to my dad, but maybe Sawyer was right: I had a lot of nerve. I didn't know if that made me good or bad, but I knew it would help me sneak into space. So would my two best friends.

PART TWO: HOW TO SNEAK INTO SPACE AND SURVIVE

June 30, 2069.

It's been fifty years
since scientists learned
how to protect astronauts
from solar radiation
using electromagnets.

It's two months
until we try
to sneak into space.

GRAWWLLL!

Okay, this is where the misguided youth with a lot of nerve might want to take some notes.

Getting into space was a million times trickier than I thought. Problem One was when and where we could actually meet to talk about the other 999,999 problems. We couldn't work at the Tirelli's house with four miniature tornado brothers swirling around and a super glued keyboard. We needed peace and a working computer. The Chakravortys' house was out of the question, too. Sunjay's mom and dad didn't snoop around our summer activities much, but his younger sister Sanjeetha did. As a third grader, she was too young to venture beyond their house and backyard, so whenever we visited Sunjay's house, she clung to us like stink on a skunk. That left a handful of other locations.

"How about the library?" I said.

"When's the last time you went to the library?" said Tabitha. "That would be pretty strange. Mrs. Stevens would want to help you find the right book. She'd make sure we were reading, too."

"Who's Mrs. Stevens?"

"The librarian."

"What about Yogurtland?!" blurted Sunjay. "Why can't we research there? We can look at maps of *The Adversity* on the 3D internet tables."

"3D Internet," said Little Bacon from the back of the room. "It offers users a chance to interact with websites without the use of a mouse or keyboard."

"Oh, sorry," I said, "Little Bacon, please shut yourself off."

"Oooh, your handroid!" said Tabitha. "I forgot about him. Leave him on. He'll be useful."

"Thank you, young lady," he said. "I am glad to help."

"Okay, but we're getting off topic, guys," I said. "Yogurtland is a cool place, but everyone will wonder what we're doing. Our whole school loves that place. Why do they serve ice cream anyway? I mean, it's a yogurt shop."

"Bingo! Bingdingalingo!" shouted Tabitha. Her eyes brightened. I could feel a Tabism coming from a mile away. "It's perfect. Why sneak around when we can sneak around sneaking around? *Cave-In!*, pancakes, and trampo. You're dad won't even think. All that kids stuff we always do. Perfect! "

I shook my head. "In English this time, please."

"Come on, guys, we work right under Commander Harper's nose in Mission Control. That way we can jump on your trampoline, play *Cave-In!*, and eat pancakes in the morning—it will seem totally normal. Only we'll be planning our own mission."

It was worth a try. Later that night, I asked Dad what his plans were for the next day. Sure enough the Space Alliance called him to a meeting. He wouldn't return until dinner. "I'll make breakfast. Can you fend for yourself for lunch?"

"There's always cornflakes," I replied. Mmm, cornflakes.

That next morning Sunjay, Tabitha, and I ate banana pancakes, gathered in Mission Control, closed the door, and began to plan. Sunjay wore jeans and a concert tee, I had on cargo shorts and flip-flops, and Tabitha was wearing a long skirt and, as she always did, a scarf. Her lucky scarf. "I wear it to all my dress rehearsals. I wore it to my exams last year and made straight A's," she explained. Did she really need luck for that?

Tabitha found the scarf in a vintage clothing store on a trip to Austin. It looked like any other gray scarf when she found it in the clearance bin.

As she flung it around her neck, the cloth suddenly burst into color. It turned sky blue, with white clouds blowing across the surface. "It's a mood scarf," she told me, "and the colors change when my moods change. But I swear it can read my thoughts! It's dire valuable and vintage, but the shop owner didn't know she even had it in stock. She said, 'Oh, my dear, you've found a lost treasure. I could never sell something that precious. I guess I'll have to give it to you as a gift.'"

Tabitha rarely wore the scarf to school because teachers found it distracting, especially when she grew excited and the scarf sprung to life with color. Today it was dark green with flashes of white flying across it like shooting stars. It did bring out the color in her eyes, but now wasn't the time for daydreaming. Now was the time for planning.

Tabitha and Sunjay both sat down on the brown couch in Mission Control and I began the day with a formal speech. For some reason, my hands were clammy and so was my forehead.

"Glad you could, uh, all make it," I said. "My friends, we have a problem: my Dad's going into space. That's sort of a problem, but it's not, uh, really the problem." On the LiveWall I pulled up a map of the United States and stood by Houston. "As you can see, all three of us have to get from here in Houston all the way to here in Florida." I leaned to reach for Florida. "But that's not the real problem."

"Correct," said Tabitha. "Not a problem. I got that one figured out already."

"Uh, really? You want to explain?" I asked.

She blew a bubble and twirled her scarf. "Nope, we can get to it later. Keep going. You're doing great."

I frowned but didn't want to get totally off track. I was building up to the important part of my speech. "Well, moving on," I said. My next map was the launch pad and runway, four square miles in the middle of the Florida wetlands surrounded by razor wire, checkpoints, and security dogs. "This is the real problem—Armstrong Field. We must evade all security and board *The Adversity.*"

"Oooh, look at all the dogs and razor wire. I bet it's like a swamp out there, with swamp water and crocodiles," quivered Sunjay. "Cats are really my favorite, you know? Cats are great. Maybe we should buy one—I can stay here and take care of the cat and you guys can go into space."

Somehow Sunjay's doubt gave me confidence. "You want to travel into space, Sunjay. I know you do. You ask my dad about his missions more than I do! You don't need a cat. You need an adventure!" I smiled and patted his shoulder, like a coach giving a pep talk.

Tabitha blew another bubble and popped it loudly. Then she laughed. "Wait, so that's the big problem, Tully? Razor wire and dogs? We can solve those problems with a shovel and some steaks."

We waited for her to explain.

"Guys, that's not a Tabism. You know, we can go *under* the fence if we *dig* with the *shovel*."

"Ohhh! Well, what about the steaks?" asked Sunjay.

"Sunjay, would a dog rather eat you or a giant steak?"

"I don't want to find out," he said.

"Don't worry. We won't have to. I've got a better idea for getting past security, too," she said, smacking her gum.

I didn't feel confident like a coach anymore. I felt annoyed. "Okay, so you solved the big problems, Tabitha. I'm super impressed. So why are we sitting here? Let's just go hop on board and wait for takeoff." I thought that would shut her up, but…

"Tully, we need to plan all this out carefully. I didn't mean it like that." She stood up and walked over to the LiveWall. We looked at the picture of Armstrong Field. Tabitha pointed up and circled the sky above. "The real problem isn't getting into space. I bet there are thousands of ways to get on board a spaceship. You will figure that out for us, for sure. No, it's *space*! We have to hide and survive on a spaceship for several days. Otherwise, your dad will send us home in an escape pod."

"Escape pods," said Little Bacon, "offer astronauts a way to safely exit a spacecraft in the event of emergencies like fires, engine failures, or structural damage."

Ugh, Tabitha was right. I sat down next to Sunjay on the couch and my butt nearly hit the ground. We watched Tabitha chew her gum and twirl with her lucky scarf for a minute before we could move.

"Astronauts get dozens of VIP passes to these launches, right?" she asked. I nodded. "Your Aunt from Alaska will take one and so will you. But if you act really lonely and we beg, maybe we can get passes, too. That will get us close to the ship, but it still doesn't get us on board. We'll have to look for that this week. Let's figure out what we need."

She wrote a list on the LiveWall: ***Get VIP passes. Find maps of The Adversity. Hiding spots on board. Learn about mission. Food? Water? Bathroom?*** "Okay, that's all. Proceed." She patted us both on the shoulder, coach-style, and sat back down between us on the couch. I was about to stand up and say something, but what could I say? I had only dwelled on a few of the problems. Sunjay must feel like this when he can't jump at the right time in *Cave-In!* For the first time, I felt frustrated with beautiful Tabitha and was about to tell her that she could just go home and forget the whole thing. Then the garage door opened. Someone was downstairs. We all tensed up and listened.

"Hey, Harper to Mission Control. Tully, you up there?" my dad called from downstairs as he entered. The stairs leading up the Mission Control began to creak, and I heard the doorknob turn. I had only a second to jump up and swipe my hand across the screen to hide Tabitha's list.

"Hey, Tully—and Sunjay and Tabitha. My meeting got canceled. Wow, all three of you, and Little Bacon. The three and a half musketeers in search of adventure!" he said, looking at us and back at the doorknob. I knew what he was thinking: *Why are they up here with the door shut?* He had a sort of unspoken "no doors closed" policy in the house—except, of course, for his office. How fair was that? He looked at the screen and frowned. "Hmmmm, that's a cute kitten," he said.

Oh, no. I remembered the last time I had used the LiveWall—I had pranked Sunjay with the kitten/zombie trick, and it was set to "kitten."

"Commander Harper, yes, that's our new kitten," said Sunjay, shrinking deeper into the couch. "His name is, uh, Button. No, Buttonhole. He loves milk, yes, he loves it. MILK!" His hair flopped down into his eyes.

"Buttonhole. You named your cat Buttonhole?" my father said, with a red glint in his eyes. "Funny, but that looks like a mountain in the background of the picture. Yes, Mt. McKinley in Washington, if I'm not mistaken. I've climbed it several times. You've already been to Mt. McKinley with Buttonhole the cat? You three have had a busy day…"

We were in the process of getting busted. Have you been there before? Sunjay sunk further into the couch and pulled his knees to his chest, looking sheepishly up at my dad. I was still too frozen to think, but the ice was starting to thaw, and an idea began to warm my mind.

Dad put down his shopping bags and brought his hand to his chin. "I hate to say it, Sunjay, but you're as transparent as a window. I can see right through you. Now, what were you three really doing?"

Tabitha jumped to her feet. "Commander, sir," she said, fiddling with her scarf, "we do have something to confess."

But before she finished, I grabbed her by the shoulder and thrust her back into the couch. I couldn't let her give away our plan before we even started. I had to do something. *I will not be left behind.* "Dad, sorry, I should explain. We, well, let me just show you. You'll need to sit down to hear this."

He frowned even more deeply but sat down anyway, sinking between Sunjay and Tabitha on the squeaky old couch. Sunjay was pale. Tabitha blew a bubble so big it stuck to her nose and hung there for a second.

I always have the controller when things get tough, I thought. *It's just like Cave-In! I just need to find the right way out of here.*

I turned out the lights and stood in front of the screen, a giant kitten peering over my left shoulder at the three people on the couch. And then I realized the way out. *If I flick the screen to the right, he'll see the map of the launch site and Tabitha's list. But if I flick the screen to the left…*

"Okay, Dad," I said. "I'm glad you showed up when you did because we were planning something. Something really big, and it involves you. You might as well know what it is. I'm going to flick my hand across this screen, and when I do, you'll see what we've been working on."

My Dad leaned forward, and so did Sunjay and Tabitha. I don't really know what any of them were expecting to see, but my dad should have seen it coming. The moment I flicked my hand across the screen, they saw it.

The picture of a screaming zombie.

"GRAAWWWLLLL!" growled the zombie. "GRAAWWLLLLLL!"

All three of them jumped back so hard they knocked over the old brown couch, their feet flying in the air. I couldn't see their faces, but I heard laughter as they rolled into a giant ball on the far side of the room. *It worked!* I thought. *We're safe.*

This was true. Sort of. Because my dad popped up, looked at Tabitha and Sunjay, and yelled, "Don't stand there, you fools. Get him!"

The three of them bolted after me as I ran for the door, but my dad beat me there.

"Tully zombie head trickster genius boy!" yelled Tabitha. She and Sunjay came from either side and grabbed my arms and my dad got my legs.

It didn't take them long to drag me outside and chuck me into the pool—shoes, shirt, wallet, and all. They spared my holophone though— Dad didn't want to replace that. As I sat on the edge of the pool squeezing water out of my pockets, I realized how close we had come to getting caught on the first day of real planning. If I had flicked my hand to the right, Dad would have seen our plans and grounded me for life. As punishment, I would have mowed every yard in the neighborhood until I went to college—unless Xanthar wanted to help. Fortunately, our secrets were safe.

Primary Objectives

After the close call with dad, we came up with some planning rules. We had to prepare for unwelcome intrusions, first of all. Sunjay programmed the LiveWall to keep all our documents on one page. If any of us tapped the wall three times, this ancient movie called *Star Wars* would start playing in the background. Sunjay's so random. I don't know where he finds stuff like this, but it's this cool old movie about a guy named Luke Skywalker. He lives on a farm in the desert with his aunt and uncle. A farm in the desert? I wasn't sure what they farm, but whatever. Also, he has these special powers that he doesn't really know about until he meets this mysterious old guy who shows him how to "use the Force" and trains him to fight with a "light saber," which is just a laser sword. The special effects are incredibly cheesy, but hey, the story is good. Of course, there's also a love story. Sunjay fell in love with Princess Leia. "Isn't her hair awesome?" he said. Tabitha had no opinions on Leia's hair but said the princess was too "complex" for Luke. "And besides, they're too much like brother and sister. She would be better with Han Solo. But let's get back to planning." Okay, Tabitha. Whatever you say.

I said that to Tabitha frequently during our planning. She kept us focused while we planned, which annoyed me for some reason. I didn't realize how often Sunjay and I just wandered off into random conversations.

Once focused, Sunjay researched harder than either of us. After I told him it was a repair mission for a space station, he wanted to know which one. He figured out some amazing stuff, too. "See, there are live cameras on every space station in the solar system. There are three stations orbiting Earth, two around Mars, one around Venus, and one even circles the Sun." He showed us live cam views from all of them. The station around Venus circled so quickly that you could get dizzy watching the surface of the planet whiz by. It was a sunrise and sunset every 45 minutes.

"But the problem is there's no problem," he said. "All the cameras work. None of the space stations are missing. There's nothing to fix, so what makes you think it's a space station repair mission?"

"I just overheard some things," I explained. I didn't tell them about all of my spying efforts.

We also read the crew profiles together. I knew them pretty well, everyone except Lincoln Sawyer. We spent some time reading his public profile on the Space Alliance website. It was written for younger kids, so it read like this:

LINCOLN SAWYER, ASTRONAUT-CLASS ANDROID
FABRICATED ON: DECEMBER 4, 2065
PURPOSE: SAWYER IS THE SPACE ALLIANCE'S FIRST FIELD-TESTED ANDROID. HE WILL SERVE AS SHIP'S DOCTOR AND SPACEWALK ASSISTANT ON THE UPCOMING MISSION TO THE MOON.
FUN FACTS: SAWYER IS QUALIFIED AS A SURGEON, BUT HIS HANDS ARE REGISTERED AS LETHAL WEAPONS! HE IS TRAINED IN MARTIAL ARTS. HE ENJOYS AMERICAN HISTORY—DO YOU SEE WHY HE CHOSE HIS NAME? SAWYER ALSO HAS UNLIMITED MEMORY, SO REMEMBER, FOLKS, IF YOU MEET THIS ANDROID, HE WILL NEVER FORGET YOU.

"Dude!" Sunjay did a roundhouse kick. "Unlimited memory! Martial arts! And he's going to be the ship's doctor. I've always wanted to meet a real android!"

"An android is a robot that looks and acts like a human," said Little Bacon, straightening his floppy hat, but Sunjay ignored him.

"Maybe Sawyer will teach us some skills," said Sunjay, chopping at the air.

"He'll be pretty busy, Sunjay. He does sound smart—kind of tough, too. Have you ever met him, Tully?"

"No, never," I said.

It was my first reaction, and it was a lie. Why had I lied? It wasn't like I needed to hide some big secret, but I thought, *Hey, they don't need to know every little detail. I didn't tell them about my weird Harper Device dream. Why tell them about my run-in with Sawyer or the trip to Hangar Two? It would just get complicated. A few secrets won't kill us.*

Despite our best efforts, one intruder interrupted our planning sessions, and it was unstoppable. A tropical storm. A few days after the Harper Device arrived in Houston, a tropical depression formed in the Gulf of Mexico. At first it headed toward Florida, but then the storm strengthened and headed straight for the Texas Gulf Coast. To everyone's surprise, the tropical storm reached Houston and then suddenly paused right over the Space Alliance Center, just a few miles from our house. We were in the eye of the storm. Of course, the eye of a hurricane is completely still with no rain and sunny skies. Our house is so close to the space center that we enjoyed perfect weather while the rest of the city was flooded and thrashed. Then, just like the storm at the hangar, the tropical storm vanished into thin air.

The rain still impacted us though. Our creek flooded the far end of the street. The Tirelli's house bordered the creek, so the flood ruined their carpet and made their house smell like old socks. My dad, Dr. Chakravorty, and Mr. Tirelli hauled the carpet outside. *Poor Tabitha*, I thought. Her brothers smelled bad enough. My dad looked at the moldy carpet and shook his head. I knew what was on his mind.

After that, Dad did seem snoopier than usual. He popped in a number of times to find us sprawled out in Mission Control watching *Star Wars*. He even watched a few scenes with us before heading back to the office again. He knew most of Han Solo's lines. I think he was glad I had company.

I was glad I had company, too. We finally found a few possible hiding spots on *The Adversity*. Most of them were in the cargo hold. Only one problem—it was frigid in there. We would need to bring coats, hats, gloves, food, water, etc. It was the best option we had found so far, but it would look suspicious if I packed my ski jacket for a trip to Florida. We also needed to know more about the mission, so I sent Little Bacon on another recon mission to dad's study. This time he found out they were planning a cover-up for the mission. Details would be announced soon.

Dad spent more and more time in his study. I couldn't help but feel resentment toward him. He may have guessed at my resentment, but he did nothing about it. Tabitha said I needed to act depressed.

"Why?"

"So he takes pity on you."

"How?"

"I'll show you."

She gave me some basic lessons in looking depressed, and they paid off with my dad. I picked at my food when he took me to restaurants or tried to talk to me about sports or school. I slouched, sighed often, and crinkled my forehead to look worried. When he asked me how I felt, I said fine. "If you shut him down, he'll get worried. Just don't talk to him very much."

I learned how to talk to Tabitha though. She was a pretty good listener as long as I wasn't trying to win an argument with her and didn't stare at her. There was something about her smile that made me feel at ease. I had to ignore how pretty she was though. That wasn't easy, but she was teaching me how to act. Sunjay would study maps of *The Adversity* while we did our acting lessons. Then all of the sudden he would fire off a question, like, "Hey, why is the sky blue if space is black?" Or he'd say, "You know, I think space might be scarier than we think."

"I think you're right, Sunjay," Tabitha told him. "Did you know that a paint chip flying through space can break a 3-inch thick window? I guess that makes sense if it's flying toward you at 15,000 miles per hour."

"Whoa," Sunjay said, "why do they even use paint?"

I could sense he was scared. I interjected. "You know what's cool, Sunjay? This one astronomer said he thinks there are a million other civilizations on other planets. A million. Maybe we'll bump into one of them in space."

I actually hadn't considered it at all.

✴ ✴ ✴

The day finally came when my dad told me what I already knew: he was going back to space. "Let's take a walk," he told me. "Leave your holophone in the house, okay?" We headed out the door, down the driveway and into the thick summer air. He didn't say anything until we were past the houses and on the dark, wooded stretch of road that led from our subdivision to a park. Luckily, the floodwater had receded. It was dusk and the crickets were chirping.

I rehearsed this moment in the mirror for a few weeks, working on my surprised and angry faces. I even rehearsed with Tabitha. I didn't expect to deliver my performance on the move though.

"Tully, I have some news you might not like," he said, looking down the street into the twilight.

"Then why don't you save it for some other day?" I mumbled.

"You don't really want me to do that, son."

"What do you know about what I want?" I shot back. That was part of the act. Tabitha told me I should get defensive and mad.

"You're right. I don't always know what you want. Somehow I think you know what I'm going to say. The Space Alliance needs me to fly another mission," he said.

"Yeah, really? Well, that stinks. I don't want to go back to Alaska." I felt a lump in my throat that stopped me from talking. It didn't matter if I was acting or not. This felt bad either way.

"I don't want to go on this mission, but they need me," he continued. "I haven't told you everything about the Harper Device. Much of it is confidential. That's why we're talking outside, why you had to leave your holophone behind. If someone wanted to overhear our conversation, it wouldn't be hard to turn that phone into an eavesdropping device." He stopped and faced me. "First, you have to promise me you won't share what I'm going to tell you with another living soul. Can you do that?"

"Uh, yeah," I said. "I guess."

He shook his head. Not good enough.

"Yes, I promise that I will not share this with another living soul."

"Very good," he said, resuming the walk. "The mission objective is clear. We've lost contact with a space station. We need to find out what happened. I will lead a small crew to assess the damage and repair the space station.

"I also have my own objective, and this is where I need your promise. When I found the Device, I didn't know what to do with it. Everyone wanted to bring it back to Earth for research, but something told me that was a bad idea. The Alliance thought it was a great idea. From what they saw, the Harper Device might have unlimited energy. New investments started coming in faster than they could believe. I got caught up in all the excitement and told them we would bring it home."

"Uh, okay," I said. "So what's your objective?"

"No, give me a moment. It turns out I was right. The research hasn't produced many results, but that won't stop researchers from trying even when things get dangerous. They see all the amazing potential of the discovery, but it blinds them to the dangers. Yes, the Device is dangerous. We only have to look down the street at the Tirelli's house to see that. So the Device produced a tropical storm. What's next—a hurricane, an earthquake, a tsunami? It's only going to get worse. So I've convinced Gallant Trackman of the danger. Fortunately he agreed with me, and he is a very influential man."

He paused for a minute. I knew what he was about to say, but tried to act confused. "What does all this mean, dad?"

"We are taking the Harper Device with us on this mission. We are supposed to drop it off at Moon Base Tranquility."

"Well, great then! Send the Device to the Moon, but why do *you* have to go? Why does it have to be the great Commander Harper on this mission?" I asked in an angry whisper. "You—you could have died last time out there! Left me alone in the wilderness!" *He doesn't have to go! I don't have to go either. We can stay here. I can convince him. All this crazy planning, we don't have to do any of it*, I thought. *Maybe I can actually convince him to change his mind.* "Dad, don't leave. Somebody else can go. You're famous enough, aren't you?"

"Famous?" There was a red glint in his blue eyes. "You should know me better than that. I don't care about fame. I care about you."

"Then don't leave me." I grabbed his arm, and he put his hand on mine.

"Nobody else can do what must be done," he explained, looking up to the sky.

"Repair a space station and drop the Harper Device on the Moon? Any commander could do that. You're not the only commander in the Alliance."

"Do you want to know my objective then?"

"Yes!"

"I'm not taking it to the Moon. I'm hiding it somewhere else."

I gasped. I already heard so much from all my eavesdropping that I thought I knew everything. I certainly didn't know this.

"What? Why?"

"Because some power is better left unused."

"Won't you get in trouble?"

"Yes, I could get in big trouble, but sometimes you have to break the rules to do the right thing. I don't mind breaking a few rules to save a lot of lives—or a planet."

That was just strange enough to shut me up. Save the planet? Was the Harper Device that powerful or that bad? The crickets chirped and a dog barked in someone's backyard. I kept thinking about his words. "To break the rules to do the right thing," he said. It was hard to understand. I imagined someone shouting "Guilty!" and putting my dad behind bars.

"So you may save the planet, but they may throw you in jail."

"If they catch me, son, and I don't think they will. Your old man is sneakier than that."

Ha! Well, I was sneaky, too, and I also had an objective—to get on board his ship. Maybe I had to break some rules to do the right thing, too.

Knowing his purpose gave me another objective in space. We might help my dad hide the Device, and that would make the world a safer place. He looked over at me a few times on the walk home, and I wanted to look back and say, "It's okay. Go save the world!" But I couldn't. I had to keep up my act.

We headed back to house. Then, unexpectedly, he started talking again.

"Oh!" he added. "I can tell you some other interesting news. We need to distract the media. We don't want them to know the Harper Device is on the mission. You've heard about the orangutan that knows sign language, right? He's from the San Diego Zoo."

"You mean Scrubbles?"

"That's his name." He told me that Scrubbles would be part of their "cover," along with an unnamed pop star. This pop star apparently wanted to write the first album in space.

"Ugh," he rubbed his eyes, "I thought things were bad enough, but musicians in space? And a primate? I wish you could come along to see it. We could monkey around in space together."

"Yeah, just what I always wanted to do, sneak into space," I said, trying to hide my surprise. However, he gave me an idea. That was the moment I knew how I could sneak on board *The Adversity*.

That night I thought about our conversation. My dad had good reasons to fly the mission. He thought he was saving the world. If I was in his shoes, I might do the same thing. I guess we both had a lot of nerve. His secrets were safe with me, but I had some secrets of my own.

Sunjay in Love, Me in Pain

The next day I perfected my lonely, only child look, keeping my eyes on the ground and answering all my dad's questions with "yes," "no," or "whatever." He must have felt bad about breaking the news to me. To lighten the mood he took Sunjay, Tabitha, and I to the flight press conference. Tabitha's acting lessons were paying off.

"Oh, I hope we can see your launch, too, Commander!" said Tabitha on our ride to Space Alliance Headquarters. "I need to get out of the house for a while. It still smells pretty gross from the flood."

"Sure, Tabitha. You and Sunjay have been keeping Tully entertained," my dad said. "I probably owe you one."

Before the press conference, The Space Alliance rolled *The Adversity* out of Hangar One. It was like watching a killer whale slowly swim past you in the ocean, with its black belly and white topside—except the ship was a hundred times the size of a killer whale and much bigger than the old Space Shuttles from the late 20th century. Its nose emerged first with two sets of windows: a Flight Deck and an Observation Deck. Next came the wings and the middle of the ship, where the crew cabins and the cargo hold were. After that, the wings broadened at the body of the ship. They kept experiments and a space lab in that section. Finally we saw the massive engines that launched the whole thing into space. It was hard to imagine those big, dark engines coming alive with fire. It was equally hard to imagine getting on board, but that's what we planned to do.

In front of *The Adversity* there stood a stage that looked small by comparison. Sunlight shined off the windows and onto the stage where my dad sat with his crew. We had front row seats by the press who were snapping pictures and filming. The "Return of Commander Harper" was a big deal in itself, but the excitement increased when the Alliance released the details. "Moon, Monkeys, and Music!" a banner read above the stage. An Alliance spokesman told the crowd that the mission had three goals. "It's a pretty standard mission," the spokesman said, "just dropping off some supplies at Moon Base Tranquility. But it's also an excited time. It has been one hundred years since Neil Armstrong walked on the Moon."

The second announcement was that Scrubbles the Orangutan would be a passenger. Primates hadn't flown in space since the early days of space flight. Back then, NASA used them to see what might happen to astronauts in space. "Primates made it into space before people," my dad explained. "Some of the them survived, but many died because of accidents like parachute failure. This mission will show how far we've come," explained my dad. "Scrubbles will have a great life on board *Adversity*. He's even worked on his vocabulary for the trip. He knows Moon, stars, sun, gravity, and liftoff." When my dad said those words, Scrubbles signed them. The media thought that was pretty cute, I guess. Scrubbles would perform experiments and practice his sign language with one of the astronauts. He sat on stage with his trainer, who was busily combing his hair. When my dad finished his brief speech, Scrubbles shrugged off his trainer and saluted my dad. The salute went viral. Who can resist a patriotic primate?

The third announcement was the big surprise—one of the world's biggest pop stars would be on board for this mission. She burst through the "Moon, Monkeys, and Music!" banner singing her latest hit, "Star Trance." She wore a dress shaped like *The Adversity* itself, with giant wings and sparks flying off the fringes.

"Oh, my gosh. Is this really happening?" asked Sunjay, grabbing his hair and pulling it out to the sides. "Is that really her?"

Yes, it was her. Queen Envy.

Sunjay's eyes almost popped out of his head he was so excited. I was also surprised but definitely not star-struck. Queen Envy was a bit of a maniac to me. She finished her song and took a bow. She flicked her glittering eyelashes and announced her new album's title: *Starboy in Love.*

With all the hype about Scrubbles and Queen Envy, there were very few questions about the actual purpose of the mission. It was a genius way to distract the media, I guess. No one asked any tough questions. No one mentioned the Harper Device or the hurricane, even with my Dad sitting right there on stage. I think that's the only reason he—or the Alliance—could bear to watch Queen Envy strutting around on stage in front of *The Adversity* and blowing kissing to Scrubbles, who didn't seem too impressed with her performance. Neither were Tabitha and I.

Sunjay, on the other hand, took about a thousand pictures of himself with Queen Envy in the background. Later that night at Mission Control he made one of his photos the desktop background of the LiveWall. Tabitha and I drew horns and a goatee on Queen Envy when he wasn't looking. He just scowled and examined his maps. "She'll write songs about me," he said.

Tabitha loved that. "Oh, so you're the Starboy she's referring to. I've been wanting to hear Queen Envy sing about a geeky space stalker for a long time."

"Me, too!" he shouted.

"Sunjay," I said, "do you remember the last celebrity that went into space? Adam Levine, Jr.? I think his dad was a voice coach on TV or something. Anyway, he wrote a song in space called "Space Maniac." Then he sort of *became* a space maniac. He launched himself toward the sun in an escape pod! 'I want to find something hotter than me!' he said. The crew caught his escape pod before he burned up in the sun, but they had to lock him up for the rest of the mission."

"My Queen won't do that," said Sunjay. "She's a normal human being."

"—who dresses up as a sexy spaceship to get attention," added Tabitha.

Well, at least he didn't seem as scared about the mission, I thought.

After the press conference, we found everything we needed to make the rest of our plans. Sunjay found blueprints that showed all the different storage areas where he and Tabitha might hide. I didn't need a spot. I already found a great hiding spot fit for one person, but not everyone felt so confident about my plan.

"You're going to do what!" Sunjay screamed, his voice cracking. His voice was changing. It felt good to surprise somebody, even if he did think I was crazy. "Stop laughing, Tully. That'll never work. Tell him, Tabitha."

Tabitha just twirled her scarf. She scrunched up her nose and squinted at me with those lovely green eyes, like she was making some calculation in her head. "Take it easy, Starboy. It won't be easy but it will work," she said, "Dire cool, Tully. You'll have food and a spacesuit. Good for you." She blew another bubble. "Now let's get *us* on board."

Sunjay pulled up a blueprint that stretched across the LiveWall. An astronaut was drawn at the bottom of the map near the nose.

"Hey, Sunjay, what's that there for?" I asked.

He squinted at the tiny astronaut. "Oh, that's to give you the scale of the map. He's about the size of your thumb, right? You can get a sense of how big everything is."

We looked down the length of the ship. Each section was labeled in small, careful lettering. The cargo hold was as big as a classroom. "No," Sunjay said, "the size of a gymnasium, but it will be packed with color-coded boxes full of equipment. We could hide in one of those boxes. I think they will put most of the food here," he pointed.

A large section of the crew cabins was blocked off in a glittery looking purple. Tabitha twirled her scarf. "Queen Envy has an entire gymnasium to herself? Look at all that wasted space. I mean, what's she going to put in there? What's she taking in to space?"

"Musicians need their instruments, Tabitha. You wouldn't understand," Sunjay said.

"Oh, good point, Starboy. If only she were a musician," said Tabitha.

"You're jealous, both of you," he said. "You know, she sent me a message last night. I opened my holophone and she popped out, right in the middle of my room."

"She sends that to all her fans," replied Tabitha.

"Of course she does, but it's still cool. She said she's bringing two full drum sets, five guitars, two bass guitars, a banjo, three keyboards, something called a 'key-tar,'" he continued listing as Tabitha and I just rolled our eyes, "two monogrammed spacesuits—purple and pink. She's going to keep those in her room for decoration, I guess. Who needs two spacesuits, right? What? What!" he said as our eyes popped open. "What? Also, a bunch of stuff I would rather not say. It's kind of embarrassing stuff, like, Tully's caveman decorations, if you know what I—WHY ARE YOU STARING AT ME?!" His voice cracked and went up and down about three octaves.

"Sunjay, you genius!" Tabitha kissed Sunjay on the cheek. He wiped his cheek and looked at his hand. "I'm not wearing lipstick, stupid. Don't you see?"

"See what?"

"Purple and pink—that's what I think," she said. "Scrubbles and Starboy and me. In space all three! Thanks to Queen Envy the celebrity hoarder."

Sunjay looked confused, but I could see Tabitha's plan. "Sunjay," I said, "how would you like to go into space dressed in one of Queen Envy's monogrammed spacesuits?" He stopped rubbing his face and realized what this meant.

"You mean it?" he said. "Oh, yeah! Strap me into a Queen Envy spacesuit and let's go to the Moon!"

To the Moon, yes! I just wish we knew our final destination. Other than that, all systems were go. Dad gave us VIP passes that allows us to tour *The Adversity* on launch day. Sunjay and Tabitha could now get on board the ship—and stay there. I wouldn't need a pass to get on board though. Finally, we created two diversions, but I'll explain those details soon enough.

Later that night dad came home and found me in Mission Control, watching *Star Wars* once again. I gave him a head nod to say, "Hello, I'm mad at you." He tousled my hair anyway and then he headed to his study. I decided to sleep on the old brown couch that night, comforted by the thoughts of what we had done.

The only thing I regretted? That I hadn't thought about those extra spacesuits. Then Tabitha would have kissed me on the cheek instead. *That* would have been dire cool.

A Moment in the Hallway

A few days later we packed into Dr. Chakravorty's hover car and headed to Florida for the launch. We drove the first few miles out of town on Interstate 10 until we reached the entrance to Hoverway 10. We drove up a steep ramp behind a few other hover cars. We reached the end of the ramp and Dr. C pulled back on the wheel. We rocketed up toward the hoverway four hundred feet above, an endless row of cars cruising between holographic yellow and white lines. I asked him to take the car "water-roading" above the Gulf of Mexico, where we could go as fast as we wanted.

He set the autopilot, turned around, and glared at me. "Water-roading? Are you crazy? These are leather seats. What if some lunatic bumps into us and we have to emergency land the vehicle in the water? The salt water will ruin the car. After that, I guarantee you that the sharks will smell the leather. They'll eat my seats for dinner and we'll be dessert." Dr. Chakravorty's new hover car was a part of our plan, a part that made Sunjay cringe. He almost fainted when we pitched the idea to him, but Tabitha convinced him it was for the best.

Dr. C acted as our chauffeur, but our chaperone was in the passenger seat—my Aunt Selma. In Middle of Nowhere, Alaska, she looked right at home in her work boots and overalls, hair pulled back into a sloppy ponytail as she chopped wood in the yard. She didn't like warm weather though. She looked out of place in her flowered dress, and she sweated constantly. "Whoo, what a swamp! Turn up that AC, Niles! I hope our hotel in Florida has a pool."

Our hotel did have a pool, and Aunt Selma swam all day. Dr. C went to visit some Space Alliance friends. The three of us tried to stay calm, but that wasn't easy. We booted up Tabitha's old laptop when we arrived at the hotel. All afternoon we played *Cave-In!* Tabitha's hands were shaking, Sunjay's voice kept cracking, but we managed to set a new high score. That distracted us for a while. "This is a really good sign," said Tabitha.

Later that night reality set in. First, I said good-bye to my Dad. Well, it was stranger than that. I had to *pretend* to say good-bye to my dad. I had to act mopey when I was really thrilled about the trip and nervous to put our plan into action. In the end, my Dad gave me the same speech he does before all his flights. He teared up, and so did I. "I love you, son, and God willing, I'll see you again."

"I'll see you soon, Dad," I said. *I mean it.* We hugged, and he boarded a hovervan with the rest of his crew. They disappeared into the damp night air. They would spend the night aboard *The Adversity*, and God willing, we would join them the next day.

Dr. Chakravorty was snoring like a freight train when I returned to the room, and Sunjay was smiling in his sleep with his headphones on. I could hear Queen Envy blasting between his dad's snores. It was going to be a delightful night. I was about to plug my ears with toilet paper and get in bed when I heard a light scratch on the door. Out the peephole I saw Tabitha in her pajamas, standing in the hallway.

"Hey," I said. I closed the door softly and leaned back against it.

"Did it go okay with your dad?" she asked.

"Yeah, fine. I don't think he suspects anything. How's Aunt Selma?"

"We're getting along. She has some wild stories about the wilderness. I guess your dad's not the only explorer in your family." *What about me?* I thought, but decided not to say anything. "Your aunt doesn't like the humidity in Florida. And she hates your dad's job. She hates space. Is it because of the last trip, the Harper Device near-death deal?"

"No, it's a long story that has to do with my mom." I blurted it out without even thinking, and Tabitha seemed surprise. I was, too. She started to apologize so I changed the subject. "No, hey, don't worry. So I think the plan is coming together fine. Dad doesn't suspect a thing."

"Of course not. I taught you how to act, didn't I?" She paused and looked down at her slippers. Something else was on her mind. "Tully, are we really going to do this tomorrow? We could get into real danger out there."

I remembered the note she dropped at school, how she doodled "Danger?" above the Harper Device. *She doesn't even know the Device is going on this trip,* I thought. *I never told her or Sunjay. She doesn't know that it caused the storm that flooded her house.* I wondered how she would feel about that, but I didn't ask. "Are you worried something bad is going to happen to us? Well, it either will or it won't, I guess." *Not the best pep talk, Tully.* She looked down again, but I put my hand on her shoulder. "No, that's not what I mean. Are you scared? Because if that's it, I think we should be scared. I'm scared that our plan won't work, but it's got to work. Anyway, you know what scares me more?"

"What?" she said.

"*Not* leaving. Being stuck in Alaska, not knowing if my dad will return. And being a thousand miles from you and Sunjay. That's really a horror story to me. I want an adventure story."

"Me, too. For the longest time I wanted to run away from home— just for a while—but I never knew where to go. So when you started talking about your plan, it just felt perfect. And you and Sunjay are my crazy fun summer friends, so I had to go. You guys are like family to me."

"Really?"

"Yes. You never let me down. You always pick me up. I just hope we haven't tried for too much."

"No risk, no reward. That's what my dad says."

Tabitha nodded. She was wearing her lucky scarf, and it turned a deep purple. *She has something else on her mind,* I thought, waiting for her to speak.

"What's your dad going to say when we come out of hiding in a few days?"

"He can say what he wants. I'd rather be yelled at in space than yelled at in Alaska. Whatever he says, it won't be 'Go cut some wood!' And whatever he does, we'll be the first people ever to sneak into space."

"And survive," she added. Her scarf went from purple to light blue.

"Yes." I tugged on her scarf. "So just wear your lucky scarf to bed and think about three things you're grateful for. It's a good habit."

"Okay," she said, laughing and sniffling.

For a moment we both stood there looking at each other in the hall-way. It reminded me of our very last game of *Cave-In!*, where we were down to our last life. We were almost crushed by a boulder, but Tabitha pointed out the danger and I dodged it. We cheated death and made it to the next level. Sunjay then found an extra life hidden under a rock, so we played the game together for another two hours. It was a perfect moment that we could never have planned. *If I said or did the right thing*, I thought, *it might be the same way tonight. Tabitha and I might hang out together for another three hours—maybe explore the hotel, sneak up to the roof, watch the stars, and take a walk. Anything might be possible.* It was a strange feeling that made my head swirl. Her scarf went from blue to bright green. Part of me said, "Go!" and another part said, "Where?"

But I couldn't decide what to do or say, and the moment sort of slipped away like a meteor blazing past and leaving behind only the cold stars. We nervously smiled. She gave me a hug before shuffling down the hall to Aunt Selma's room. I tried to get some sleep, but between Dr. Chakravorty's Snorefest, Sunjay's elbows, tomorrow's mission, and thinking about that moment in the hallway, I didn't sleep a wink.

How to Sneak into Space in Three Easy Steps

The next morning went as planned. Sort of. By the end of it, we would be aboard *The Adversity*, but not before I scared an orangutan, wrecked a hovercar, and had a run-in with an angry swamp monster.

We arrived at the launch site, which looked like a music festival hosted at an airstrip on the fourth of July. A holographic banner flew above the entire event—about a mile long and a mile off the ground, it was clearly visible from the ground or from space. "100 Years Since Man First Walked on the Moon!" One hundred thousand people poured through the gates in every sort of vehicle—bicycles, mopeds, cars, hovercars, hoverboards, and monstrous hoverbarges blaring dance music. We flashed our VIP badges and found a place to park Dr. C's hovercar.

Inside, an enormous grandstand towered over one side of the airstrip and boomed music to the huge crowds. A hangar stood next to the grandstand, and in it was *The Adversity*, full of people wanting a closer look at our ship.

Some people came for the launch. Some people came for the music. The Space Alliance booked some of the world's biggest acts for the festival: The Rolling Tombstones, the Stone Cold Breathmints, and the Hypertones were all there. Queen Envy was the closing act the night before the launch, of course. Sunjay couldn't believe he had missed her performance, but we all knew we needed our sleep. We had a busy day ahead of us.

"But she wore hover shoes and floated over the audience when she sang 'Nothing Can Hold You Down!'" he said.

Tabitha shrugged. "Sunjay, you don't need to hear that song. We're going to live out those lyrics when we get on board *The Adversity*."

For the last few nights the crew slept on board: Redshirt Anderson, Buckshot Lewis, Gallant Trackman, Sylvia Moreline, and my dad. Lincoln Sawyer was on board, too, but Androids don't need sleep. Queen Envy slept in her hoverbus, enjoying one more night of luxury. And Scrubbles, well, I knew exactly where Scrubbles would be.

He was my ticket on board.

After we parked the hovercar, the three of us walked ahead of Aunt Selma and Dr. C to talk about our plan.

"Everybody say what you're going to do," I said.

"Okay," said Sunjay, with a gulp, "I'll get the keys to my father's hovercar. Then we'll meet back here and we'll drive it into—oh, stars, daddy's going to kill me—"

"—You'll be in space before he knows, Sunjay," I reminded him. "Once we've ditched the car—"

"—Tully will do his orangutan thing and Sunjay and I will use our VIP passes to get on board and hide. We get Queen Envy to take us on board *The Adversity* for a tour of her room and we don't leave," said Tabitha, smiling and flipping her scarf.

"I can't believe we're doing this!" Sunjay squealed. "To hang out in one of the Queen's spacesuits and watch her write the first album ever recorded in space—"

"—will be Heaven for her space stalker. And why I brought earplugs." Tabitha grabbed his shoulders. "Time for the tour, Space Boy. Remember, I get the purple spacesuit."

Step One: Ditch the adults and ditch the car.

Sunjay and Tabitha took Dr. Chakravorty to *The Adversity* hangar. I grabbed Aunt Selma by the hand and made for the grandstands. "Tully, slow your caboose down!" she said. Beads of sweat popped up on her forehead. I kept dragging her. We needed to tire her out.

"Wow, Aunt Selma, let's check out the grandstand seats before we see the hangar." She grimaced but tried to keep up as I pushed through the crowd, past the concessions, up the first set of stairs, and began bounding up the steps toward the VIP seating at the very top. "Come on, Aunt Selma!"

She looked like she had just jumped out of the pool by the time she made it past the vendors to the VIP seating, and she was breathing like she swam the 400-meter butterfly.

"My stars, what's gotten into you? Let your old aunt rest a minute," she said, puffing. "Can't we just take the elevator?"

"Come on, Auntie. We'll be sitting down all day. Oh, they've got the best lemonade in the VIP area. Let's get some," I said. It didn't take much more than that to get her inside the air-conditioned booth. It looked like a huge press box at a football stadium where people can watch the game, eat, and drink. And that's what Aunt Selma wanted to do. She sat down and ordered nachos and a lemonade. By the time her food arrived, she convinced me that we should stay in the VIP. Perfect.

I ran back to the car. Sunjay and Tabitha were already there.

"Your aunt is drinking lemonade," said Tabitha. "Good! We lost Dr. Chakravorty in the hangar. Sunjay, give Tully the keys please." Sunjay reluctantly handed me the keys to his father's car. We all got in. I started the engine. There was no turning back now.

"Okay, Sunjay. Where's that pond?"

Sunjay pointed the way. I slowly brought the hovercar off the ground. Carefully, we made our way down rows of cars until we reached a little forest. There we found a pond surrounded by cypress trees, just like we had pictured it on the LiveWall. It's the kind of place my dad would take me bass fishing, but we weren't here for the catch of the day. We were here to dump a car.

Tabitha and Sunjay hopped out of the car and onto the shore of the pond. I stayed in the driver's seat. When we decided no one was around, I coasted Dr. C's brand new hovercar over the water. It was just deep enough to submerge the car. I would have to swim back to shore once I dumped the car.

I guess that's the first mistake I made—I didn't bring a swimsuit for this operation. I put the car in "Park" and it started to descend to the water. A few alarms sounded. The car wouldn't land on the water.

"It won't land!"

"Try to surprise it!" yelled Sunjay. "Bring it back over land and then nosedive it in before it has time to think."

For a guy who didn't want to destroy his dad's car, Sunjay knew what to do. I put the car in reverse, aimed the nose at the center of the pond, and hit the accelerator. In a moment I went from seeing blue sky to seeing fish swim beside the windows. I checked my pocket. Sure enough, Little Bacon was there, holding on to my shirt, wondering what I was doing.

"Hang on, LB. We're about to get wet." I took a deep breath, opened the sunroof, and water filled the car. Drenched, I swam for the surface. After that, I started to swim back to shore.

Behind me, I heard a deep, rumbling sound, like a gasoline-powered engine roaring to life. It was an odd sound for a sinking hovercar to make. That's because it wasn't the sinking car.

"Tully, swim faster!" yelled Tabitha, looking panicked. I heard the rumble behind me again.

"Okay, gimme a minute. It's not easy swimming in jeans."

"You don't have a minute. Crocodile!"

I looked behind me and sure enough, it was an...

"—Alligator," said Little Bacon. He had climbed from my shirt pocket to my shoulder to avoid the water. "Florida is one of the only places where both alligators and crocodiles coexist in the same habitat," he explained calmly.

"That's not helpful!" I yelled between strokes. The alligator swam behind me with a hungry look in his eyes. I was so scared I almost forgot how to swim.

"An alligator has a bite force of 3,000 pounds, three times stronger than a lion," he continued.

"Tully, you can't die before we get on the ship! Swim for your life!" shouted Tabitha.

I turned for the dock and did my best freestyle stroke, which isn't very good. The alligator was still coming at me, but I was making good enough time and almost to the shore now.

"Stars!" I shouted. "Throw something at him."

The alligator was about five feet from me as I got into the reeds at the edge of the water. I started bounding through reeds. *This wouldn't be so hard if I was taller!* I heard him snap his jaws but didn't turn around. I just kept running like a mad man and thinking, *This thing will not eat me! I'm going into space!*

"Tully, watch out!" I didn't turn around, but that was for the best, because the danger came from right in front of me. I ducked as a giant rock sailed over my head. Clunk! I hoped that was the sound of an alligator getting hit by a big rock. For once, I was glad I was short.

I sprinted from the swampy water and tried to catch up with my friends. The three of us ran back to the parking lot before we turned around. Tabitha and Sunjay looked at me wide-eyed. I had to keep my cool, even though my heart was beating like a snare drum. This was no time for a freak out.

"Well, I'm glad those swimming lessons paid off. Tabitha, are we on schedule?" I said between breaths.

"If we hurry," she said.

"Thanks," I said. "And good shot, Sunjay. Next time aim a LOT higher."

Tabitha smacked her gum and flipped her scarf. "Rock tossing, hover car wrecking craziness! No time for congratulations! We're not on board and you're not an orangutan yet, Tully Harper. Come on, you guys. We're wasting time!"

Step Two: Do the orangutan thing.

I dried off quite a bit on the way to the hangar. Tabitha brushed the swamp weeds out of my hair. I looked almost normal.

"We're off to travel the universe with Queen Envy!" Sunjay yelled, excited and scared senseless at the same time.

"Space Boy, take a deep breath," said Tabitha. She turned toward me and hugged me. "Stars, Tully, you smell worse than my house! We'll see you on board."

The enormous hangar loomed in front of us. They headed for *The Adversity*, and I walked toward the Space Alliance offices. It was just a few hours until the launch. A lot of people were leaving the hangar and headed down to the field toward the runway and bleachers. As most of the crowd left the hangar, I made my move. *It's time I met Scrubbles,* I thought.

Tabitha taught me two things: first, how to act mad and depressed around my dad. Second, she taught me some sign language, because that's how Scrubbles communicated with people. I knew just enough to make the rest of our plan work.

Scrubbles was with his manager, Corbin Belafonte. I found them in their dressing room on the second floor of the hangar. Corbin had agreed to let me play with Scrubbles for a few minutes before the flight. When Corbin came to the door, he wore a gold tuxedo shirt, camouflage pants, and purple sunglasses. So did Scrubbles. I flashed my VIP pass when he opened the door. He didn't seem too thrilled to see me, but the famous Commander Harper had asked the favor for his one and only son. How could he refuse?

Bubble's spacesuit was thrown into a chair beside him. Scrubbles sat on the couch, and Corbin stood behind him, combing his hair one last time before he boarded the ship. Scrubbles seemed to be enjoying the attention as well as the sunlight coming in through the second floor window. He had stubby legs and freakishly long arms, but he was about my height, as I had hoped.

"So Commander Harper's son is here to see you, Scrubbles," he said. "Give the lad a fist bump, dear." Scrubbles and I awkwardly fist bumped. I'd never fist bumped an orangutan.

"Isn't he about to put on his spacesuit?" I said.

"Oh, in a minute! My gosh! Scrubbles loves to have his hair combed. It relaxes him, and he's been a wreck all day with all these photographers. Just look at him! Biting his fingernails, scratching his armpits. He hardly ate a thing this morning," explained Corbin, looking frazzled. "I don't know how he'll survive in space without his Bong Bong."

"His what?"

"Me, you fool!" he shouted. "I'm his Bong Bong."

"Uh, okay. Do you want some help, Bong Bong?" I said, reaching for a comb.

"It's Mr. Belafonte to you!" Corbin yanked back like I was trying to rob him. "No no no! No help! He simply freaks out when other people comb him. He's so stressed right now," he said and then yelled out the door to the photographers. "All of you, shut your filthy paparazzi faces! You are upsetting the talent!"

Scrubbles didn't seem to share any of "Bong Bong's" worries though. He gazed out the window calmly, looking over his shoulder at me once in a while, and then at the comb. Corbin looked like he was on the caffeine high of a lifetime. I didn't need the manager to freak out though. I needed Scrubbles to freak out in a big way. Soon.

Bong Bong combed Scrubbles' hair for several minutes. I asked him several questions: What would Scrubbles eat in space? How did he train? What would the ship's doctor do if Scrubbles were sick? This last question made him stop combing "the talent." "Listen, Commander Harper's kid. I'm sure it was great for you to meet the talent, but I need to get him into his suit now. Could you go ahead and, uh, blast off?" he said.

"Yes, that is my plan," I said, "but my dad, Commander Harper, said I could help you first. Could I, please?"

Corbin wrinkled his nose and took a deep breath. He threw up his hand, "Look, kid, Scrubbles and Bong Bong need some time together, okay? He's going into space and I can't go with him and this has all been such a mess and...." Just then, the door flew open and a photographer poked his head in for a picture. Corbin jumped up and hurled a comb at him. "Away from here, you filthy paparazzi devil! If you open that door again I will end you! You will curse the day your mother bought you that worthless camera!" He went on and on with his execrations.

In the meantime, I calmly opened the window behind him. Then I turned to Scrubbles and delivered the hand signals I had been practicing for the last several days.

Scrubbles looked at me calmly until I gave him the first sign.

"Fire," I signed.

He sat up straight and sniffed the air loudly. He looked out the window.

At the second sign, he let out a loud screech and jumped on his couch, jerking his head frantically.

"Lions," I signed.

I heard Corbin slam the door behind me. Time had run out. Scrubbles jumped into action when I gave him the full message.

"Fire. Lions. Window. Pond. Go!" I signed and pointed to the window. Scrubbles leapt out the window into a tree. He ran for the woods.

Corbin screamed. "Beautiful Scrubbles, nooo! What did you tell him, you smelly reprobate troll!" He grabbed me by the shoulder and pushed me aside.

I hoped Scrubbles' manager would pass out from the stress. That always happens in the movies, but that didn't happen. I should have known. For a second, I thought I might need to knock him out. He pushed me out of the way and ran for the door. Just as he passed me, he tripped on the coffee table. Whack! His head hit the table with a thud, and he didn't get up. I poked him to see if he was alive, and he seemed to be breathing. Well, I didn't mean for that to happen, but I stuck with my plan. The orangutan was gone. I was in the room with an unconscious man and an orangutan-sized spacesuit—my ticket on board *The Adversity*.

I could now become Scrubbles.

I closed the window and pulled on the awkward space suit. It had long arms and short legs, but it fit well enough to move. The helmet had a gold visor that covered my face. I pulled it on and headed for the door. Bong Bong was still unconscious. The paparazzi devils met me in the hallway. I pointed into the room and they saw Scrubbles' manager passed out on the floor. They started snapping pictures, but one of them finally said, "Someone get a doctor!" Half of the paparazzi ran into the room and the rest followed me as I waddled down the hall toward the hangar.

The crowd of crazed photographers grew as I reached the main hangar. People applauded the space orangutan.

"Look at the brave space monkey, dear! Here's getting on board all by himself!"

There was a set of stairs on the side of *The Adversity* and a door into the cargo hold. The crowd roared as I clattered up the stairs. I viewed the sea of cheering faces and took in the scene. For that moment, I looked like an orangutan but felt like a rock star. Sweet victory. "Scrubbles" saluted the crowd. That surprised them all. They saluted right back and cheered even more. With a few final waves, I made my way toward my orangutan cage, using the route that Sunjay suggested would be the fastest. After all that craziness with the car, the crocodile, and Bong Bong, I sat down and finally caught my breath.

I couldn't believe that our plan worked. I could only hope that the orangutan would be lost in the forest where we dumped Dr. C's car. I hoped he was safe. I imagined that crocodile scaring him pretty good, but the orangutan would spend his time in the trees. He would watch for fire and lions for a few days, just long enough. After a few days, Corbin Belafonte would find Scrubbles, and we would come out of hiding and tell my dad we were aboard. In the meantime, I would pretend to be the orangutan while Sunjay and Tabitha were Queen Envy's pink and purple spacesuits.

In the midst of these thoughts my dad showed up to check on his living cargo. I expected that, but it still shocked me, seeing him in his flight suit standing in front of me. Sylvia Moreline accompanied him. She climbed into the cage with me and strapped me into a seat for takeoff.

"Sylvia, that manager must have hit his head pretty hard," my dad said. "Did he really say that Tully threw his orangutan out a window?"

"That's what he said. The poor guy," Moreline looked at me, er, Scrubbles. She gave me the okay sign and I signed back that I was okay. "I will report back that the orangutan is fine," she said. "We can check on him in a few hours when we are in zero gravity."

"My son attacking an orangutan?" said my dad. "Well, I'll have something to tell Tully when I get back," he said, shaking his head. He turned and left with Moreline. I could breath again.

Everyone was now in place. I was safe behind bars. With any luck, my two friends were in Queen Envy's spacesuits.

Step Three: Send everyone on a wild goose chase.

I had one final job—to send out the video we'd made as a distraction for our families…and the authorities. We didn't think anyone would believe the story completely, but at least they wouldn't think we were kidnapped or in serious danger. Whatever they thought, they would never guess we were in space.

In the message, Sunjay, Tabitha, and I sat on the saggy, brown couch in Mission Control. I had memorized the script while I was writing it. It went like this.

CAMPING SCRIPT

Tabitha: "Hey, mom, dad, brothers, everyone. We don't know how to tell you this, but, well, we got inspired to do something really cool and crazy these last few weeks, and Tully just doesn't think he can go back to Alaska yet, so we are going camping for a week."

Tully: "I know you're probably freaking out about this, but we'll be fine. Aunt Selma taught me a lot of survival skills. I'm basically a professional woodcutter. And Dr. C…"

Sunjay: "…Daddy, I'm soooo sorry about taking your car. If we damage it in any way, we will pay you back—"

Tully: "—or maybe you have good insurance. Anyway, we'll check in with you in a week. Just don't start searching every park in Florida for us. We promise to be back by the beginning of school. You can ground us forever if you want, but this just had to be done. We'll call you next week."

All three: "WE LOVE YOU!"

The three of us waved at the camera.

END OF SCRIPT.

With any luck, people would see that message and start searching in Florida—on the highways, in the national parks, in hotels, in motels, everywhere. But no one would think to look for three misguided youths in space.

My finger hovered over the "SEND" button for a second. I knew this would cause trouble back on Earth, but we had already come this far.

There's no going back after this one, but I won't be left behind. I reminded myself of all the lonely nights in Alaska, all the missed dances and parties, all the times I wondered if my dad would make it home. And I remembered my dream, and that faint whisper that gave me the courage to do this: *Go, and do not delay.*

It took a lot of nerve, but I was done delaying. I hit "SEND" and turned off the phone.

At that moment, *The Adversity's* engines came to life. They weren't like an airplane or a hyperplane's engines. The slow rumble made my teeth rattle like on a cold day in Middle of Nowhere. We turned onto the runway and picked up speed. I imagined the audience cheering outside. I pictured the takeoff from my dad's point of view. He was seated on the Flight Deck ready for takeoff. He pushed in the throttle and pulled back on the stick. The rumble increased and the nose lifted first. Then the entire ship lifted into the air. He gave *The Adversity* more throttle, and the massive engines pushed everyone on board back into their seats. We ascended quickly through the thin clouds. The blue sky blackened. The horizon came into view, the curve of the Earth. The ship no longer rumbled with power but cruised with grace. We were almost in space.

The plan had worked. This time I wasn't left behind. I felt so satisfied, almost like I was floating in mid-air. All the troubles of getting on board were floating away. Then I realized what was happening: I *was* floating. Gravity was letting us go. We would be weightless soon. It was a beautiful sensation. I picked up my arm and watched it slowly fall back onto my leg. I shook my head and my hair didn't fall back right away.

What brought back the weighty feeling was something Tabitha had said weeks ago in Mission Control: "Getting into space isn't the problem, Tully. It's surviving once we get there." *No reason to worry about that right now,* I thought. I pictured dad again on the Flight Deck. He knew what he was doing, and he would take care of the mission like he always did. After a few days we could come out of hiding and watch the crew perform spacewalks to repair this space station, our unknown destination. Maybe we could even help my dad on his personal mission—to hide the Harper Device. That was my greatest hope. If he was going to face death and danger again, at least I wouldn't be that helpless, little kid who thought he lost his only parent.

How little I could see of the future at that time.

PART THREE: THE CONSPIRACY GAME

August , 2069.

It's been three days
since we did it.

Three days since
we boarded a spaceship
and became the first humans
to sneak into space.

SAVING MY BACON

I did a lot of wishing the first few days in space.

I wished that Tabitha and Sunjay had hidden closer to me. I had no idea how they were doing. We couldn't use phones—they could track our signals, and we wanted everyone to think we had run off in Dr. C's car. It's hard to leave your holophone behind, but sometimes it has to be done.

I also wished for some entertainment. Tabitha had just finished those old Harry Potter books, and I meant to borrow one of them before we left. What I wouldn't have done for a few books!

We did each bring a few items: Tabitha brought her lucky scarf. Sunjay brought a picture for Queen Envy to sign. Since I was all alone in a cage, I brought Little Bacon and a sketchbook.

I sketched the entire ship, from nose to tail, but I had to work from memory on most of it—at the front, the flight deck, the observation deck, and the crew members' quarters. In the middle, the payload bay, which was pretty empty on this trip. Finally, the space lab, my home.

The space lab was spacious and bright. The lights felt warm and looked like sunlight. That was probably intentional because there was plenty of life in the space lab. In the middle of the lab there was a garden. All sort of plants and grasses grew there—bamboo, tomatoes, different varieties of vines and fruits. Little Bacon knew all of their names and told me more than I ever wanted to know about each one of them. Next to the garden was a group of glass cases filled with green slimes and blue fuzzy fungi that grows on rotten vegetables and fruit, also known as bacterial experiments. Finally, there was a colony of mice that looked really nervous, bunching up and burrowing in their woodchips. They had reason to be nervous. Beside them was an owl that never stopped looking at them. He clung to his branch so he wouldn't float around in his cage.

"A hoot owl," said Little Bacon. "Hoot owls hunt at night and feed on a variety of small rodents."

"Like those poor guys?"

"Yes."

"Why is there a bird in space, Bacon?"

"Possibly to see how a bird digests food in space."

"Poor guy can't even fly. I bet he didn't volunteer for this job."

"Neither did those mice," said Little Bacon.

I did a few sketches of the mice and named the owl "Owlbert." I know. Pretty creative. He flapped his wings occasionally and spun his head around in all directions. The mice didn't find much of this entertaining.

Finally, across the garden from me was the Harper Device. An enormous white room housed the Device, and a clear plastic wall with a door separated it from the rest of the lab. I could just make out that familiar red glow through the garden. I sketched it from memory though, imagining the mist trailing onto the white floor.

Between sketching and writing about my surroundings, I stayed busy. I took breaks to watch my pen rotate slowly in mid-air, or see how fast I could spin my sketchbook. I never took off more than my helmet even when I was alone.

Scrubbles had a specific diet—fruit, fruit, and more fruit. Apparently one astronaut was supposed to feed him three meals a day. I don't recommend eating fruit three meals a day, but feeding time was when I met my "handler," Sylvia Moreline.

She seemed worried about her orangutan. I couldn't blame her. I mean, he wouldn't take off his spacesuit or even open his visor! She got over it though, and we worked into a routine over the next few days. I looked forward to seeing her, but the first feeding almost gave me a heart attack.

I did not have on my helmet when the hatch opened at the far end of the space lab. Little Bacon was floating a few feet in front of me, so I shoved him into a bunch of vines in the back of the cage and threw on my helmet. Sylvia floated down the length of the walkway and past the garden. She had a smile that put me at ease, and her long, black ponytail stuck straight up on top of her head in zero gravity. Watching someone float weightlessly toward you is a real thrill the first time you see it, especially if it's the friendliest astronaut in the world, Sylvia Moreline. I almost answered her when she said, "Hola, chiquito! You want food? Lift up that visor and I'll give you this jaca."

A jaca? What the heck is that? I thought. If I lifted up the visor, we would both be in for quite a surprise. Instead, I sat back in my spacious cage. Then I scratched my head and made a throwing motion.

"You want me to throw you the jaca? Well, okay, chiquito, you got it!" She reared back and slow-pitched the fruit to me. I caught the football-sized fruit. I laid it aside and pointed for a banana.

"Yay, look at you!" She motioned for me to eat the *jaca* first, but I did the same thing as before. "Okay, you want to play with your food first, huh?" The banana came spinning slowly across the cage as well. *She's not very strict. She would be a good mom,* I thought.

"That's it. Eat up now," she said, signing to me. I signed back to her: "Alone, please." I gathered the fruit in the corner and pretended to protect my *jaca* and banana. I tried to shoo her away. "I see," she said, "so shy. Well, hasta luego, chiquito. You know where to put your hands when you're done eating, like we practiced, remember? And don't forget to do your experiments!" She floated back toward the hatch.

She knows Scrubbles! The idea dawned on me. Of course she did. *The Adversity* had no space for extra workers, like a crazy orangutan manager, especially since Queen Envy took up three cabins to herself. Moreline probably practiced with Scrubbles for weeks or months, feeding him and training him. She "knew" me. I would need to be careful around her.

I removed my gloves so I could peel the banana. The banana was easy to eat and clean up, but my stomach still growled. I looked at the spiky football she had thrown me next.

"You can come out now, Little Bacon," I said. "Could you tell me what this is?"

"Certainly, sir. It's a jackfruit, or jaca in Spanish. Jacas can grow up to 80 pounds."

"Is it edible?"

"A jaca can be opened with a knife or, with some effort, human hands."

It did take some effort, but I broke open the jaca, and immediately my hands felt like they were coated in glue. It tasted sweet, but I couldn't get the sticky off my hands. *If I put on my gloves now, they'll be nasty forever,* I thought. I didn't feel safe with them off. Feeling frustrated, I threw the banana peel at Little Bacon.

"How am I supposed to get clean?"

"Soap and water act as traditional cleaning agents for human hands," he said.

Thanks, Bacon. So helpful.

With no solution in sight, I decided to get a better look at my cage. The cell was green and brown, and some type of grass covered the walls. Vines and trees grew up to the ceiling thirty feet above. At the top of the cage was a huge skylight, about the size of a queen-sized bed. I pushed myself toward the skylight, which opened up into a black canvas dotted with tiny colored lights. Space. The entire universe of a septillion stars was just four inches from my nose, and for who knows how long I stared out into the vacuum of space and lost my thoughts there for a while. We were circling the Earth now, and I saw my first sunrise in space. It was amazing, watching the sunlight burst over the blue curve of the Earth. All the blackness around it made the Earth look that much more special, like a jewel that someone wanted the universe to see. The jewel got blurry though. There was a tear in my eye. I blinked and it floated in front of my face, a perfect sphere that reflected the sunlight. I had planned to sneak on board a spaceship, but I had not imagined the beauty of space.

I would have stayed there longer, but when I wiped the tear, my sticky hands reminded me to get clean. From the ceiling, I saw where I was supposed to perform my "experiments," as Moreline called them. I also spotted a slot in the wall, just big enough for furry orangutan hands.

I pushed myself toward the ground and stuck my hands into the slot. *Maybe it's a hand sanitizer.* Oh, it was. Immediately the slot clamped down on my wrists. I was handcuffed to the wall. I guess that wasn't the end of the world, but my visor was up. Anyone could see me. "Tully, you idiot!" I said, wondering when this thing would release me.

Well, it wasn't a hand-sanitizing machine. It was a full-body, orangutan-washing monster, and it was just getting started.

"Orangutan secured," a robotic female voice said. "Beginning preparation phase." *That doesn't sound good.* I struggled to free my wrists again, but no luck. I heard some loud clanking sounds. *That sounds even worse.* The monster freed my wrists, but four large clamps grabbed me and removed my spacesuit. There I was, in my jeans and t-shirt, clamped in place in the middle of the room. I struggled to get away, but it was no use. The monster had me. I looked everywhere for help, but all I saw was Little Bacon, Owlbert, and the mice, watching me with growing interest.

"Little Bacon, get me out of this thing!"

"As you wish." He pulled on my hands but couldn't do anything for me.

A high-pitched whine began. "Cleaning apparatus engaged," said the voice.

"No, hey, no need for cleaning apparatus. I'm not that sticky today, really. Uh, abort! Stop! Scrubbles says no!" I struggled to free myself, but there was no use. Suddenly streams of warm water shot from the green walls around me, soaking my jeans and t-shirt. A jet of water blasted Little Bacon across the cage.

"Okay, whoa, no more! You're making Scrubbles mad!" I yelled. Next came soapsuds in the same way. Then four arms with scrub brushes. For about a minute, I got the most thorough cleansing of my entire life. By the end of it, my jeans, t-shirt, shoes, arms, face, and hair were cleaner than they had ever been.

"Orangutan clean," commented the robotic voice.

At just that moment I heard the hatch open once again, and a familiar voice.

"Hola, chiquito!"

"Oh, you've got to be kidding!" I was soaked and suspended in my jeans and t-shirt. Sylvia Moreline was coming to visit me again. In a moment she would be in front of my cage. I did the only thing I could do. "Little Bacon, you've got to distract her," I said. "She can't catch me yet."

"What sort of distraction would you recommend?" he asked, floating toward me.

"Sorry about this, buddy, but figure it out." With that, I kicked him. He flew through the bars of the cage and landed in the garden. He disappeared into the vines. *I can't believe this is how I'm going to get caught,* I thought, struggling with the clamps. Moreline was almost to my cage before Little Bacon "figured it out."

"Oh, say can you see, by the dawn's early light!" Little Bacon began to sing "The Star-Spangled Banner" at the top of his Android lungs. Sylvia Moreline floated toward him to see what was singing in the space lab. He ducked behind the vines and kept singing. They played a bit of cat and mouse.

"Ultrasonic dryer engaged," said the robotic voice. Ultrasonic sound waves hit me and in an instant the water popped right off my clothes. It was amazing. Droplets of all shape and size were suspended all around me in mid-air. Then a burst of air hit me from one side, blowing the droplets into the vines. This happened three times, and in less than ten seconds the whole cage, including me, was dry.

"And the rockets red glare / The bombs bursting in air..." Little Bacon kept singing as the dryer did its job. Moreline kept searching for him.

Thankfully, the suit returned. The metal clamps tried to jam my arms, legs, and head into the suit. "Adjusting suit," the voice said. "Still adjusting." Two metal claws emerged from the vines, poking, prodding, and tightening the suit to fit my non-orangutan body. After a painful readjustment, I was completely clean and dry and back in my suit. And just in time. Sylvia Moreline appeared in front of my cage a moment later. "Scrubbles, have you been hiding a toy on board? How in the world did you keep him hidden from me?" Little Bacon was about to say something, so I put my finger up to keep him quiet.

I nodded at her.

"Well, no more hiding things from Sylvia. Okay, chiquito? I'll give him back to you in a few days."

I reached out for him, but she wouldn't budge.

"You've been a bad boy, Scrubbles. You won't take off your suit and now you sneak toys on board. You think about all the bad things you did and I will feed you later." With that, she left.

My visor was down, my gloves were on, and I felt like a team of angry hairstylists—or bears—had attacked me. Little Bacon was lost, and I felt bad about throwing the banana peel and kicking him—even though I was a jerk to him, he saved me. He "saved my bacon," like my dad says. As long as he didn't start spouting random definitions, the rest of us might not be discovered.

The rest of the day I spent a lot of time laying near the skylight with my sketchpad, enjoying the best view in the universe. I could see so many stars that the sky looked dusty and stained, with big blotches of color. I remembered how many stars were in our galaxy—300 billion. A million stars for every living thing on planet Earth, if you think about it, and I had some time to think. Our gigantic spaceship, our whole planet, it was just a drop in a drop in a drop in a big glass of frosty milk—The Milky Way. 300 billion. How could there be that many stars? Was there some other blue jewel just like ours circling a yellow sun? Was there a boy with a sketchpad looking at a sunset like this one somewhere in the Milky Way? Did he have good friends? Did he help his dad? Did he think these exact same thoughts? It all made my head spin, a little like Owlbert's, but the sunset made me tired at last.

The Earth was at first a big green and blue globe, but pretty soon it would be only a shiny blue speck. That brought me back to our mission. We would spend two days circling the Earth, three days on the way to the Moon, and then what? We knew so little. My goal was to hide for at least three days. Then the crew couldn't send us home in an escape pod. As I discovered, easier said than done.

Oxygen Leaks and Uninvited Guests

Everything went along "orangutan style" for the first day. I entertained myself in the enormous cage by playing games on a computer (Bubble's experiments), watching the sunrises and sunsets out my skylight, and doing flips in zero gravity. Owlbert wasn't impressed, but I was having fun. It's about as much fun as you can have while locked in a cage. Still, I was locked up, surviving on *jaca* and banana, and counting down the days until I could reveal that I was a human.

The second day I watched several astronauts on a spacewalk outside *The Adversity*. Two of them guided an enormous, circular tube into place around the ship's mid-section. It was the DSWM (Deep Space Workout Module). It wasn't a very good acronym, so everyone called it the "Hamster Wheel," which pretty well described its purpose. To stay healthy, humans need gravity, even in space—the Wheel simulates the effects of gravity and the faster it spins, the more gravity they experience. The astronauts ran at least a mile every day in the Hamster Wheel. When they were on longer missions, there was room and equipment for team sports. I always wanted to play basketball in the Hamster Wheel. My dad told me he and Buckshot had a dunk contest on the way to Mars—on a 20-foot basketball goal. "We played at half of Earth's gravity," he said. "Buckshot won with a quadruple back flip dunk." I wanted to try that myself.

But far below us was a more amazing scene: the Earth itself. Every 90 minutes we orbited, watching the land below shift from dark to light and back again. I saw the outline of North America lit by a billion pinpoints of light. I saw red and yellow deserts and blue rivers that ran across entire continents into the sea. I saw the Great Wall of China, the only manmade thing you can see from space, other than Nouveau Eiffel Tower in New Paris. And I saw a hurricane in the Atlantic, with lightning jumping from cloud to cloud like it was recess time for electricity. I could hardly take my eyes off our world long enough to sketch the scenes.

But I was being selfish. *How are Tabitha and Sunjay?* I wondered. We had worked out how to get them on board, but they had some serious challenges, like how to sneak food when Queen Envy wasn't around.

Later that day my thoughts of food, friends, hoops, and sketching were drastically interrupted. I was looking out the skylight when I was surprised to hear voices drifting down the corridor. *It's not feeding time,* I thought, *who would be coming to see me?*

It turns out no one was coming to see *me*.

Two people floated into the space lab and stopped in front of the Harper Device. I recognized their voices and caught glimpses of them through the garden between us. First was Lincoln Sawyer. I had not seen him since he helped me escape from the crazy events at Hangar Two. I could see his cold, blue eyes glowing through the vines. Gallant Trackman was beside him. He was on board as "Mission Advisor." My dad wasn't a big fan of advisors, but Trackman had supported his decision to take the Device into space. I had no idea what Trackman and Sawyer were doing in the space lab. Neither did Trackman.

"Lincoln Sawyer, you fool of an Android, why meet here?" The high, steady voice traveled across the garden.

"My apologies, Mr. Trackman. We could not meet in the cabin areas safely. No one is here to listen, except for a few plants and an orangutan."

Yep, the orangutan was definitely listening.

"You have a point, Sawyer, but you let me worry about those things. I'm the Space Alliance's eyes and ears on board *The Adversity* for a reason. I am the brains. You're just the hands. When the brains need information, the hands deliver it immediately. You follow me? Is that clear enough for your miniscule robot mind?"

"As clear as clearest crystal, sir. Now let me show you—"

"Sawyer, don't show me anything. Update me on Operation Close Encounter."

Operation Close Encounter? It was the first time I heard the phrase, but not the last.

"As you wish, sir. Stage One is nearly complete. Arrangements have been made. A distraction is planned. We will not need to stop at the Moon base before we proceed to our destination."

"The base beyond the far side of the Moon," said Trackman. "Fine, fine."

What base? In all of our research no one mentioned a space station on the far side of the Moon. It seemed like a bad spot for a station, too, a lonely place so far from home.

Trackman continued. "Fine, fine, but you've left out the most important piece, Sawyer, or have you forgotten about our good commander? What about him?"

My dad? I thought.

"Ah, yes," said the Android. "The man is very cautious and watchful. His heart rate increases when I approach, as if he is ready for a fight. He does not trust me."

This "operation" sounded more like a conspiracy.

"Stupid Android, you've given him no reason to trust you. You must earn the trust of a man like that," said Trackman. "He trusts me. When he wanted to remove the Harper Device, who do you think supported him? I did. You earn trust by finding a common need. Unless you earn his trust, Operation Close Encounter will not succeed."

"Thank you, sir. You are wise. Now for what I wanted to show you. Here." He pointed across the room toward my cage. The two of them floated toward me.

I had no time to think but a lot to think about as they approached my cage. They stopped and stared at me: Lincoln with his long, somber face and bright blue eyes, glowing with cold fire.

Trackman looked like some boring uncle whose name you always forget. He had tiny features—small, black eyes, thin eyebrows, a receding hairline, and enormous, sharp, pointed teeth. On second thought, maybe he ate boring uncles for lunch. He frowned as he looked into my cage, then back at Sawyer.

"It's an orangutan, Android. An orangutan in a spacesuit. Thank you for this amazing revelation." He sucked air between his teeth suddenly with a scary hiss. "We should go to the zoo together more often."

"Yes, a perfectly normal orangutan," said the Android. I backed away from the sound of his voice—it had a probing quality, like he could see right through my suit. "But that's not what I'm here to show you." They moved past my cage, but the Android continued looking at me. "This gauge right here shows the oxygen levels in the ship. Not that I care very much about oxygen, since I don't need to breathe it myself…"

Trackman rolled his beady eyes and threw up his hands. "Oh, splendid! I always wanted to know what that gauge was for. Oxygen. Wow. And you don't even need any? Of course not, you inorganic fool. We're done here." Trackman turned to leave, but Sawyer didn't move.

"Sir, we are not done here. You will hear this. The brains, as you call yourself, need to know something. None of the crew has noticed yet, but we are 2.94% above expected oxygen use levels. We are using more oxygen than we should."

Trackman looked annoyed. "Which means?" he said.

"Which means we may have an oxygen leak; however, another possibility is that we have uninvited guests on board."

That startled me, and for a split second, Sawyer glanced at me. It felt like he was toying with me somehow—or maybe I was just worried about getting caught.

"Orrrrr," said Trackman, "it may mean nothing. That's the problem with you Androids. You're smart, polite, strong, can follow directions, but you don't know how to focus on the right things. So there's a rat or a possum or a unicorn on board. Big deal! We'll feed them to Scrubbles here." He tapped on my cage.

"You are probably correct, sir. It may be nothing."

"Leave me now, Android."

Sawyer left. Trackman stayed behind. He floated over to the Harper Device for a moment. "Oh, the plans I have for you, the places you will go. If only they knew how valuable you are," he said, looking at the Device, sucking air through his teeth. It was a creepy habit. Fortunately he didn't talk to himself for very long. He left me alone at last.

I didn't know what to make of their conversation. What had I just heard? A distraction? The base on the far side of the Moon? Operation Close Encounter? A speech on earning someone's trust? The whole conversation made me feel very alone, like I heard a mean joke about someone, and maybe the joke was on me. Or my dad.

You're all alone out here, Tully, said the small voice in my head. *The Android will figure this out and Trackman will probably make Tully Stew out of you.*

But I pushed that voice out of my head. I had learned to do that much. Androids don't eat meat either, and I had friends on board.

Sunjay and Tabitha. The thought of them calmed me down a bit. We needed to make contact. A few days more and we could come out of hiding without being launched home, but I needed to talk to them now. Sunjay would ask the right questions. I needed Tabitha to come up with solutions. I might even need to tell my dad about Operation Close Encounter. But to do any of that, I needed my freedom. The only problem? A locked cage.

"My Secret Friend"

A few hours later I was still pondering all these problems when someone opened the hatch at the end of the dark corridor. *Sylvia?* I thought. In the dark of the far end, I could only make out a shadow and two bright blue eyes. Floating toward my cage was Lincoln Sawyer. He stopped in front of my cage, smiled politely, and folded his hands behind his back. He stayed there for a minute, as still as if he was made of wax. I pretended to play chess by myself and let him study me. Finally he sprang to life, speaking in a polite, even tone, like a waiter at a five-star restaurant.

"Uh, Scrubbles, could we talk for a moment? I heard you have been acting strangely—not taking down your visor, eating meals in private. Space will do that to an orangutan, I suppose. Anyway, I brought you something that might make you feel more at home."

I turned my head and looked at him. He pulled a cheeseburger from behind his back. A cheeseburger! Wrapped halfway in foil, I could see the steaming meat patty and cheese melting on the edges. The suit insulated me from the smell, but my mind recalled the aroma of a cheeseburger just fine. Next he produced some sour gummy worms from his jumpsuit pocket. They were crusted with all that beautiful sour sugary stuff, some of which floated through the bars of the cage. Man, I love candy. I didn't realize that I was drifting forward with an outstretched hand. I came to my senses and tried to think like an orangutan, but the damage was done.

"Hungry, my friend? You don't have to hide now. I guessed you weren't an orangutan earlier. When I said we had uninvited guests on board, you jumped. You reacted like an uninvited guest, and therefore my suspicions were confirmed. Of course, I wasn't sure of your identity, but Sylvia Moreline showed me something that solved this puzzle. A particular Handroid that I had seen before. Unlimited memory comes in handy in times like these. Of course, who else might fit into an orang-utan-sized spacesuit? Probably a 5'2", 105-pound teenager, with a slight build and light brown hair. I thought candy would prove irresistible to you. Yes, a simple equation for me to solve, but what a plan! I was right about you. You've got nerve, Tully Harper."

From behind my visor, I said nothing. Nothing. What could I say? He stuck out the hamburger and sour gummy worms again. "This hamburger was also made with the brand-new organic 3D printer. This particular recipe was highly recommended. If only I had taste sensors. Haha. You must be in shock. You just overheard my conversation with Mr. Trackman. Part of a game we play. I can explain later. Just eat your burger before it gets cold."

"What are you going to do with me?" I asked in a muffled voice.

"Feed you, Tully. I kept your secrets once, did I not? I see no reason to change my course of action. You can stay in hiding. If anything, I thought you could eat your hamburger and then get some exercise with me. Please accept this food as a token of my trust."

"How did you know I loved gummy worms?"

"You don't remember? That day in the hangar you had a light crusting of sugar on your fingertips. When you tried to escape my grasp, you touched my jacket. I analyzed the sample and discovered its origins. These are also fresh off the organic printer."

Darn Android! I flipped up my visor and took off my gloves. I didn't have much choice. After a few days of fruit, my stomach growled at me like an angry Doberman. The burger tasted so good that I ate half the wrapper. Sawyer looked amused—not that Androids can feel amusement. He punched the code on the cage and let me out.

"Good to see you still have an appetite. By all means, bring your gummy worms with you. Would you like a bit of fresh air? The Hamster Wheel is free right now."

A burger, my favorite candy, and a trip to the Hamster Wheel? I felt like a fool for getting caught, but apparently my secret was safe with the Android.

We pushed ourselves from the space lab floor toward a small hatch on the ceiling that led into the Hamster Wheel. Moments later we stood beside each other in an enormous curved room with thirty-foot ceilings. Along the walls were windows, and between the windows were screens that showed movies, concert, lectures, sports, anything you wanted. All sorts of exercise equipment lined the walls—weights, jump ropes, yoga mats, basket/foot/volleyballs, but I had my eyes on the half-court basketball court.

"We're at normal gravity right now. Try to jump." I jumped and didn't go very high, which was normal for me.

"So this is 1G—normal gravity," I said.

"Yes, we produce this with centrifugal force. You can't feel it, but the Hamster Wheel is spinning around *The Adversity* right now, about one rotation every thirty seconds."

"My dad told me about this before. He said the Hamster Wheel helps astronauts survive."

"If humans don't experience normal gravity, they run into problems. They lose muscle. Their bones become weaker. Humans need to exercise daily to avoid this. That's why we're here. We could also try 2G." He turned the switch again. Nothing happened quickly, but I started to feel heavy. I took off the space suit. Still, I felt twice my weight.

"So that's what 210 pounds feels like," I started to sweat. "Can we do 1/2G?"

"Certainly." After a few minutes I felt like I was on my trampoline in Houston. I jumped and almost touched the ceiling—about 30 feet from the floor. I bounded toward the basketball court. Grabbing a ball, I took off from the 3-point line and dunked. Then I tried some of the crazy dunks that mascots during halftime shows—a windmill dunk, a back flip, and a flipping two-handed jam. I tossed a ball up in the air and yelled, "Hey, Sawyer, what can you do?" He stood motionless at first, and then with incredible speed he launched toward the ceiling. He caught the ball on the way up, pushed off the ceiling, and on the way down threw the ball through the hoop. The net barely moved, and the ball hit the floor so hard that it bounced back to the ceiling. He landed, bowed, and caught the ball behind his back without looking.

"Whoa," I said, as he tossed me the ball. "I don't even know if that was a dunk, but it was pretty insane."

"Thanks, I believe."

"I could get used to this."

"Yes, you could, but your legs would get weak. 1G is best."

I was pretty warmed up by then. Sawyer switched back to 1G. I felt like a human again. He walked over to a stand and picked up a stick.

"This is a bo staff," he said. He put the staff in front of his face and pretended to attack an invisible opponent with amazing speed. Then he spun the staff over his head like a propeller and brought it down on the floor with a whack. "Do you want a lesson?"

"I know how to use these. Sort of. My friend Sunjay taught me. He likes martial arts."

"Oh, and where is he?"

"He's back in Houston," I lied. "I thought you could figure that out."

He tossed me a staff and backed away. He spun the weapon above his head again, then put the staff behind his back, where it kept spinning like a helicopter blade. The amazing feat distracted me so much that I held my staff loosely—until he spun his staff forward and knocked the weapon from my hands. Then he tapped me on the head with the staff.

"Rule #1: never let your guard down, Tully. Round One is over."

"Hey, I didn't know we began Round One! Let's see how I do in Round Two."

We tried again. This time I chopped at him with all my might. When he counterattacked, I fought off a few blows but couldn't keep up. He whacked me on the head harder.

"Take it easy!" I said, rubbing my head.

"Rule #2: No pain, no gain," he said. "Science tells us that people learn how to avoid pain. This should make things a bit more fun for you." He switched the wheel to 1/2 gravity again. My legs felt great. Without warning he attacked, and this time I kept him away. He chopped at my staff with more force, but he couldn't get through my defenses. I jumped one of his attacks and landed on the basketball hoop. "You defend better in low gravity. We will call Round Three a draw."

"Thanks," I said, standing on the basketball hoop. I looked down at him and remembered the strange conversation from earlier. "So what is this game with Trackman? You talked about the far side of the Moon and my dad."

"Ah, yes. I apologize for not explaining. On every trip the Space Alliance plays 'The Conspiracy Game.' Two crewmembers pretend to be conspirators—or bad guys—and they make up a plan to take over the ship. The other crewmembers must find out who they are. As you may have guessed, Mr. Trackman and I are playing the conspirators. It is rather amusing. Sort of a game for Rule #1."

"Never let your guard down."

"Correct. Of course, I cannot tell you much more about our plan. Commander Harper and his crew are quite adept at finding conspirators."

"Well, I made it on board. Maybe they're not *that* good." I stood on the basketball hoop and thought about it for a moment. The Conspiracy Game made sense—the Alliance kept the crew "on their toes" with games. My dad liked games, but I had more questions. "You said something about the far side of the Moon?"

He paused, like he was performing a calculation. "Listen closely. I will tell you something you do not know. Beyond the Moon there is a secret space station called LG Alpha. You see, it is located at a Lagrangian Point, which is an area in space with almost no gravitational pull. This particular point, technically known as Lagrangian Point Two, is our destination."

"So let me get this straight. The Lagrangian Point is sort of a dead place in space where you can leave stuff and it won't float away?"

"That is a basic understanding, yes."

"And the Alliance has a secret station there?"

"Yes."

"Why did they do all this?"

"Because the Alliance has big plans for deep space exploration. We have bases on Mars, and the moons of Jupiter are next. LG Alpha will be a fueling station on the way to those distant places. Also, it's an excellent observatory. There's a clear view of the rest of the solar system. Maybe too clear."

"How could it be too clear?"

"Never mind," he said. "Any other questions?"

"How did the Space Alliance keep it a secret? Anyone with a telescope could probably find it."

"That is true, but LG Alpha has an advance cloaking device. It is invisible from Earth. One would have to get quite close to actually see it."

"So you're worried this secret, invisible space station is destroyed?"

"Androids don't worry, Tully, but we have lost contact with the station. It may be damaged or destroyed."

It all seemed to make sense with what I already knew. I wanted to ask Sawyer some more questions—especially about the Lagrangian Point—but he didn't give me a chance. Before I could react, he dashed under me and hit the basketball hoop. It cracked in half. I fell, and before I hit the ground, Sawyer swept my legs out from under me. I landed on my back. A second later his staff was on my throat. I thought for a second this was the end, but he withdrew and pulled me back to my feet.

"No fair!" I yelled. "We were talking."

"Rule #1"

"That hurt!"

"Rule #2."

"Yeah, no pain, no gain. Thanks for the lessons."

"You should be returning to your cage now anyway, my secret friend."

We exited the Hamster Wheel, but before he locked me in the orangutan cage, Sawyer wanted to make a deal.

"Tully, I will propose this: we keep each other's secrets. It's in everyone's best interests. Mr. Trackman and I need to play The Conspiracy Game, and you want to play the orangutan as long as you can, don't you?"

"Definitely."

"Then I have your trust?" he asked.

"Isn't that what you wanted from my dad for The Conspiracy Game?"

"Of course."

"Okay," I nodded and put on my helmet. He smiled. It looked like such a human smile.

"Now, if there's nothing more to be said, Commander Harper is expecting me in the Flight Deck. Ah, yes, what do you need?"

My friends! I held up my hand to stop him. Then I pointed to the cage door.

"How long do you need to be out?" I held up four fingers. "Four hours? If you're caught, you cannot share our secrets." He hit a few buttons on the cage door and I floated out beside him.

"Here's the sequence to access the cage," he said. "Your next feeding is at 7 o'clock, so you have the afternoon outside the cage. I wouldn't wander far though. No one expects to see Scrubbles wandering around *The Adversity*. Maybe Queen Envy would enjoy your presence though. Her album isn't going very well."

I nodded yes.

"Oh! Queen Envy. You want to see her. Well, I could accompany you there, if you like."

He grabbed my shoulder in his powerful, Android grip. We were face to face. His long, gaunt face reminded me of every picture I ever saw of Abraham Lincoln, except for his eyes that shined with a cold, blue light. "It would be ever so unpleasant if we were caught," he said, "but you seem to be ever so good at keeping secrets."

Something about him made me nervous. We trusted each other, I guess, but I would need to remember Rule #1 around him. We headed down the corridor to visit Queen Envy in her cabin, and hopefully two good friends.

The Celebrity Snowglobe

Floating out of the space lab, Sawyer and I passed through a door that led into the cargo bay. *The Adversity's* supplies were all packed into boxes and cylinders that were held to the wall magnetically. The Android must have read my thoughts.

"Impressive, isn't it? Everything is labeled and color-coded: green for food; blue for drink; purple for parts; gold for Queen Envy; and black for military hardware." It was all well ordered but dire crowded. The Android made his way smoothly through the obstacle course of cargo, but it was harder for me. Just one good push off the top of a container and I was flying to the ceiling or the floor. I read the colored cargo labels on my way: "Orangutan food," "thruster rebuild kit," "Queen Envy's acting props," "Restricted—Commander Access Code Required."

Once through the bay, we came to a long corridor with red carpet. Lincoln went first. Feet first. As he landed, his feet seemed to stick to carpet. *Oh, the magnetic walkway.* Sunjay had pointed out this feature in the blueprints. My feet contacted the carpet with a thud, and suddenly I felt like I was walking on a floor covered with glue. We clomped down the corridor.

I could feel and hear something, too. It was hard to identify at first, but then I recognized it—drums.

"Well, here we are." Lincoln stopped in front of a gold door. "Queen Envy is listening to music right now, as you probably noticed. I don't think she'll mind the interruption though."

The airlock slid open and several pairs of shiny pants and shoes began floating into the walkway. Lincoln caught them, gave those items a polite shove back into the room, and shoved me in as well.

Compared to the cargo hold, Queen Envy's room was a mess, like a snowglobe that had been shaken too hard. A million bits of celebrity debris floated around me like those fake plastic snow pellets—guitars, sitars, a keytar, keyboards, glowing blue wigs, fake eyelashes, and even a piece of sushi slowly spun past my visor. *I'll take the orangutan carwash over this dump any day!* I thought.

In the midst of all this mess, the world's most famous diva floated cross-legged, her pink wig bobbing to the beat of the music. She wore a shiny black jumpsuit with an enormous black collar and was totally unaware of my entrance.

A thump came from the ceiling. I looked up and saw Queen Envy's two spacesuits floating there. One of them gave me a thumbs-up, the other a friendly wave. Yes! I wanted to float right up there and hug them both, but that's not what an orangutan would do, and just at that moment...

"Scrubbles, baby bear, it's about time you visited your Queen," said Queen Envy above the music. She spun herself around to face me but just kept spinning, making us both feel dizzy. "The sweet robot said he would bring you to me soon."

She held a golden rope that was tied to the floor. She pulled herself to the floor, then pushed herself toward me. She gave me a bear hug. A baby bear hug. "When I was on my 'Glitter Pop' tour last year in Europe, I had the most fabulous choreographer. He was also my yoga and sign language instructor. He told me you knew how to sign, so let me try to say something you'll understand. Your Queen knows your language."

Oh, no, I thought. She made several signs and frowned when I didn't respond. What was I supposed to say? My sign language vocab included few words besides "Fire. Lions. Window. Pond. Go." I had been a lot more focused on Tabitha than I was on learning sign language. Now I regretted it because a superstar in a glowing pink wig and leather jumpsuit was trying to communicate with me while microphones and slices of pizza plunked against my helmet. I was about to blow my cover again!

Queen Envy reached for my visor. "Let me get a look at you, baby bear. You are acting dire strange. You don't remember how to sign with me?"

Boom! A big boom had come from the ceiling by the Queen's spacesuits. We both looked up.

"Oh, did they scare you, baby bear? I think my spacesuits are possessed or something. The pink one kept floating into me earlier this week when I was singing. I think it was flirting with me," she laughed.

Oh, it was, I thought.

"Now pop off this crazy helmet and let the Queen see your sweet monkey face." Just as Queen Envy reached for my helmet, the purple spacesuit (Tabitha), gave me a sign. Literally.

I performed the sign, not knowing what it was.

Queen Envy frowned. "More what, baby bear?"

That's it! I thought. I made a talking sign with my hand.

"Oh, more talk? Well, sure, you like my voice. Everybody does. Okay, baby bear. You want an update on your Queen? I haven't been able to get into the flow of my music yet. Sometimes it's like that—the creative process. I'll just go a few weeks and all I've done is gone dancing in clubs, worked through my yoga poses, and holophoned with some fans. They eat those up, you know? Me popping up as a hologram in the middle of their room. Sometimes I let them hologram back. I had a hundred holograms fans in my studio before the launch! We had a mad karaoke sing-along. It was dire fun, baby bear. I wore this outfit that made me look like I was on fire. Swaggy beautiful. Anyway, after that night, a song just fell in my lap from outer space, and then the Space Alliance call and told me they wanted me on this mission…"

She paused. *More, more,* I signed.

"It's good to have somebody to talk to, baby bear. Talking to Sawyer is about as interesting as looking out the window at all these stars. No, no, wait. That's not like me. The stars are beautiful. Everything is beautiful, isn't it? Everything, even crazy boring Androids!"

Stars sparkled outside her window, the slash of the Milky Way. We had left the Earth's orbit, and the Moon was getting closer. It was gorgeous, a better view than my cage.

More, more, I signed.

"Anyway, I haven't seen enough of that Commander Harper since takeoff. He's an absolute space babe, but he's always so busy. Maybe I should write a song for him. That could slow him down. I wish he had found me on Mars instead of that crazy red thingy. Oh, that's it! You crazy sweet baby bear, that's it!"

Queen Envy hugged me and yanked herself over to a microphone floating on the other side of the room. She turned on her drum machine and began to sing:

I tracked you down in outer space
Space Boy
You bring me back and watch me blaze
Space Boy

The purple spacesuit covered its ears. The pink spacesuit had its hands above its head like on a rollercoaster, rocking out to Queen Envy's new song.

Could this get any weirder? I thought. *Queen Envy is writing a love song about my dad.*

The music absorbed her. She floated around the room singing:

I blew a crater in your heart
Space Boy
Now we can never be apart
Space Boy

I'll glow red, red, red, red, red
When you kiss my f-f-f-f-face
Red, red, red, red, red
F-f-f-f-face

She forgot her orangutan audience, so I pushed myself toward the ceiling and lifted my visor. Sunjay popped his open as well. He was smiling ear to ear and said above the music, "Free concert every night!"

Tabitha rolled her eyes and removed her earplugs. In zero gravity, her tight curls filled her entire helmet, giving her a big, curly brown halo of hair. We yelled over the music while Sunjay kept grooving.

"Queen Envy return to sender, my brain in a blender," she said. "I can't take much more."

"You won't have to," I said.

"Good! And you don't have to be an orangutan much longer."

"Uh, that kind of already happened."

"What?"

"I'll explain later. What are you eating?"

"Whatever floats by. She eats a lot of pizza and sushi."

"How do you go to the bathroom?"

"Very carefully. Whenever Queenie goes searching for your dad."

Tabitha stared at me with those lovely green eyes. It was the first time I had stared into human eyes for days. Queen Envy sang on:

You can't hold me, I'm burning inside
Space Boy
You're in a trance nowhere to hide
Space Boy

Tabitha laughed and smiled. "We're surviving, right? It's so good to see you."

"Uh, yeah, so is for you for me also." With the drum booming in the background, The Conspiracy Game on my mind, and Tabitha staring at me in her purple spacesuit, it was hard to get the right words together. "So it's seeing you that's good for me, too."

"What does that mean? Was that supposed to be a Tabism?"

We had an awkward pause, so I changed the subject.

"Uh, no. A Tullyism. I've been talking to Androids, not, uh, girls. Listen, I know more about the mission. And this Conspiracy Game—," but there was no time to talk. Queen Envy was wrapping up her song.

"Okay, we'll talk about the mission and your game later."

"No, I don't know if it's a game. It's—"

"Tully, visor down! We'll talk later."

"Don't let Sunjay get us caught! No more hugging the Queen!" I shut the visor.

"Don't worry. The pink spacesuit gives her dire creeps. She uses me for a pillow. Ugh. Now go."

She flipped down her visor and gave me a shove, which propelled us in opposite directions. I floated toward the door and she to the ceiling, right beside the dancing pink spacesuit.

Space Boy, I thought, as I left the messy room. She could have at least called my dad "Space Man" or "Space Commander" or something. I wondered how my dad would feel when we revealed ourselves. It probably wouldn't go very well, but he would realize the truth, too. He was stuck with me and would have to make the best of it. Anyway, if he could put up with Queen Envy, he could put up with the three of us. Her "Space Boy" song faded as I made my way to my tidy cage, planning to sketch Queen Envy's room and Tabitha's poofy space hair and brilliant green eyes. I took a nap instead.

RED, RED, RED, RED, RED

When I awoke, three things replaced my plan to sketch Tabitha in space. Well, not replaced. You can't replace Tabitha's eyes, but you can have distractions. Distractions are like waves that surprise you at the beach. They lick your heels while you scramble for safety, but every once in a while a rogue wave appears, dragging you into deeper water, where the coral grinds and your mind loses track of which way is up. The problem is the waves all look about the same until it's too late. It's the same with distractions.

First distraction: Lincoln Sawyer's cold blue Android gaze. He tapped on my cage, handed me another steaming cheeseburger, and bowed. I ravenously ate. After that we returned to The Hamster Wheel for more basketball and bo staff fighting. I fought much better, especially in 1/2 G, where I could flip and spin away from his vicious attacks. I asked him more about Operation Close Encounter, but he said nothing—just caught me off guard again and whacked me in the stomach. I almost lost my burger. "Rules #1 and #2," he said.

Second distraction: stargazing. I looked out the skylight for a while and tried to make out constellations, but it was really hard. Not because I couldn't see any stars. No, it was the opposite. I saw too many stars. Slowly though I figured it out—there was Polaris, the North Star, and from that I made out Orion, with the three stars on his belt. He always was my favorite constellation—Tully Orion Harper is my full name.

Then I thought about 300 billion again. I guess I got completely lost in my head, thinking about how big the universe was. But eventually my mind wandered on to the third distraction.

The Harper Device.

As I looked out the skylight, I started to picture the Device, how it glowed red, or "red, red, red, red, red" as Queen Envy sang. The only time I really saw the Device was back in Hangar Two. Lightning and lots of scientists kept me from inspecting it then. Now they were all gone, and the Harper Device was all by itself, just a beautiful glowing orb, and another addition to the space lab. I looked out the skylight, but I had a sudden urge to see that red glow up close.

I punched in my cage code and floated across the garden toward the Harper Device, locked in its enormous clear plastic case. Such a huge cage for that small item. My dad was a really careful packer. As I looked into the case, shades of red filled my mind. Just as my mind wandered while looking at the stars, I felt lost in the beautiful red sphere spinning in front of me. Red wasn't just one color but a thousand, and each one of them had its own personality, meaning, and mood.

Red, red, red, red, red.

The orb spun slowly in place, with tongues of mist that flicked the air and then disappeared. Something about the color, the movement—the Device mesmerized me. I don't know how long I watched it floating there. I felt calm, and it didn't matter that I was out of my cage or that the Android knew my true identity. The Conspiracy Game, Operation Close Encounter—everything melted away into a red haze. The Device inhabited my mind. It seemed larger, closer, more interesting with each rotation, with each wisp of red mist that reached toward me. It was like being next to a star, or being with a star, almost like becoming a star. I could almost feel jets of vapor rising from my skin. And then, suddenly, my nose bumped something.

Without even noticing, I had removed my helmet and gloves. My nose was against the case, just a few feet from the Device.

Maybe I had just lost myself again, but this felt different. *I wasn't drifting around aimlessly, I was floating toward something. No, the Device is drawing me toward itself.*

That was a startling thought. I turned around and headed toward my cage, but all the trees and vines in the garden and in my cage were also reaching toward me. No, they were reaching toward the sphere that was in the case behind me.

I turned back toward the Device.

It seemed to be spinning a bit more quickly, and I could feel myself being drawn to the glass case again. For some reason, I wanted into the room. *It wants me in there,* I thought. *This isn't close enough. It needs to tell me something, show me something.*

My heart pounded. I floated toward the access panel. *If only I knew the code,* I thought.

You do know the code, whispered a voice. It was the same voice I heard in my dream of the Harper Device weeks ago. *Go, and do not delay.*

I tried my cage code. Nothing happened. I tried again. Nothing. *Backwards,* said the voice. So I tried the code backwards. The door silently slid opened.

My heart skipped a bit. Adrenaline rushed through my veins. The Device seemed brighter, closer, and more real than anything I had ever seen or felt.

Red, red, red, red, red.

It was pulling me toward itself, spinning quicker, and flicking mist farther.

Red, red, red, red, red.

The spinning increased and the mist reached my hand—a cool mist that made my fingers feel frostbitten. The sensation moved up my arm, and I could see the mist move through my suit, toward my chest, and I felt cold. Cold but alive. My mind felt the same way, like it was taking in some big new idea. *How did I ever live without this feeling?* I thought.

"Show me something," I told the Device. "Show me something I need to see."

The Harper Device stopped spinning, like it was listening to me or trying to make up its mind. Then the Device pulsated, and each pulse produced an electrical current that ran through my entire body. Once, twice, three times—each pulse felt more powerful. A red mist filled the room. All I could see was red.

Red, red, red, red, red.

Through the red haze, dreams emerged. Not dreams, visions. Red Visions. First I saw Trackman and Sawyer appear amidst the haze. They stood in the space lab talking about the Conspiracy Game. Then Trackman disappeared in a puff of red dust, and the scene changed. A man stood in front of the escape pods, his back to me. Someone else was with him, but this person looked limp and pale, attached to the magnetic walkway by his feet. My heart skipped a beat as Sawyer turned toward me with cold blue eyes. I was thankful when that dream vanished. It was so real, but another rose up in its place, stranger than the first. The Moon appeared, and beyond the Moon in a field of stars I saw a strange sight—a fish gulping for air. The fish looked deeper into space, and as it did, I looked upon what was approaching. A jellyfish emerged from the depths, its tentacles brushing the stars on the approach. The fish wriggled but couldn't move. The jellyfish reached for him, but just as he did so, the Moon blocked out my view of the terrible scene.

That scene disappeared, and a final scene emerged. I saw myself back in Alaska at the foot of Mt. Denali, all alone with the cold wind in my face. A mountain towered over me. I looked up to the peak and heard a crack. The mountain was moving. No, it was the snow! An avalanche. I ran, but the avalanche tumbled down the face of the mountain toward me—an avalanche of red snow.

Sawyer with the body. The fish waiting for his death. The avalanche booming down the mountain. These were my first Red Visions.

Just as the avalanche hit me I came back to my senses. My mind couldn't take any more. The visions vanished. The real world reappeared. There I was, spinning in the cage with the Harper Device. My mind returned to my body, which was freezing cold and spinning in the red mist. The Device and I were one.

"No, enough! Too much!" I yelled. Then, suddenly, the red mist vanished. I was thrown against the door with a loud pop.

I screamed in pain. My body felt broken. My hands felt like they were both frozen and on fire. I saw nothing but red, red, red, red, red.

Somewhere an alarm sounded. I could hardly hear it and couldn't move.

Through the pain and blindness, I heard a voice: "Attention Flight Deck—emergency in the infirmary. All crew stand by." Then I felt strong arms scoop me up and carry me out of the space lab. The contents of the cargo hold flew past in a flash of color, and Lincoln Sawyer's steady voice drifted into my mind.

"One to infirmary. Commander Harper, please report."

"No, Sawyer. Help me." My words came in spurts because of the pain. "Hide me. Keep our secrets."

"Tully, you are going into shock. I cannot help you and hide you simultaneously. Not if we want to keep you alive."

Lightning Flowers

I awoke from the blackness of sleep into a red haze. A steady beep droned on and on inside my head like a metronome. Tick-tock. Tick-tock. Beep-beep. Beep-beep. Before I opened my eyes, I remembered the Red Vision again—clear as crystal. Not like a dream, not like living, but not like a fantasy either. That vision of someone floating beside Sawyer came back to me. What had I seen? The beeping accelerated, and as my eyes opened, I realized it was a heart monitor. I was in the infirmary, a dozen monitors strapped to me, and me strapped to an examination table.

Sylvia Moreline floated beside me. "Hola, niño. How are you feeling?"

My brain feels like grated cheese, I thought, but I remembered I was an orangutan in a spacesuit and could not speak. I was dire thirsty, so I motioned for water. Through the red haze my hand came up to my mouth, but there was no glove, only my swollen fingers. I reached for my helmet. No helmet. I felt my hair instead. I looked down and didn't see a spacesuit at all—just my jeans and t-shirt. Of course I did. I was Tully Harper, and Sylvia Moreline knew me. She handed me a water bottle with a straw.

"What is that?" I asked.

"It's water."

"Why is it pink?" I asked.

"It's not pink, Tully. Does it look that way to you?"

"Uh, no." I lied, looking around the infirmary. Everything looked off-color. The white lights and the ceiling looked pink. The red Space Alliance logo looked black. I saw the world through a red haze, like the Harper Device warped my brain, which was pounding with a terrible headache. From that day forward, this red haze came and went in waves, like fog blowing over the ocean.

"What happened to me?" Sylvia just smiled and stroked my hair. Someone else answered.

"You interacted with the Harper Device." Lincoln Sawyer emerged from the corner of the room. "I was getting some tools from the cargo hold when I heard a thud. When I went to inspect, I found you beside the Device. It seems to have electrocuted you—among other things. Notice the entry point of the electricity—your hands."

Faint lines ran across the backs of both of my hands. They looked like the henna tattoos I had seen Sunjay's mom wear one time. The lines reminded me of the lightning I had seen jumping between clouds as we orbited the Earth. "Are these scars? They're white."

"Those are Lichtenburg's figures, or lightning flowers."

"Lightning flowers?" I flexed my hand. The skin crinkled painfully.

"They sometimes occur when electricity enters a conducting material. In this case, your hands were the entry point and you were the conducting material. They show where the electricity first entered your body. They aren't scars. They will disappear with time and treatment. How do your hands feel?"

"Not that bad. They just look weird. But you said 'Among other things.' What else happened?"

"I ran some tests. You had some strange brain activity while you slept—overactivity, really. Your mind showed evidence of being awake and asleep at the same time. Very strange. Also, your heart stopped beating for a moment."

"Stopped? Like, I died?"

He smiled. "No, but you would have. I defibrillated your heart to start it again. No damage occurred, which is fascinating. You are fortunate that the ship's doctor was the closest person to you. And how is your head? Do you remember what happened right before the incident? How you came to interact with the Device?"

"Uh, no."

"Are you sure?" He stared at me with his cold, blue gaze.

"I'm sure. Stars, my head is pounding." I didn't want to tell him too much, especially after seeing the strange visions, but I don't think Sawyer believed me. He was about to ask me more when Sylvia interrupted.

"Tully, your father wants to see you as soon as possible. It's a miracle that you're okay," said Sylvia, stroking my back.

But I wasn't okay. The water looked like pink lemonade, my ears rang, every part of my body ached. Even my hair follicles. Not to mention I saw some strange visions before the Harper Device tossed me across the room. On top of that I was discovered. Nothing was going to be okay.

I ripped off the monitors and pushed myself away from them both, floating toward the ceiling. Immediately I felt dizzy and sick, but I tried to hide the feelings.

"No, dad can't know."

"He already does, honey."

"He, he can't," I mumbled. "But he does. Wait, how many days since we launched?"

"Four days, Tully," she responded, floating toward me. "Now take my arm. We need to get to the Flight Deck."

Four days. It was too soon. I couldn't believe our bad luck.

Several things are about to happen, I thought. *First, my dad grounds me for all eternity. I will never leave my room again. Second, I confess about Tabitha and Sunjay. Everybody will learn about our whole plot. Third, the crew crams us in an escape pod and sends us to the Moon Base Tranquility. We then ride back to Earth on a lunar mining vessel, which is probably like being stuck on a city bus for an entire week. I go back to Alaska and survive the rest of my life on asparagus and caribou meat. And all because of that stupid Device.*

My body felt sluggish, like I couldn't move in all this red haze. Sylvia seemed to understand. She gently took my arm and steadied me on the magnetic walkway, passing the crew quarters on our way to the Flight Deck. My head throbbed and each step on the walkway seemed impossible.

Urgency and Discovery

Dark thoughts floated through my mind as Sylvia Moreline and I stumbled through *The Adversity* toward my doom. The ship was empty and quiet, like we were the only people on board.

That all changed when we emerged from the walkway onto the Flight Deck. I floated there for a moment and took in the surroundings. The Flight Deck was a semi-circular room. All the seats pointed outward from the center, and in front of each seat was a holographic workstation. When it was turned on, the crew could focus on the hologram in front of them—sometimes it was a blueprint of an engine, other times they watched video from cameras inside *The Adversity*, and occasionally someone from the real Mission Control on Earth would call them for an update on the mission. No one looked at us at first.

Everyone was hard at work in the cramped room: Redshirt Anderson was looking at a 3-D image of the cargo hold. Buckshot Lewis plotted the rest of our trip. He drew one red line from *The Adversity* to the Moon. "ETA: 12 hours," it said. Then another line, from the Moon to a point in space. "LG ALPHA— 3 DAYS." Our destinations.

My dad was strapped to a chair in the center of the room that was slightly taller than the others, watching their progress, asking questions, and spinning his pen. I always wanted to see the Flight Deck in action, with my dad in command—but I wanted to be here as a guest, not a captive. In a minute, his attention would be on me.

"Buckshot, give me an update on LG Alpha. How much time until we arrive?"

"Thirty-six hours to destination from the Moon. The space station is still cloaked though. We won't see it until we are practically standing on top of it."

"How confident are we of its flight path?"

"Certain, but if it's damaged, it could be off course."

The base on the far side of the Moon, I thought. *Sawyer had explained it to me already. And he also saved my life. I didn't even thank him.*

My dad grabbed the pen without even looking. Then he turned around and looked at me. The red haze had faded, so I saw him clearly. He frowned and studied me for a moment, like he was making some calculations in his head. I shoved my scarred hands into my pockets, which hurt like crazy. What was he thinking? Something like, *"Buckshot, I need to launch my son into space for eternity. What would you recommend?" "Leave him on one of Jupiter's moons, sir."* But dad didn't say a thing. The pen twirled. No emotions showed on his face. He was in command of the ship and of himself. And of me. Finally he spoke.

"Okay, let's go ahead and get this over with. Sylvia, escort Tully to the Observation Deck. We'll be right behind you."

A hatch popped open below our feet. Sylvia gave me a gentle push and we descended to the lower level Observation Deck, a spacious, tidy room without all the buttons, levers, screens, and holographs of the Flight Deck above. A dinner table and eight leather chairs filled the room. The walls seemed to be solid steel at first, but they turned into clear glass as soon as we touched the magnetic floor. It was a beautiful view of space from all sides, but I wasn't interested in the view. Sylvia seated me at the middle of the table. The rest of the crew took their seats. Gallant Trackman sat at one end, my dad at the other. Even Queen Envy was there, wearing a formal black evening gown and glowing, heart-shaped earrings. Lincoln Sawyer didn't look my way, but all others eyes descended upon me. I wondered what was going on in his Android mind.

My stomach had gone ice cold, my throat tightened, and my heart was pounding. My dad sat at one end of the table. Once again, he spun his pen. Finally, he pretended to poke something in the air with the pen, at which point I heard the voice of the on-flight computer: "Recording has begun, Commander Harper."

"Very good, DORIS," he said, in his "on the record" voice. "Commander Harper, crew, and one stowaway present—four days since liftoff, 36 hours to final destination," he stated. "Now, the facts are as follows: on board *The Adversity* we found one of the three children that authorities have been searching for on Earth for the last several days. Apparently they created a diversion and made people believe that they were camping. Tully, is that correct?"

"Uh, yes."

"So I am assuming you had help getting on board. Correct?"

"Yes."

"And since the other two are nowhere to be found, could you tell us their locations?"

The red haze clouded my vision for a moment. I didn't say anything. *He hasn't even asked if I'm okay. He's just grilling me with all these questions like we don't even know each other.*

"Tully, where? We don't have time for secrets."

"Okay. Queen Envy's spacesuits."

Everyone seemed shocked, especially Gallant Trackman, who shot a look at Lincoln Sawyer. I remembered their conversation about using too much oxygen. Sawyer smiled faintly, as if to say, "I told you so." My dad, on the other hand, was not smiling. He twirled his pen. Queen Envy laughed and slapped her forehead.

"Oh, Baby Bear, you wild crazy thing. Your friends have been hanging out in my spacesuits? And you came to visit—oh, that is just wild! Commander Harper, your son is just the wildest beastie in the whole zoo. I should be mad but whatever. My fans will go roasters for these crazy stowaways. Oh, I can't wait to tell them…or can I?"

"Your fans will love this story, but for now you can't breathe a word of this. Redshirt, would you mind fetching the other stowaways? DORIS, as

I was saying, all three stowaways entered *The Adversity* in spacesuits: two in Queen Envy's extra suits, and one, well, pretended to be a monkey."

"Sir, an orangutan, to be precise," added Sawyer. I could feel my face getting red.

"Yes, an orangutan. The three stowaways kept on their suits until one of them, Tully Harper, engaged the Harper Device, at which point he nearly died. Sawyer saved him. He appears to have recovered almost completely. Now, the solution would seem simple. We could still carry out our mission—drop off our stowaways on the Moon as well as the Device. Then we could continue to LG Alpha to investigate and repair the station. However, we can't do that. I've received information that changes our mission." Everyone in the room stirred. The mission changed? "This is now a *rescue* mission. Mr. Trackman, would you like to share?"

Gallant Trackman sat at the other end of the table, looking composed. He cleared his throat to speak.

"Certainly. This is a surprise to us all. LG Alpha is a secret space station. We all knew that. However, the Space Alliance told us something more today. It is a *manned* space station," said Trackman.

"There's a crew on board?" Buckshot yelled. "Well, we've got to get out there right now and help."

"My thoughts as well," said my dad. "There's no time to delay. We'll skip the Moon and head straight to LG Alpha. We can drop off the Device on the return flight." Everyone nodded in agreement except for Sylvia.

"What about the children?" asked Sylvia. "Let's not put them in harm's way. We could still send them in an escape pod to the Moon."

"That's the problem. We only have two pods. If we launch one, we put our lives at risk. We may need them for injured people or for the rest of the crew," said my dad. "We're stuck together, it appears. So Tully, Tabitha, and Sunjay decided to stow away. They'll have to share in the risks, same as the crew, same as Queen Envy."

Moreline looked frustrated but nodded.

The crew headed back to the Flight Deck. My dad stayed behind. He sat at the table for a minute staring out the window at the Moon, running his hand through his hair.

"It's beautiful, isn't it? When you're this close, you can really see the all the features. The asteroid craters, the hills, even the miners if you look through that telescope." I didn't know what to say, so I listened. "Son, you must know how angry and disappointed I am, but I just want to know if you're okay."

"Yeah, I'm fine. Just a headache."

"You don't look like you have 'just a headache.' You look like you need some rest. Why don't you head back to the infirmary? We can talk later."

"Dad," I said, "I'm glad we're still on board. We can definitely help out with the mission. Just let us know what we need to do."

"Oh, you've done plenty already," he said. "You almost got yourself killed. You are just three more problems in a difficult mission right now."

"No, we're not," I said. "I already found out some important stuff that I need to tell you."

"More important than planning a rescue mission to a damaged space station?"

"Yeah, maybe," I said, but I didn't get to finish. Behind me the door slid open. In came Redshirt with Tabitha and Sunjay. They both looked shocked, and they both looked at my dad, not me.

"Commander Harper," said Tabitha, "we're really sorry to cause you all this trouble. You just don't know how miserable it is for Tully when you're gone. We just wanted to help him."

Sunjay raised his hand. My dad nodded for him to speak. "Are you going to throw us into prison when we get back to Earth, sir? If so, for how many years?"

Commander Harper sighed. "I'm an astronaut, not a judge, so don't worry about that. Besides, you're a bit young for prison, Sunjay. You will get the grounding of your life, I'm sure. Look, I understand what you were trying to do. I know Tully doesn't like Alaska, but this wasn't the best solution. It's not the end of your lives, but don't expect a very warm welcome from me or from anybody else in the universe." He looked my way. "Especially from your Aunt Selma. You scared her to death. Redshirt and I will leave you three here for now, but you should all know where to go afterward."

There I was, alone with my two best friends on the Observation Deck. Not exactly a happy reunion.

"We're going to jail," said Sunjay. "I'll never be a free man again. I'll never get my doctorate in Physics or become an astronaut. We probably won't even survive. We'll get hit by flying paint chips and never even make it to the space station."

Tabitha didn't say anything at first. She didn't have to. The colors in her lucky scarf swirled around like an angry hurricane of green and blue. Then the entire scarf burned bright red. She grabbed my scarred hands and looked at them. Then she gave me a big bear hug and punched me in the arm. Hard.

"Why did you do it, Tully!" hissed Tabitha.

"What?" I said.

"You told me not to blow our cover, and then you go off and hug the Harper Device? You could have died. Device hugging space idiot. Nice work!" she yelled. "And you knew it, too! You knew the Device was on board weeks ago and didn't even tell me. Stars, how stupid can you get? What else don't we know?"

"Nothing—just a lot has happened to me." I thought about Trackman, Sawyer, and the Red Visions. *How was I supposed to tell her any of that?*

Redshirt poked his head down from the Flight Deck. "Uh, guys, the doors aren't that thick on board the ship. There might be a better place for you to talk."

We nodded okay, but Tabitha's green eyes burned right through me. "Tully," she hissed, "don't talk to us again unless you want to explain. Come on, Sunjay. Queen Envy expects me in her room and you're supposed to stay in Redshirt's room. Tully can go wherever he wants. I guess we'll do what we're told for once."

"Yeah, go ahead," I said, "but meet me in the Hamster Wheel in an hour if you want to know what happened to me in the lab. We might also have some fun, too. That's part of why we came anyway, right?"

"Oh, sure, we'll have tons of fun," she said, grabbing Sunjay by the arm and floating away.

With that they left me alone on the Observation Deck, hurt and angry, looking at the lightning flowers on my hands, trying to figure out what to say.

New Problems, New Skills

Two hours passed before Tabitha and Sunjay arrived in the Hamster Wheel. Before they arrived I shot free throws, practiced with the bo staff, and tried to sort out what I might tell them. I made a mental list that would make me sound like a halfway normal human being.

Now Tabitha stood there with a death-ray stare and her scarf on fire. "Okay, Space Boy, story us. Sunjay and I are ready." Sunjay looked around the Wheel, amazed by all the endless possibilities for entertainment, just like I had, but Tabitha pinched him. "Sunjay, remember prison. Remember our discussion."

"Oh, right. Sorry." He scowled at me and crossed his arms.

"Okay, okay, I blew it. I got caught."

"That's not why we're mad. Queen Envy would have found us soon anyway. Sunjay was jealous that he wasn't her pillow."

"Then why are you mad?"

"Because we planned this for weeks and you didn't tell us everything you knew. The Harper Device was on board? Just a little detail."

"It didn't seem that important at the time. I didn't want y'all to freak out."

"Well, here we are, freaking out!" yelled Sunjay. "Freaking out in space! I'll never breathe the free air again. And what I did to my dad's car—"

"What else haven't you told us, Tully?" asked Tabitha. "There's no room for secrets out here. Secrets cause problems. Secrets kill. Tell us everything that happened, everything you know."

Everything I know? *I don't know anything anymore,* I thought. *I have a weird secret friendship with an Android. I see Red Visions about space jellyfish.* I wasn't about to tell them that. They would think I was crazy.

I began my story. I took them through the facts of my journey—getting the orangutan spacesuit, finding my cage, getting fed by Moreline, stargazing in the cage, and the first orangutan carwash. They asked about Little Bacon. I told them about how he saved me.

"You kicked him across the lab? That was a jerk move," Tabitha said.

"It was my only hope," I explained.

"Yeah, he did save your bacon!" Sunjay laughed. "Did you shout 'GOALLL!' when you kicked him?"

Tabitha shot him another look and he scowled again. It felt good to tell them some things, even if I did feel guilty for kicking Little Bacon. Still, it wasn't enough. Tabitha popped her gum. She wanted more. I took a deep breath and told them about Sawyer, how he discovered me, fed me, kept my secrets, and took me to the Hamster Wheel. I did not tell them about our conversations back on Earth.

"You practiced martial arts with him? Nice!" said Sunjay, looking over at the equipment again.

"Why did Sawyer keep your secrets?" asked Tabitha.

"Because he likes me. He says I have nerve."

"What a creeptastic Android," said Tabitha. "I never want to talk to him—his eyes are so bright and hollow at the same time. He looks possessed."

"Yeah, Androids have that freaky look, but he also saved me from the Harper Device. Just because he's unusual doesn't mean he's dangerous." I could have told them he also appeared in my Red Vision, but what would that do for us?

The scarf around Tabitha's neck finally shifted from bright red to faint pink. "Ha! Maybe Sawyer thinks *we* are dangerous. I don't blame him. We sneaked—or snuck or however you say that—on board. Anyway, they decided to keep us on board. I guess we'll wait and see what happens."

We all let that sink in for a moment.

"Never trust the Android," said Sunjay, thoughtfully. "In the old science fiction movies, the Android always goes crazy. He always saves you early on but then turns on you and pushes you out into space or he pulls off your helmet and you suffocate. Or! Or he tries to smother you in your bed with a pillow or twist your head sideways like this."

Sunjay grabbed Tabitha's scarf and twisted it like he was wringing out a wet towel.

"Horror movie neck-wringing crazy fanboy!" Tabitha said. "Easy on the accessories. I only have one lucky scarf. So, Tully, Sunjay says we can't trust the Android. But can we trust *you*?"

"You can trust us both," I said, offended by her question.

"I don't know. There's one thing you haven't said," she told me. "One phrase in Queen Envy's room you said was important."

"What phrase?"

Before she had time to answer, the portal to the Hamster Wheel opened again. In came Redshirt Anderson. He was as surprised to see us as we were to see him. He was on a break and looking for some peace and quiet. *Man, he's in the wrong place at the wrong time,* I thought. He could tell we were in an argument because he didn't interrupt us. He nodded toward us and walked toward the basketball court. He picked up a ball and dribbled between his legs a few times. I remembered that he played college basketball and turned down a professional career to go into the space program. He started sinking free throws—one after another, never missing. His presence pulled us out of our intense conversation. I was glad because I couldn't remember any phrase. *What did I say in Queen Envy's room?* Sunjay sighed and flopped his hair out of his eyes.

"Guys, can you continue your argument later? I want to play basketball in space before my prison sentence begins."

Sunjay hopped up and walked over to Redshirt. They started shooting. Tabitha wouldn't look at me, and after an uncomfortable silence, I decided to shoot some baskets, too. Redshirt tossed me the ball and pretended to guard me, so I passed the ball to Sunjay, who missed a lay-up. We played a game of 2-on-1 for a while and started to work up a sweat.

Redshirt gave us enough space to shoot, but he also swatted a few of our shots. We lost track of the score after a while and just shot around.

"Is your friend okay?" he asked, nodding to Tabitha.

"We're in an argument," said Sunjay.

"Hmmmm," said Redshirt.

We played a little longer. At first my hands ached, but they loosened up the more we played. After a while Redshirt swatted one of my shots in Tabitha's direction. She passed the ball back to Redshirt, but he smiled and threw it right back to her.

"That wasn't a bad pass," he said.

"I haven't played since I was in kindergarten," she said.

"Perfect. These guys have never played before."

"Hey," said Sunjay, "we're not that bad!"

"Oh, no?" Redshirt smiled again and motioned for her to come over. He put Tabitha on the free throw line. He nodded toward the rim. She shot the ball two-handed and threw it over the backboard. Sunjay and I laughed. Tabitha could dance and sing, but she wasn't a baller. Redshirt frowned at us. "Hmmmm," he said. He repositioned the ball in her hands. Then he put his hand on her head and pushed down to make her knees flex.

"Don't let these boys make you feel small," said Redshirt. "Now shoot again, and leave your right hand up in the air at the end, like you're reaching into a cookie jar on the top shelf." She tried another free throw. It hit the rim. And another. Swish.

"Wow, that works!" she said.

"Form, focus, and confidence." Redshirt spun the ball on his finger. "You think we can take these two boys to school now?"

"Bring it on!" yelled Sunjay, so we started a game. I guarded Redshirt. He still gave me enough space to shoot, but I missed. He never even needed to shoot to beat us either. He dribbled, faked, and nodded to open spots. Then he would set a pick on Sunjay, and Tabitha would be wide open. Every time she hit a shot, she would say a different kind of cookie. "Macadamia nut...chocolate chip...oatmeal raisin...chocolate covered almond biscotti..."

"Hmmm, biscotti," said Redshirt. They beat us so easily that she nearly ran out of cookie names. By the end they were high-fiving like old pals.

"I guess we are that bad," said Sunjay. "Or you're like a pro."

"When I'm back home my daughter and I always play my two sons. She and I always win, but I gotta say, Tabitha shoots better than my daughter. We may need to print some cookies on the 3D printer after this. I'm hungry."

Tabitha's scarf turned a warm yellow. I smiled, even though they crushed us. Sunjay needed to get out some frustration though. He left the basketball court for a moment and returned with a bo staff for both of us. Tabitha and Redshirt were our audience, but they were pretty distracted talking about basketball and baking cookies.

I walked over and turned the knob to 1/2G. Moments later, Sunjay jumped and touched the ceiling with his staff.

"This is awesome! Who cares if we're going to prison! You ready to feel the wrath of Sunjay?" he asked, spinning his staff.

Oh, I was ready. We faced off on the free throw line. On Earth Sunjay always beat me with a bo staff, but Sawyer taught me some things. Sunjay flew into attack mode. He held his staff with both hands and threw attacks at my chest, head, and legs. Our weapons clanked together loudly. I blocked everything.

"Whoa, not bad," he said, backing away. "But I'm just warming up." He came at me again—this time more ferociously. He somersaulted over my head and continued his attack from the other side, pushing me back under the basketball goal. I blocked most of his strokes, but one of them caught me on the hand. That's when everything changed.

Pain bloomed in my mind. A red haze blinded me for a moment. My ears rang. My hands felt like they were on fire again. Sunjay kept attacking though, pushing me almost to the wall, not realizing he had hit me so hard on my injured hands. I remembered Rule #2—no pain, no gain.

I ignored the pain. The red haze still filled my mind, and as I focused, it seemed like time slowed down. I could see all the details of his movements. *Is this how Sawyer feels when he looks at me?* A bead of sweat flew from Sunjay's black hair and I watched it suspended in front of his face.

He glanced at my right leg, giving away his next attack. His muscles tensed in his right hand, and I knew he was about to swing his staff. Instead of blocking, I raised my leg. His strike missed completely, spinning himself around and almost falling on the floor. Sunjay prepared for another attack. His left hand tensed, and I dodged again.

"You never dodge," he said. He looked angry and confused, so he threw a roundhouse kick at my head. I saw it coming from a mile away. I dodged, swept his leg with my own kick, and before I knew what was happening, Sunjay was on the floor and I was perched on the basketball rim, holding both of our staffs and looking down on my defeated opponent.

"Rule #1: never let your guard down," I said.

"I didn't! You broke through my guard. You cracked my staff!" he said, pointing. I looked at his staff and there was a split in the wood. "What was all that? Dude, my head!" Sunjay pulled back his hair, and there was a red whelp on his forehead with a dab of blood. I must have hit him without even noticing. Redshirt and Tabitha seemed interested now. I hopped down from my basketball goal perch.

"Sorry, just a few new tricks," I said, stretching my hands.

"You were so fast, and your hands, your hands..." Sunjay stammered. I dropped the staffs and crammed my hands in my pockets. They felt hot but didn't hurt anymore. "They were glowing—"

"How hard did I hit you? You're seeing things," I said, but he was right. Something happened when Sunjay attacked me that second time— that red mist had filled my mind and done something to me. Had our audience noticed? Redshirt just shook his head, looking relaxed, but Tabitha looked stressed, like she had the night before we left. Maybe she noticed. Maybe not.

That's when I realized that Redshirt and Tabitha weren't the only people in our audience. We had an uninvited guest of our own in the Hamster Wheel. Behind them, walking briskly on a treadmill, someone else had appeared without notice. Gallant Trackman.

"Yeah, your hands looked like they were on fire—" Sunjay stammered on. I didn't know how to quiet him, but I didn't have long to worry about that. A loud alarm sounded, like a tornado alert. The lights in the Hamster Wheel flashed. Redshirt sprang to his feet immediately.

"That's an emergency call from the Flight Deck. You should come with me."

The four of us left the Hamster Wheel together. But not Trackman. Like a phantom he vanished before anyone else saw him. So did my opportunity to check in with Tabitha.

NO SUCH THING

The moment we appeared in the Flight Deck, Redshirt took his place beside my dad. The crewmembers stood in a semi-circle. The three of us stood behind them. In the middle of the room a holographic image of the Moon held their attention. Out the window the real Moon loomed. In both cases, there was a tiny white speck in the distance, with a long wispy tail that trailed into the deep black of space. Anderson took in the scene.

"Hmmm, that is what I *think* it is," he said.

"Yes, it's rogue," Buckshot said. "Came out of nowhere. We just plotted its course. And you won't believe it." Buckshot pointed to a spot beyond the Moon labeled LG Alpha. "First no one can contact LG Alpha. Now there's a rogue comet headed directly for it. Unbelievable. It's like the perfect storm out here."

"It is a perfect storm," said my dad, "but we won't see this storm make landfall. You see what's happening here? The comet may intersect the space station, but we won't know."

"We won't see if there's an explosion?" Sunjay asked.

"If there is an explosion, the Moon will block our view. DORIS, run Scenario One."

The image in the middle of the room sprang to life. The Moon rotated slowly. On one side we saw *The Adversity* slowly approaching the Moon. In the distance, quite far away, we saw the small space station LG Alpha sitting in space like a speck of dust. Then the bright white comet sailed into the picture, its tail flaring. It was like watching a bullet fly through the air in slow motion. Tabitha grabbed my shoulder as it approached LG Alpha. Sunjay stared wide-eyed. It gave me a queasy feeling, just like the animation that the media did with my dad getting hit by an asteroid on Mars.

However, the comet passed right by LG Alpha, so close that the images blurred together. Moments later it appeared on the other side of the Moon. "That's the best case scenario—the comet reappears in thirty minutes. That much we can see. Now here's Scenario Two."

The image reversed. This time the white bullet of the comet hit the space station. It was a glancing blow, and pieces of the space station flew in all directions. The comet also split into chunks, which appeared on the other side of the Moon.

"If that comet hits anything, we'll know it alright," said Buckshot. "In thirty-four minutes."

Tabitha tugged on my shirt. She motioned to the Observation Deck.

✳ ✳ ✳

"This is getting crazy," said Sunjay. "Hey, why does your dad always answer my questions but not yours?"

"I don't know, Sunjay. Look, that's not important right now. Tabitha, what is it? Is it Trackman?"

"No, well, kind of. What about him?"

"Well, I just thought he might have freaked you out earlier?"

"When?"

"When he was on the treadmill behind you in the Hamster Wheel."

"He was? Stars, no. It's something else."

"What?" I pleaded.

We were on the Observation Deck, just the three of us, but not for long. When the portal opened again, Trackman descended into the room. He kept popping up everywhere. He hardly acknowledged us and drifted over to the far side of the room. Still, we couldn't talk with him there. We needed privacy. I nudged Tabitha and said, "Hey, weren't we supposed to check on Queen Envy?"

Sunjay piped up. "Oh, great idea!"

We drifted through the ship until we arrived at her door. It was strangely quiet. Only a faint guitar played inside. I knocked. She opened the door. I would not have recognized her if it wasn't her room. She wore no makeup, a pair of jeans, and an ancient Rolling Stones t-shirt.

"Hey, Baby Bear, what brings you to my room?"

"Uh, we needed a place to talk."

She scrunched up her nose at us. "I'm not recording, just messing around and trying to not to think about those poor people on board LG Alpha. Come on in. Would you like some chai tea or a scone?"

Tabitha and I didn't want to take tea with Queen Envy. Sunjay did. The Queen brought us tea and scones, and we sat there making small talk and sipping tea through straws for a few minutes. We told her about the comet as we batted away all the celebrity space junk that kept floating into our faces. Finally Tabitha floated up to the ceiling and I followed her, leaving Sunjay to entertain the Queen.

"Now, what did you find out? I bet it's about—"

"The Conspiracy Game," she said. "First, tell me what you know." I told her about Trackman and Sawyer's strange conversation and how it seemed suspicious. Then she filled me in. "Redshirt and I talked while you were beating up on Sunjay. He told me all about his family and his first two missions with your dad. He really admires your dad. Anyway, I asked him what other games the crew played in space. That's when I remembered the name. He listed off sports. Then I asked him about The Conspiracy Game."

"And?"

"There's no such thing."

My heart accelerated. "What do you mean?"

"He's never heard of it. The Android is lying to you. You know, the same one that saved you? Sawyer and Trackman may be playing a game, but nobody else knows the rules."

"What if they're trying to take over the ship, Tabitha?"

"They sound sketchy, but I don't know about that. What if they're just messing with you? Maybe we should just tell your dad."

"He's got enough problems right now. I can't tell him some stupid thing about a Conspiracy Game while he's trying to save a space station. He'll think I'm crazy."

"Tully, nobody thinks you're crazy, but maybe you're right. We don't know enough to say something right now."

"Exactly. So let's just play it cool and see what happens."

We pulled Sunjay away from tea with the Queen. That wasn't easy. She was in the middle of some story about being on tour in India, riding an elephant and bathing in a river. Sunjay's mouth was open, he was shaking his head and grinning like a hyena at the zoo, like someone just told him the secrets of the universe. Tabitha grabbed his arm and pulled him toward the door.

"Sorry, Queen Envy. The comet should almost be visible," I said.

"Ooh, Baby Bear, I almost forgot. Your friend Sunjay is such a sweetie for listening to me. Tell Papa Bear I'll be up there in a while. I just need a costume change first."

On the way back to the Flight Deck, we told a distracted Sunjay about The Conspiracy Game. He was surprised.

Not nearly as surprised by what happened next.

✳ ✳ ✳

Back on the Flight Deck, everyone gathered around the hologram. It showed the "progress" of the comet behind the Moon. The comet—or what remained of it—would soon be visible.

"Three minutes to go," said Redshirt. He gave us an update every thirty seconds. Everyone watched quietly.

I looked at my hands and thought about my Red Vision again. *If The Conspiracy Game wasn't real, Sawyer might just be messing with my mind like Tabitha said. He's an Android though. People program Androids to follow instructions. Androids obey. They're not like humans. They don't make or break the rules. They follow them. So why does he always break the rules? He kept me in hiding and called me his "secret friend." He betrayed my dad, but he was loyal to me. And Trackman? Maybe that's who makes the rules for Sawyer's game.*

"Two minutes."

Then there was the fish and jellyfish thing. It was weird that ocean creatures appeared in the Red Vision. *A perfect storm. Maybe the vision makes some kind of sense. There was a fish gasping for air in space. It was scared. That could be the space station. The people on board don't have enough air. Then there was the jellyfish with the deadly tentacles. That would be the comet about to destroy them. Maybe it's a prophecy. But what's the purpose of seeing this stuff if I can't do anything about it? What did the Harper Device do to me?*

"One minute now." Anderson watched the seconds tick down. "You can ignore the hologram." We all looked out the window at the horizon of the Moon. In moments we would see a whole comet or its fragments.

I should just explain the Visions. At least to Tabitha. She won't think I'm crazy. She always listens to me, and right now she doesn't trust me because I haven't told her everything. Sunjay will listen, too. If I cry 'Wolf,' they'll listen. They have to. Then we can get to the bottom of The Conspiracy Game.

"Five, four, three, two, one."

The three of us looked out the window, floating close to the glass to get a good look at the comet.

Nothing appeared.

"Redshirt, are those calculations—"

"Completely accurate, Commander. It's simple math."

"Well, there's no use waiting. It appears that our rogue comet has gone missing on the far side of the Moon," my dad said. "Mr. Trackman, any other information you can give us to help with this? Does LG Alpha have a defense system? Could it have destroyed or captured a comet?"

Trackman shook his head. "I'm afraid not."

My dad twirled his pen and looked out the window. "Well, I guess we discovered Scenario Three. So the fact that the comet disappeared doesn't change what we need to do, does it? We might explain the rogue comet later, but it's not important for now. We'll proceed on our rescue mission. Crew, back to your regular duties. You three, please stay in your quarters the rest of the day. That is all. We'll see you at lunch."

BURDENS

Back to the orangutan cage. Back to square one. I hoped the comet would give me some idea of what to do next. Everything was "as clear as mud," as my dad liked to say. I worked my way through the ship and was on the magnetic walkway when I heard a portal open behind me. It was Trackman.

"Ah, Tully Harper. Our stowaway. I don't think we've ever properly met. I'm Gallant Trackman. I am on board as an observer and consultant to your father. This mission was my proposal, as was bringing the Device."

"That was my dad's idea," I said.

He sucked air through his teeth and got this ferocious look in his eyes for just a moment. Then he relaxed his face into some sort of smile. "Hmm, so you say, but how would you know whose ideas it was? At any rate, you've seen some strange things in space already. I wish I could explain them all, but one thing I can explain: our Android. I'm training him, you see, to interact with people well. He's learning to earn people's trust. He must have seen his opportunity with you on board the ship. I know this would be awkward to report this to your father right now—all his babblings about The Conspiracy Game."

"And what about Operation Close Encounter?" I asked. "He talked about that, too." The fury returned to his eyes and disappeared in a flash. *That got his attention and hit a nerve!* Sawyer never said anything about Operation Close Encounter to me, but I thought that might get Trackman talking. If he was making the rules for the Android, I had to figure him out. Trackman regained his composure and smiled his shark-like smile.

"Ah, he mentioned that as well? It's nothing. Don't bother your father with all that. I wouldn't lose any sleep over it. Sawyer appreciates history, and I've always been a big fan of spies, double agents, Benedict Arnolds. I find them enthralling. Conspirators treat life like it's a game that you can win or lose. Don't you like games?"

"How do I know it's just a game, Trackman? Why shouldn't I tell my dad?"

His eyes narrowed. "Get a grip, boy. It's ludicrous. Why would I plot to take over this ship with the Android as a sidekick? What am I going to do—fly us all to the moons of Jupiter? What's out there but empty space? And where are my supplies for such a trip? Insanity. You want to pester your dad with this after all the trouble you've caused? I'm sure you feel guilty, like a burden to him. Children can be such a burden. I'm glad I never had any."

He picked at his big teeth with a fingernail. My heart sunk as I thought about his words. I had burdened my dad. Still, something didn't sit right with me about his explanations.

"Ah, sorry, that was inconsiderate of me. I didn't mean to be so harsh. Your father speaks highly of you. So does Sawyer. He says you like martial arts, and I saw you battle your friend. You're quite good with that bo staff. How are you with your mind? I'm not interested in hand-to-hand combat, but we should play chess sometime. I'll stop by your cage when things settle down. Hopefully that will be sooner than later."

He exited the space lab. I went back to my cage and set up the chess-board. Trackman seemed to love games, and I felt the urge to practice if he ever wanted to play me. With no one to play against, I got bored pretty quickly. My stomach growled. It was still an hour to lunch. On the other side of the room the Harper Device softly glowed.

"Hey," I said, "you in the other cage, what's the deal with the Visions? You could have at least told me something useful, like 'There's a rogue comet out there and it's going to disappear.' Or what about Sawyer and Trackman? Are they telling me the truth? Instead you gave me weird visions and glowing hands. Thanks. Really useful stuff."

The Harper Device must have been listening because that night I had another Red Vision. This one started the same as the first, with everything turning red, and then out of that red haze appeared images. My mind seemed to detach from my body and floated through the ship. I floated through the cargo hold and onto the magnetic walkway. Someone was there again. This time it looked less like a human being and more like a body, swaying lifelessly in zero gravity. Sawyer was nowhere to be seen.

Then, a new scene. I hovered above an ocean for a moment. A storm was raging above the water. Waves crashed everywhere. They didn't faze me at all. I felt like a god. I decided to dive beneath the waves. The ocean was dark but not deep. A reef full of coral glowed at the bottom. As I approached the reef, I saw it again—the jellyfish. It swam deliberately toward the reef. There again was the fish, gasping for air. I swam to help, but the current pushed me away. Just as the jellyfish reached its victim, an enormous white whale cut off my view. By the time the whale passed, the jellyfish had its tentacles wrapped around its prey. The fish struggled to survive. *If the current wasn't so strong, if the white whale hadn't cut me off, and I would have arrived just a little earlier,* I thought. It was a perfect storm. A perfect storm! I heard that phrase just hours earlier, and now my dream made sense.

I jolted back to the present and found myself floating in the middle of the dark, orangutan cage. Maybe it was part of the Red Vision, but the lightning flowers on my hands seemed to glow for a moment before they looked like scars again. I looked through the bars toward the Device.

"I get it now," I whispered. "These are dreams with hidden meanings. I said 'Show me something' and you did. The white whale is the Moon. The fish must be LG Alpha. The jellyfish is the comet? I want to understand." Still, I couldn't bring myself to tell anyone, especially not my dad. Like Trackman said, I was a burden. I sat there until morning, rerunning the images in my mind.

Phase Two

"Lunch served. Report to Observation Deck," the voice of DORIS announced.

I cheered up at the thought of food. Everyone was there for lunch on the Observation Deck except for Buckshot who was piloting us past the Moon. It was an amazing view. Since the Moon has no atmosphere, the craters were clearly visible from hundreds of miles away. Moon Base Tranquility was just visible from space, too. No one felt like talking about the beautiful view though. The weight of the rescue mission was on us. What would we find on the far side of the Moon? Deadly scenes of exploding space stations and jellyfish kept popping up in my mind.

We sat on the magnetic chairs. The middle of the table opened, and covered platters of food appeared. The meal was "breakfast for lunch." The food—bacon, eggs, orange juice, and oatmeal—was kept in steamy glass containers so it wouldn't float away. If any food did float off, a mechanical arm grabbed the larger particles and a small vacuum grabbed the leftover bits. All the drinks had straws, and they filled from the bottom up if you placed them in the right spot on the table. It was all a bit tricky at first, especially keeping everything on the metal sporks—you know, those spoon/fork things. I never liked sporks and Tabitha felt the same. She tried to lighten the mood.

"They aren't good spoons and they're not good forks either. What's the point?" she said.

"A spork doesn't have a point," said Sunjay. "You're thinking of a knife."

"Oh, haha, Sunjay. Seriously, they should make one that has a spoon on one side and a fork on the other," she said.

I watched Tabitha. She, like me, had to snatch her eggs out of mid-air several times so they didn't float to the ceiling. It took my mind off our problems for a moment, even though the beady-eyed Trackman sat next to me. A spork looked dangerous in his hand. It slowed my appetite down, but not much.

Sunjay was even hungrier than I was. We passed dish after dish down the table toward him. "Could you pass this? Pass that?" he said, with a mouth full of fluffy eggs that would occasionally float out of his mouth toward one of us.

Finally, Redshirt looked at Sunjay across the wide table and said, "Hmmm, please open your mouth wide just like you would at a dentist office. Just don't say 'ah.'"

Sunjay obeyed. Redshirt pinched a piece of bacon, aimed it like a dart, and launched the projectile toward Sunjay. We all watched the slice of bacon float through the air toward its target. The bacon dart reached Sunjay's mouth and went right in. A perfect shot! Everyone applauded, and Redshirt grinned.

"You ought to see Redshirt shoot free throws," dad said.

Yes, we had seen that.

"That mouth is an easy target," Redshirt replied.

"Commander, how long until we can see the base?" asked Sunjay.

"We'll be there in about 48 hours," my dad said. "But remember, the base has a cloaking device. It will be hard to detect, and we won't see it until we are very close. If the cloaking device is damaged, we should see it much sooner."

"Is there a Scenario Four," I asked, "where something else happened to the rogue comet?"

"I seriously doubt it, Tully," he said. Once again, my questions always seemed to be wrong. Dad didn't seem interested in answering me, just Sunjay.

After lunch the three of us disembarked for the Hamster Wheel and left the crew to do their jobs. For once the Wheel was ours. We played more games: basketball, volleyball, and just jumping around in 1/2 G. Volleyball was amazing. At 1/2 G, I could jump over the net. For a short guy, that was heaven. I felt like an Olympian, flying through the air and hitting the ball straight down, watching it bounce back to the ceiling. So Sunjay and I hit volleyballs at each other for a while. Tabitha set us and laughed when we hit each other, which wasn't that often. Our aim wasn't very Olympian.

Sunjay and I also battled with bo staffs again. This time, like the last, went in his favor until he hit my hand. I actually put my hand into harm's way on purpose. At that point the pain brought back the red haze. Then I felt untouchable, unstoppable. My hands and head throbbed with power and pain, but I easily knocked him down again. My hands glowed, but I shoved them in my pockets to avoid any strange conversations. Tabitha frowned at me, like I was holding something back from them both, but we had bigger problems to solve. In 48 hours, we would arrive at LG Alpha.

"Guys, we need to figure out if there's anything to this Conspiracy Game." I looked at Tabitha. She looked out the window, but I knew her now. She wasn't distracted. She was deep in thought—probably deeper than Sunjay and me. "Any ideas?"

"Divide and conquer," she said. "Here's what we do. Sunjay follows Trackman. Tully, you follow Sawyer—because I don't want to. I'm going to have some girl time with Queen Envy."

"Girl time? What's the point of that? Why don't I get to have girl time with Queen Envy?" said Sunjay.

"It's not worth explaining, Sunjay. I'm going to 'pull a Tully' and not tell you right now."

"Haha," I said. "Let's figured this out. It's the one thing we might be able to do for my dad."

I didn't learn much though. Sawyer stayed on the Flight Deck most of the day, the one place I could not stay for long. Observing him I didn't learn much, other than he did not eat or sleep, so his days never really ended or began. He left the deck occasionally to check something else on the ship or to check my vital signs, if he noticed me with my sketchbook.

"How's The Conspiracy Game?" I asked, sketching the Observation Deck. "Are you winning?"

"Oh, Tully, I wish I could tell you, but since you have been discovered, I have to keep my secrets. By the way, are you still keeping mine?"

"Of course," I said.

"Then I have something for you."

"What?"

"Follow me."

I felt tense as we made our way through the ship. When we reached the magnetic walkway near the escape pods, my mind raced. The vision of the body returned.

"Is something wrong?" he asked.

"Nothing," I said.

Every muscle tensed up and I clenched my fists. I prepared for the worst—maybe I was the body in the magnetic walkway. I let Sawyer walked ahead. I wished that Sunjay or Tabitha were there with me. But he didn't stay on the walkway. He opened the infirmary door. I slowly made my way down the empty walkway and turned into the infirmary. There was a camera on the wall. Maybe Redshirt was watching. I would be safer there than on the walkway. Once there, he retrieved a box from a drawer and held it out to me.

"What's in the box?" I asked.

"A token of our friendship," he said. "You should be more gentle with him in the future."

I opened the box and expected something to pop out at me—a scorpion, maybe? Instead, Little Bacon stared up at me.

"Bacon! I thought I lost you!" I patted Little Bacon on the head.

"You did lose me. Actually, you kicked me," he said.

"He was a bit damaged. I repaired him," Sawyer said, "just like I repaired his owner."

✳ ✳ ✳

Little Bacon was back in my shirt pocket when I met Sunjay and Tabitha later. They were happy to see him, but I had nothing to show for my afternoon with Sawyer. Tabitha had more.

Queen Envy sent the new song, "Space Boy," back to Earth. It was an immediate hit.

"She's in dire love with your dad, Tully, and the world knows by now," Tabitha said, smiling. "Queen Harper sounds kind of nice, doesn't it?"

"About as good as Tabitha Trackman," I said. The whole thing creeped me out. I couldn't imagine Queen Envy with my dad. He loved his job more than anything else, except, hopefully, me.

"I wish I was her Space Boy," Sunjay said.

"That makes two of us," I said. "So is that all?"

Tabitha twirled her lucky scarf. Clearly she had more.

"Oh, it's dire crazy. Crazy question of a comet hurling through space. And it just veered off course. Boom, you know?"

We both looked at her. She took a deep breath.

"Okay, here's the thing: Queen Envy and I kind of bonded this afternoon. We talked about music and fashion, but there's more to her than that. Did you know that she knew about the mission before we left? The Alliance told her it was dangerous, and they needed a cover story. She agreed to be the cover, as long as they kept her posted on what was happening. She's cooler than I thought," said Tabitha. "Well, maybe not her music or the glowing eyelashes, but she's got guts."

"So *now* you like her! Finally. What more about the mission?" asked Sunjay.

"It's about the comet," said Tabitha, quietly. "The crew reviewed the recording of the comet. Before we lost track of it, the comet *turned*."

"Comets don't turn," I said. "Comets might orbit or get pulled by gravity—"

"—Right, comets don't do that. But what does?" She let that question hang there. I pictured the jellyfish.

"A comet with a mind of its own?" said Sunjay. I wouldn't have believed it a few days before, but ever since the Harper Device drew me in, anything seemed possible. It was just another piece in a growing puzzle. We asked Sunjay about his day.

"Oh, Trackman? He just hung out in his room and on the Observation Deck. He looked out the window at the Moon and muttered to himself, like my dad does when he's trying to fix something in the garage."

"Could you hear him?" I asked.

"Nope."

"Could you see his lips?" asked Tabitha.

"Uh, no."

We hadn't made much progress. We had Little Bacon, and we knew more about the strange comet. "Guys, we've got to get to the bottom of this. Let's meet again as soon as we can. We need to get ready."

"For what?" said Sunjay.

"I don't know." I floated back to my cage, determined to find out but having no idea how to find out. That changed when I touched the hatch to the space lab. A shot of fear and excitement shot through me. The lightning flower on the back of my hand glowed. Someone was in the lab, I could feel it. I didn't even need to peek through the window to see who. I picked Little Bacon out of my pocket.

"Hey, LB, I have another adventure for you. I promise, no kicking. Just sneaking. Go hide in the garden and listen. No talking."

I slid open the door ever so slightly for him to enter the space lab. Two figures were talking in front of the Harper Device. You know who. *More games,* I thought. Sawyer and Trackman had not noticed the door.

Little Bacon scooted down the corridor just inches off the floor, trying to catch their conversation.

"I returned the Handroid to the boy. His trust seems to be growing."

"Well, bravo, you walking piece of hardware," said Trackman. "Finally you do something right. But how could you tell the boy the access code to his cage?"

Apparently Trackman had found out about my earlier conversations with Sawyer and he wasn't happy.

"Who knows what he thinks?" Trackman continued. "Telling him some story about 'Conspiracy Games'? Is that really what you called this? What a fool! Better to have done away with him while you had the chance. And you had your chances…"

"That would have made quite a mess, sir. Someone would soon notice the missing pod…"

"Yes, they would, and Tranquility Base would find him. They would have quite a surprise when they found a missing child in an escape pod," laughed Trackman. "Yes, it could have come back to haunt us, but this Tully bothers me. He's your responsibility now. You make sure he keeps his secrets. It's too early for anyone to discover Operation Close Encounter—and don't you dare utter that phrase again to anyone."

"I haven't," said the Android.

"Yes, you have."

They debated the point for a minute. *That worked out well*, I thought. *They're arguing. As long as I stay quiet about their plans, I'm safe. At least they aren't going to launch me into space, dead or alive. Maybe my Vision of the body was all wrong, or they had nothing to do with it.*

But I realized I was wrong moments later.

"Phase One of Operation Close Encounter ends now," said Gallant Trackman through his sharp white teeth. "The comet was right on schedule. Now Phase Two. Weaken the crew. The children can be used as pawns. Humans love to protect their young, like any other animal."

My heart was in my throat. I couldn't swallow. His words paralyzed me. They had no such effect on Sawyer.

"Yes, sir," he said. "I know my assignments. Now, if you please, I would like the details of our arrival at LG Alpha."

"You're so eager, Sawyer," said Trackman. "You will receive your reward in full, if it's really what you want so badly. You will become more human than you will ever believe."

"When? When? I want to know when!" shouted Sawyer.

At that point, Little Bacon peeked through the vines to get a good luck at Sawyer. A crease appeared between Sawyer's glowing eyes. An attempted frown, no more effective than an attempted smile. His voice sounded urgent, like he wanted something so badly he could taste it, but Androids can't taste. Neither could they have real emotions.

"Oh, sir, when and how can I become more human?" mocked Trackman. "Listen to you, begging like a dog, shouting like a child that dropped his ice cream on the sidewalk. I guess you were fabricated just four years ago. You're a child to me, and about as dangerous. So here's your answer: soon. Soon is all I will tell you. Simply complete Phase Two, and then we can discuss this again."

"Certainly. I am sorry, sir. I lost control of my emotions."

"No, you didn't. You don't have emotions. You tried to frighten me into telling you something. It didn't work. Remember that. You can frighten children, but you can't frighten me. And you certainly can't frighten Commander Harper. He will not be easy to deal with, I assure you. If you do as I instructed, everything will go according to plan. Now, begin Phase Two. And change that access code on the cage before you leave. No more trouble from your misguided youth."

With that, Trackman turned and looked at the Device. Sawyer floated toward the cage, and Little Bacon was smart enough to keep a visual on him. He began punching in a new access code. I memorized the code and quickly realized I had to hide myself! I dove behind one of the black boxes in the cargo hold. I heard the door open and Sawyer stopped right in front of me. I held my breath. I felt the box move. Then the lid opened. He pulled something out, locked the box, and left. I waited a few more minutes behind the box and finally Trackman left, too. I returned to my cage with my mind spinning.

There never was a Conspiracy Game...just a conspiracy. Phase One—something to do with the rogue comet, if that's what it was. Phase Two—weaken the crew and use us as pawns...

I needed to tell what I knew. Everything. Not yet though. It was late. I couldn't just go barging through the ship. Trackman and Sawyer might notice. My dad was still mad, my friends were sleeping by now, and I was worn out, too. I needed to get my thoughts in order before I made my move.

CASSANDRA

That night, as I slept on the grass in my orangutan cage, the Red Visions returned. It started like a lot of my dreams—a dark night sky with tiny stars hanging over my head. Actually, I was hanging there in the stars, floating in space. Slowly I began moving, passing bright stars along the way. I watched a gray-black chunk of ice and rock zip by me. The comet. *The Adversity* appeared next to it. The comet grew a bright tail, but the tail split into glowing tentacles. The ship struggled to break free, but it couldn't. I saw three people with armor emerge from *The Adversity*. One held a flaming sword. They launched toward the jellyfish.

Next I was on board *The Adversity*. All was quiet, but the red haze was so thick I could hardly see. I was looking at something I had already seen—the magnetic walkway. The last time Sawyer was there, but this time it was Gallant Trackman, with a scorpion in his hand. He stood beside a limp body. "My secret friend," he hissed through his oversized white teeth, turning toward me. The scorpion raised its tail. "Soon, very soon." The image froze in my head and I couldn't pull myself away for a moment.

Finally, I found myself back in the space lab. Someone else was in my cage, which was filled with red haze. The figure emerged from the haze. It was Tabitha.

In the background I heard a voice. A familiar voice sang an unfamiliar song:

> *Boy who doesn't know his gifts*
> *Girl who flies into the mist*
> *Cassandra cries to the skies*
> *but no one listens anymore.*

> *Blue-eyed demon, green-eyed girl*
> *Man with a plan that changes the world*
> *The hand that holds open the door*
> *will have to let it close.*

"Who's Cassandra? Who closes the door?" I asked. It was as confusing as any Tabism. I floated toward her, but she said nothing to me. Red mist furled around her. She retreated deeper into the cage. No, a hand pulled her deeper back. I reached for her, but the bars were between us. I put my hands on the bars and they began to melt, but I was too late. She and the voice disappeared.

I woke up still and silent, but my head was full of terrible images. Have you ever looked at the sun and then looked away? There's this strange black spot where the sun used to be. That's kind of how it was: I could see all those weird images—of jellyfish and walkways and Tabitha—all swirling in front of my open eyes for a moment. They began to fade. I saw my surroundings once again—the cage, the garden, the space lab.

The garden had grown. Lemons, oranges, tomatoes, and jackfruit sprung from the branches and vines. Those were real. That sort of brought me comfort. So did Little Bacon, sitting in my pocket.

"What's Cassandra, Little Bacon?"

"Cassandra. A small town. A small town in Pennsylvania."

"No, Cassandra. Isn't she from mythology?

"Ah, yes, a Greek princess. She is given the gift of prophecy by Apollo."

"What happened to her?"

"She was a queen and prophetess."

"What happened to her?"

"She tried to warn the people of Troy about its destruction. She even warned them not to accept the Trojan Horse because it was full of enemy soldiers."

"She warned them? But didn't the Trojan Horse work? The Greeks took the horse and the Trojans surprised them and killed them, right?"

"Right. Cassandra warned them. She had the gift of prophecy, but she also had a curse...no one ever believed her words."

"Well, I would have. I wonder if she dreamed about jellyfish, too."

"Jellyfish consist of a gelatinous umbrella-shaped bell and trailing tentacles."

"They sure do."

"Scientific name—Medusozoa."

"Really helpful. Thanks."

"At your service."

Little Bacon shrugged at me and buried himself back in my pocket. I could only glimpse the Harper Device on the other side of the room, all the plants bending in that direction. I peeked my head around a large vine to see the Device, but it didn't seem to be doing anything, as usual. I almost felt like it was, well, ignoring me. I turned away and floated toward my skylight to escape the garden for a moment. The Earth was a shiny blue speck in the distance—so small and alone and helpless and lost.

I couldn't escape the visions. They appeared again as I peered out into the vast field of stars, crazier and scarier than ever. A single figure with a sword. Tabitha yanked into the mist. But the one that troubled me most was the magnetic walkway. I didn't expect to see it again. I thought I was out of danger, but there it was again—this time with Trackman instead of Sawyer. Was it a vision of the future?

Stars, I hope not, I thought, *but at least I'm ready to tell someone about it.* I drifted back to sleep.

What Happened in the Hallway

I was sound asleep near the skylight when a shrill, pulsating sound startled me. An alarm. It was different than the one we heard earlier in the Hamster Wheel. What was it for? The voice of DORIS explained. "Lockdown alert, lockdown alert. Commander Harper and Lincoln Sawyer report to escape pod area. Code Red."

Escape pods? I nearly jumped out of my skin. *Escape pods!* The Red Vision came back to me like a lightning bolt. They were about to send my Dad and Sawyer to the escape pod area. *What if I'm not the one who dies!* I thought. *Dad!* I pushed myself toward the door.

"A lockdown alert," said Little Bacon, "suggests that people should take cover, possibly behind a chair or desk in the corner of a classroom."

I ignored Little Bacon and threw myself out of the cage, floated through the space lab and across the dark cargo hold. Light poured from the hatch to the magnetic walkway. The door was closed. I pushed off one of the walls and threw myself toward the light, with my arms stretched out in front of me like a diver. The alarm grew louder. "Code Red, Code Red," said DORIS. "Civilians stay in your rooms." After an eternity I finally reached the magnetic walkway. *I have to stop him!* I thought. *He can't take my dad!*

My chest heaving hard with fear, expecting the worst, but it wasn't what I imagined. I threw open the hatch and hesitated, not putting my feet down on the walkway yet. On the walkway a tall man swayed life-lessly, attached to the magnetized floor, his arms floating out at his sides like a scarecrow's. Lincoln Sawyer stood beside the body with something like a remote control and aimed at the lifeless form. Beside Sawyer stood my dad. He was safe, but someone else wasn't. I didn't feel surprised—I'd seen this scene before—but I did feel weak and jumpy. I hate to say it, but I also felt relieved—the man suspended in the hallway wasn't my dad. It was Redshirt Anderson.

My dad was there though, and so was Lincoln Sawyer. They were positioned in the hallway on opposites sides of Anderson's body, and they seemed to be discussing what had happened to him.

The Android spotted me first. "Tully, please be so good as to return to your cage," he said, as if he were a flight attendant asking me to put my seat in the upright position.

My dad looked grim but guarded, like he was ready to be attacked. "No, stay, Tully. Whatever happened here, the danger has passed. I could use your help."

Lincoln couldn't overrule my dad. My dad moved Lincoln back and gestured me forward. We took the lifeless body between us.

"We're moving him to the infirmary. Remember when you sprained your ankle? How coach and I helped you off the track?" I understood what he wanted. I pretended that Anderson was just a wounded athlete that needed our help. Lincoln went ahead of us and opened the door to the infirmary, where we laid Anderson's body on an examination table.

"Please step aside, gentlemen. Thank you kindly," said Lincoln, put-ting on a pair of latex gloves. He pulled the gloves on tight and then released them, which made a loud snap. I jumped. Nothing about his demeanor said to me, "Wow, there's a dead crew member in front of me." After all, Sawyer was just a machine with artificial intelligence. Trackman said he was emotionless, and that made me sick. It seemed like Anderson deserved something more than an autopsy by a heartless Android, especially one that might have murdered him. Not that I was sure about that.

He motioned for the onboard computer to begin recording. "DORIS, it's Lincoln Sawyer, here to perform autopsy on crew member

Anderson…" he said, preparing for an examination, ignoring my father and me.

"Come on, son. Leave Sawyer to do his duty," my dad said, pulling me out of the infirmary and into the hall. On the way out, he squeezed Anderson's arm lightly. I took one last look at Anderson's gray face, his body strapped to the table, before we left the room.

It was the first time my dad and I had been alone in days, standing on the magnetic walkway. I knew it was time to tell him what I knew.

"Dad, after I touched the Harper Device, something different inside me sort of clicked," I said.

My dad looked tired. "Son, I'm so sorry you had to see this."

"But I already saw this. Trackman and Sawyer are plotting against you."

"Redshirt is gone," said my dad. "I don't know how or why. I wish there was something we could do."

"Yes, there is! The Red Visions. Trackman and Sawyer, they did this—" but I could tell he wasn't following me at all. He was looking down the hall to where Redshirt's body had been floating.

"Redshirt was a good man, Tully. We will do a full investigation of his death."

"But they did this, dad. I know it!" I urged him, grabbing his sleeve.

"Tully, settle down. Your letting your emotions control you. I understand your feelings, but this is no way to act in a crisis. Trust me. Now, we can't blame others for no reason." He paused and ran his hand along his hair. "Also, we shouldn't raise our voices so loud that everyone on the ship can hear what we're saying."

He looked at me like I should understand something, but I didn't get it.

"The entire universe should hear it!" I yelled. "That Android is in there with the body right now and who knows…"

My dad put up his hand. I stopped and took a breath. He placed a hand on my shoulder. "Son, I think this shook us up a great deal. We'll have time to talk later about Anderson's death."

"You mean murder."

"I mean for you to return to your cage, where you should have stayed when the alarm sounded," he said. "I need to make some decisions here.

One of my crew is dead and both escape pods have been launched. That means you're stuck here on board with us, and so is everyone else. Now please follow orders," he said, turning back toward the Flight Deck. "Collect yourself. Then go find your friends."

What could I do? Redshirt was murdered, our chances of escape were gone, and my dad wanted me to collect my thoughts. I *thought* he would do something! I turned to go without saying another word, angry and confused and disappointed. The one time I could help my Dad, and he didn't want to hear a single word.

Instead, he had one last thing to say.

"Tully, remember what I told you when we went on that walk," he said, looking back at me. We were exiting the walkway on separate ends. "Remember my words."

The garden seemed to be growing by the hour. I had to push a few vines out of the way to make it down the corridor. Almost invisible behind all those vines was the Device.

The stupid Harper Device.

"Hey, gas ball! What good is a vision if nobody will listen to it, huh?" I muttered across the garden. "Yeah, I'm talking to you, you red freak. What are you, some sort of reject planet? You make my brain go all haywire and all for what, huh? I should never have come out here."

Why had I come out here anyway? It had been a stupid idea. Exploring the universe with my dad and bringing along a brainy drama queen and my so-called best friend. Like that would really be fun. Sunjay was right to doubt this. So was Tabitha. The best we could hope for now was to survive long enough to find out about Operation Close Encounter. Most likely it would be the last thing we would ever learn. I locked myself in the cage.

Remember my words, my dad said. I couldn't remember anything just then, but his words kept wandering through my head, along with all the Red Visions.

I launched away from the floor and headed toward the skylight, hoping a good look at the stars would clear my head. Instead, my head hit the skylight because I pushed myself too hard. I cursed. Then I realized I was acting like a lunatic. I forgot about the walk completely until then, but I finally remembered a key word: *objective*.

That walk we took near our house. It was a month ago. My dad told me to leave my holophone behind. Why? Because you never know who could be listening. Then he said that this mission needed him as commander. He told me about his objective.

Objectives! There were two. The first—the Alliance wanted to repair a space station. But he also had a personal objective. He needed to get the Harper Device off the planet before something terrible happened, and he had his own plan for that. What was his plan?

In the midst of all the other things that had happened on board, I lost track of my dad's objective.

The escape pods. Oh, stars! I thought. *We didn't just need those for the rescue mission. Dad was going to launch the Harper Device in the escape pod, and now he can't. We might accomplish the mission objective and save the space station, but his objective has failed.*

Things were getting clearer now. His plan wouldn't work.

He knows we are all in danger now. Does he think it wasn't an accident? Why wouldn't he listen to me? He just kept trying to shut me up.

I stared back at the Earth, a tiny blue marble in the distance, and stewed over how badly things turned. I half-expected to see Sawyer float down the corridor at any moment, snapping a pair of latex gloves.

Nothing happened for a long time. I floated around, looked out the skylight, puzzled through all the scraps of information I had about our situation. Occasional announcements from DORIS startled me.

I thought about Redshirt, how he played basketball with us and cheered up Tabitha. He was a really good dad. It just didn't seem fair. Thinking about his kids back on Earth really saddened me, but then sadness turned to anger when I pictured Trackman and Sawyer, all their scheming. If only I had known how bad things would get.

Time passed.

"Crew on alert, code orange." Little Bacon began to babble about different types of codes and their meanings, but I hardly noticed. My mind spun in circles, wondering where it should go. If only our situations was as straightforward as *Cave-In!*, where I could spot bad guys instantly and fight them with my friends—or die trying.

"Crew to standby, civilians stay in your rooms."

And more time with my spinning mind.

"Crew to stations, civilians move only with permission. There has been a problem on board, and Commander Harper will explain soon."

This last announced wasn't DORIS but Sylvia Moreline's comforting voice. My mind began to clear, but I wanted to figure out this whole mystery as soon as I could. I needed to ask the right questions and find some answers. I needed Sunjay and Tabitha.

In the meantime, I turned back toward the Harper Device, glowing softly through the vines. "You lousy excuse for a planet. I'm starting to understand the Visions, but I may be too late. The next time you show me something, help me save someone, will you?"

PRAYERS

"We are gathered here today to pay respects to a dear colleague, a great father, and a trustworthy friend…"

This was my first funeral, and it occurred to me this was the first funeral in space. Plenty of people had died trying to get into space, but they had never been mourned out here in the stars.

There was a lot to mourn, too. Redshirt helped us feel at ease on board. Sunjay sniffed a bit to hold back tears. Tabitha wept silently. Her tears didn't flow anywhere—they clung to her eyes in growing droplets. I leaned over and daubed them away with a handkerchief, then used it for myself.

The ten of us stood around Anderson's coffin, a storage container that once held Queen Envy's extra recording equipment. Everyone contributed to the ceremony. Sylvia Moreline used a laser cutter to print a Bible verse on the lid. Buckshot and my dad had guided the container in to the Observation Deck. Sunjay, Tabitha, and I had arranged the chairs and moved the table. Lincoln helped with arrangements, so I could not tell my friends what I knew.

"…He served the Space Alliance well, for eight good years we had him. He took care of this ship with a sense of duty that inspired us all…"

Trackman brought a bouquet of flowers to place on the coffin. He covered up the Bible verse with the flowers, and I wanted so badly to push those flowers off the coffin. He didn't deserve to put flowers there, as far as I was concerned. My dad pushed back the flowers to reveal the verse: *I have fought the good fight, I have finished the race, I have kept the faith.* 2 Timothy 4:7.

Now all of us stood there, the crewmembers wearing their uniforms, Sunjay and I wearing the jeans and t-shirts we wore the day we left, and Tabitha wearing a simple black dress she had borrowed from Queen Envy. In the dress Tabitha looked about five years older than either of us.

"...Anderson flew with me on my first mission to Mars. He was there for the discovery. He was the kind of man who didn't take credit for things, just did his job, raised his family, and lived the best life he could."

If you haven't guessed, my dad spoke. It was his duty to deliver the eulogy. He stood at the head of the coffin and spoke the words over his fallen friend, his eyes and voice steady like a general who has lost a faithful soldier.

We all held hands around the coffin as he spoke. I was sandwiched between Sunjay and Tabitha in her black dress, and any other day my heart would have beat double-time to hold her hand. Today my heart just skipped beats whenever I looked to see who held her right hand—Sawyer.

I noticed a camera in the corner of the room. It hadn't occurred to me, but this funeral would be recorded. No one knew about the death yet. *His family will hear these words and see these images if we make it home.*

"...And now we send him out on his last mission. We will miss you, old friend."

Before we saw Anderson off on his final mission, Queen Envy stepped forward, wearing a plain black dress like Tabitha's. She began to sing a song I had heard before.

May the road rise to meet you
May the wind be always at your back.

Her voice sounded different, sort of personal, like she wasn't singing in front of fans anymore, but for someone she knew, for Quentin

Redshirt Anderson. I began to remember where I had heard the song. My dad used to sing it to me at bedtime before he left for missions:

> *May the sun shine warm upon your face*
> *The rains fall soft on your field.*

It was an Irish blessing. My grandmother taught him the song when he was a boy. Queen Envy closed her eyes and sang:

> *And until we meet again*
> *May God hold you in the palm of His hand.*

The words kept ringing in my head after she finished. I hoped that Anderson got to hear the blessing somehow. I hoped the blessing was for us, too. I didn't know what road we were on, and the sun grew dimmer every day as we approached LG Alpha, but maybe God would hold us in the palm of His hand. I hoped and prayed that He could reach all the way out here into the darkness of space.

SPEECHES

As far as I was concerned, we were now at war. The first soldier had fallen. My dad didn't believe this, but would my friends? I found out soon enough. After the funeral they moved the body into the cargo hold and the three of us stayed on the Observation Deck. We floated to the dining table and Tabitha and I sat down. Sunjay made a peanut butter and jelly sandwich before joining us. When we were all situated, I told them what I saw in the hall and heard in the lab. This was murder, plain and simple to me, but to them...

"Murder?" asked Tabitha. "Sawyer said it was a heart attack."

"Well, of course he did. Sawyer and Trackman committed the crime. They're covering their tracks."

"I don't know about that. They're both creepers of the direst degree, but murderers?" asked Tabitha.

"Trackman's weird," Sunjay chimed in. "He mumbles to himself all the time, but he just seems like that kid that kept talking to himself during tests, the one who licked that frog during bagel break."

"You're comparing Trackman to a kid who licks frogs! Are you crazy?"

"Are you, Tully?" Sunjay shot a pretty nasty look my way. *If only I could bring myself to tell them about the dreams,* I thought.

"I just don't see it," said Tabitha.

"Well, I did—I mean, I do. Anderson probably caught them as they were releasing the escape pods. Or he found out about Operation Close Encounter and decided to do something about it."

"No, he would tell your dad, like we should have. And anyway, why would 'they' want to release the escape pods?"

"They wanted to trap us all on board."

"I thought you said they wanted to get rid of us, Tully. Maybe Redshirt launched the escape pod on purpose," she said. "I mean, if he was dying, he probably tried to get everyone's attention the only way that he could."

"An astronaut wouldn't do that!" I said, pounding my hand against the table. "I'm trying to get your attention right now, and it doesn't seem to be working. How can you guys be so blind? Lincoln Sawyer did the autopsy. He's lying through his perfect white teeth about the heart attack. I'm telling you, it was Trackman and Sawyer."

I tried to keep my frustration in check, but at some point emotions took control. I was breathing heavily and felt faint. My friends disappeared for a moment. I felt like I was going to black out, only everything went red again. In that moment the words from the Red Vision returned to me: *Cassandra cries to the skies / but no one listens anymore.*

When I came back, they were both still looking at me, so I guess I hadn't blacked out after all.

"…I know you have all these theories about what's going on, but how do you *know* it was Trackman and Sawyer?" Tabitha asked.

"I just do. Look, you're right. We should just sit back and relax. We'll make it to LG Alpha soon, and then our lives will end just like Redshirt's, and I can say 'I told you so' when we get to Heaven or whatever. It's going to happen. That's all." How could I tell them about my visions? *Hey, guys, I see dead people. Also, we're going to run into a space jellyfish pretty soon.* I would go from being "frustrated Tully" to "crazy Tully" in a nanosecond. I looked around the deck for inspiration. The camera in the corner. "Wait, I can prove it."

"What, cameras?" Tabitha asked, looking at Sunjay. "There's one in here. Is there one in the hallway?"

"No," said Sunjay, "there are a lot of cameras on board, but none for the hallway."

Tabitha shook her head. She was always one step ahead of me, but I couldn't give up.

"Sunjay, when did you see Trackman talking to himself?" I asked.

"Oh, the other day I was making a PBJ when he entered the room. He floated to the window over there and looked into space. He started talking to himself, like this."

He pushed himself over to the bay window and kept his hands behind his back, like a soldier addressing a general. We could see his reflection in the window, a serious look on his face.

Tabitha grabbed my arm. The wheels were spinning. "Sunjay, did his lips move like that?"

"Yes."

"So he wasn't mumbling," I said, "he was giving a speech."

Tabitha spun her scarf. "Well, that pickles the cat then. Just jump right into the tape recorder and press play, right?" she said, seeming proud of herself.

"Huh?" Sunjay said.

"Try to keep up, Space Boy! It was your idea." She pointed at the camera in the corner of the Observation Room. "We have the whole thing on camera now. I just need to see it. Maybe we can figure out what's going on in his creepy crawly brain."

"But I copied him perfectly!" said Sunjay. "Why do you want to see Trackman do it?"

"Because he was giving a speech, and I can read lips."

Finally! I was glad Tabitha could read lips but not minds, because my mind would have embarrassed me. I would have been redder than the Harper Device. Finally someone believed there was at least one lunatic on board bent on destroying us all. He already killed a good man. Now we could prove it.

"So Tabitha needs to see the recording. Where are those kept?"

"On the Flight Deck," Sunjay said. "It won't be easy. She'll need to access DORIS's files."

"Not easy?" said Sunjay. "How about impossible? There's no way we can just walk in there and ask your dad."

"Of course not, Sunjay. We'll need to distract my dad. That should be easy for you."

"Okay, and if I distract him, where will Tabitha access the files? Redshirt was in charge of monitoring those cameras."

Tabitha looked out the window toward the passing Moon. "You two just distract Commander Harper. I can handle the rest."

"How?" we asked her.

"It will work better if you don't know ahead of time," she said.

PROOF

When the three of us arrived on the Flight Deck, my father gave Buckshot a few commands and turned his full attention to us. He offered a tour of the deck while Sunjay warmed up his question cannon. I watched Tabitha. She seemed really down, distracted and staring out into space, like her heart was still at the funeral. My dad noticed. He put an arm around her. She looked at him.

"Where did he do his work?" she asked.

"Here's Redshirt's station. From here he was the eyes and ears of *The Adversity*," he said, pointing to a chair behind his own command chair.

Tabitha looked pretty shaken. When she saw Anderson's empty chair, she squeezed my hand hard. She grew pale. Tears pooled in her eyes. *Is she acting?* I wondered.

My dad seemed worried, too.

"Tabitha, maybe this is too much. You can see all this later," said my dad.

"No, I want to stay, Commander. It's just so sad," she said. Either she was about to fall to pieces, or she was putting on a very good show. Or both. "Could I just sit down for a minute? Please, just give me a moment by myself."

My dad offered her his chair, but she took Redshirt's command post instead. My dad continued the tour with me and Sunjay. She looked at me a moment and then picked up something from the armrest. It was a pair of hologlasses—more advanced than mine—that could project images and audio from all around the ship. Anderson's hologlasses. In that moment I saw Tabitha's plan taking shape.

My dad continued the tour. Tabitha leaned forward with her head in her hands. She wasn't sobbing, she was motioning in mid-air whenever my dad turned his back. She flipped from scene to scene, skimming through holographic videos, looking for video of Trackman. All the while, Sunjay fired questions.

"No, we probably won't run into any black holes or—what else?—supernovas? No, Sunjay, you know that. Anyway, here's where Buckshot pilots us. If we can dock at LG Alpha, if it's even there, Buckshot will use the piloting headset you see here. Right, Buckshot?"

I was paying more attention to Tabitha. She swiped past video after video. Finally she must have found a video of Trackman. She grew very still and intense. Not Sunjay though. He had forgotten our plan entirely and was wrapped up in every word my father said. He even had some questions for Buckshot.

As quickly as they could, the two men threw out answers:

"No, piloting is not hard if you practice."

"Yes, I've piloted dozens of missions."

"The only other pilots on board are Commander Harper, Lincoln Sawyer, and myself."

"No, Sunjay, uh, you can't *try* to fly it. Well, you could try, but that would be an expensive mistake. Wait until you graduate from the Naval Academy, or at least high school."

"Bananas."

"Grapefruit."

When he asked them about their favorite fruits, I figured he was almost out of ammunition, and so did dad and Buckshot. After answering about three thousand questions, both men turned to each other and shrugged.

"Guys, you should get some sleep now," my dad said. "It's been a long day. Tabitha, are you better, hon? You still look pale."

I turned to look at her. She looked *paler* than when we arrived.

✳ ✳ ✳

We slid through the portal on our way to the Observation Deck. Tabitha explained what she saw. Well, she delivered a classic Tabism.

"What a speech! You should've heard. Who's the Commander? Commander Observation Deck Sharktooth Turncoat Benedict Arnold."

"Thanks for that, Tabitha," I said calmly. "Now please repeat in some form of English."

Through the headset, she flipped through a number of rooms until she found the Observation Deck. She found the recording of Trackman with Sunjay in the background, chomping his sandwich.

"It didn't make much sense at first, but I realized Trackman was not looking out the window. He was looking at his reflection in the window. Just like we thought, Trackman was preparing a speech. He bowed toward someone, then he gestured to stage left and smiled. He pretended to give something to somebody," she explained. "Stars! He has those terrible sharky teeth."

"Well, what did he say?" I asked.

"I couldn't catch everything, but he said something like, 'Greetings, Lord blah blah blah. We've long awaited this day. I am Commander Trackman, *Commander* Trackman, here to blah blah blah the Harper Device. Then he said something about 'the arrival of the lion's mane'? I don't know what that could be, but that's what he said."

"The lion's mane," interrupted Little Bacon, "is a medicinal mushroom in the tooth fungus group."

"That's not helpful, LB," I said. I forgot he was in my shirt pocket. He turned around and poked me in the chest. I tried to shove him deeper into my pocket but he resisted.

"It is also the largest known species of jellyfish," he said.

Trackman's words suddenly became clear to me, as if I heard them myself. It all came together in my mind in a flash.

"So that proves it. The jellyfish is the *Lion's Mane*—it's a ship! It ate the fish. The fish was the space station—or maybe it was *The Adversity*! Either way it's planning on eating us. Little Bacon, you're a genius!"

"At your service," he said, burrowing back into my pocket.

Operation Close Encounter was now revealed. Sunjay gave me a strange look when I high-fived him.

"Okay," I whispered, hiding my mouth in case others could read my lips, "we've got to keep this secret. Trackman plans to take over *The Adversity* and give away the Harper Device to Lord Somebody. Obviously we'll meet them at LG Alpha. We need to act now before it's too late." My friends listened to me in silence, waiting to hear the rest of the plan. "He probably plans to kill us all before he gives the Device to the aliens. It's aliens, right? Of course it is! Ha! We have to stop him. Do you believe me now?"

It was one of those strange pauses, like when you space out and ask a teacher the same question someone else just asked. Everyone in the class stares. Everyone knows the answer but you.

Tabitha had pity in her lovely green eyes. "Tully, okay, that's possible—minus the aliens. Now what was all that about a jellyfish?"

"Don't you see? He's clearly working with aliens," I said.

Tabitha shrugged. "But what if he's, he's just, you know, pretending? He delivered an odd speech, but he's an odd guy."

Sunjay nodded his head. "Yeah, maybe he is pretending. He could just be crazy."

"Operation Close Encounter? A dead crewmember? That's what's really happening right now!" I whispered. "This is a conspiracy. Now keep your voices down. People might be listening."

They look at each other. Tabitha said, "This could be a conspiracy, or it could be a lonely, weird guy talking to himself. Aliens and jellyfish, Tully? You sound a little…"

"What? Worried? Yes, that's the word you're looking for, Tabitha. Worried. Sunjay, back me up here."

Sunjay sighed. "Tully, what if you're wrong about all this?"

Those words stung. Sunjay always had my back, and now I was alone.

"This has to make sense to you! I've seen things. I have imagined things." I pointed to Tabitha. "You got sucked away in a red mist."

"You imagined things?" said Tabitha. "Was this after you almost died with the Harper Device? Why don't we get Sawyer to check you out again?"

"What? He's a murdering lunatic," I said. "No way he's examining me."

Tabitha frowned, Sunjay shook his head. I took a deep breath and thought about why they didn't believe me. It dawned on me that my explanations would sound crazy unless they knew about the Red Visions, and I had done everything in my power to hide them from my friends. My friends thought *I* was insane, not Trackman. I was seeing things, over-reacting to things, and apparently believed in aliens, which was now quite true. Talking more wouldn't help in the least. It was just like Cassandra talking about the Trojan Horse.

"Okay, when we reach LG Alpha in a few hours, if there's anything weird, or, like, wrong, just remember this conversation. And be ready for anything. I'll be in my cage, sleeping."

"That's probably a good idea," said Tabitha. Nothing to argue there.

I shook my throbbing head and headed back to my cage.

A Chess Match

I settled down into my cage and prepared for bed, but only a few minutes passed before the hatch opened at the far end of the cargo bay. I thought it might be Tabitha, coming to see if I was talking to myself about aliens.

Instead, in floated Gallant Trackman.

My heart skipped about twelve beats, and by the time he floated to my cage, I could feel a cold sweat starting on my forehead.

"Did I catch you sleeping?" he asked, his big sharp teeth gleaming.

I didn't answer, just glared at him. Was he here to kill me or to tuck me into bed?

Neither. In his hand was what looked like a briefcase. "Dr. Chet Chan's Space Chess" was written on the lid.

"I haven't found a single opponent on board worthy of playing against me, not even our dear Commander Harper. Let's play a game, Tully."

It wasn't a request. It was one of those "offers you can't refuse." He opened my cage and floated inside. He released the briefcase, which folded open to reveal a chessboard. The red and black pieces began to arrange themselves. At the same time, the bottom of the board transformed into a high table, with one leg that attached to the floor and two seats on either side for the opponents. We sat across from one another.

"This has been quite an adventure for you," he said, as the board finished arranging itself. "You know, I went on some adventures when I was a boy, too. I never impersonated a primate, of course, but they were quite memorable."

"I'm sure you did. Where did you go?" I asked.

"Oh, you know, here and there. Met some very intriguing people, saw some things that I will never forget," he said, adjusting the knight and rook. His beady black eyes gleamed like his teeth. "I imagined you'll see some things out here that you won't forget either."

"I already have," I said.

"You don't have to tell me," he said. "I know what you've seen. Ah, why don't you take the first move in our game? I'll be black. That makes you red."

It appeared he was here just to play and talk, but I would rather have fought him hand to hand. He wasn't that much bigger than me, but I had a feeling he was a lot smarter. I looked over the army of red pieces on my side. Aunt Selma and I sometimes played chess back in Alaska. She taught me some basic strategies. Now I wished she taught me more. I took a gulp and moved a pawn. He did the same.

The first game didn't last long. He always seemed three moves ahead of me as we played in silence. When it was his turn, Trackman kept his eyes on the board. When it was my turn, his eyes never left me. He took my knight with a pawn, then took my castle with his rook. And so on until...

"Checkmate," he said, sucking air through his teeth.

The first game was over. He clearly had a lot more experience than I did, but after that game I knew my opponent much better. He liked to make dramatic moves with his rook, and he gave me one hint before an attack: the wicked hiss of air going through his teeth.

"Well, you're really not terrible," he said. "Maybe not a worth adversary, but I'll play you another game. Maybe you were just a little, hmm, nervous."

Well, he had that right. I was fearful. But something else pumped through my veins when he said that. I could feel my pulse quicken, but it wasn't from fear this time. It was anger. I was *right* to be angry, too. I looked at Trackman, and the red haze seemed to fill the room.

Set it aside.

Those words echoed through my mind. What did I have to set aside? My fear, my anger, everything? *Just focus. Set it aside.* Was he a killer, conspirator, alien, and spy? Whatever he was, he was just an opponent, and an arrogant one at that.

"Nervous?" I said. "Someone once told me I have a lot of nerve."

"Ah, that's not news to me. You don't think Sawyer tells me these things?"

"I'm sure he tells you everything. Still, you've got reasons to be nervous."

"So what in the wide expanse of space should I be concerned about, boy?" he said, setting up the pieces again.

"Operation Close Encounter," I said.

He stopped putting the pieces back in place. "So you heard the Android and I chatting one day in the garden. You know nothing."

"Plotting, you were plotting Phase Two. It seems everything has gone your way so far. Congratulations," I said.

His face reddened. His clenched his teeth yet didn't suck in air like he had earlier. He broke into a grin, and I saw uncertainty on his face.

"Well played, boy," he said. "It has gone brilliantly thus far."

Game two began. Once again, Trackman motioned for me to start. This time the board looked different to me, like I hadn't really seen it before. I had been looking at each piece instead of the whole board, but now I could picture them all moving together, like an army going to war. There were so many options. Several moves gave us advantages for a moment, but they wouldn't last. I looked for a slower strategy. I focused.

Before long, most of the pawns disappeared from the board, but I held back my best pieces. Then Trackman began to move his rook again, and when I heard that sucking sound through his teeth, I tried to look a few steps ahead. I moved my knight just in time to avoid his attack. He nodded in approval.

"Oh, much better," he said. "You have something going here. You know the only, uh, person I haven't tried to play on board beside you?"

"Tabitha or Sunjay?"

"Oh, I wouldn't even consider your two playmates. Just children. No, I haven't played Sawyer."

"You're scared that you would lose," I said, taking one of his bishops. He looked annoyed.

"Oh, I know I would lose. All Androids are programmed to play chess perfectly. If I did beat him, it would only be because he let me. And I don't like that idea. I don't like it when people hold things back from me."

He sucked air through his teeth. His rook took my castle, but I took his rook with my bishop. Then the red haze in my mind swirled around several pieces on the board, showing me where they could move next. There were hundreds of different moves, from boring defensive plays to overly aggressive attacks, but Trackman's strategy seemed simpler now: to make aggressive moves that would make me doubt my abilities. If he kept doing that, he would overreach and I could counteract. I tried to look a few plays ahead, and I saw that I had a chance in this game.

"Much better indeed," he said. "So, Tully, what do you think we will find at LG Alpha anyway? Nothing? Aliens? I mean, really," he laughed and then hissed. I didn't respond.

His queen took my castle, but two moves later I took his queen with my own queen.

"I think you may have some wrong ideas about what all you have heard," he said. "This is just another boring trip into space. I've been on a few. I'll go on a few more. Too bad Anderson won't," he said, moving his other rook. "Check," he said.

I lost my cool.

"Who do you think you are?" I yelled. "You come into space, kill people, plot to take over my dad's ship—"

Trackman looked at me with his beady eyes shining.

"Yes, go on, what else, boy? What else? Tell me!"

"—You promised the Android he'll be like a human, that they'll help him—"

I stopped myself just in time. Trackman was sucking air through his teeth like a snake. *This is why he's visiting me,* I thought. *This is the real game.*

He wants me to get angry and spill my guts. Well, now I can see a play ahead. I have an advantage.

So I continued, with a bit of a lie. "—You, you're horrible! You send your Android to play games with my mind just because I spied on you that one time. Then he caught me in the hangar back on Earth and let me go."

"He caught you? What hangar?"

"I bet you gave him the orders. Then, when I finally get on board, he told me about The Conspiracy Game and made me keep all those secrets."

Trackman looked confused. "Sawyer has no secrets from me, boy."

"Oh, I know that now. You were both just playing games with me, trying to 'earn my trust,' like he said. I should have just done what he told me."

"What did he advise you to do?"

"To tell my dad about The Conspiracy Game."

Trackman jumped to his feet and accidentally floated to the ceiling. "Damn," he said, pushing himself back to the floor of the cage. He shook me by the shoulders. "What did he say? Tell me more."

"No," I said. "He didn't say anything else. I said enough. Coming to play chess with me? I'm just a kid, Trackman. Leave me alone. I'm sorry I got on board this ship, I just wanted to be with my dad, and you hate me because I messed up the mission. I get it. I'm just a waste of space. The Harper Device messed me up. And you want to mess me up just as bad." I started crying and rubbed my eyes. My tears floated in salty blobs toward Trackman. He brushed them away like they were flies and frowned at me. For a moment I thought he might leave. Instead, he blew out a frustrated breath that smelled like stale coffee. He watched me closely, trying to see if I was telling the truth.

"It's my move," I said after a minute of tense silence. I sniffled and moved my queen. We played out the last few moves. I played poorly, too, right into one of his traps. He took my queen with his other rook in a few moves and once again…

"Checkmate," he said. There was no look of triumph in his eyes even though he had beaten me. "Well, much better that time, boy. You fell apart at the end though. Just absolutely collapsed," he said, eyeing me carefully. "Almost like you *meant* to."

"Just leave me alone, will you?" I pleaded.

"I don't know if I should. Something seems wrong here. If you're lying to me about Sawyer—and you, you could have played better there at the end." He pushed a button on the board, which collapsed into a briefcase again, and prepared to leave. "If we ever play again, try to think several more steps ahead. You showed great promise—just too little too late."

He was right. Getting a few steps behind Trackman would mean losing at more than chess. I nearly spilled my guts about everything I knew. That's what he wanted, but the world turned red for a moment and helped me turn the tables on him. I hadn't convinced him completely that I was just a confused kid, but maybe he would doubt Sawyer and wonder what we discussed in private. That might turn his focus away from me and from his goal—taking the ship and the Harper Device. A glimmer of hope goes a long way sometimes in space.

Tabitha and Sunjay wouldn't understand the importance of the chess match. "Maybe he was coming to keep you company," they would say. "That was his awkward way of trying to help you."

However, I was starting to see the whole board now. The chess pieces were all in place, we were almost at LG Alpha, and the real Conspiracy Game was about to begin.

PART FOUR: LG ALPHA

Lightning strikes are so hot
that they can turn your sweat
into steam. That's why victims
sometimes lose their shoes and socks.
They find them twenty feet away,
blown off their feet by the steam.
Lighting strikes can also cause mood swings.

At least that's what Little Bacon said.

THE DIRTY SNOWBALL

I didn't sleep long or well. A shadowy blur with long, flowing tentacles reached for me in my dreams. I woke early and made my way to the Observation Deck for breakfast. The lights stayed dim when I entered, so it must have been before 6 a.m. No one else was there that early. The stillness of the room made me uncomfortable, so I started to hum. I looked out the bay window at the Moon in the distance. Beyond it was the Earth, a white and blue marble. I stretched my aching hands. We were now at the Lagrangian Point.

The whole idea of the Lagrangian Point reminded me of a scene I once saw in an old pirate movie. One day the sails on the pirate ship went completely slack. The wind died. There was no current, and the ocean looked like a mirror without a single ripple of movement. The pirates sat there for months, running out of water and praying that the winds would wake up. Finally the winds blew the pirates on to their destination…only after some guy apologized to the sea god. Hey, it was a movie. I guess I had the ocean on my mind. Either way, the Lagrangian Point was the same sort of place, where if you stopped, you had to find a way to start moving again.

My father's voice came from the intercom. "All personnel, good morning. We have arrived. We will start the search for LG Alpha today. Gather on the Observation Deck in a quarter hour. Commander out."

Still alone on the Observation Deck, I worked through a rough plan in my mind that went something like this: *My dad knows something's wrong. Trackman or Sawyer will make a move. I will be ready for anything. Tabitha and Sunjay will probably just say, "Oh, Tully. Stop overreacting! They just want to chop off one of your arms, not both!"* I thought about the karate moves I knew from watching cartoons and all those kung fu movies that Sunjay loved. I imagined myself fighting Sawyer, taking down Trackman with a round-house kick. What I really wanted was a light saber. How scared would Trackman be when he saw that in my hands instead of a chess piece?

Queen Envy interrupted my planning. Her outfit didn't really look like clothing. It looked like an angry, golden octopus was attacking her. On second look, it *was* a golden octopus, and it had her wrapped in its tentacles. She noticed that I was "admiring" her outfit.

"Morning, baby bear," she said. "You like this outfit? I saved it for today. I tried to beam back an update to the fans that we were all doing okay on board, but the transmission failed. I need to talk to your dad about it."

"He'll be down in a while."

"So will your girl Tabitha, I think." She raised her eyebrow, like we had some secret between us.

Tabitha isn't my girl. That's the last thing on my mind, I thought. Queen Envy could tell.

"Oh, baby bear, I didn't mean it like that. She didn't sleep well last night, I don't think. Still upset about the funeral. She helped me film a message for the Envy Squad last night and that took her mind off things for a while, but like I said, the transmission just cut off half way through." She turned toward me. She wore gold contacts that glittered when she spoke. "How you holding up?"

"Fine," I lied. "My dad says you have to do the best you can with what you have. I think we're all doing that."

"We certainly are, baby bear."

It *was* sort of flattering, having Queen Envy called me "baby bear." I wasn't sure why she picked that name for me. She didn't have a nickname for anybody else. Except my dad. *Space Boy.* Even when she was wearing a gold octopus and calling me nicknames, I could still picture her singing at the funeral—she seemed like a real person now. She wasn't just a crazy egomaniac—that was part of her act. I knew the difference.

"Uh, thanks for yesterday," I said. "The song. It was—it reminded me of my grandparents and church."

"Oh, I love that old hymn, Tully. My grandma used to sing it to me when I was a baby."

"My grandma did the same thing to my dad."

"Yeah, your father told me," she said. "Those old hymns always set my mind at ease when things get crazy. 'May the road rise up to meet you.' That's such a great line. I mean, can you imagine what that would be like? If the road just rose up to meet your feet, like the whole universe was guiding your every step?"

I didn't know what to say to that. It was a cool thought. Queen Envy gazed thoughtfully out the window beside me, her gold eyes twinkling like stars. I didn't think she would be so deep, and I wondered if Tabitha had talked to her about me. Was she trying to make me feel better? One of the tentacles from her dress wrapped around my arm. I peeled off the suction cups carefully.

"Maybe you should update that song. You could write some new lyrics," I said. Like pop stars need my input, like she would have time to do that before we made it to LG Alpha, or our deaths.

"That's such a flash idea, baby bear, but I don't know if I can write stuff that deep. I'm more glitter and glam than heart and soul."

"You could try."

"Maybe just for you," she said, smiling at me, her gold lipstick sparkling. "I see a lot of good in you. You're like your dad, just working to make things good like they ought to be. That's hard work because life always goes crooked just when you want it to be straight." The door at the far end slid open just as the lights brightened the room to indicate morning. "Oh, there's your girl and your hungry friend."

"Oh, she's not my girl. She thinks I'm crazy."

"Welcome to the party," she said. "Everybody says the same about me."

"No, it's true, they both think I'm crazy and—"

"—And there's that dad of yours. Just the man I wanted to see."

Queen Envy floated toward him with her octopus dress, which grabbed at everything in sight. My dad looked at her with a weary smile. He wasn't sleeping much. His forehead wrinkled and creases formed around his eyes. We were too near LG Alpha to rest. There was no time to be tired. Queen Envy asked him about the failed transmissions.

"Right, we're having the same problem," he said. "We lost communication with Earth and Moon early this morning. We prioritized rescue mission preparations but need to get that fixed. You'll be the first to know when it's done."

Tabitha and Sunjay both entered about the same time, but we really didn't talk, just nodded at each other like we were between classes in school. I just didn't have much of anything to say to them right then, nothing that they wanted to hear, anyway.

Trackman and Sawyer entered last, but they entered separately. *That seemed promising,* I thought. *Maybe my lie did some damage to Operation Close Encounter.*

The hatch to the Flight Deck opened. Buckshot poked his head through. "Well, we're at the Lagrangian Point and we've got a visual on something. Y'all get yourselves up on this Flight Deck and have a look-see."

Breakfast could wait. It would be pretty cramped with all ten of us in there, but I guess we could all get a good look at our destination. We crowded behind and around the chairs on the Flight Deck and looked out the window at an unidentified object. We could also see a 3D model of the object in the middle of the room.

It looked like, well…

"…Is that supposed to be the runaway comet?" Sunjay asked. "It just looks like a big, dirty snowball."

He was right. Smudges of brown and gray splattered the comet's white surface, which looked grainy and rough.

"That's our comet, alright. It's just too far from the sun," said Buckshot. "That's what our instruments suggest. See the comet symbol here: ☄." He pointed to the 3D model and a list of elements popped up beside it with the wave of his hand. "You can see here: the rock and dust keeps it all stuck together. But there's plenty of methanol, ethanol, formaldehyde, and ammonia near the surface, too. Those gases all start burning off when she gets closer to the sun. Then you'll get that big ole tail that you can see from Earth."

"That does look like a comet. That's the simple answer," said my dad. "The only problem is…"

"How does a comet stop?" blurted Sunjay.

"Right," said Buckshot, "comets don't have emergency brakes."

"Where's LG Alpha?" asked Trackman. "Any signs of it at all?"

"None," my dad said.

"That's disappointing. The fuel on board was worth billions of dollars. The Alliance will have to hear that news immediately, Commander."

"You don't seem too concerned about the folks on board," said Buckshot.

"Well, that goes without saying. Of course I am."

"We won't be making reports either way," said my dad. "As of a few hours ago, we lost communication with Earth and Tranquility Base. We'll keep trying to contact them, but we ran into some kind of interference."

"A solar storm could interfere with communication," Moreline said.

"Or mechanical failure. That would be the simplest explanation," my dad said.

Why do you keep looking for simple answers? I caught myself before I asked that question. Things were only getting more complicated as we went along. We had no escape pods and now no communication. Sabotage was the simple answer. Operation Close Encounter seemed to be working perfectly.

My dad continued, "Let's scout the Lagrangian Point for a few hours. The space station is cloaked, so it could be hidden nearby. If not, we set a course for the Moon. We can deliver the Device as promised."

"No, Commander, we won't," said Trackman.

He pushed his way from the back of the room toward the front where my dad sat beside Buckshot. "As Alliance Field Operative, I am authorized to deal with such unforeseen circumstances, particularly those that might benefit the Alliance."

"How can a stationary comet profit us?" Buckshot said. "It's interesting, but we don't have the equipment to tow it back home."

"That's true, but you haven't told us the full story here. I'm looking at your 3D model and wondering one thing. Why can't I see below the surface of this comet?" He pointed to the center of the 3D image, which looked completely hollow. "This is not a normal comet. If it were, I would agree with you that we should continue our search for LG Alpha immediately. However, this is an anomaly. We need to explore, so I propose we send an away team to the surface to collect more data."

My dad shook his head. "That's an unnecessary risk, Trackman. This comet isn't going anywhere. That might just be a faulty readout on the computer. There will be time for research later."

"Quite the contrary, Commander. This 'comet' already moved once. We *will* make time for research now."

My dad rubbed his arm and popped his knuckles. I could see he was digging in for a fight. "The Space Alliance has always lived by a code, and part of that code is 'Safety Before Profit.' We put profit before safety with the Harper Device, and I will not do that again."

"Point taken," he replied, "but an empty comet looks harmless to me. I say we explore."

"On whose authority," said my dad.

Trackman laughed. "Stars, not mine! I'm merely an advisor. But I do have this."

He reached in his pocket. Who knew what he was about to pull out? I didn't want to find out. I launched myself across the Flight Deck and kicked him into the control panels at the front of the ship with my best karate kick.

"Dad, get him before it's too late! Sunjay, grab Sawyer!"

I held Trackman in a bear hug for a moment, waiting for him to fight me. He wasn't going to take down my dad and act out his evil plans without me stopping him! My adrenaline went through the roof, and I expected a brawl would occur behind me in a matter of seconds. I prepared for the worst.

No one else in the room moved, including Trackman, who just sort of let me squeeze him. Then he coughed.

"Ouch," he said, calmly. "Commander, could you tell your son to unhand me? He has a surprisingly strong grip for his size."

"Oh, stars," said Tabitha. "Tully, let him go."

I opened my eyes and looked around. Trackman was sandwiched between me and the control panels. I felt my father' hand on my back. He pulled me away gently and gave me a polite shove back toward the rest of the group, whose eyes were all the size of Jupiter's moons.

Trackman straightened his uniform.

My father lit into me. "Tully, what in the name of the solar system! Control yourself, son! One more outburst and I'll…" My dad paused. "We'll talk about this later. For now, if you can't stay calm, get off my Command Deck. Trackman, you were saying—"

"Before I was tackled, yes." He reached in his pocket and pulled a small black cube from his pocket. An image of a man in a three-piece suit sprang to life—it was Charles Meteroff, the President and CEO of the Space Alliance. He wore a black jumpsuit with the Space Alliance logo on his shirt pocket and three gold stripes on each arm. His black beard and bushy eyebrows moved more than his mouth when he spoke.

"To whomever it concerns," he said, with a slight Russian accent. "I issue this directive, Number 3.14, on behalf of Gallant Trackman in regards to *The Adversity*. If at any time during this mission he sees fit, he has permission to direct the mission's efforts and change objectives to achieve Space Alliance priorities. To the commander and crew of *The Adversity*, my greatest thanks. Godspeed to you all. I sign and authorize this statement, CEO Charles Meteroff."

The image hung in the air for a moment. My heart fell through the floor. Trackman hadn't been reaching for a weapon, he had been reaching for something just as deadly. I thought I had checkmate, but the game was far from over. Trackman adjusted a ring on his finger and addressed my dad.

"So you see, Commander, this mission is still in your hands, I suppose, but I will be calling some shots from here. Space is a business, and you'll agree that businesses require a certain amount of risk to be successful, and people willing to take those risks."

"We came out here on a repair mission. Then it was a rescue mission. Those were our concerns. I don't think landing on the surface of an uncharted comet is in anyone's best interest."

"I suppose you will find out soon. Please make plans for your away team, sir, and please try to control your son."

SWIMMING IN THE AVALANCHE

We all pushed back through the hatch toward the Observation Deck and dispersed. Everyone avoided me, like my space madness was contagious. Tabitha and Sunjay pulled me aside.

"Tully, what in the world?" Sunjay said. "You still have jellyfish on the brain?"

"I thought he had a weapon," I said. "I know it sounds crazy to you guys, so don't worry about it."

"You've got to get back to reality here, Tully," chimed in Tabitha. "It's just adults trying to work out what to do in a pretty shifty situation. It's going to be okay."

"Yes, you're both right. We'll all be fine. The Device fried my hands and my brain. Cut me some slack. I'm going to catch hell from my dad about this already."

He called me into his quarters about an hour later. It was the first time I had even been there since our holophone conversations months ago. His room wasn't much larger than the infirmary, tiny compared to my cage or Queen Envy's monstrous room. I sat on his bed and he took his chair.

"Tully, I know you've got this conspiracy all worked out in your mind. It's obvious to me what you're thinking. I just need to remind you of what I said the other day: 'Remember my words.'"

"I do, dad. I remember," I stammered, "But what am I suppose to do when some guy reaches into his pocket and pulls out—"

"…A video cube?" he finished. "Well, you should watch the video. Listen, you've been through a lot out here already. It probably doesn't help that I'm a bit on edge about this exploration. There are lives at stake, but that does not excuse me either. I shouldn't have lost my temper with you in front of everyone. I am sorry about that, but we've got to stay calm out here."

"Easier said than done," I said.

He nodded. We looked at each other for a moment. He looked tired again, like he had when he returned from his last mission. The streak stood out in his hair under the bright lights in his cabin. He rubbed his hand along that red line and sighed.

"Did you know that I survived an avalanche once?"

"What's that got to do with anything?" I said, securing myself to the bed with a strap. Then I remembered the avalanche from my Vision.

"If you have ears, use them right now, okay? It happened before you were born when I was a ski instructor in Breckenridge."

"You were a ski instructor?"

"For a few months to earn some extra money after college. So I was skiing in the backcountry in Colorado all by myself. It wasn't the best idea, being out there all alone. Nobody knew my location. It was peaceful afternoon until I heard this enormous crunching sound behind me. I looked back and saw the snow behind me starting to move and realized what it was. My first instinct was to ski away, but the snow would have caught me. Fortunately they had trained all the ski instructors on avalanche procedures, and I knew my only chance was to follow my training."

"What did you do?"

"As the snow caught up to me, I threw away my poles, kicked off my skis, and prepared to swim. That's what they trained us to do in an avalanche. Snow acts like water when it is moving, so I closed my eyes and imagined myself in a turbulent ocean. I was swimming in the avalanche."

"Weren't you scared?"

"Sure, but I didn't panic. I trusted my training. I kept my head above the snow and struggled to stay afloat. When the avalanche finally stopped, my nose was barely above the height of the snow pack. I dug myself out of the avalanche and walked the rest of the way back to safety. I could have died that day, but my training saved me."

He pushed himself further into his chair. A wave of calm washed over me. I could see where he was trying to go with his story.

"So what happens if all my conspiracies are right? What happens if Trackman wants to take over the ship?"

He tousled my hair. "One avalanche at a time, Tully. Now I need to prepare for this comet exploration," he explained. "Just don't go tackling anymore Space Alliance employees and things will be fine. And I won't tell you what to do about Trackman, but I think…"

"…I owe him an apology," I said.

It was true. I had tackled him pretty hard. Of course, he was still plotting our doom and I would tackle him twice as hard the next time he reached in his pocket for who knows what. Hopefully someone else would follow my lead, but that didn't seem likely.

If I can stay calm, I might figure things out in time to save us. Besides, the chess match backfired on him. Trackman may think I'm confused about whether he is evil or not. And if I apologize, I thought, *I'll seem more confused. That's my only advantage—to make him think he has the advantage.*

The bed held me in place as I closed my eyes. The smart fabric sheets wrapped around me—or maybe my dad tucked me in—but before I knew it I was fast asleep. When I awoke, the room was empty.

THE RING

found Trackman on the Observation Deck. He took my apology as I thought he would. "I expected you might come to your senses, Tully," he said, holding out his hand. "Sometimes boys get the craziest ideas in their heads. All is forgiven—if you will kiss this ring."

For the first time I clearly saw his signet ring. It was made of white gold, and an image of the Earth was carved onto the top. *What is above the Earth though?* A strange flying object hovered, with three red rubies for its lights!—*No, wait, it's just a crown.* None of the other crew members wore jewelry, not even wedding bands. Who did he think he was, some sort of king? And I was supposed to kiss his ring? Oh, stars. I didn't see that coming.

"Problem, Tully?" he asked.

"No, sir. I am sorry for how I behaved." I guessed this was part of swimming in the avalanche. I bent over and kissed his ring.

"You should be. Now I have to check with Sawyer on Operation—I mean, our comet exploration. You are dismissed," he said, smiling.

"Thank you, sir," I said, and floated calmly away. My hands trembled. I wanted to punch a hole in the wall, but that wouldn't do any good. I might need my hands later.

It wasn't long before the away team donned their spacesuits to explore the unidentified dirty snowball that was still about a mile away.

They—my dad, Sylvia Moreline, and Lincoln Sawyer—would take the last of *The Adversity's* only small transportation vehicle, the CERBERUS. Like a lot of the Space Alliance's vehicles, CERBERUS was an acronym, but I couldn't remember what it stood for at the time. It did look like the three-headed dog from Greek mythology though. My dad operated the steering and thrusters from the middle head, while Moreline and Sawyer fit into the other heads and operated the arms (or paws) of the vehicle. Of course, no one needed to "man" Cerberus at all. The Flight Deck could control the vehicle, but with all the communication problems and no escape pods, nobody wanted to risk losing our only remaining small craft. They brought a laser drill to bore into the snowball to see what was below the surface.

The rest of us—Sunjay, Tabitha, me, the Queen, Buckshot, and His Creepiness—gathered on the Flight Deck and watched the Cerberus depart. It looked like a big ship up close, but as it crossed into the deep space between *The Adversity* and the snowball, I got an icy feeling in my stomach. My dad was on board that tiny craft with a psychotic android. He was about to land on the surface of a mysterious stationary comet. I caught Tabitha glancing at me once or twice. I only hoped she would be ready to back me up if this was part of Operation Close Encounter. She was probably worried I would tackle someone without any warning.

"What's the rate of travel? How long will it take for them to reach the surface? Will the drilling take long?" Sunjay was beside himself with excitement and worry.

Buckshot sat in his chair in the Flight Deck. "Shoot, this whole operation may take a few hours, Sun. It just depends what they find when they get over to that chunk of dust and ice. Lemme ask *you* a question: why don't you just sit back and enjoy the show?"

Sunjay was about to ask another question, but Queen Envy patted him on the shoulder. Sunjay kept a lid on it for the most part after that.

Things happen slowly in space sometimes, not like in the movies, where you see a rocket ship do a 180 degree turn and fire off into the distance with its laser cannons blazing. Those guns usually make sound—there's no sound in the vacuum of space. It took the vehicle half an hour to reach its destination. A few thrusters fired as the Cerberus approached the surface of the snowball, bringing it almost to a standstill for what seemed like five minutes. Touchdown was so slow we didn't notice it. We only noticed when the three cockpit doors opened and the away team stepped out. They stood on the comet.

"Hmm, I'll be darned," said Buckshot. "That's a lot of gravity."

"Agreed," said Trackman. "That almost seems impossible. This object appears to be only about a mile across and shouldn't have much of a gravitation field."

Tabitha tugged my arm. Sunjay leaned in. "That's really weird. Tully, isn't that weird?"

"Yeah, it's, well, impossible," I explained. "Things have to be enormous to have much noticeable gravity, like a planet or a sun. Unless there's something unbelievably heavy in the middle of that comet—"

"—Which is also impossible," said Sunjay.

"You probably want to keep your eyes on the 3D model now, kids," said Buckshot. "They just started drilling."

We watched the 3D model in the middle of the Flight Deck. A red beam appeared to show the progress of the laser drill. The red beam crept into the crust of the comet. Arrows popped up on the screen: "graphite" and "water" and "methanol," all the ingredients of your usual comet.

"About what we expected," said Buckshot. He put his hands behind his head and leaned back in his seat. Queen Envy plucked at a tentacle on her dress. It looked like we were in for a few hours of boring programming—like golf on Aunt Selma's television. Very slowly the drill bit through one layer, then another, then another. That's when it happened.

We saw a faint trembling in the 3D model, and the model switched off.

"Shoot, more tech problems," said Buckshot.

We all looked out the window. Nothing appeared to be happening, but I looked over at Trackman. He looked nervous or excited, beads of sweat on his forehead, clutching the arms of his chair.

Drilling continued in the distance.

And then, very slowly, the dirty snowball began to turn. The Flight Deck went completely silent. We all sat forward in our seats.

"Mike, come in," said Buckshot. "We've got rotation. Repeat, rotation." The away team didn't seem to notice, but it was clear to everyone on board that the comet was moving.

"Ah, we got a problem here, folks," Buckshot explained. "I won't try to explain it—just see for yourselves. I've still got a visual on the away team, but not for long. They will be out of sight in a few minutes."

"Oh, stars, what if it takes off? We'll lose them," Queen Envy said.

"No, no," said Trackman, grinning at her naïveté and tapping his ring. "It doesn't appear to be moving anywhere, just rotating. I guarantee the away team will notice when we lose visual contact. They'll also lose the light of the sun."

Sure enough, a few moments passed and my dad looked up, tapped Moreline on the shoulder, and pointed in our direction. No sooner had he done this than the three of them disappeared over the horizon of the dirty snowball. They were on its dark side. They were gone.

This is it. Trackman's going to start killing us all right now, I thought, getting ready to tackle him again, but something made me hold back. *You did something crazy once. Don't overreact, Tully. Swim the avalanche. Your dad's going to be fine.*

Sunjay and Tabitha watched me with fear in their eyes. When I didn't freak out, they looked at each other and breathed a quick sigh of relief.

Buckshot wasn't in relief mode though. He was in crisis mode, but I've never seen anyone look calmer in a crisis. "Listen up, folks. We may be facing a life-threatening situation here. This object is putting itself in motion. I need everyone to sit tight and stay quiet."

"They are in danger! Why did it rotate like that?" Queen Envy said. "Do something, Buckshot!"

Buckshot sat motionless, deep in thought.

"You can stay on deck but stay quiet, Ursula," he said. "We wait three minutes and then I take *Adversity* around the backside of the comet. If it spins again, we approach. If no contact, I will arm laser cannons and weigh my options. We need to assume the worst. We may be dealing with hostile forces here. Then again, we may not."

Tabitha looked at me and mouthed something. I didn't understand at first, but she did it again: "Trackman. Watch Trackman."

"Yes," I mouthed back. A wave of triumph washed over me. Finally she believed me! Tabitha nudged Sunjay and whispered the same thing. It took a moment to dawn on him, but I could tell he understood.

At long last we were all on the same page. That's when the wave of triumph became a rogue wave and washed the book straight out of our hands.

Something big, bright, and purple exploded out of the surface of the comet. Chunks of rock shot toward *The Adversity*, pelting the ship and bouncing off the Flight Deck windows. It sounded like a hailstorm. Alarms sounded. Warning lights flashed.

"Hang on!" Buckshot yelled.

Then the streak of purple shot toward us. *The Adversity* lurched sideways. On the screen we saw something latch on to the ship, yanking her forward. We all flew forward in our seats and crashed into each other—everyone except Trackman, who had fastened himself to his chair.

The 3D model suddenly sprang back to life. On the far side of the comet we saw a red dot on the map...the away team. They were falling through a crack in the skin of the dirty snowball. The snowball was opening up.

"Dad, no!" I shouted. Our eyes fixed onto the model as we watched the red dot disappear.

In that moment I saw a gold flash out of the corner of my eye. I turned and saw Trackman's signet ring. He raised his hand and brought it down quickly on Buckshot's neck. Whack!

"Ah! What was—," Buckshot didn't finish. He slumped over in his chair.

Trackman raised his hand again, and we all saw a small needle on the bottom of his ring. All of us scrambled away from Trackman sitting in the commander's chair. He sucked air through his teeth and smiled.

A pause.

Trackman held Buckshot close to him. "Feelin' sleepy there, cowboy?" he said, mocking Buckshot's Texas accent. "That's okay, old friend. I'll take over from here."

Then he turned to us. His beady eyes shined like his teeth. "Tully, you expected something, didn't you? Probably not this. Operation Close

Encounter is now at a close. I didn't expect them to disguise the ship as a comet, but bravo to my good friends. Commander Harper and the rest will be captives—oh, don't worry, they're not dead—not yet."

"Who do you think you are?" I yelled.

"I'm so glad you asked. I've been waiting to say this for a long time. I am Gallant Trackman, Commander of *The Adversity*, Arch Spy of the Ascendant."

"Arch Spy for who?"

He pointed toward the comet. "For whom, you mean. The Ascendant. You'll meet them soon enough, but I don't want to waste any more time on you at the moment. I have only one word for you, Tully Harper—checkmate."

Trackman laughed long and loud. Angry and humiliated: that's how I felt. Sunjay and Tabitha both looked the same. Queen Envy started crying.

"Stop sobbing, you ridiculous, loud-mouthed diva! Don't give me a reason to launch you into space. You'd make a much better popsicle than pop star. I've only put this idiot to sleep. We may still need a pilot. And you children, stop plotting. I don't know what you actually believed about all this, but that doesn't matter now. There's plenty of poison left in this ring, but I would prefer to keep all of you alive for now. I want you to see this."

On the 3D model, a long purple tentacle now held on to *The Adversity*. The snowball opened into two halves. I expected it would be empty, but it wasn't. Each half was shiny and black on the inside, with glowing purple letters and designs. We could make out a dark shape in the center.

"That's not a comet. That's a space ship," said Sunjay.

"Oh, bravo, Commander Conspicuous," said Trackman.

I looked out the Flight Deck window and watched the shell open even more. The center was now visible. It was a purple and black sphere about half a mile across. The tentacle was attached to us from the black surface.

"Who's on board that thing, Trackman?" I asked.

"You'll address me as Commander Trackman," he said.

"Where are you taking us?" Queen Envy shouted.

Trackman laughed and shook his head. "So many questions and me with no interest in answering them. Lady and children, I give you the *Lion's Mane*. It may be the first and last Ascendant ship you ever see."

UNBREAKABLE GAZE

"**I**f any of you makes a move, Buckshot never wakes up." Trackman held his signet ring at Buckshot's neck as we stared out the window of the Flight Deck at the massive black ship in front of us. A lengthy purple tube stretched between the ships where the escape pods once were. It glowed with a purple light, and there seemed to be dark figures moving toward us from the other ship.

"It looks like we'll have visitors soon," said Trackman. "Splendid."

My fury began to boil. I wanted to lunge at Trackman, but he held the signet ring closer to Buckshot's neck.

"So it was you who launched the escape pods," I said.

"That was part of the plan. I didn't want anyone to escape, and we needed a spacebridge to the *Lion's Mane*."

"And you killed Redshirt."

"Oh, I wouldn't say that. Accidents happen in space. Redshirt was a bit too curious about some of my activities during the mission. In the end, he simply found himself in the wrong place at the wrong time. Just like you. Now, before we proceed, I would like to say that it has been a pleasure working with each one of you. I'm terribly honored to be your new Commander. If you want to continue breathing, you will follow my orders without hesitation from now on. Understood?"

No one responded. Trackman took a deep breath through his teeth.

"I would have preferred a 'Yes, Commander Trackman. We live to serve you,' but I will accept your silence as an assent. It's probably best for now. Just remember. When you see him, do not break his gaze. The Lord Ascendant would take it as an insult."

"Who is that?" said Sunjay.

"Really?" said Trackman. "You can't shut that mouth for ten seconds? Make that your last question for a long time, boy."

Trackman produced the black cube from his pocket again. He threw it into the middle of the room. Immediately all the instruments blacked out. A glow surrounded the cube, and in a few moments it began to brighten into a ball of blue static. We all shielded our faces. *So this is how we die*, I thought, watching the ball of static expand to fill the room. Then it morphed into an image. A black room with three purple thrones. On each throne sat a muscular figure. The room was so dim we could hardly see their faces. Behind the thrones was an image of our ship trapped by the *Lion's Mane*.

"Go along with whatever they say," whispered Queen Envy. "No anger, no questions. Baby Bear, you hear me?"

I nodded. She was right.

The center throne towered above the other two, and in it sat a cruel-faced giant. He extended his index finger and motioned toward us. The image of his face filled the Flight Deck. I wanted to look away, but I couldn't. He held us in his gaze, and his gaze was unbreakable. He had a deep crease between his eyes, which had purple irises. His face swam with moving images. They were animated tattoos— sea creatures scuttled across his tanned skin. A jellyfish grappled with some sort of fish on his narrow forehead. A crab with twenty claws crept across his cheek and attacked the jellyfish from behind. It was a war in some alien ocean, projected on the stone face of the Ascendant Lord.

It would have been a distraction, but his eyes locked onto us. The deep crease between his eyebrows hardened. Trackman put both his hands across his chest and bowed at the waist. He nodded at us to do the same and we followed his lead. Without a word, the Ascendant Lord had silenced the room.

"This is the son of Harper then," said the lord, speaking to Trackman. His voice was hollow and deep. "This runt of a boy survived an encounter?"

"Yes, Lord," he said.

Who are you calling a runt, aquarium face? And how do you know English? I thought, but before the thought had left my mind, he narrowed his eyes. He looked from my face to my hands. I could feel the weight of his stare running up and down my body. *Did he just read my mind, or maybe my face?* A shark swam from his chin to his forehead, chasing a school of fish. He was like that shark, trying to hunt down my thoughts, to read my body language. I let my hands loose at my side and kept my calm. *Don't give him anything, Tully. Not a thing.*

He sneered. "Hmph. Sometimes it's the smallest thing that creates the greatest problem. But I have an eye for such things. Commander Trackman, cause him to suffer," said the figure, tapping the back of his hand. "I will watch."

What? I had only a second to think about his words. I remembered what happened when Sunjay hit my hand in the space lab. My hands had glowed. *If he sees my reaction, he will know something. I can't let that happen.* I focused all my energy on one thing. *Feel no pain,* I said. *Feel nothing at all.*

"To me," Trackman said. I floated toward him. Sunjay and Tabitha grabbed at me, but I pushed them away. "Stick out your hands." Trackman looked at the backs of my hands, reared back, and slapped them hard. I focused. *Feel nothing. Do not flinch.*

"Again," said the Lord Ascendant.

Feel nothing, I thought. Trackman slapped again, but I didn't flinch. It was like a weird prank—Trackman playing slaps with me on the Flight Deck. It didn't seem funny for long.

"Now dig," said the Lord Ascendant in a growling voice. This time Trackman gripped my palm and dug his thumb into the back of my hand. The Ascendant tried to sense my feelings. The pain bloomed in my hands. In the edge of my vision I could see the red mist begin to form and grow. But I pushed back. *No, feel nothing. Stay in control. The pain is a million miles away.* The pain was there, but it felt far away, as if I was watching someone else hurt. *This is nothing,* I thought. Trackman pressed harder and harder. *He's trying to prove something. He's not going to win this game.* The scars ached and itched, but I did not look at the frustrated Trackman. I locked my eyes onto the Ascendant Lord's. Underwater landscapes scrawled across his face. A tentacle reached out for a fish, but at the last second the fish hid itself behind a glowing chunk of coral. I buried my secrets deep down inside my mind. They couldn't make me reveal a thing. *He thinks I can't take this. I can take anything. For my friends, this crew, my dad, Redshirt, he can squeeze the blood out of my hands, but I won't let them glow. I'm in control.* After a moment, Trackman threw my hand back toward me. I let my throbbing hands hang at my sides and pretended they weren't even there.

"Lord, earlier I saw his hands, his movements. I saw the glow—" started Trackman, but the Ascendant Lord stopped him.

"This one does not concern us for now," proclaimed the Ascendant Lord, snapping his staff on the ground. "We will give him full trial when we return to the Chaos. Until then, carry on with your operation, Commander."

"Thank you, sir," said Trackman. He crossed his arms once more, extended his hand, and the image disappeared. Trackman turned to me and whispered, "You won't hold your secrets forever, boy, but I've wasted enough time on you. On to bigger and better things."

Trackman grabbed Buckshot and motioned toward the hatch.

"Where are you taking us?" said Queen Envy.

"Ice skating," said Trackman. "Wait, no, that's not right. How about the orangutan cage?"

JUMPER

Trackman stayed behind us with his ring on Buckshot's neck. We left the Flight Deck and walked down the magnetic hallway where I had seen Redshirt's body. In place of the escape pods was a glowing portal about five feet high. There seemed to be some dark figure moving toward us.

We floated through the cargo hold. Back to the space lab. Back to the orangutan cage. Back to square one. Trackman changed the code, locked the five of us in, and said, "There's no need to panic. Just sit tight like a bunch of frightened little mice for a while. That's an order." He glanced in the direction of the Harper Device, which faintly glowed through the jungle that had grown toward its storage area. "Soon," he said. With that, he exited the space lab, leaving us in dismay. Queen Envy laid Buckshot in the corner and stroked his hair.

"Stars, I have no idea what's going on," said Queen Envy. "One minute we're watching a comet in space and the next minute a maniac has taken over the ship."

"Who was that guy?" said Sunjay.

"You mean the monster with the purple eyes and the fish swimming on his face?" asked Queen Envy. "I have no idea. That could be the devil, for all I know, but I'm talking about the maniac that crushed Tully's hands and knocked out Buckshot."

"How is he?" asked Tabitha, floating toward them.

"I think he's just in a deep sleep." She stroked his hair for a moment. "What just happened? None of this makes sense."

I squeezed the bars of the cage so tight that my fingers hurt. *Yes, it did make sense! If only Sunjay and Tabitha had listened we wouldn't be here, we would have found some way to stop this whole thing before it started!* All the emotions and pain I had hidden earlier came bursting out. Tears welled up in my eyes.

"Tully, you, you saw it coming. We were just too late," said Tabitha.

"Do you really think we could have stopped this, Tully? If only we had seen some real proof," muttered Sunjay.

"If only we had proof! Yes, that would have been great," I yelled. "Yeah, if only Trackman had talked about the conspiracy in front of one of us. If only they threatened to murder someone and then actually did it. If only we suspiciously lost communication right before we reached LG Alpha. Boy, *then* we would have had proof, right?"

"It just wasn't ever clear—"

"—Oh, not clear," I said, throwing up my hands. "One of them should have written you a nice letter, Sunjay: 'Dear annoying kid, we are evil genius murderers who want to take over *The Adversity*. Please don't try to stops us. Oh, and PS—You'll love our friends. They have moving facial tattoos and a ship named after a jellyfish. Hugs and kisses, Trackman and Sawyer.' You didn't get that letter, huh? And now we're all doomed and who knows what will happen with the ship and the Device in their hands?"

Nobody had anything to say to that.

I floated to the skylight and stretched my hands. The *Lion's Mane* dominated my view, blocking the Moon and stars. The exterior of the ship was covered with glowing purple letters, an alien language I could not read. *No, the letters look red. Now they're purple again.* I took a few deep breaths and realized the red mist had returned.

"Well, we're swimming through the avalanche now."

"What's that, baby bear?" asked Queen Envy.

"Swimming through the avalanche. My dad said we would have to swim through a few more…before…the mission was over." I repeated his words.

"Do you think he saw this avalanche coming?"

I closed my eyes. Through the red mist I could picture us trapped in the cage, Trackman on his way through the tentacle to the other ship. It was a spacebridge. My dad couldn't have seen any of this coming. He would have done something. As stressful as the situation was, something was calming me down from the inside out. I wanted to rage at my friends, but I knew it wouldn't do us any good. If only Buckshot was awake. He was so good in a crisis like this.

Trackman didn't come back. We waited a while, all huddled together in the cage saying nothing, but exhaustion took me more quickly than I expected.

✳ ✳ ✳

Once asleep I began to dream, and my dreams became a Red Vision. The feeling was becoming more familiar now. It wasn't like sleeping. I felt conscious of my surroundings. They were encased in the red fog that slowly opened to show a new world around me, and this world included *The Adversity*, the *Lion's Mane*, and the purple tentacle connecting them. I noticed an astronaut on a spacewalk outside of our ship. He stood on the side of the ship and looked into space. Without warning, he leaped into space! *Why would he do that?* I wondered, but it seemed he had a target in mind…the *Lion's Mane*.

Tell me who it is, I demanded of the Red Vision. No response at first. I concentrated like mad, and the Vision granted my request. I began to fly through space toward the jumper and as I did, two other jumpers passed me. *Who are they? Tell me!* I demanded. Just before I caught up to them, the vision faded.

Another Vision took shape. It pulled me into the space lab, and it seemed like a battle was raging. Two combatants attacked each other. Purple sparks were exploding like fireworks all around them. It was too much to take in all at once. *No, not yet! Back to the jumper! Show me. Please.* The lab flew out of my mind and I returned to space. I finally reached the first jumper as he was about to land on the side of the *Lion's Mane*. His hands began to glow. Then I understood.

CLEAN

The Vision of the space jumpers filled my mind. I opened my eyes, feeling calmer than earlier. I took in our situation in the cage. Buckshot was still unconscious beside the sleeping Queen Envy. Sunjay was by me near the skylight, Tabitha far below. She stirred and looked up at me. She must have sensed that I was back in my right mind—as right as my mind gets.

"Well, what now, Scrubbles?" said Tabitha, smiling and wincing at the same time.

"Would you believe me if I told you?"

"Tully, I'll believe anything you say."

"That would be a nice change."

Tabitha floated toward the skylight and took my hand. She gently ran her fingers along the lightning flowers. I tried to pull away, but she held on. "No. You've been holding something back from me this entire trip. That's the same thing as lying to a friend. Don't you get that? You're a hard guy to trust."

It made me angry. I yanked my hand away. "What are you talking about? I did what?"

"You heard me. Look at what you just did. You keep pulling away. Now don't make me say it again." She stared right through me.

A hard guy to trust? I wanted to be angry with her for doubting me, but looking into her sharp green eyes, I knew exactly what she meant. I had held back the truth from her. Then, when I finally had the truth to tell, she didn't believe me. I had no right to be angry with her. I had been hiding secrets for so long, and finally I couldn't hide any longer. I didn't want to. At that moment, I started talking as honestly as I could—

"You're right. I held things back from you, and that's just as bad as a lie. I thought it would make things easier for us, but it only made them worse. I don't even know why I did it. You're the smartest person I know."

"Save your compliments for another time," she said.

"It's not a compliment, Tabitha. It's the truth. We'd be lost without you. Anyway, enough. I'm about to change, if I can. I have an idea of what to do next, but first you need to hear some things about me. I don't care if you think I'm nuts. It just doesn't matter."

"No, it doesn't. And no, I won't think you're nuts."

"We'll see. Let me tell you about the Red Vision I just had…"

"You had a Vision?"

"I've had lots."

She was listening. I shared everything: starting with last Vision, then all the previous ones, even the one in which she disappeared into the mist. She wanted to know more about the weird song that she sang in that Vision.

"Well, sing it for me," she said.

"No way. I can't sing."

"Yes, you can."

"Dangit. Okay. Here's the first verse." So I sang, quietly:

Boy who doesn't know his gifts

Girl who flies into the mist
Cassandra cries to the skies
but no one listens anymore.

"I'm so getting you into the musical next year," she said. "So I guess you were Cassandra, huh? We didn't listen to you. Who's the girl that flies into the mist? Me? That doesn't sound so great. So what's the second verse?"

Blue-eyed demon, green-eyed girl
Man with a plan that changes the world
The hand that holds open the door
will have to let it close.

I stopped singing and explained. "The demon must be Sawyer, and the green-eyed girl is you. I don't know about the last two lines though."

"The man with a plan. That could be Trackman. Or you. And the hand that closes the door? That's definitely you." Her face seemed to darken for a moment. She stared out the skylight, repeating the words.

"Are you okay?

"Just thinking. So the Visions are like bits advice or something," she explained. "They are clues to the future. I'll keep that in mind."

We moved on. I told her about my complicated "friendship" with Lincoln Sawyer and how it started on Earth. All the secrets poured out of me. The truth poured out of me. As guilty as I felt about hiding it, she just nodded her head and listened patiently.

When I finished, she said, "And that's all of it?"

"Except for one secret between me and my dad, that's it," I said. And it was true.

"I trust you," she said. "I'm still hurt, but I trust you."

"Would you have thought I was crazy earlier?"

"Maybe. It doesn't matter now," she said. "You came clean. Friends have to do that for each other. I never want anybody but the real Tully that's right in front of me, even if he is insane. That's the only way to be *us*. This is the real *us*, the *us* that plays Cave-In! and sneaks into space and figures out how to survive and stands up for each other. I love this *us*—forever and for all time."

Then she hugged me tight. I could feel myself relax. She released me and her green eyes looked soft for the first time in a while.

"Tully, I'll always be your friend. You better be mine."

"I will."

"Even if I pop up in your dreams and sing weird songs."

I laughed and wiped away a tear. I had my friend back. That was it. I don't know if telling the truth always goes that well, but this time it was awesome. I felt like I had taken some sort of bath, like I was clean for the first time in so long. I wasn't wearing any more disguises, not an orangutan space suit or a bunch of lies either. I was just me in a t-shirt and jeans, and Tabitha was herself again, and apparently Sunjay was listening in, because he cut short all my deep thoughts. He swooped in and hugged us both. We didn't have much time for a hugfest though. Tabitha was already thinking a step ahead of us. Sunjay, for once, just listened.

"So the jellyfish in your Red Vision was the *Lion's Mane*," she said. "Trackman must have killed Redshirt with his ring, like he knocked out Buckshot."

"Right, and Sawyer covered for him," I said. "He's the doctor."

"Now, it sounds like we're supposed to make a spacejump from *The Adversity* to the *Lion's Mane*. Do you think you should use your powers to do that or what?"

Sunjay and I both looked at Tabitha.

"Who has powers?" I asked. "I have Visions and glowing hands."

"You have more than that. The Ascendant Lord thought so."

"I knew he was examining me," I said, "but I thought he just wanted to know if I touched the Harper Device."

"No, think about it. He said that the small things could do great harm, sort of like David took down Goliath. Something like that. He wanted to know if you were a *threat* to him. You are, but you hid it. Good job."

"So Tully has powers?" asked Sunjay.

"Of course. Sunjay, when you two fought in the Hamster Wheel, Tully was so fast you couldn't kick him, right?"

"Uh, yeah. That was like magic."

"And remember how Tully's hands glowed red?"

"Wait," I said, "you noticed that?"

She nodded. "Yep. You stuck your hands in your pockets, but you weren't fast enough."

"Yeah, but how are Tully's super-fast hands going to help us jump through space without dying?" asked Sunjay.

Tabitha twirled her scarf. "I'm not sure, but first we have to escape the cage. Tully, here's a test. Break us out of here. Then we can do the spacejump and save everyone else."

"Oooor maybe we should stay here and not die," said Sunjay. "A spacewalk is hard for an astronaut. How are the three of us going to do a spacejump? We'll be spacejunk unless someone rescues us. What if the *Lion's Mane* just takes off or something and—whoosh!—there goes our target? Who's going to save us? We'll be space popsicles before you know it."

"No risk, no reward," I said. "It's either take our chances in space or take them with Gallant Trackman. We have to make the spacejump. The Vision says so. We've got to save my dad, and he's over there."

"Yep, let's jump to the jelly," said Tabitha. "He's not looking for little minnows. Anyway, the Ascendant won't go anywhere without their big prize." She pointed across the garden to the Harper Device. We couldn't see it because of the vines, but it glowed a steady, dim red.

We looked out the skylight. A quarter mile stood between the two ships. *That's the emptiest place I've ever seen, and we have to cross it by ourselves.* There was nothing there. No air, light, or life. Nothing except for the tentacle, full of dark spots moving toward our ship.

"Something's coming," I said, floating toward the bars.

A Presence in the Hallway

In a matter of minutes the hatch opened at the far end of the storage area. We peered down the corridor to see what was coming. Our hopes jumped immediately when we saw who it was.

"Moreline!" Tabitha said, "Get us out of here!" Sylvia Moreline floated down the corridor slowly, with a grim look on her face. She shook her head. Our hope turned to fear. Behind her floated Sawyer and Trackman, who grinned like a thief after a robbery. That was bad, but it got worse.

Behind Trackman and Sawyer I *felt* another presence—something that seemed to make the space lab darker. The presence became a shadow; the shadow became a form; the form took on flesh, which bulged with muscle and crawled with tattoos. For the first time we saw an Ascendant warrior in person. He didn't float like the rest of us. He walked into the space lab—in zero gravity. How? Who knows?

He was a tower of muscle. Black and purple armor covered his chest but not his arms—they were covered with tattoos. I recognized one of his tattoos—our solar system. Each of the planets was in motion, spinning at different speeds. Unlike the Ascendant Lord, this warrior's tattoos were heavenly bodies—spinning galaxies, shooting stars, and ringed planets. An open-faced black helmet hid most of his features. He wore a tunic like a gladiator, and his legs, like his arms, rippled with every step. However, the thing that terrified me most was in his right hand, something that sucked the very light out of the space lab and obscured the features I just described—a black staff as tall as he was, covered in strange writing, glowing purple at each end.

"What is that?" whispered Sunjay.

We watched the Ascendant warrior looming in the dark. We all backed away from the bars of the cage. Sawyer opened the cage and pushed Moreline inside. Trackman had obviously made her enter the lab first on purpose.

"'Oooh, come save us!'" he mocked us. "Help us, Moreline, you're our only hope!"

Moreline grunted in pain and struggled to catch her breath. She had a black eye and bruises around her neck.

"What happened? Is he an Ascendant, too?" Sunjay asked.

"Wrong time to talk," she wheezed.

"Wrong time indeed!" Trackman turned his gaze on Sunjay and sucked air through his teeth. "Question boy, I have a question for you. Would you like to find out what happened to Moreline?"

"Uh, no, I'm okay. I can ask her later, really. No problem. Sorry," he said.

Trackman turned toward the Ascendant, said something, and the warrior's black staff lit up with purple flame. He flicked his wrist. That's all it took. Sunjay flew forward and stuck to the bars of the cage, like a magnet on a refrigerator. I can't imagine how bad that hurt, but Sunjay didn't yell.

"You get the idea now, boy? Any more questions for the Ascendant warrior? You'll find that they prefer action to speech." The Ascendant flicked his black staff again, which sent Sunjay smashing to the back of the cage. He couldn't catch his breath for a minute but waved us away.

Trackman continued. The darkness behind him drew the light out of the room. Even the Harper Device seemed dimmer than usual. "Well, I hope you all slept wonderfully well in your cage. It looks like Buckshot is still in never-never land. The rest of us should get down to business."

"What kind of business is that, Trackman? Selling out your friends, maybe the whole world?"

We all turned and looked at the owner of the voice, who looked equal parts scared and angry, flipping her lucky scarf, which turned bright green.

"Tabitha, are you crazy?" I whispered.

"Yes," Trackman said, "I think she is. And, yes, that about sums it up. I sold you out. All for the price of the Harper Device."

"Well, aren't you a good dog?" she continued, "Did the Ascendant tell you to fetch the Device like you're a sweet little poodle? Little poodle labroodle give a dog a bone."

We're all about to die. I should have clamped a hand over her mouth. The Ascendant's black staff glowed. Somewhere under his helmet his eyes lit up with a purple light, too. I don't know if he knew English, too, but he knew one thing: this girl insulted Commander Trackman. Trackman kept those teeth shining and put up a hand to stop the Ascendant from tossing Tabitha into the bars. "Say all the rhymes you want, girl. You're in a cage. I'll be on a throne soon."

"I doubt that," she said. "They'll give you a doghouse."

Sawyer floated forward. "Would you like me to eliminate the girl now, Commander Trackman?"

That cooled Tabitha down. She pushed away from the bars. My fear gave way to anger, and I started to see the world through the red mist again.

"Ha, no. Such a clever girl," Trackman told Sawyer. "I may retain her as a servant in my mansion, if she can tame that nasty tongue. Yes, I'm going to build a mansion on Liberty Island, right in front of the Statue of Liberty. What a great lawn ornament that would make."

"Generally lawn ornaments are more diminutive," said Sawyer, "such as rabbits or gnomes."

"Don't interrupt me when I'm picturing my life of luxury, you mechanical misfit!"

"And how are you going to get this big mansion? By fetching the Harper Device?" Tabitha asked, gripping the cage bars.

"The Harper Device. Yes, that's what you call it," he said. "You named it after the great Commander Harper. How arrogant! The Ascendant know its real name, and its real purpose—to claim the Earth for their own." He floated back over to the cage and eyed me. "Your father had no idea what he found on Mars, Tully Harper. But now I'm giving it back to its rightful owners, and they have plans far beyond building my dream house. Now, where is that prize?" Trackman and Sawyer struggled through the vines in the space lab on their way toward the dim, red glow. They didn't struggle for long. A flick of the black staff and the vines parted for them.

In the meantime, Sunjay looked at Tabitha and me. "Didn't you see what he did to me? Why did you say all that?"

"It was worth the risk," Tabitha said. "We know more about his plans now, more about the Device. That could be helpful if—"

But she was interrupted by Trackman.

MELT

"What? What is this? Where is it?" He shouted from across the jungle. He crawled back through the vines tangling him with every movement. The Android followed. "You did this!"

We all jumped back as he approached. Trackman's face glowed red and his eyes twitched. In his hand he held an LED light covered with a red cloth. No wonder the Device had seemed dim. It wasn't just the presence of the Ascendant warrior. The Harper Device wasn't there at all. Trackman reached through the bars and pulled me up to his sweaty red face.

"Where have you hidden the Sacred? Where?"

One part of me was thrilled. Someone had foiled his plan. But another side of me was petrified. A vein of Trackman's forehead thumped like a bass drum. Lincoln Sawyer stood beside him, calmly observing me with his cold, blue gaze. In the background the Ascendant warrior's tattoos glowed and swirled.

"Boy, you did this," he sputtered. "You give me that thing or I swear…I will make you feel pain you can hardly imagine."

The black staff glowed. I lurched forward. The Ascendant stuck me to the bars of the cage. It felt like a heavy weight was rolling up and down my body, crushing my legs, then my pelvis, then my chest and head. I wished that I could just melt through the bars because they were pressing deep into my skin. Everyone yelled for the Ascendant to stop, but Trackman would not relent. My ears started to ring. And just when I thought I would black out, the Android saved me.

"Uh, sir, if I may," said Sawyer, calmly, "I checked on the Harper Device just an hour ago, as you suggested, before I deployed with the away team. Everyone else on board was in the Flight Deck. The boy couldn't have taken it."

"Oh, yes he did. He's a sneaky one. Look at him!" yelled Trackman.

"Sir, be reasonable. Only one person could have taken the Harper Device, which, by the way, we should continue using that nomenclature until the Ascendant Lord allows us to use its real name."

"Get on with it, Android. Who took the Device! You?"

"Me? No, sir. I was with Moreline preparing the Cerberus. Only, well, Commander Harper left us for a moment. He told us he wanted to say goodbye to his son before he left."

"Oh, did he? And you let him do it?" yelled Trackman.

"Yes," said Sawyer, "it would have been suspicious to go with him. So we finished loading equipment into the Cerberus until he returned."

Trackman flicked his hand. The Ascendant released me. I fell away from the bars of the cage. Air returned to my lungs. Trackman turned toward Sawyer. "So it's *your* fault. Brilliant, Android. Just brilliant. If the Lord Ascendant doesn't receive his gift, we are all doomed. I will assume that your robot brain can't tell me where the Device is, so get busy. Search this ship. If we can't find it, we will pay Commander Harper a visit. If he won't give us what we want, I'll be back for you," he said to me.

With that, the three of them left. The Ascendant walked behind them, and as he left, the room brightened.

"My dad did see the avalanche coming," I said. "He knew that he was walking into a trap."

"If those Ascendants find the Device, they'll make us all slaves!" said Queen Envy.

"Mike won't say a thing," Sylvia Moreline grunted.

"Well, if we're going to swim an avalanche, we should get started," said Tabitha. "Trackman will search the ship before he asks Commander Harper."

"You're darn right." Buckshot said that. He was only half-way coherent, but we were happy to have him back. Queen Envy held up his head. "Get us up to date, Sylvia."

✳ ✳ ✳

Moreline told us what happened on the "comet." They had been on the surface trying to drill, as we had seen. My dad first noticed the comet was starting to rotate. They began to get back into the Cerberus to return to *The Adversity*. Then Lincoln Sawyer grabbed them both by the arm and said, "Keep drilling. We're almost there."

After a few moments of drilling, my dad turned the laser drill on Sawyer. The drill burned through the arm of Sawyer's spacesuit. That depressurized his suit momentarily, which would have killed a man. Not an Android. Sawyer grabbed Moreline and made a motion as if to rip off her helmet. My dad had no choice but to put down the drill. Sawyer tied a hose around his arm to keep the rest of his suit pressurized. At that point, a crack opened in the surface of the "comet," and the three of them fell, along with the Cerberus, until they were hauled into the Ascendant ship. There they were taken captive and beaten.

"They split us up," she explained. "No plots that way."

"Well, they're wrong about that," said Tabitha. "More people, more places, more ways to bring them down. Where did they keep you? Tell Sunjay everything you can."

Moreline described the ship's interior in detail. Sunjay made mental notes. I was only half-listening. *It won't matter if we can't get out of this stupid cage.* I kept clutching the bars. *Need to get out. These bars, these bars. We need to break these bars. No, we can't break them. Need to melt them. Yes, they need to melt.*

In the background, Moreline and Buckshot brainstormed about how to reclaim the ship. *This is pointless unless I can do something about it.* The bars seemed to grow hotter the more I thought about them. The red haze clouded my vision. I closed my eyes and pictured the bars turning red. Red, red, red, red, red. I could hear something sizzling. Beneath my hands the metal felt soft, like molten lava, and squished between my fingers. The bars were no longer in the way, and I pictured myself grabbing Sunjay and Tabitha and floating out of the cage. Everything grew strangely quiet as the Vision faded away.

When I opened my eyes again, there were no bars in front of me, only the overgrown garden and the empty cage where the Harper Device once was. I turned around to see what had happened. My hands were glowing. So were the bars, which were molding back into place. My friends stood beside me. In the cage everyone else looked at us.

Tabitha and Sunjay looked at me with wide eyes. "Tully, you, we just…"

"I can't explain it," I said. "I don't know what I just did."

"Tarnations, Tully!" said Buckshot. "Do that again!" I tried again, but the red haze was gone. The bars wouldn't budge. I couldn't make my hands glow on command, apparently. We tried to override the locking system but Trackman had planned ahead. It was useless.

"Listen to me," I said, "we've got work to do. We've got to save my dad. He was smart enough to hide the Harper Device. He's got to have a plan."

Buckshot shook his head. "Godspeed," he said, still looking dazed. Moreline grabbed my arm through the cage. She smiled weakly. "Tully, the ship is full of guards with those black staffs. Watch for them on the spacebridge. It sounds impossible, but you three do impossible things all the time. Now it's in your hands."

Moreline's words gave me courage as we left the lab and made our way through the ship, looking around every corner for an enemy. Finally we reached Queen Envy's room. We needed some spacesuits. Moreline didn't realize it, but we wouldn't be crossing over to the *Lion's Mane* through the purple tentacle. Sunjay donned his pink suit, Tabitha her purple, and I floated across the hall and grabbed the first suit I could find. "G. Trackman" it said on the helmet. I returned to the Queen's room wearing Trackman's spacesuit.

"I'm burning this suit when I'm done with it," I said.

"Only if I can help," said Sunjay. "Only if we survive."

"Everyone ready for the spacejump?" I said, ignoring him.

Tabitha gave me a thumbs-up.

"Wouldn't the spacebridge thing be safer?" said Sunjay.

"We've got to go with the Vision," I said.

"Space is cold, Tully, and we won't have any way to maneuver once we jump. And how are we supposed to get in even if we make it?" he asked.

"Do you know the Elvish word for 'friend'?" Tabitha asked, adjusting her gloves. Sunjay looked confused.

"You're the map genius. You'll figure it out," I told him. "Maybe we can just knock. One of the Ascendant warriors might direct us to the nearest entrance."

I had no idea how to answer his questions. Still, my dad needed help and I had seen a Red Vision. This was no time for doubt.

HANDS

Tabitha and Sunjay had already worn human spacesuits, but it was the first time I had worn a spacesuit designed for my species. The orangutan suit was hard to move in, but Trackman's suit was a perfect fit. The suits had magnetic footpads, which seemed to turn every surface in the ship into a magnetic walkway. That came in handy. We were going to need to stick to the side of *The Adversity* before we jumped—or float into outer space.

The suits also had ABA, Active Biomechanical Assistance, which supercharged all of our movements—I felt like a mini version of Hercules. It was good to feel strong, and we might need that strength if we ran into any of the Ascendant warriors.

We walked from Queen Envy's room toward the airlock on the opposite side of the ship from the *Lion's Mane*. We carried our helmets and discussed the plan on our way, peeking around every corner and hoping not to see our enemy.

"We can't hesitate when it's time to jump," I said. "I give the count-down and then we go. We get one shot, and we either make it or miss it."

"One more thing," said Tabitha. "We might not be able to com-municate out there. Remember, your dad couldn't contact Earth or the Moon." We put on our helmets to check. The radios didn't work. As usual, Tabitha was right.

"Tabitha, you can read lips, and you and I both know some sign language now. That should help."

"What about me?" said Sunjay, throwing his helmet. "Stupid radio! I won't know what's going on if you start signing or talking. What if I float away into space and can't even talk to anyone before I freeze to death or run out of oxygen or, or, AHHH!" Sunjay grabbed his hair and yanked. Because he had on the ABA space gloves, he pulled out a chunk of hair on accident and screamed again.

Stars! Sunjay is already freaking out and we haven't even started the jump! I thought. His hair floated past my face. He was probably picturing himself like that hair, floating off into darkness. He must have seen my concern because he took a deep breath. I was about to give him a pep talk, but he put up his hand.

"No, no wait. Tully, I trust you. You had a Vision. Queen Envy always says 'When you can't be anything else, be brave.' So I'll be brave. At least if I die, I'll die in one of her spacesuits."

"Did you really just say that?" asked Tabitha, punching him. "What about dying with two of your best friends? Creepy crawler death wish spacestalker. Now I'm glad we can't talk in space."

He laughed. I laughed. We both snapped on our helmets. I kind of understood how soldiers manage to joke around before a battle. It felt good. The tension was gone for the moment.

We gave a final thumbs-up to each other. It was time to walk into space. I gripped the airlock handle and opened it with easy strength.

We floated into the small room and waited for it to depressurize. After a few minutes a light turned green. The outside airlock opened. There, looming like a black curtain, was outer space. It stretched out before us, dark and sparkling.

Floating around in a ship was a strange experience. Being weightless outside the ship made my whole body tingle with fear, like I was looking over the edge of a skyscraper. I attached my feet to the body of the ship and tried to keep my eyes focused on my movements rather than black expanse that surrounded us. Even with the ABA and the magnetized soles, it was awkward to move. For the crew the suits were a second skin, but I felt like a little boy trying to walk in his father's cowboy boots. On a tight rope.

Tabitha followed and Sunjay came last. He tried to crawl out of the airlock on all fours, but I picked up one of his feet and put it on the side of the ship. He waved his arms as if he was falling. Then he steadied himself and put the other foot down. All systems were go.

We clunked along the side of the ship until we could see the *Lion's Mane*, its purple tentacle stretched between the two spacecrafts. I reviewed the plan in my head. Pretty simple: *jump, land, and enter.*

We looked at the giant ship in the distance. I decided not to push off too hard. I mouthed to Tabitha, "Not a big jump, just a little push." She read my lips perfectly and pantomimed to Sunjay. Her drama classes were coming in handy in space because Sunjay understood. He gave me the okay sign. We were ready to launch ourselves. I pointed to the center of the giant black and purple sphere. I wedged myself between them and began a countdown.

"10, 9, 8, 7...."

My hands trembled as I counted down, but the gloves hid my fear.

"6, 5, 4..."

When the count reached four, we clasped hands: Sunjay on my left, Tabitha on my right. I nodded with the last few numbers.

"3, 2, 1, 0..."

And with that, each of us gave a light push. I felt my magnetic foot-pad stick for a second and then we were adrift in an ocean of stars.

I looked back at *The Adversity* for a moment. It was the strangest feeling, moving away from something so slowly and having no way to change course. We seemed to be on target, but we had a long way to go and weren't going to get there quickly. There was absolute silence except my breathing inside the helmet and the blood pounding in my ears.

Sunjay had a death grip on my left hand, and he kept repositioning his grip. Soon I felt a squeeze on my right hand. I turned toward Tabitha. Her head looked tiny in the helmet, but her hair filled up the rest of it. "Your hair looks crazy!" I mouthed. She smiled at me and shook her head, like bad space hair and facing certain death were what she signed up for when we decided to do this. How cool is that? My breathing slowed down and was quieter. The more I thought about her, the more awesome she seemed to me. Tabitha the scarf twirler. Tabitha the problem-solver. Tabitha the tough and beautiful and tall.

I squeezed her hand back. I felt like the luckiest guy in the world. With the ship in the background, it seemed like we were the only two people in the universe, doing a dance among the stars. For some reason I thought about the mystery doodle she drew when we first learned about the Harper Device.

"What did you write on that doodle?" I mouthed to her. "The one I found. I couldn't pick it up."

"Oh my stars, you *did* see that!"

"Not the whole thing. What did you it say about me?"

"Ha, no way! I have a secret from you now!"

She mouthed something else to me, but I got distracted. It felt like that moment in the hallway back on Earth. I looked into her green eyes and forgot all the dangers that awaited us when we landed.

I didn't have long to admire her though, because suddenly her eyes widened with fear. She squeezed my hand so tightly with the ABA that she almost broke my fingers.

"Tabitha, ouch!" I yelled.

With her other hand, she pointed across my body.

I turned to my left and gasped. I wasn't holding Sunjay's hand! He flailed his arms, trying to grab my hand. We touched fingers for a moment, but inch by inch, foot by foot, we were drifting slowly away from one another. There was no way to bring him back. Terror was in his eyes. He was screaming, but I couldn't hear a thing. We weren't even halfway to our destination, and our plan was ruined.

I looked to see if our aim was okay, and to my surprise Sunjay was headed toward the center of the *Lion's Mane*. He swung his arms like he was drowning, but he wasn't the one who needed help. Tabitha and I were. I tried to look as calm as possible, but it was clear that we might miss the target completely. *My foot stuck for just a second,* I remembered. I wish we could have radioed someone for help, just so we could say something, but who would we call, even if we could? Lincoln Sawyer? The Ascendant Lord? All I could do was mouth things to Tabitha.

"He's on the right path. We're off target. My foot got stuck for a second. It's going to be close, Tabitha."

She shook her head. "We're going to miss."

"I'm sorry," I said.

"Don't be. Figure it out, Tully. You can do it."

"What?"

"You have power. Use it. Use it."

She was pleading with me, like I was holding something back from her again, but I wasn't. Sunjay kept swinging his arm wildly in the distance. Behind him the *Lion's Mane* looked shiny and smooth like black glass. I could picture him landing and us grabbing for the surface and sliding off into the darkness. It wasn't a pretty picture. Tabitha and I crossed the halfway point, holding hands. Our moment in space had become a jump to our deaths.

Space opened up before us, twinkling and uninviting and cold. I focused and thought, *We didn't come all this way to fail. We are going to get my dad. I won't let everyone down. I can swim in the avalanche. If only I had had some training…*

I focused on that idea. The three of us could do this. The three of us. That's when I felt Tabitha struggled away from my grip. She released my hand and pushed me as hard as she could. I reached for her, but she pulled her hand away from me. Now all three of us were alone in space.

It took me a moment to realize what she did. She was floating farther off course into space, and I was closing in on Sunjay. I panicked. She could read my lips.

"Calm down," she said. "You'll be fine."

"No! What did you do?" My voice echoed in my ears.

"Go help your dad. You and Sunjay."

"We won't be able to get you in time. You'll run out of oxygen."

"Then you'd better hurry."

"I'm not going to lose you."

"Then bring me back," she said. "Use your power."

"I don't know how!" I yelled. "You have to live!"

"Then save me," she said.

"How?"

"It's in your hands."

Sunjay and I slowly moved toward each other. He looked back and saw me coming toward him. He looked thrilled until he realized what was happening. His hands went to his helmet and he opened his mouth to shout. The weight of responsibility almost crushed me. This was my fault. I turned back toward Tabitha. She signed something to me that I did not understand. Then she turned her face to the blackness beyond the *Lion's Mane*.

I screamed at the top of my lungs. "Now! Now, now, now! Now or never! God, she has to live!"

There are times when you think you're focusing on some idea, but then you realize you really weren't focused at all. I closed my eyes. She was right. There was no use in panic, no use in what I could not do. I pushed everything else out of my mind except for this: *She has to live.*

As I said those words, the whole world turned red again. I saw the situation from all of our perspectives—Sunjay headed on course, me headed toward Sunjay, and Tabitha floating to her doom. No. No, we would go where we needed to go. I heard a voice in my head repeat her words: *It's in your hands.*

My clenched fists felt red hot, as they did when I gripped the bars of the cage. They felt powerful, like they could hold or catch or grab anything. When I opened my eyes, my hands were glowing again, right through Trackman's white suit. *This is in your hands, Tully. Do what you need to do.*

I extended my right hand toward Tabitha, like I wanted to grab the back of her space suit. She was so far away now, just a white speck among the stars. *Make a way,* I thought. *Make a way.*

I repeated the word again and again, like a chant. Each time I said this, the red glow in my hand brightened, pulsated, just like the Harper Device. After several seconds—it felt like an hour—a thin red beam of light emerged from my glove. Then a second beam. A third. Soon hundreds of thin red beams extended from my glove. The beams slowly extended like a net toward Tabitha. I continued my chant. With a big mental push, the beams spread out and reached around her. She turned around and saw what was happening. I captured her. Now I had to pull her back. I pulled the beam toward us like it was a rope, hand over hand. It shouldn't have been so hard. There was no gravity to fight. It was something else. Sweat beaded on my forehead. My lungs heaved against the space suit. It was like the universe was fighting to keep her away from me, and I wouldn't let it win.

About that time I bumped into Sunjay. Well, he grabbed me around the waist and held on to me as I pulled the glowing net toward us. My arms were burning by the time she finally reached us. The red beams disappeared. The three of us clumped together in a giant group hug after the scariest ten minutes of our lives. Nobody was floating away again.

Tabitha stayed cool. She tapped us both on our helmets. "Get us in," she mouthed. We looked at the enormous black ship. There was one red band around the middle...a walkway. We saw an Ascendant warrior walk past us there. Getting on board there would mean capture for sure.

"No, not there! Lower." Sunjay pointed just below the walkway to a row of hatches on the side of the ship. Most had windows. He took my hand and pointed it toward a hatch with no windows. I had to guide us there. What were we going to do? Kick it down?

Wait, I thought, *a portal! Why not make a way?* It was worth a try. "Hold on," I mouthed.

"Stay together!" said Sunjay.

My arms felt weakened, but I brought both my hands together overhead as if I was diving into a pool and aimed them at the windowless hatch. A red glowing circle appeared right where my hands pointed. The circle expanded.

I spread my hands, as if I was diving into the ocean. *Portal,* I said, *portal, portal.* The glowing circle on the ship became a hole.

We dove right through the black skin of the ship and landed in a heap in our spacesuits. I looked up, expecting to see an Ascendant warrior with a black staff pointed at my face. Instead, I flipped open my visor to see a dark cell. On the far side sat my dad.

TWO AND TWO TOGETHER

I spend more time locked up than anyone else in the universe, and I've never even been convicted of a crime. At the moment, I was in a new cell—small, dark, and alien—that also contained my two friends and my dad. The whole room was lit with a black light. Everything white shined brightly, like eyeballs and teeth and my spacesuit.

My dad didn't seem surprised to see us, but he did seem injured. It was hard to see well in the black light, but he had a gash above his right eye. His uniform was ripped in several places, and he limped out of our way when we landed in the middle of his cell. I'm glad he moved. Our suits were so cold from outer space that they would have given him serious freezer burn on top of all the other problems.

We pulled off our helmets and looked at each other. Tabitha looked calm, but Sunjay punched me in the mouth.

"What was that for?" I yelled.

"You let go of my hand, you idiot! I was floating out there all alone and you and Tabitha—"

"Yeah, me and Tabitha were floating to our deaths!" I yelled back, rubbing my jaw.

"You left me! And then you came back. You and your crazy powers—Tully, why didn't you tell me you had a plan to get in?"

"I didn't! That just happened. How did you know that this was the right hatch?"

"It was a good guess. I was making an imaginary map of the *Lion's Mane* in my head right before you let me go. If I were an evil alien pirate, I would put the prisoner's quarters just below a main walkway for easy access. My prisoners wouldn't get windows. I had it all figured out like you asked, but then you let me go and I hyperventilated and I might have peed in this spacesuit!"

"Stars, I'm sorry. What about all that stuff about being brave?" I said. "It all worked out."

"Only because Tabitha pushed you toward me. I saw that much."

We stopped arguing and turned toward Tabitha. She was waiting patiently for us to stop bickering, and the revelations that she saved us was enough to get us back on track. "If you hadn't pushed me toward Sunjay, I would be dead. You pushed me to safety. You saved me—"

"—Us," she said, "*You* saved *us*. Sometimes Baby Bear needs a nudge, but he comes out of hibernation and flies just right." She smiled again, like she knew things I didn't know. It usually frustrated me, but this time I was in awe of her.

"If I'd lost you, I'd, I couldn't—" I stuttered. I grabbed her gloved hands.

"How did you know he could save us?" asked Sunjay.

"I didn't. I just had hope," she explained.

"And hope does not fail." We all turned toward the soft, low voice of my dad. He sat with his arms resting on his knees. We were still a big tangle of spacesuits on the floor. I jumped up and gave him a big hug. Fortunately my spacesuit had warmed up.

"We're here to save you!" I said.

"Careful, Tully. I've got some pretty deep bruises," he said. "Did you consider using the door?"

"Aren't you surprised we're here?"

"My crew always gets the job done when I need them, and you're part of that crew. It looks like you had a successful spacewalk."

"It was more of a jump, but that doesn't matter right now. Did you hide the Device?"

"Of course."

"Where?" I asked. "Trackman is coming for it."

"He's not here yet and probably won't find the Device."

"But he'll find you! I can't believe he's not here yet. He's furious. I think he might—"

My dad put his hand on my shoulder. He seemed calm and sure of himself, just like he was sitting in his commander's chair—only he was in a jail cell with some evil conspirators coming to beat the truth out of him.

"Let's all slow down for a moment. The three of you just went on quite a journey. Tully, apparently you opened that portal into the room. Whatever powers you used, whatever Tabitha did to get you here, whatever Sunjay is upset about, those things we need to set aside for a moment. You accomplished your goal. That's all that matters, right?" We nodded in agreement. "Now, I need to gather some information from you. First, give me an update about *The Adversity*."

We told him everything that happened. His crew was locked in the orangutan cage. Buckshot and Moreline were in bad shape. The Ascendant warrior literally scared the living daylight out of the space lab. Trackman freaked out when he didn't find the Device.

"They're searching the ship now," I said. "Will they find it?"

"No," my dad said.

"I hope not," said Sunjay. "And I hope we don't run into one of those warriors on our way back."

"Better than Sawyer," said Tabitha. "He has icebergs for eyes."

"I'd rather face an Android than a giant with an glowing bo staff. Who are they, Commander?"

"Well, they're about 6'5", muscular, and aggressive. So is their captain. He interrogated me on their Flight Deck. He speaks English. He seemed to know all of our plans. They knew we had the Device. Trackman must have been—"

"—Their spy on board the ship," I interjected. "He called himself the Arch Spy. What did they ask you, dad?"

"A lot about you. He knew that you interacted with the Device. He wanted to know how you survived and what powers you had. I told him you didn't have any, and that's when he sent us away and started beating us. He thought I was lying. Well, I guess I was.

"So, tell me about these powers, Tully. Tell me what you've done so far. Give me a list and I will ask for details if needed. This may be useful for later."

I described everything—the Visions, the escape from the cage, the net, the portals. My dad ran his hand across his hair as I spoke. He asked for more details about the melting the bars and nodded his head.

"So, you're learning to control them. And if you focus and remain calm you can accomplish the most?"

"Yes, sir."

"Well, that's a good lesson," he said.

"This isn't the time for lessons, dad."

"But using these powers also makes you tired, correct?"

"Yes, a little."

"I'd say a lot, judging from how you look. Use them only as needed. I'm telling you this as your Commander, not your father."

"Okay," I said, annoyed, "if you put it that way. Now you know what we know. If we are your crew, tell us what *you* know."

My dad nodded. "I can tell you some now and hopefully more later. Most of their plan I learned while Trackman and the Ascendant Lord were interrogating me on their Flight Deck. From the moment I started talking to them, it was clear that they came for the Harper Device and didn't care about anything else.

"First of all, this was all carefully planned. Operation Close Encounter, as Trackman called it, was meant to recapture the Harper Device. They lost it—maybe it escaped from them. I'm not sure. So the Ascendant disguised their ship as a comet. They knew the Alliance would notice a comet headed toward their space station and send us as quickly as possible. Therefore, we could not drop the Harper Device on the Moon."

"And they could capture us here in deep space with no one else to see," said Tabitha. "When the comet didn't reappear from behind the Moon, we might assume that a collision had occurred."

"But where is the space station? The crew we were coming to save?" asked Sunjay.

"The space station is in the belly of this ship. There never was a crew."

"So Trackman is a liar and a spy," I said, "and this whole mission was a way to recapture the Harper Device."

"Trackman called it 'the Sacred,'" said Tabitha.

My dad nodded.

"And it's a weapon?" asked Sunjay.

"It's more than that!" I said.

"Well, whatever it is," Tabitha said, "the Ascendant are planning an invasion. They want to rule the Earth. Remember what Trackman said to me about having the Statue of Liberty for a lawn ornament?"

"They need the Harper Device so they can attack," explained my dad. "Their plans must depend on it. Now you know what I know." He sat for a moment and considered our situation and my powers. "Before I say anything else, I should thank you for coming. You weren't the three crewmembers I expected, but you were the three that I needed. Whatever happens next, remember that. You've earned my trust. We've got a chance to get out of this thing alive, but we have to make a plan.

"We need to get you three back on board *The Adversity* as soon as possible. You can help me on board that ship…not this one. After you free me, go back and free the others. Use your powers as best you can, Tully. It sounds like Tabitha gave you good direction on that."

"Why can't we help you here, dad?" He ignored my question.

"They probably left someone on board to guard you. We need to get you back there as soon as we can to avoid suspicion. That will give me a chance to do my job. They have a reason to keep me alive. They don't need a reason to do away with the three of you. So break me out of this cell. I need to get to the Cerberus. Tully, this door leads to a walkway. Give me a portal. Now let's get moving."

"What are you going to do, Commander?" asked Sunjay.

"Good question, Sunjay," he said, in the same easy tone he used for all his other orders. "I intend to blow up this ship."

SEVER

I was speechless. Sunjay's eyes almost popped out of his head. Tabitha's mouth dropped. My dad sat there waiting.

"So, can you get me out of this cell?" He felt along the wall, looking for the seams of a door.

"Oh, yeah, one minute." I lifted my hands and tried to focus. Then I dropped them. My dad didn't notice. He was staring at the wall, probably planning how to blow up the *Lion's Mane* without being killed by aliens with electric bo staffs. How did he stay that cool?

"Dad, it's almost like you expected to see us here," I said, "like this was part of your plan."

He leaned toward me. I could see the red streak in his hair, that strange red light in his eyes. He didn't respond, just tousled my hair and patted Sunjay and Tabitha on the shoulders.

"Let's hope that we can discuss that someday," he said. "Now can you make me a portal about halfway up the wall?"

"I can try," I said.

"Oh, just like getting to the next level in *Cave-In!,* Tully!" said Tabitha.

Huh, great point, Tabitha. It was like *Cave-In!* A few deep breaths and I pictured us all inside the room. Then I imagined the empty walkway behind the wall. *This not a wall anymore, not a wall, not a wall.* I could picture the metal disappearing. *Portal,* I thought, *portal.* I opened my eyes this time to watch the wall sizzle and melt away. In the middle of the wall was a perfectly round portal. I stood aside. My dad poked out his head slowly and scanned for the enemy. "Now back to the ship the way you came, the three of you," he whispered, crawling out of the cell. I raised my hands and shut the portal like it was a heavy door.

Sunjay and Tabitha both turned toward the other wall. They didn't want to stick around, especially if my dad fulfilled his mission and blew it into space dust. None of us wanted to run into an Ascendant warrior armed with a black staff with no reason to keep us alive.

At the same time, I felt like there was something else I needed to do. We helped my dad escape his cell. Was that enough? Hopefully he could escape back to *The Adversity*, but it seemed like the odds were stacked against him.

"Guys, what if my dad runs into one of those warriors?" I said. "We need to create a distraction."

"We need to leave," said Tabitha.

"We need to *live*!" said Sunjay. "Your dad gave us a command."

"I know that, but something tells me we need to stay."

"How can we create a distraction that doesn't draw attention to us?" asked Sunjay. "That's not the right word. We need to create a diversion."

We sat there under the black light, looking at the incredibly bright whites of each other's eyes. Tabitha hopped up.

"Oh! Chop off the hydra's head! Gigantic fantastic diversion!" She chopped her hand through the air. "Tully, chop chop the noodle!"

It only took me a moment to realize what she meant. "Uh, I can try, but I think I need to see it to cut it."

"Oh!" said Sunjay. "That tentacle thing! If you need to see it, we should follow your dad. There is a window that runs down the length of the hallway. We'll have a great view of the spacebridge and *The Adversity*. You guys didn't notice that on our way in?"

"No, but thanks, Sir Maps-A-Lot," said Tabitha.

"Grab your helmets," I said, "and follow me."

I reopened the portal and we emerged into the hallway, my suit and eyes shining white in the black light. We looked left. No one was there. We looked right. My dad was carefully making his way forward. Out the window loomed the spacebridge.

"Keep a lookout both ways. Let me see if I can create that diversion," I told them, closing my eyes. I couldn't imagine chopping the spacebridge in half, so I had to get creative. I thought of an image that would help me cut the spacebridge. A picture came to me—a jellyfish held onto a fish with one long tentacle. It was just like in my Red Vision. I imagined diving into the ocean and swimming toward the jellyfish. I focused on that tentacle and raised my right hand—my hand held a glowing red sword. *Sever*, I thought, *sever. Sever.*

This was harder than creating the portal. The jellyfish somehow knew my plan and fought me. A second tentacle shot toward me and grabbed my arm. My arm seared with pain, but I lunged with my sword and cut that tentacle in half. I was free again, but the fish still struggled to escape. I swam forward. Then I swung my sword overhead and brought it down on the first tentacle. Again and again. Sweat dripped into my eyes. My heartbeat quickened and lungs worked overtime. *Sever, sever, sever,* I said.

"It's working," Tabitha said. "Keep going!"

A few minutes passed, or maybe a few seconds. I lost track of time. My heart beat like mad and sweat fell into my eyes. In my mind the sword slashed again and again. My arm felt like it was on fire. Finally, my arm snapped forward all by itself, like I had thrown a thunderbolt. I opened my eyes in time to see a red flash shoot across space and chop the tentacle in half. *The Adversity* was free.

"Stars!" Sunjay said. "I think you burned my eyebrows off!"

I was exhausted. Sunjay grabbed me before I fell over. Tabitha scooped up my helmet, looked down the hallway, and hushed him.

"Tully, someone is coming. Get us out of here!" she said.

The red haze blurred my vision, but not enough to miss a tall, muscular shape with a glowing staff turning into the hallway. He had not noticed us yet, and we didn't need to give him the chance. I was still breathing heavily.

"Make a portal. Get us out!" whispered Sunjay.

"Never mind the portal," said Tabitha. "Helmets on. Now."

She shoved on my helmet. Without a moment's notice, Tabitha grabbed us both by the arm and threw us out the window! But it wasn't a window—there was no glass there at all—it was just a hole in the side of the ship. We were outside the ship in a moment, hanging onto a thin ledge.

The Ascendant warrior in the hallway approached. I could only see the top of his black staff and his purple eyes. We pressed ourselves tight against the ship. The warrior clicked the staff with each step, but when he made it to where we had been standing, the clicking stopped. We edged farther down the ship, looking for any handhold we could find. We could have launched ourselves on another spacejump, but if the warrior saw us, we were captured.

A few seconds passed. I peeked over the ledge to see if the warrior was still there. He was, but he was looking over our heads. He yelled something loudly in a deep voice. His staff started to glow purple, and the warrior sprinted down the hallway out of our view. *That was a close call,* I thought, looking at the others.

BOOOM!

It wasn't a sound but a vibration that almost knocked us off the side of the *Lion's Mane. Oh, no!* The tentacle whipped against the side of the ship a few feet from us. The second thud made me lose my grip. Sunjay grabbed my arm and pulled me back. Clearly it was time for us to move.

Now! I mouthed to them. *Jump.*

This time we all grasped hands and didn't let go. We pushed away from the side of the *Lion's Mane*…just in time. The tentacle smacked our takeoff point, leaving a dent. We would have been space junk if we waited a second longer.

It was probably the adrenaline, but we pushed off with a lot more force than last time. Our aim was great though. *The Adversity* was quickly approaching, and behind us we watched the tentacle flopping wildly, leaving dents in the side of the ship. *That should keep them busy for a while,* I thought, *and hopefully it won't knock us into the next solar system.* We were still well within its reach but somehow avoided a death swat. My breathing was under control, but the journey wasn't over. We needed a portal when we arrived. I collected myself and pictured the space lab inside the ship. I aimed for a spot just to the side of the orangutan cage. A portal began to emerge, and a thin red line extended from my hand, guiding us toward our target.

Moments later we tumbled into the space lab. This time the vines in the garden caught us, but we ended up in a pile nonetheless. I slid the portal shut.

"Everybody okay?" I said, removing my helmet.

All thumbs were up. Tabitha rubbed her hands across my forehead where my hair fell in sweaty tangles. "Tully, you look tired."

I was. The suit felt heavy, even with the ABA, but we had work to do. Buckshot floated forward, rubbing his neck. He had recovered his senses.

"Where's the Commander? Gimme a report."

"Dad's alive. He's going to blow up their ship. He sent me to release you."

"Can you do it now?"

It was a chore to lift my hands, but I calmed myself down and focused. Once again, the bars softened and began to bend, but a soft noise interrupted my efforts. A chill ran down my spine.

The hatch at the other end of the space lab opened. Slowly, methodically, a dark shape made its way into the light, stealing our hope with every inch it moved forward.

"Oh, no," said Tabitha. "Not those eyes."

DUELS AND DEALS

Lincoln Sawyer's blue eyes illuminated his face, a faint grin on his pale lips. He moved up the corridor toward us. On his left was the orangutan cage. On his right was the garden. He pushed past the vines and plants, past Owlbert and the mice, and stopped at the far end of the cage. In each hand was a black staff, both ends popping with purple electricity. The captives retreated to the back of the cage. They knew what those staffs could do. Sunjay, Tabitha, and I retreated to the back of the space lab. Sawyer clicked the staffs together.

"Well, children, what a surprise," he said, calm as usual. "Three of my captives are free. I didn't expect to see you outside the cage. And in spacesuits no less? Where have you been?"

"Space," I said. There was no hiding that information from him. His Android eyes could determine the temperature of our suits.

"Ah. I do not suppose you brought me the Harper Device, did you? Commander Trackman would be ever so pleased if I brought him the Device. He went to find your father and left me in charge of *The Adversity*."

"Congratulations," Tabitha said, "your mother would be so proud."

"I have no mother," said Sawyer, "just like someone else I know."

As tired as I was, that insult pumped me full of adrenaline. It seemed that Sawyer knew how to be just as cruel as Trackman or any of these Ascendant warriors.

"I thought you wanted to be more human," I told him.

"Yes, that is affirmative," he said.

"Then why did you betray us?" I asked. "Why are you fighting against us?"

"Humans treat each other like this all the time." He clicked the staff together and purple sparks flew. "Don't you know your own history? Look at all the wars you've fought, the crimes you commit, the lies you tell. Humans treat each other worse than I ever have. Yes, I do want to be more human. The Ascendant will help me do this."

"How are ruthless aliens going to make you more human?" Tabitha said. "You've lost your mind."

"Quite the contrary. Your mind is not developed enough to understand this situation, young woman. The Ascendant know much more of humanity than you do, and they can fulfill their promises. They promise to fight the war to end all wars. The war to bring a lasting peace to planet Earth."

I didn't like the sound of that at all.

"What are you talking about?"

"Don't you understand? The Ascendant are returning to Earth, and they will rule."

"You mean bringing war to Earth," I said. "To a place where they don't belong."

"Do they not? You think they are evil, but they simply want the greater good. More so than Earthlings. But no matter. The Ascendant will conquer you, and I will join them in their triumph. Only they need one thing before they start their war."

"The Harper Device!" yelled Sunjay.

"They have other names for it, and they understand its value."

Sawyer clicked the staffs together and tapped them on the ground. Then he pointed them in our direction. Jets of purple lightning crept toward us from the deadly weapons.

"You're not going to lock us in the cage again," I said, backing away from him.

"Correct. Commander Trackman gave me permission to punish those who cause problems. You already broke out of this perfectly good cage a number of times, so why should I trust that you will stay there? I suppose that you, my secret friend, have violated my trust for the last time."

Purple sparks flew through the air like mutant fireflies. He looked at me with that same knowing gaze I first saw months ago in Hangar Two. There was a new intensity to him.

"There's only one game left to play, Tully," he said. "It's called Fetch."

"Don't hurt them, Sawyer. They're just kids," yelled Buckshot. He reached through the bars, grabbing at the Android. "I swear if you hurt those kids…"

"No need for swearing, Buckshot. I won't harm a hair on their heads…" But quick as a whip, one of the staffs sparked. A blinding purple jet of sparks headed our way. Sawyer aimed for me but hit Sunjay, who was enveloped in a purple mist and flung toward Sawyer. The Android seized him by the hair. "Like I was saying, I won't harm a single hair on their heads, as long as Tully fetches the Harper Device for me."

"Let him go!" shouted Queen Envy, floating forward. "Take me instead."

"That's not how this game works," replied the Android. "Now, Tully, do as I ask."

"But I don't know—"

"Of course you know where the Device is. Do I need to explain this to you? This much is clear to me: the Device gave you some sort of power to escape the cage. You can almost assuredly sense its location. Now you retrieve the Device or I will break his arm." Sawyer ripped the sleeve off Sunjay's spacesuit and twisted Sunjay's arm behind his back. Tears welled in his eyes, but Sunjay didn't scream. "Funny, that should hurt more."

I was blind with rage and tired beyond belief. I had to do something. *There must be a way to delay him from destroying us. Ride the avalanche*, I thought, *ride the avalanche*. Sawyer twisted Sunjay's arm farther behind his back, but I held up a hand to stop him.

"You're right, Sawyer, I do know its location."

"Well, don't keep me waiting then. Where would that be?"

"Let's make you a deal," I said. "I will give you the location, but show me something. Prove to me that you want to be more human."

He looked at me with a cold smile. "Prove that I want to be more human?"

I looked at the two black staffs in his right hand and nodded.

"Oh, you propose a duel? I see. You do have a flair for the dramatic," he said. "If I win, I gain the location of the Harper Device. If you win, you can live for a few more hours. What a shame you have never used one of these black staffs before."

"I learned how to use a bo staff from a pretty good teacher, and I'm a quick learner."

"So you did, but I am afraid the only thing quick here will be your death, my secret friend."

Lightning covered Sunjay's ripped spacesuit again, and Sawyer flung him toward us. I pushed my friends behind me. This was now my fight, but I wanted their advice. Buckshot, Queen Envy, and Moreline shouted execrations at Sawyer, who waited calmly for our duel. I turned my back on him and faced my friends.

"Tully, you can't be serious," said Sunjay. "He'll crush you like a bug. Even in these suits we're still no match for him."

"I'm not going to fight him in this suit."

"What? That's insane?" said Sunjay, rubbing his wounded arm.

"It's crazy either way. The suit gives me strength, but it will slow me down. I have to be fast."

I pulled off the gloved to reveal my scarred hands.

"Tully, you look so tired," pleaded Tabitha. "Can't we find some other way?"

"We're done sneaking around and hiding from these guys. It's time to face them."

Sunjay patted me on the shoulder.

"He's stronger, faster, and smarter than you are. Good luck."

"Is that supposed to be a pep talk?" I asked, stripping off the rest of the spacesuit.

"I tried." Sunjay shrugged and looked at Tabitha.

"Sunjay is right. Sawyer has all the advantages," Tabitha explained. "But, Tully, that *is* your advantage. He doesn't know your powers."

"Well, I don't either," I said.

"Yes, you do. You just have to trust yourself. He knows what he can do. You can do things that none of us can imagine. I have faith. You can defeat him."

"That's what I meant," Sunjay jumped in. "Here's your pep talk. When you can't be anything else—"

"Be brave," I said. "That's better. Thanks."

I took one last look at my friends. Then, wearing only jeans and a t-shirt, I faced my enemy.

The Next Level

66**F**rom where I stand, this does not seem like a fair fight," said Sawyer. "This looks like three against one. Let me change that before we begin this duel. Tully, you might watch how I do this as well. Here is the push/pull maneuver—"

Sawyer flicked one of the staffs. A cloud of purple sparks flew out of the top of the staff and hit Sunjay. The shot knocked him across the lab into the vines, which were so thick no one could see him. He stayed in the vines and didn't reappear. Everyone shouted insults at Sawyer again, but he paid no attention.

Sawyer tossed a black staff toward me. The moment the staff hit my hand, I could feel its electrical current. Tendrils of purple lightning hissed at either end. The staff felt alive with energy, and it was so cold that my hand tingled. The hairs on my hand stood up, and my feet latched to the floor. It wasn't quite gravity but I could walk. I tightened my grip and tried to get used to standing instead of floating.

"Ah, and now we have two against one. Let me demonstrate the stun maneuver. This is a bit more difficult, but I will attempt it." Sawyer held his staff in both hands. A purple lightning ball appeared in front of him.

"TABITHA!" His voice was ear-splitting, louder than a human's. As he yelled her name, he lunged forward and made his eyes glow terribly bright.

We had been huddle closely together, but she jumped back at his sudden move, floating away from me.

"Tully, take us to the next level, please. Where you—" I wondered what she was talking about—*the next level?*—but she couldn't finish her sentence. The purple lightning ball zoomed past my head and froze her. Sawyer flicked his wrist and she floated toward him, finally pinned against the wall behind him.

"Oh, that worked wonderfully well," he said. "A grab and stun. Do not worry, she is fine for now. My, but you do love this one, do you not? Look at your face turn red. An emotional reaction indeed. I will offer you a chance to win back your trophy."

"She's not a trophy. She's my friend," I said, clicking the staff on the ground.

"As you say."

We faced off at either end of the orangutan cage.

"Round One," he said.

Sawyer wasted no time. He bowed toward me. Immediately he spun the staff over his head and charged. I hardly had time to react. His attacks were ferocious, each one creating a purple flash that sent me a few steps backward. It was all I could do to block and keep my balance. He retreated as quickly as he came, quicker than any human could.

"Not bad. I did not wish to kill you on my first pass. You can now attack me, if you wish. No need to be nervous. Whenever you are ready."

"I have permission to attack you?"

"Yes, please do."

"You're always so polite."

"Yes, I am."

Sawyer crouched and prepared for my attack, but I paused. The staff felt heavy and cold in my hands. Sweat popped up on my forehead. I looked at Tabitha frozen behind him. Only her eyes moved. She looked at the bars of the cage, like she wanted me to see something. What was it?

"Round Two," I said.

I unleashed an attack on the Android, aiming low at his legs. He was about a foot taller than me, so his legs were an easier target. If I could knock him off his feet, he wouldn't be able to use his speed against me. He would float in mid-air until he reached something to push off and fly at me again. It was a good idea. He saw my plan though. He blocked, blocked, and blocked again, never taking his feet off the ground. Purple sparks flew everywhere. Then he leaped. I missed him and hit the bars on the cage instead. There seemed to be a crack in the bars—*So that's what Tabitha meant! To hit the bars and free everyone,* I thought.

I didn't have time to hit the bars again though. I needed to watch Sawyer, and he didn't come down from his jump! Of course not. He hung on the ceiling above me like a vampire bat. His staff glowed and shot a purple flame toward me that burned my shirt. I put the flames out, dodged a few more flaming shots from the ceiling, and hid behind the glass containers in the middle of the room. Sawyer landed back in front of the cage and smiled.

"You didn't teach me that!" I yelled.

"Oh, the incinerator maneuver? I am under no obligation to teach you all the tricks, Tully. It appears you damaged the cage. Trying to free your friends? I may have to end you more quickly than I intended."

Now I understood why Trackman didn't want to play chess against the Android. He was one step ahead of me in everything. How could I possibly win?

"Round Three!"

With that, he leaped from the ground to the ceiling again. He stood there on the ceiling, upside down, and launched a few more shots at me. This time one of the shots hit me right in the chest. My lungs felt like they collapsed, and I expected to see fire consuming my body. Instead, my muscles froze. A stun shot. Sawyer leaped off the ceiling and landed in front of me like an eagle jumping onto a field mouse. He was toying with me now. *I won't be his toy. He doesn't get to kill me!* I concentrated all my thoughts. *Recover*, I said to myself. *Recover.*

"You only lasted three rounds. Well, it appears you owe me an answer. Where is the Device? I wish this had lasted a bit longer, but—"

"ROUND FOUR!" Sunjay burst from the vines.

He kicked Sawyer in the chest and tackled him, disconnecting him from the ground. They flew across the space lab.

Recover, I thought. *Recover.*

"Oh, this simply won't do," Sawyer said. He broke Sunjay's grasp and threw him across the room. Then he stunned Sunjay and pinned him against the far wall. Poor Sunjay. Sawyer had zapped him three times already, and he wasn't even supposed to be fighting the Android! Sunjay bought me just enough time. My body came back to life. I launched a stun at Sawyer, who had his back to me. The purple sparks hit him in the small of his back. Yes! For a moment he glowed purple, but the sparks disappeared. My stun shot had no effect on him at all. He grinned over his shoulder at me.

"You cheated. You should be frozen!" I yelled.

"So should you," he said. "Something is different about you, Tully. What secrets do you hide?"

He spun around, launching a dozen stun shots at me. I retreated and blocked each one, hiding behind anything I could find. I hid behind a storage box and Sawyer tossed it aside with his black staff, then shot a dozen more. I could feel my staff starting to heat up, like it was going to melt. If the staff broke, I was in trouble.

"You're all defense, Tully. You'll never win like that."

That's when it struck me. The black staff was *his* weapon—I had weapons of my own. I just needed to find a way to use them. I needed to calm down for a moment, and I couldn't do that with shots coming at me every two seconds. I looked at Tabitha. Once again she was looking somewhere—this time at the ceiling. No, the Hamster Wheel! If I could get Sawyer out of the space lab, we might have a better chance. I just had to get there without being blasted. Only one way to do that—I calmed down even as purple sparks flew all around me. The red mist covered everything. I could see what needed to be done. I just needed more speed. *Faster,* I told myself. *Faster.* Sawyer fired again, but suddenly I could dodge most of his shots. I blocked the rest. He cocked his head sideways, like a dog listening to a strange sound. He shot. I dodged again. We danced around the garden, him firing and me dodging.

"Tully, I understand now. The Harper Device gave you some of its power, but not near enough to defeat me. Let me demonstrate." He grabbed his staff with both hands and lifted up. Glass shattered. Plants were uprooted. The space lab vibrated, and Sawyer's staff flashed. Everything that stood between us flew toward the ceiling. It was my chance! I used the garden as cover and leaped toward the ceiling. Purple balls of flame exploded all around me, blowing shards of glass and soil at me from all angles. Before he landed a shot, I reached out my hand and created a portal that took me into the Hamster Wheel. I closed it quickly. Sawyer would have to use the hatch, which would give me a moment to prepare. I ran to the other side of the Hamster Wheel, getting as far from the entry hatch as possible. We wouldn't be able to see each other because of the curve of the room.

Moments later I heard the hatch open. Sawyer made his presence known. He shot a few stun shots that bounced off the walls and landed near me. The red mist was still with me though. The shots seemed slow compared to moments ago.

"This is Round Five," I said. "You didn't expect me to get this far."

"You do have nerve, and now you have something more. Shall I explain?"

"Sure," I said. If it bought me more time, anything was fine.

"It was the morning I found you with the Harper Device. I came down to the Space Lab to bring you to this very room for exercise. Between training you and feeding you, I had gained your trust. That morning you weren't in your cage though.

"I looked across the room and saw the Harper Device had grown to three times its normal size, and inside it I sensed a lifeform. You. The Device must have sensed my presence because it cast you out immediately, as if it wanted to keep a secret of its own. I don't know if you could have survived any more exposure to it anyway."

"So you think you saved me from the Device?"

"Of course. The Device intended to kill you, but instead the exposure gave you some of its power. Tully, this could change everything." He shot a few more stun shots my way. I backed away from his voice, hoping to keep him out of sight on the other side of the Hamster Wheel.

"Like what?" I asked.

"Your powers would give you standing among the Ascendant. If you had shown them to the Ascendant Lord, he would have freed you right then. They would award you with Exceptional Status. When they return to Earth, they will reward those with special abilities. Your powers would make you useful. They might even spare Sunjay and Tabitha in return for your loyalty."

I hadn't thought of that. With my powers, the Ascendant might make me an offer to live. I wouldn't have to fight Sawyer to the death. I could probably find some sort of place among them. But it was a deal with the Devil. I knew that. If I had to betray the world to survive, I didn't want to survive. Then again, maybe survival was all we could hope for now.

"If I reveal the Device and put down my weapon you'll let us live?"

"Yes. You have my word."

"And if I don't?"

As an answer, a giant purple fireball roared around the corner. A massive incinerator shot. I jumped into the air to avoid the heat and found a familiar landing spot—the basketball hoop. The last time I stood there Sawyer swept my feet and knocked the air out of my lungs.

Another fireball rounded the corner. It singed my jeans, and I beat out the fire with my hands. The moment I touched the flame, the red mist returned to my mind and an idea formed in my head: *he's shooting from one direction. He'll come from the other.* By the time I turned around, he already had his staff in the air.

"Where is the Device? We made a deal." He aimed his staff at me. I could feel the hairs on my arm stand up.

"You were right about a few things, Sawyer. You're stronger and faster than I am. I never had a chance. You were also right about something else—my powers are useful. But I'm not Gallant Trackman. I won't use my powers against my own people."

He didn't hesitate. He launched an enormous purple ball of flame toward me. But I was ready for his move. I threw my black staff in the way of his shot. The staff exploded on impact, an explosion that blew us away from each other. I carved another portal and was in the space lab before he could react.

Everyone watched as I flew through the ceiling and landed beside the cage. Sawyer would be right behind me with his staff set to kill, like an avalanche that would be upon me any second. I said a quick prayer and focused on what I needed to do.

Sure enough, Sawyer came right behind me. He was cautious though. He came through the hatch and stayed on the ceiling, his staff loaded for another shot.

"You fought valiantly, boy, but you are unarmed now. So we made a deal. Tell me the location of the Harper Device."

"I can do better than that. I can show you. Just unfreeze my friends. Then follow me."

"So be it. Gather beside the cage." Sawyer turned off his staff. The purple glow around Tabitha disappeared. Her scarf, which had been black as midnight, turned a bright red. She slowly regained her senses.

"Sunjay always has a map for the next level. Right, Tully?" She floated toward me and held on to my arm to steady herself. Sunjay came from the other direction.

"I don't have—"

"Tully must have it then. He must," she said, yanking my sleeve. *The next level? What was she saying? What was she*—then it struck me. I knew exactly what to do.

Sawyer's gravity disappeared. He drifted in our direction.

"Where is this next level?" he asked, slowly floating toward us as we gathered beside the cage.

"I forgot the map, but I can still find it," I said. "It's you who forgot something."

"That's impossible," he said, laughing. "I have unlimited memory."

"Really? Which rule did you teach me first?"

"Rule #1, of course. *Never let your guard down.*"

"Exactly," I asked.

Sawyer was almost upon us when I sprung my trap. *Find the next level,* I thought, *the next level.* I pushed Tabitha and Sunjay nearer to the cage. Sawyer shook his head. He thought I was just dodging him for no reason. But I wasn't.

The next level. I set aside everything else and focused my attention on the interior of the *Lion's Mane.* With some effort, my mind penetrated the ship's walls. *There are no walls, no walls,* and with that they seemed to melt away. I saw the skeleton of the ship and everything on board—rooms full of Ascendants with black staffs and cold faces; hangars crammed with all sort of weapons and smaller spacecraft. I found my dad working his way through the ship, probably trying to plant his bomb. I didn't have time to follow him though. I had to find another room.

The search continued until I found what I was looking for—a black lit room with three thrones. In the middle of the room sat the Ascendant Lord, his face swimming with strange images and his mind full of rage. He leaned forward onto a black staff, barking orders left and right. His black braid of hair flew back and forth. Trackman stood at his side, looking angry and nervous. The Device was still missing.

I opened my eyes. In my mind the trip had taken hours, but only seconds had passed. Nevertheless, Sawyer was about to land, but right at his landing spot a red circle appeared. He saw it, as did everyone else in the space lab.

"What is this? Tully, this is an impossibility." The red circle widened and turned into a portal to the throne room. Of course, this worked both ways. Everyone on the *Lion's Mane* could see through the portal on their end, too—me with outstretched hands, Sawyer floating toward them.

"But it's the *Lion's Mane*," said Sawyer. "Wait, I understand. Unbelievable, you've created an interspace portal between the two ships. But where is the Device? You must be using it."

Sawyer floated toward the portal. Our side had no gravity. The other side did. The captain stopped shouting when he noticed the portal. He advanced toward us, as did a few other warriors. Trackman looked relieved. "Well, greetings, *Adversity.* This is a bit surprising but convenient. Did you find the Device, Sawyer?"

"No, it's the boy," he said. He was now only a few feet from the portal. "I don't know how he's doing this."

Sawyer looked at me with a question on his face. It was a question he never got to ask.

It was time to launch my trap. My hands glowed red again as Sawyer was about to touch down. He gasped in shock. It was the most human noise he ever made. No longer did he see his friends on the command deck. Instead, the portal opened into the cold void of space.

Sawyer turned back to me. "No!" he said. "Stop me! Stop me! I can't stop myself!" He was right. He swung his limbs wildly trying to grab at anything that could stop him. I widened the portal until it filled the half of the wall.

Tabitha and Sunjay edged away from him toward the orangutan cage. We all watched Sawyer pass within inches of us on his way to outer space. He wrenched his head around to see me and kept flailing for a moment. There was nothing he could do. Before long, his limbs stopped moving. The cold of space turned him to stone. His bright blue eyes stayed fixed on me until, at last, their light ran out. He was lost in an endless canvas of stars.

Fatigue finally caught up with me. I was breathing fast and my hair was soaked with sweat. All that was left was to close the portal. My hands trembled as I pushed the portal. *Close,* I thought, *close, close.*

The portal began to shrink, but it didn't close. It was like trying to shut a door that had flown open in a hurricane. My hands struggled and the lightning flowers shimmered with power, but the portal wouldn't budge. Suddenly a horrible image reappeared in my mind—the *Lion's Mane's* command deck. Nothing could make the image disappear. I lost focus. The portal swung free of my control and through it reached a familiar hand with a deadly golden ring.

Trackman.

He grabbed the first person he could touch.

Tabitha.

"No!" I gasped. "No!"

It happened so fast we had no time to react. Sunjay grabbed one of her arms and Trackman held the other. I reached for her as well, but a black staff emerged from the portal and knocked me back across the lab. Now it was Sunjay and Tabitha fighting Trackman, but the staff knocked Sunjay back. Tabitha was through the portal in a moment, Trackman's signet ring pointed at her neck. He sucked air through his teeth and pointed toward me.

"Check mate again, Tully," he said. "The Conspiracy Game is over now. You can open all the portals you want, but you can't fight the entire Ascendant army. I'd like to see you try." Trackman put his other hand on the edge of the portal. He was about to come through and retake the ship.

"Tully, my song!" said Tabitha.

"Not the right time for showtunes, girl," Trackman said, laughing at her.

But I remembered the lyrics she sang in my dream: "The hand that opened the door/Will have to let it close." Trackman held the ring closer to her neck. I hadn't been able to save her in my dream, and I wouldn't be able to now. A terrible choice was in my hands: to give us all up or to let her go. We both knew what I had to do.

Close the portal.

"Tully, I trust you!" yelled Tabitha. "It's always been in your hands!"

Energy streamed into me from somewhere. I could feel it, like a river of fire running through my veins. I took one last look at Tabitha's lovely green eyes and raised my hands. The river of fire rushed into them. The lightning flowers became a blinding white light surrounded by red flame. The light and heat caught everyone off guard. Trackman was closest, and Tabitha took cover behind him. The sleeve of his jumpsuit burst into flame. With a scream, he tried to put out the fire with his hands. With one huge push the portal expanded, glowed red again, and then slammed shut. The river of fire was gone, and with it every last ounce of my energy. I started to black out.

At that moment, *The Adversity* was rocked by several explosions—more like shockwaves that knocked us all against the side of the ship. I heard Buckshot yelling orders, Sunjay grabbing my arm, and Queen Envy screaming. The noise and shouting around me faded into a red mist. The last thing I remember was a strange vision—I saw half of Tabitha's lucky scarf floating in mid-air, and near it was Gallant Trackman's burned hand, reaching for me with that deadly ring on his finger.

LOST AND FOUND

I was in a dream, a beautiful dream. I laid under a tall, green tree in my jeans and favorite t-shirt. Fields of purple flowers stretched across the hills near me. A small stream gurgled beside the tree, its green leaves rustling gently in the wind. I propped myself on one arm. In the distance loomed beautiful towers of purple and black. Someone was stroking my hair. I expected to look up and see Tabitha, but it wasn't her. The freckles on her cheeks, that black hair brushing across my face. I hadn't dreamed of her in years, but those soft grey eyes belonged to only one person. My mom.

She whispered, "Look at you, all grown up. The man I hoped you would become."

She pointed across the fields. Miles away from us stood the towers. On top of one I saw a girl. Yes, there was Tabitha, standing by herself, scanning the horizon for something or someone. I wanted to jump up and shout to tell her I was coming, but she was so far away. My mother kept stroking my hair. "Shhh, rest. You don't have the strength. There will be time for that. Each day has enough trouble of its own."

"She needs me now."

"And she will need you later, and you will need her."

"When?"

"Be patient. Do as your father says."

"But he's gone."

"He's never gone, neither is Tabitha, neither am I. Tully, you passed through fire once. You must pass through fire again to find her."

I wanted to hear more, but the purple flowers, the tree, the towers, they all faded into a red mist. A familiar beep sounded in the background.

When I woke up, someone was stroking my hair. I opened my eyes, hoping to see Tabitha, expecting my mom, but the kind eyes of Sylvia Moreline met mine instead.

"Hello, Tully. You're in the infirmary. Don't say anything just right now. Just rest for a minute. Just rest."

She gave me a sip of water and another, but I could hardly hold up my hand without feeling dizzy. I drifted in and out of my dream world. Each time I was by the stream with my mother and Tabitha stood in the tower. I didn't want the dream to end. I wanted to clamber over those purple hills and break down those purple towers, but I didn't have the strength. Finally the dreams ended. I opened my eyes and saw Queen Envy beside me. The infirmary bed wrapped itself around me and tried to keep me still.

"Dad and Tabitha, where are they?"

My mind was still numb, my body ached. The bed fought to keep me in place but I pushed myself free. I felt faint but had to get up.

"Baby Bear, you're supposed to stay here. We're about to leave for Earth." I pushed myself off the bed. My shoulder felt numb and my head ached. She put a hand on my shoulder to keep me in place.

"Help me to the Flight Deck," I said. "We can't leave. Tabitha and dad, they're on the other ship. We can't leave."

"Tully, that black ship is gone. It just started spinning and smoking, and that purple thing flapped everywhere. Then it flew away. I'm sorry."

"The *Lion's Mane* can't be gone. Tabitha and dad are still on board."

"Honey, you gotta be brave now. The ship is gone. We are on our way back to Earth."

"Okay, and I'm on my way to the Flight Deck. You can help me or not."

I couldn't believe what she said. I had to see it. Queen Envy helped me down the magnetic walkway. My legs hardly moved, and my mind didn't work much better.

When we arrived on the Flight Deck, Buckshot had just powered the thrusters and set a course for Earth. The *Lion's Mane* was nowhere in sight but it had left behind the comet shell, now split into two pieces. We coasted between the two halves of the enormous shell. In the distance a chunk of the purple spacebridge floated like driftwood down a river. The 3D model showed the scene as well. Buckshot turned toward me once he punched in the last coordinate.

"Tully, there's just nothin' for it," he said. "The *Lion's Mane* disembarked. Your dad did just enough damage to cause them to retreat. He saved our lives."

"But we couldn't save his," I said. "Or Tabitha's."

"We don't know that, Tully."

"But I could've saved him. I could've saved her. I just..."

"...You saved us, and your father kept the Ascendant from getting the Device," he said. "No one could have done more."

✳ ✳ ✳

He was right. I did everything I could, and it wasn't enough. I bought my dad some time to save us but not enough to save himself. I defeated the Android but lost Tabitha. I tried to ride the avalanche. Somehow I survived, but everyone I loved was missing under layers of cold snow.

Snow. The 3D model of the "dirty snowball" still blinked away in the center of the room. I looked at it as Buckshot worked. So much had happened since we first encountered that dirty snowball. I knew Trackman and Sawyer were playing The Conspiracy Game, but I had no idea how big that game really was. Sometimes you don't see how bad things are going to get, and then suddenly they are upon you. You can only hope that you'll have some friends to rely on.

Moreline reached to switch off the 3D model of the snowball. She must have seen me staring at it miserably, but before she switched off the model, I grabbed her hand. Something on the surface of the 3D model caught my eye. A tiny red dot drifted along the edge of the shell.

What is that? My heart leaped. *It couldn't be!* I closed my eyes and tried to use my Red Vision to see it, but dizziness stopped me. I was just too tired to see anything but what was right in front of me.

"Wait," I said. "Buckshot, wait."

He didn't turn toward me. "Thrusters are a go, Tully. We need to go. I'm sorry."

"Just look." I pointed to the model. "We can't leave without the Device. I know where my dad hid it."

"You do?"

We looked at the surface of the 3D model together. The red dot drifted and grew brighter.

"Well, I'll be derned," said Buckshot. "DORIS, thrusters full right, turn back 180 degrees."

The Adversity wheeled around. We watched the edge of the snowball for any sign of the Device. There was no glow at first, only a white and grey wasteland. We waited to see the dim glow of the Harper Device floating somewhere in space. That's not what we saw though.

"The Cerberus!" yelled Sunjay, entering the room from below.

We saw the beat-up remains of the small spacecraft. It crept toward us like a wounded animal. From inside the vehicle came a familiar glow. In the dim light I could just make out the Device…and a pilot.

Buckshot let out a hoot that scared us all to death.

"Oooooh-weee! Son of a gun! Will you look at that! There's your Harper Device. And there's your Harper!"

Sure enough, on one side of the ship the Harper Device faintly glowed, and in the middle, piloting the Cerberus, was my dad.

THE WAY HOME

"**Y**ou mean the Ascendant had the Device on board their ship and didn't even realize it?" asked Sunjay.

"It was right under their noses."

After a trip to the infirmary and an ultrasonic shower, my dad met us on the Observation Deck to debrief about his experience.

He had not destroyed the *Lion's Mane*, but he did some serious damage to the ship. After we set him free, he searched until he found the ship's enormous hangar, filled with well-armed, smaller spacecraft. There was the Cerberus. Two Ascendant were examining it. Just as they discovered that the Device was on board, my dad crept behind them, knocked out one, fought the second, and won. The Cerberus was full of mining equipment, including small explosives, which he attached to a large fuel tank of some kind in the hangar. *That must have been the explosion we felt in the space lab,* I thought. He then piloted the Cerberus through one of the escape hatches and hid the Harper Device elsewhere.

"I knew Trackman and the Ascendant would search every inch of both ships for the Device, so I opted for a new hiding place—The Lion Mane's shell. But the Cerberus was too damaged to return to *The Adversity.* Still, I couldn't come back. It was in our best interest—and the best interest of the world," he said.

"Tully found the Device," said Buckshot, stretching his bruised ribs. "The boy convinced me to turn this ship around. You'd have froze out there if your boy hadn't looked at that model." My dad grinned and tousled my hair. At long last, I had done what I came to do.

Of course, "feeling good" didn't feel great. After his story ended, everyone asked about our adventure, too—escaping the cage, identifying the traitors, outsmarting Trackman, creating portals, and on and on. They peppered us with questions. When we got to the part about the battle in the space lab, it caught in my throat. I could only picture those that weren't with us anymore—all four of them. Two people I never wanted to see again, one person who didn't deserve to die, and one that I could never replace. Eventually my dad said, "Why don't we leave Tully to his thoughts for a while? He's been through enough." He was right.

I had a lump in my throat that wouldn't go away. That night Sunjay decided to sleep in the orangutan cage with me. When I closed my eyes, I could still see Tabitha reaching out to me, telling me to close the portal. The scene replayed a hundred times in my mind—if I had been faster or stronger, I could have closed the portal while she was still on our side. She would still have been with us. I couldn't sleep, so I let myself out of the cage and decided to wander through the ship alone. Before I was out of the space lab, I felt a tug on my sleeve.

"Hey," said Sunjay, sticking right by my side.

That night Sunjay and I visited Redshirt's room. It was almost exactly like my dad's. There was a quote on the wall: *A noble man makes noble plans, and by noble deeds he stands.* We looked at his family picture for a while—one of those beach photos where everyone is wearing khakis pants and white shirts with a perfect sunset in the background.

"We could have saved him," I said. Sunjay looked at me and shook his head.

"No, Tully. We would *never* have figured out the plot without him. It's not your fault."

"I guess not."

"No, it's not, Tully. You did everything you knew how to do."

"And Tabitha? What about her, Sunjay? I could've saved her if only—"

He grabbed my arm and stopped me.

"Tully, didn't you hear what your dad said earlier? He didn't come back to the ship because it was in everyone's best interest. Well, Tabitha did the same thing. She *wanted* you to close that portal, and you *had to* close it. What if you hadn't? It gives me shivers just thinking about the Ascendant coming on board and, and taking over *The Adversity*, and then what? Returning to Earth to make us slaves?"

"Yeah, I guess you're right."

"I know I'm right, Tully. Don't you get it? You did exactly what your daddy would have done, and he's my hero."

I tried to let that sink in. We returned to the orangutan cage and slept.

✳ ✳ ✳

A Red Vision interrupted my sleep. In the Vision, I stood in the middle of an ice-covered plain. The terrain wasn't familiar, but in the distance I saw those enormous purple towers. I walked toward them. Everything glowed with a strange purple light. *It's the Ascendant's planet,* I realized. The icy plain stretched for miles. There were enormous cracks in the ice, which groaned, squeaked, and shifted beneath my feet. I had a feeling this place was once full of life. Something was wrong. Nothing could live here now.

Something sprouted from the ice in front of me—first it looked like four enormous snakes were leaping from the ground, but then a fifth shorter one emerged, too. *A hand,* I realized, and on one finger a gold ring—the ring of Gallant Trackman. The hand towered above me, and with a menacing gesture, pointed one finger toward the sky. I looked up and saw a star in the distance, and beside it a faint, blue speck. *Where are we?* I wondered. *This must be our solar system.* The hand seemed to feel my presence though. The hand became a fist and tried to swat me like a fly. I barely dodged that giant fist, which crashed into the ground behind me and shattered into icy chunks.

I continued on toward the towers. Getting closer, I could see a figure on the parapet. She held a ribbon in her hand. No, a scarf. "Tabitha!" I shouted. Just as I began to run toward her, a black staff grew out of the ground, its purple head buzzing with energy. Then another and another. They formed a barrier and wouldn't let me pass. I couldn't create a portal. High on her tower I could see Tabitha searching the horizon. The vision faded into darkness. I tried to remember all the detail of the landscape—the icy plain, the seven high towers. Was there a city below them? Had I heard people cheering in the background? It was hard to say.

The next Vision was the first hopeful scene I had seen in a while. I found myself back in Houston. It was spring and bells were ringing in a church tower. Everyone I knew—from Aunt Selma to Dr. Vindler and my classmates—sat in the churchyard at an outdoor wedding. Tabitha was missing though.

At the front I could see a bride. Beside her, a groom. Their backs were to me, but I could see the groom's hair: a red streak went through the center. *My dad's getting married?* I jumped out of my seat and ran toward the front. The groom began to turn toward his bride, but before he could lift her white veil, the Red Vision dissolved into nothing and left me wondering what the future held for us all. There might be some happy ending waiting for us, but it was a long way away.

All these Visions drifted through my mind when I awoke. I looked out the skylight at the Earth growing closer by the hour. Sunjay stirred, and for the next few hours, we stargazed together.

FOOTPRINTS

"I brought you something," I told my dad the next morning, floating up beside him on the Observation Deck. He ran his hand down the red stripe in his hair and looked at the Moon behind us. We were nearly home.

"I have a gift for you first," he said, reaching into a pocket of his blue jumpsuit. It was a piece of dingy gray cloth the length of my arm. One end had fringe. The other end was blackened but trimmed, like a hot blade had cut it. I had no idea why he brought me the old scrap of cloth until I touched it. At that moment the cloth sprung to life with color—purple and black began to swirl around the cloth, mixed with an occasional bright red flash.

"How did you get this? Where is the other half?" I asked, but the answer came back to me. I pictured the portal in the space lab—the Ascendant Lord holding Tabitha, Trackman preparing to climb through the portal, Tabitha's scarf positioned between the two sides. When I closed the portal, her scarf was severed. Maybe she held the other half even now, locked away in a cell on the *Lion's Mane*. I tied the scarf around my right arm and watched it radiate with color.

Then I remembered the rest of that scene. The terrible sounds. The chaos. But something else had frightened me before I blacked out. *Maybe*

I was hallucinating, I thought. There had been a horrible thing floating beside the scarf in the space lab that day. *No, it was as real as the scarf.*

"Dad, what else happened when the portal closed? I remember seeing something else. Did Trackman lose—"?

"Yes, I wasn't there to see it, but you took Gallant Trackman's hand when you closed the portal," my dad explained, staring into space.

"Like he needs more reasons to hate me."

"He sure doesn't. Neither do The Ascendant. They lost the Device and their ship was nearly destroyed. I lost a good man. They captured your friend. There are a lot of scores to settle here."

"I don't care about scores. We've got to save Tabitha."

"You're right." He turned toward me. "That's one thing I promise you: no matter what comes next, we'll find Tabitha. We're not going to lose another..." His voice trailed off and eyes flashed red with old memories. "She's as much my responsibility as yours. First, we must prepare. The Ascendant will come first for you and the Device, and then for the world."

"Why me? You're the one that blew up their ship."

"I crippled it. That makes me a threat," he said, "but you're the danger. You can use the Device in ways they didn't expect."

"Or it can use me."

"Either way, you can wield a terrible weapon. Who knows what they could do with it—or you? I don't want to find out. So I've warned the Alliance about the Ascendant. Every government on Earth went on high alert when they heard me say 'hostile alien invasion.'"

It made my hair stand on end. I hated the thought of seeing one black ship floating in space. How many would they bring to Earth?

"Did you tell anyone about me?"

"No. I told them that the Device is lost."

"You lied. Why?"

"Because the Ascendant aren't the only danger. The world will prepare for war, and they'll want to use every weapon they have. They would want to use the Harper Device."

"Well, what's wrong with that?"

He took my hand and looked at the scars. "Do you think a weapon that powerful is safe in anyone's hands? Maybe it would help us defeat the Ascendant, but it could also destroy us all. So we will keep these things secret for now."

I can keep secrets, I thought, handing him my unofficial account of what happened. He read over the first few pages.

"A 'misguided youth,' huh? That's what Sawyer called you. You look like you've got good direction to me."

"You think so?"

"Definitely," he said. "You might need some guidance, but that's different than needing direction."

"He also told me I had a lot of nerve."

"Well, that's true, too," he said. Then he pursed his lips. "This account isn't final yet. There's one thing you haven't written."

"I wrote everything. The whole truth. What's missing?"

"I haven't completed my personal objective. It was something that needed to be done, but I could never do the job, no matter how hard I tried. Now I know why. I have a few requests before we return to Earth."

"What requests?" I said. My heart started to pound. *What more could I do?*

"First, you can't use your powers when we return to Earth. I know you'll want to. You'll want to try to locate Tabitha. You'll want to practice," he said.

Why hadn't I thought of that? I could keep looking for her in the Red Visions, I thought.

"I need to practice," I said. "The Ascendant will come for me first, like you said. I'll need to fight them."

"But I forbid you from using your powers," he commanded. "They could create chaos just like the Device."

When did he decide all of this? I wanted to yell it out loud, but I just listened.

"And the second request?"

"Second, before we land, I need you to put the Harper Device to sleep."

I rolled my eyes at that. "I don't even know what that means. It's not awake. And when did you become an expert on my powers?"

"I'm not."

"It sure sounds like you are."

He rubbed his hand along the red streak in his hair and floated over to the bay window. He took out his pen, clicked it three times, and let it spin in mid-air. "You remember when I discovered the Harper Device. Those images of me standing in the crater? I was standing in the light and the Device was in the shadow. There was one thing that no one noticed. I still can't believe it."

I imagined the crater, the Device, and my dad with a helmet in his hand. It was an impossible scene, but it was simple. There was nothing to miss. He stroked the red streak in his hair again. "I wish I had understood them then. It was all too baffling, and I only saw them once—those strange dreams of exploring space with you, of strange objects on the far side of the Moon. I returned home and forgot about those dreams—until the day you boarded my ship. Then it all started to make sense. When the portal in my cell appeared and you tumbled through it, everything came together. Still, I can't believe no one noticed."

He turned toward me with a red glint in his eyes.

"You're talking like Tabitha. What didn't we notice?"

"My footprints in the crater, Tully. My footprints led up to the Device, but there wasn't a set of footprints leading back to where I was standing. That's because I didn't walk back into the light—I was thrown there," he said, rubbing his hand along his hair again. Then I began to understand—the streak in his hair, the glint in his eyes, why he didn't seemed surprised by our space jump or my powers.

"But you're saying—"

"—You're not the only one who has seen a Red Vision. The Device gave me none of its power, but I have seen things in dreams."

Every hair on my body stood on end as I realized the truth of it. My heart was in my throat.

"So, so you knew—"

"I knew enough. The mission was in some sort of danger, but I wasn't sure how bad," he said. "I knew that Scrubbles' manager was upset for a good reason. There wasn't really an orangutan on board. And I knew that we needed that boy in the cage."

"Why?"

"Because part of this mission was in your hands."

He trusts me more than I ever imagined. It made me feel like a whole person all over again, like when I had come clean with Tabitha.

My lost friend.

"We have to save Tabitha," I said. "Promise me."

"I already did, but I will again. Now will you help me finish my objective?"

"It's the Beginning Again..."

The space lab was empty and in shambles when I arrived. I had been too tired to notice until then, but Sawyer had destroyed the garden in our battle. Chunks of dirt and plants were suspended throughout the lab, making it difficult (and disgusting) to enter. Owlbert was in the middle of the lab, flapping his wings and looking confused. I plucked him out of the air and placed him on the bars of my cage. He turned his head toward me and hooted, thankful to have his talons on a solid perch. My attention turned toward the Device, back home in its spacious room.

I didn't really have a plan, only that it must be put to sleep. I adjusted the scarf on my arm, punched in the access code, and entered the room. It seemed like months ago that the Device had drawn me toward this room, along with every living thing in the space lab. Entering the room this time I felt the opposite effect. The Device seemed to hold me at a distance. I tried to float toward the swirling red globe, but I found myself pressed back to the glass door. Behind me I heard something that sounded like rain. Turning around I saw all the soil, the plants, everything in the lab that had been suspended in mid-air was now pinned against the other side of the lab. This wasn't going to be easy. I set my mind on moving forward, putting my hands in front of me, reaching for the Device. The lightning flowers began to glow, and I drew the Device toward myself. It was a strange feeling. I didn't feel like the Device was moving. Instead, the entire ship seemed to move sideways so that I could reach the Device. As my fingertips reached the mist, my hands went cold and disappeared, as did my wrists, then my arms, and then all I saw was red.

Red, red, red, red, red.

I was buried in a Red Vision. It looked like a red fog bank, and I emerged from it into a small garden. There was a stone bench in the middle. A trellis lined with flowers arched over the bench. From the far side of the garden a figure came into view. More like materialized. The form seemed human but remained cloaked in mist as it walked toward me. Red mist streamed onto its shoulders like hair flowing in the wind. It sat down on the bench and motioned for me to do the same. I couldn't tell if it was man, woman, or something else. The being spoke in a soft voice.

"You came and did not delay."

"It was you who spoke to me in my bedroom," I said, sitting on the bench.

"Of course. Are you young now, Tully?"

"Yeah, pretty young. Where are we?" The words felt strange on my tongue, even though I understood them. *Are we speaking some other language? This creature seems to know me, like we're old friends.*

"Ah, it's confusing to you," said the being. "Yes, young you are indeed. It's the beginning again…before the Chaos. Sometimes I can't tell. We are in my garden."

"It was you who drew me into the Device."

"The Device? That's no way to refer to an old friend," it said. *Was there a smile on its lips?* A thousand questions popped into my mind.

"Who are you?"

"I have many names—some will never be spoken again. Some should never have been used."

"Names like the Sacred? That's what the Ascendant call you. Trackman said that." The being nodded, and mist cascaded onto the bench. "So who are the Ascendant?"

"I cannot say. They must speak for themselves, but do not hate them. Fight them, but do not hate."

"Why did you cause problems on Earth?"

"I didn't. It's just the way some things respond to me. I upset them. Sometimes things are so wrong that they must be remade to be made right. It is my nature to realign things, to make them right. "

"Did you 'realign' me?"

"No. I met you, and we left an impression on each other. Everyone leaves some sort of impression, for good or bad. To meet me means to leave space and time, and that leaves a deep impression, doesn't it? You have seen this—glimpses of ever-presence—your Red Visions."

I held up my hand and observed the lightning flowers. "So this is part of the impression you left on me?"

"Yes, it is. My power, but you had to endure pain to receive it. You will have to endure more. I wish it were not that way, but my wishes hardly matter."

"What did the last Vision mean?"

"Of the purple desert? Of your mother, Tabitha, the wedding? You know me better than this by now, Tully. What if I answered all your questions and left you with nothing to discover? Far be it from me! I will not steal your future like that. I am no thief. I am a gift and a giver. But come now. You haven't traveled all this way to quiz me on things you can uncover on your own. What do you really seek?"

A million questions ran through my mind. I wanted the being to explain everything to me, but none of the answers seemed to help me learn anything new. *At that time*, I reminded myself. All those Visions had helped me uncover Trackman's conspiracy, but I had to put the pieces together myself. *What's most important?* I asked myself, and that was the key to understanding the Harper Device.

"I seek wisdom," I said.

"Ah, now we are getting somewhere." The being leaned forward and rested its arms on its legs.

"My father told me to put you to sleep," I explained.

The mist cascaded off its head and covered the ground. We both remained silent for a while.

"And for once, you chose to listen to him," it said.

"But now I'm worried. If you sleep, what will happen? I don't want to lose the Red Visions or give up my power."

"Some people will do anything for power when they would be happier if they gave it away. Look at Gallant Trackman, so power-hungry that he would sell his entire world into slavery. He lost himself in his quest for power, you see. Don't lose yourself like that, Tully. Don't be afraid to lose what you can't keep. Power is temporary. Don't let it define you. It's only good if you can give it away and remain a whole person."

"But I can help the world."

"You already have. Tully, I can't tell you what to do. I can only say this: it is right for you to seek wisdom. It is right for you to choose. Your choices will define you in the age to come, and I won't steal your choices from you."

The figure walked into the middle of the garden. It knelt and wrote in the dirt while I thought about my choice. Finally, I spoke.

"If we are in need and I call on you—"

"I will try to awaken before you descend upon the Chaos. In the meantime, love your friends, your family, fight for your world. And do not hate the Ascendant—they are more like you than you know."

Tabitha's scarf unraveled from my arm and floated through the air. The figure held it as a scroll, then reached down into the mist, rubbing some red dirt on the scarf.

"Chaos awaits you," said the figure, tying the scarf onto my arm, "but do not fear. You will pass through ice and shadow before you see her again, but see her you will. Now I must prepare to rest." The figure stood to leave. I could almost make out a face beneath the mist, staring down at me. "May the universe rise to meet you, my young friend. It is always good to see you. It always will be."

The figure returned to the red mist and left me to reflect on those words. Then the mist surrounded me, and before I knew it I was in the space lab again, my scarred hands stretched out toward the Device.

I turned and looked behind me. The entire space lab had somehow been cleaned—the plants were replanted in their soil, Owlbert and the mice were back in their cages. Everything was restored to its right place.

I knew what I had to do. I turned back toward the Device and felt my hands getting colder, glowing with a blue fire. I ran my finger along the singed edge of Tabitha's scarf and tightened it on my arm. The scarf turned a deep blue. The Device began to dim from red to green to blue to gray, spinning more slowly with each rotation. The mist stopped flowing. Before the spinning stopped, I heard a faint whisper, "When you descend upon the Chaos, bring order. You were made to make things new."

That's exactly what I wanted to do, but I had to prepare for the Ascendant first. And figure out what the Chaos was. Apparently both of them were coming for me. *Soon*, I thought. *Very soon.*

✳ ✳ ✳

Thus ends The Conspiracy Game...and begins the Tully Harper Series, which will continue with....

...The Rathmore Chaos.

"Chaos awaits you, but do not fear. You will pass through ice and shadow before you see her again, but see her you will."

Where have the Ascendant taken Tabitha Tirelli?

The Conspiracy Game is a thriller that, in the end, scrapes the surface of a solar system on the brink of unexpected war. The Harper Device reveals some of its power and wisdom to Tully, which he will need on his descent into the Chaos.

Book Two, *The Rathmore Chaos*, sends Tully on a sweeping adventure: to discover the Ascendant homeworld to save a friend. Some of the heroes and villains you met in this book will reappear. Gallant Trackman will return—well, most of him. **The Rathmore Chaos** is set for release in 2015.

At least one other book will follow before this series is complete.

In the meantime, clever readers can predict Tully's destination if they search for Chaos in a faraway place. If they'd like to know more about the Ascendant, they need only think about that peculiar name. Until next time, may the Universe rise up to meet them.

-Adam

ABOUT THE AUTHOR

Adam Holt grew up in Friendswood, Texas, near the Johnson Space Center, where his father worked. He attended Baylor University for his undergrad and SMU for his grad degree; taught Middle School English at Greenhill School for a decade; coaches and plays volleyball when he has the time; travels abroad when he has the money; loves Victor Hugo and C.S. Lewis; and respects Rick Riordan. He left a great job to write his debut novel, and he hopes you enjoyed the journey as much as he did.

Got questions about *The Conspiracy Game*? Follow Adam on Twitter: @adamholtwrites.

Adam is available for readings, workshops, and speaking engagements about his novels, the writing process, and science fiction. Please direct all questions to adamholtwrites@gmail.com.

Made in the USA
Coppell, TX
24 October 2021